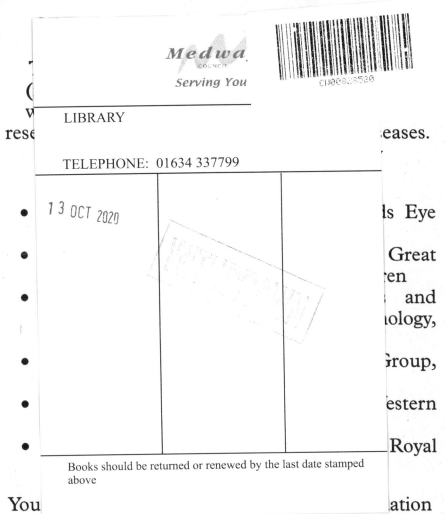
...ls Eye

...Great
...en

... and
...iology,

...iroup,

...estern

...Royal

You ...ation
by making a donation or leaving a legacy.
Every contribution is gratefully received. If you
would like to help support the Foundation or
require further information, please contact:

**THE ULVERSCROFT FOUNDATION**
**The Green, Bradgate Road, Anstey**
**Leicester LE7 7FU, England**
**Tel: (0116) 236 4325**

**website: www.ulverscroft-foundation.org.uk**

# TWO HEARTBEATS

When Jess heads west for a fresh start in a small mining town, she soon learns that the dusty outback plains are a far cry from her former life in the city — but she finds herself loving the isolation and local people she lives with. All she has to do is keep her head down and work hard to create a better life for herself and Johnno, the only person she has ever truly cared about. As relationships develop and change, Jess discovers the warmth of a welcoming family and a circle of friends who look out for her. However, problems arise when she collides with her new boss Daniel, who is suspicious of her background story. Has Jess told him everything, or is there a hidden secret to justify his earlier distrust of her?

RHONDA FORREST

---

# TWO HEARTBEATS

*Complete and Unabridged*

## AURORA
### Leicester

First published in 2018

First Aurora Edition
published 2020

The moral right of the author has been asserted

A catalogue record for this book is available
from the British Library.

ISBN 978–1–78782–438–6

Published by
Ulverscroft Limited
Anstey, Leicestershire

Set by Words & Graphics Ltd.
Anstey, Leicestershire
Printed and bound in Great Britain by
T. J. International Ltd., Padstow, Cornwall

This book is printed on acid-free paper

# 1

Towering office buildings cast shadows across the bustling city street, a cold August breeze using the thoroughfare as a tunnel to push its chill across the throngs of workers and slow-moving cars congesting the area. Lights flashed as impatient drivers sounded their horns, while pedestrians weaving their way in and out of the traffic searched for the quickest way to the other side of the street.

Peak hour. Bumper-to-bumper cars. Groups of men in suits, briefcases swinging at their sides, strode next to women with immaculate make-up, their hair neat and slick, tight pencil skirts stretched over legs that paced briskly; the click-clack of high heels a rhythmic noise heard only intermit-tently amidst the din of the morning rush.

The wind picked up and pedestrians tucked their heads lower to ward off the icy chill on their faces. A young man and woman ducked into an alcove off to the side of the tallest building in the street, both with heads down and hands pushed deep into their pockets.

'Jesus Christ, Jessie, I didn't know it was going to be this cold in here. It feels like it's going to snow.'

'I told you not to come in, Johnno. I could have found the place; it's the fanciest building in the street. Now you're going to have to hang around until I'm finished. Why don't you get on a bus and go home? I'll meet you back there.'

'Hey, I know how much you want this. You know I'm with you one hundred percent.' His solemn eyes looked into hers, and they stared hard at each other before hugging tightly, pressing against one another, relishing the warmth emanating from their bodies.

'How do I look? Is this dress formal enough?'

Johnno held her at arm's length, looking her up and down. Brown wavy hair that fell naturally onto her shoulders framed a delicate face, a faint hint of makeup covering high cheekbones that were flushed from the cold air. Thick eyelashes highlighted dark brown eyes that stared at him, waiting for his reply. 'Um, you look a little nervous and bloody hell, get rid of that coat. It's got holes in it.'

'I know that.' She hugged the coat tighter around her slim body. 'I'll take it off just before I go in. I didn't have a choice, you know.'

'The dress is okay, and the shoes. I think you look all right.'

Pushing the dress down nervously, she smoothed over the tiny floral print that flowed down to just above her knees, fitting snugly but not too tight across her body. Scrunching her toes up, she tried to settle her feet into the shoes that although only having a small heel, were causing her all sorts of discomfort.

'Okay. Wish me luck, Johnno.' She kissed him on the cheek, sensing his agitation from standing still in the cold.

'I love you, Jess. I'll be here waiting for you.'

Turning and waving, she watched as he pulled

his worn coat around him, head down and hands dug deep into his pockets, his trousers dragging on the footpath as he made his way back up the street. She knew he'd hang around and wait for her; he had nothing else to do, and somewhere there'd be a sunny area in a park where he'd relax until she finished. Now she needed to focus, think about what lay ahead, and yes, now was the time to get rid of the coat. Taking it off carefully, she folded it up, and after removing a manila folder, placed the coat neatly in the small bag she carried.

An imposing sign, *Seelo Mining*, stared down hard as she entered the building, deep breaths doing nothing to calm her nerves. Reminding herself to walk with confidence, she looked straight ahead, eyes fixed on the signs that led to the enquiry desk. Her icy hands held the manila folder and bag as she tried not to slide on the slippery tiles that seemed to accentuate the clatter of her shoes as she walked.

The receptionist on the other side of the desk raised her eyes as Jess approached. 'How can I help?'

'Um, thank you. I'm here for the interview, that is the job interview.'

'Which interviews are you referring to?'

Jessie realised that the woman, who looked like a model out of one of those glossy magazines, was raising her eyebrows as she spoke, her tone condescending, as if she were talking to a child. 'Are you sure you're in the right building? Perhaps you were after the Centrelink Office? It's further down the street.'

'No, I have the right place. I'm here for the mining interviews.' Jess tried hard to control the tone of her voice, reminding herself that this was not the time or place to use her typical street language and tell the stunning brunette woman in front of her what she thought of her rudeness. The receptionist's eyebrows arched higher, and she peered over the top of the counter, staring down at the shoes on Jessica's feet. Jessica's eyes narrowed and she pulled herself up straighter.

'The interviews we are conducting today are for the Seelo Mining Corporation,' the woman behind the desk said, tapping her bright red fingernails impatiently on the marble counter, speaking slowly, once again as if she were talking to a child.

'That's the one,' Jess replied. 'Thank you so much, and if you could tell me which direction I need to go . . . ?'

'Firstly, I'll need to check your name is on the list. We don't just let anyone walk in and out of the building. We have strict security protocols in place. Name, please?'

Jessica bit her lip to hold back a sharp remark. 'Jessica Bailey.'

Marking her name off the sheet, the woman, whose lips were now tightly pursed, handed over a plastic folder, the name 'Jessica Bailey' printed on the top and further details of the instructions for the day listed below. 'Take the lift on the right over there, 42nd floor. There are toilets up there to try and fix yourself up before the interview.'

'Thank you so much, you've been so kind. I hope you have just the most wonderful day.' Jess

4

smiled sweetly and then squinted at the woman's nametag before saying the name slowly in syllables as if she was having trouble reading it. 'Mir . . . i . . . am.'

Miriam glared hard at her before turning her back, ignoring the last comment.

Jess's brown eyes flashed, revealing the direct antagonism that the woman had so easily provoked in just a few minutes. The clip-clop of her cheap second-hand shoes echoed as she tried to walk steadily across the glossy tiles, her hands now full with her bag and folders. For a moment she felt nauseous, the nerves kicking in as she realised the grandness of the building and those walking through it, so at odds with her life.

The woman at the front desk had not helped her anxiety. Perhaps she was out of her league and this was a huge mistake. Today might only make her feel less confident and confirm that it was just not going to happen for her. Pushing her shoulders back, she straightened her body, admonishing herself for the hundredth time. *I've got nothing to lose. This is my one big opportunity to get out and make something of my life. To get a decent job, to be my own person, earn money, and most importantly get my own place.*

Stairs next to the lifts offered a few extra moments to calm herself, and she walked slowly, each step allowing her to breathe evenly and gather her ideas. Words that had been practised repeatedly resounded with the echo of her footsteps in the empty stairwell as she paced herself, eventually pushing open a heavy door that led out onto the fourth floor.

# 2

Outside the building, a bright orange taxi, patiently waiting its turn in the line of traffic, squeezed into the drop-off zone directly outside the highest building in the street. The thick glass panelling covering the front of the building reflected the blinking indicator light as the passenger opened the door and cautiously eased out beside the moving traffic. The driver opened the boot, reaching in and handing a small travel bag to the passenger, who was conspicuous in his fluorescent navy-blue and orange work gear, amidst the formality and darker colours of workers who passed around him.

The two men shook hands. 'Thanks, Harry. I don't know how you fellas navigate all this and stay so calm. It feels like everyone is moving at a million miles an hour.'

The taxi driver laughed. 'I've been driving around this city for so long I could get you here with my eyes shut. It's a bit different from where you come from, though, Dan. From what you've told me, there's probably more people on this street than in your entire town.'

'Too right. Our biggest problem on the roads out home is avoiding the wildlife.' Dan looked up at the imposing skyscrapers and then back to the streets filled with choking traffic and endless throngs of people moving along the pavements. 'Everyone here's in a rush. They're all trying to

6

get somewhere, and as quick as possible. It's just as well I'm only here for one more day.'

Harry chuckled and reached into his pocket. 'Take my card, and don't forget — when you need to get to the airport tonight, just give me a ring and I'll be out the front here to pick you up. That's of course if you don't change your mind and decide to stay and have a look around.'

'No chance of that! This is a strictly fly in and fly out trip, two-day turnaround. Just business. I'll be ringing you later tonight.'

The two men shook hands again and Daniel watched as Harry's cab pushed its way back out into the traffic, the beeping of horns heralding the irate disapproval of other drivers. Dan shook his head, always shocked at the hustle and bustle he experienced when he was forced to come to the head office for work.

A large sign above the rotating glass doors declared the name of the mining company that Daniel worked with: Seelo Mining, one of the largest businesses in Australia. A corporation that ran its open-cut mining operation in Gowrie, Central Queensland, currently extracting millions of tonnes of coal per year, destined for use in steelmaking applications around the world.

Daniel had grown up and lived in the Gowrie region all his life, so had jumped at the opportunities that Seelo brought to the area when they first opened up. Over the years he had seen bare, dusty areas turned into expansive mining camps: sheds, dongas, admin buildings and even swimming pools adding to the instant towns that consisted of the fly-in fly-out workers, commonly known as FIFOs. Before the mining boom, his workshop mainly repaired farming equipment and local machinery, and although it had always operated successfully, he now enjoyed the continuity of well-paid work that the mines provided. Living further out from the small town and camp, his workshop and life remained somewhat distant from the workers and mining executives who usually flew home as soon as their shifts finished.

On one hand, he enjoyed watching the area fill with hundreds of workers, equipment and sites that were state-of-the-art, and the constant work for anyone who lived in the area. On the flip side, he knew that the boom wouldn't last forever, that one day the coal or the need for it would wane, and then the tiny town of Gowrie would return to as it was before, a quiet desert outpost.

Daniel kept the work in his camp specialised and at a small scale, not wanting the business to become too large or entirely dependent on the mines, instead leaving that to the main workshop near the camps and the multitude of workers they employed.

Coal mining was riding the crest of a wave in Queensland, evident by the luxurious foyer that met him as he stepped inside. The lavish furnishings and expensive interior designs left no doubt as to the wealth and prestige of the company. He reminded himself to be thankful that these visits didn't happen often and then tried hard to remember the name of the stunning brunette who was looking straight at him as he approached the front desk.

She greeted him, her voice friendly. 'Daniel Smith.' Her manicured red nails gleamed as she reached over the counter to shake his hand, her company badge luckily reminding Daniel of her name. 'How lovely to see you again.'

'Miriam, great to see you also.' His rough, burly hand closed over hers.

'Are you in town for long?' she asked, her voice sultry as she passed him some paperwork and a folder with a schedule for the day attached. 'If you're staying overnight, maybe we could go out again. We had so much fun last time.'

'Thanks, Miriam. We did. Unfortunately, I'm leaving tonight so I won't have time to catch up.'

He thought she appeared to be a bit put out and realised he could have gone out with her last night, instead of enjoying the fact that there were numerous TV channels to choose from in his city hotel room. Miriam had been a fun companion last time he was in town and had made it clear to him that she was only interested in casual relationships. 'Maybe next time I'm in town.' He threw her his best smile and winked, the attractive Miriam placated as she fluttered her long eyelashes at him.

'Maybe you'll have time for a drink after you finish this afternoon. I can see your schedule ends at four. Just a quick drink?' She leaned over the counter, her voice sweet and inviting, a hint of perfume wafting over the counter.

The scent reminded Daniel of the night they

had spent together last time he was in town. 'I guess, maybe just a quick drink before I go to the airport.'

'See you back here at four, then.'

He nodded politely, his slow deep voice sounding out of place in the foyer where everyone talked quickly, their words business-like and efficient. Looking up, he was thankful to see one of the managers he knew coming his way. The young man, wearing a perfectly fitted wool suit, shook his hand, happy to see a ground worker come into the office. Although Dan ran his own business, he'd worked with the company for years and was well respected, his opinion highly valued, a straight down-the-line regular country worker who told it exactly how it was.

'Good to see you, Dan. How did you go with the traffic this time?'

'G'day, Phillip. Great to see you again. It gets busier every time I come in here.' Dan walked alongside, picking up his pace as the younger man steered him over to one of the offices on the far side of the foyer. Phillip had already climbed a long way up the corporate ladder of the company, and it always amazed Dan how someone who he guessed was probably only in his late twenties displayed so much knowledge and confidence, obviously using it to the utmost to get to such a high position at such a young age.

'I see you didn't escape the clutches of Miriam.' Phillip chuckled and handed Dan a stack of folders. 'She was excited to hear you were coming into town.' He smiled as Dan grimaced before turning to business matters. 'We've got an hour

10

before we start, time for you to go over the folios that relate to your section; and then if you've got time you can scan the others, just to give us some backup with decisions we make today.' Phillip held open the door to his office. 'The main thing now is coffee and a quick briefing before we start. After you, Daniel.'

# 3

Phillip's office provided a quiet area for Daniel to read the folios he had been given and he appreciated the silence, allowing him to focus on the paperwork in front of him.

Using the large mirror that adorned one entire wall of the office, Daniel observed the fact that the curls at the front of his head were receding a little. He ran his hands through his hair, annoyed at the bright lighting in the room that accentuated the wrinkles around his eyes. Thirty-four years of laughter lines, he told himself, the lines creasing out from the corners of his dark blue eyes that stared back hard at him. Early-morning stubble was already forming on his tanned cheeks, and he rubbed his face before straightening his heavy cotton shirt. His work clothes, even though they were new, seemed out of place in the professional city office, and he flattened the fabric, ensuring no creases were visible.

The company always insisted that he wear his regular work attire and not the formal getup of the others on the panel. 'It just opens up communication a bit better,' Phillip told him. 'A lot of the workers are more at ease with someone in work clothes than they'd be with us in our suits.'

*Bloody huge mirrors*, he thought. *Who'd want to look at themselves all the time?* He collected

12

his thoughts and pushed open the office door, making his way across the foyer to the lifts on the other side. A few workers stepped into the lift behind him, briskly tapping the buttons for their required floors, a couple of the elegantly dressed women smiling warmly as they entered.

On the fourth floor, he noticed a young woman join them, and he moved over to allow her some room in front of him. He smiled at her, but she didn't respond, instead turning around, her back positioned directly in front of him. The lift stopped and started, emptying a little on each floor, and eventually the two office women, who had spent the entire time whispering and laughing, their clicking high heels briskly and efficiently, left also. Now only the young woman remained, and he observed her as she stood with her back to him, noting that she was fidgety and continually looking up, checking the numbers that lit up on the screen above the door. Floor 24. The light flashed, and she tightened her grasp on her belongings.

Daniel leant forward and held down the open button before speaking to her. 'Miss, I'm not trying to be funny or anything, but there's a major problem with the back of your dress.'

Angry brown eyes flashed at him as she turned around. 'I beg your pardon, what did you just say?'

He raised his eyebrows. 'I'm not being weird, but it looks to me like your zip has busted.'

Twisting her head around, she tried to see what he was talking about, but to no avail. Christ, here she was on the twenty-fourth floor,

13

her hands were full, and there was a guy who looked like he was the cleaner telling her that her zip was busted.

'Do you want me to do it up for you? Although it looks like the entire zipper has come apart, not like when it's just not done up. I'd say it's busted completely. Regardless, whatever has happened, I can see your entire back.'

'Shit, are you joking with me? I have a job interview in thirty minutes, how the fuck am I going to fix that?' She noticed Daniel tilt his head on the side, looking more closely at her back. Peering around, she took in the fact that there was no one else around. She turned back to Daniel, continuing with her abuse. 'If you so much as fucking touch me, I swear you'll be sorry you ever got into the same lift as me this morning. I know your fucking type.'

Daniel raised his eyebrows further. 'What a foul mouth you have. I was going to suggest that I could have a go at fixing it. But I guess you'll just have to forget about the appointment you have.' He watched in amusement as she twisted her body around again, trying to get a glimpse of the broken zipper.

'Shit, I can't forget about it. I need to go to this interview.'

Daniel stepped outside the lift into the deserted hallway. 'Look, I promise you, if you stand out here, I can have a go at fixing it for you. Unless you have a friend here that you could ask?'

Scowling at him, she thought for a moment before stepping out of the lift. Daniel followed,

14

both of them standing in the corridor on the twenty-fourth floor. He pointed to her bag. 'Is that a coat in there? It's freezing today — why don't you just put that over the top.'

'You're just full of brilliant ideas, Mr Fix-it. It's full of holes. Otherwise, I could wear it and then I wouldn't need to ask a bloody cleaner, or whatever you are, to fix my dress.'

Daniel looked hard at her and saw a skinny kid, probably not much older than twenty, with a pretty little face, fine features and delicate skin; features that belied the angry brown eyes and aggressive language that flowed so smoothly from her mouth. 'Are you always this rude to people, or have you just saved it up for me this morning?'

He was staring straight at her, his voice stern and deep, the bluest eyes she had ever seen, daring her to continue with her tirade of abuse. She glared back at him, her anger bubbling to escape. However, she thought about the time ticking past and her tone changed somewhat. 'I really do need to be on time and attend this job interview, so if you think you can fix it, I'd appreciate it.'

*So she does have manners*, he thought, just before another tirade was directed at him.

'If you so much as even dare touch me, I'll fu — '

He interrupted, 'How about you keep your mouth closed before I change my mind about helping you? You're holding me up also, so be quiet for a minute and let me see if I can fix it.' He placed the pile of folders on a nearby desk.

'Stand still and get your hair out of the way, the zipper bit is up the top still.'

It was obvious even to Daniel, who wasn't right up on the fashion stakes, that the dress had seen better days. Frayed edges caught the zipper as he carefully pulled the clip part back down through the zipper teeth that ran almost the entire length of the dress. He noted her slimness and thought how nicely the pretty floral material fitted over her body. 'Okay, now I have it at the bottom, so it should zip up again and hopefully stay together long enough to get you through the day. It's not that tight, so as long as you're careful it should last. Just don't eat or breathe out.' Holding the bottom part of the zip firmly, he pulled the zipper up slowly, careful not to catch the fabric as it held together, pulling the sides in neatly, the dress once again intact. He smiled as the young woman turned to him, her eyes glaring, annoyance written all over her face, clearly irritated that she didn't have any other choice in the matter.

'I promise I didn't look.' He winked at her before picking up his folders. 'It must be an important interview. Best to go in fully dressed, though, and . . . ' He knew he couldn't help himself, her scowling ungrateful face lending itself to further comment. ' . . . it's so good to see that you have nice underwear on.'

'I knew it, a creep. My luck I get into a lift, my feet are killing me, my dress breaks, and my only help is a pervert of a cleaner with a smart mouth.'

'No need to thank me. Have a lovely day,

young lady.' He laughed out loud as she strutted off down the corridor, the zip holding together, but her ungainly walk testament to the pain her shoes were causing her. Stepping back into the lift, he wondered how long it would take her to realise she was on the wrong floor. It had been on the tip of his tongue to tell her that floor twenty-four was strictly storage and maintenance division and that perhaps it was the forty-second floor she was after. He was still smiling to himself as he wondered what position she was applying for. These interviews that were about to begin could make for an interesting morning.

# 4

Daniel entered the spacious room where the interviews were being held to be greeted by Rosalie, who gave him her usual welcoming smile.

He nodded his head politely, always the gentleman, and somewhat in awe of the middle-aged woman who was in charge of human resources at Seelo Mining. 'Good morning, Rosalie,' he said. 'It's lovely to talk to you in person instead of over the phone.'

'It's our pleasure, as always, to have you here, Daniel, and you know we do so appreciate you coming in to help out with the panel decisions. I am aware that the city is not your choice of places to be.'

'It's fine, Rosalie. It's important for me to have input, particularly with quite a few of these today, and I'm looking forward to chatting with the ones I'll be working with.'

Phillip joined them both and spread some folders out on the desks in front of them. 'So for Seelo, we have six vacancies at the main maintenance section, one in the office and two more working out with you, Daniel. Then also to share between Seelo and yourself, there's a courier driver and one gate man for the store area.'

Daniel pulled one of his folders out. 'I think I saw Hoppy's name down here again for the storeman. He's due to come back out again. From memory, he said he'd want to be back out around August.'

Rosalie looked at both of them. 'Run that past me again.'

Daniel continued talking as he pulled out a chair for Rosalie. 'You remember Hoppy, the old guy with the prosthetic leg. He's worked back and forth for us for years. We sort of keep that job for him because he likes to have a long break every so often to visit his elderly sister.'

Rosalie smiled. 'Oh, you mean old Reg, of course. I forgot his name was Hoppy. Why do we make him go through this process each time if the job is his?'

Phillip explained, 'He says he won't take any favours and doesn't want any special treatment. This way he feels important, like he wins the job each time.' He shrugged. 'He's such a lovely old guy, and he does a great job for us. I like him, so we do it this way. It keeps him happy.'

Rosalie pretended to look surprised. 'Sometimes you really shock me, Phillip. I mean, you can be utterly ruthless with some applicants, and then, well you must have a soft spot somewhere in there.' She fondly patted his shoulder.

'That's why we all work well together, hey, Daniel,' Phillip said. 'We all know you won't put up with any trouble from workers. Let's hope there's some good ones in here today because we've got a lot to get through, so let's get started.'

Daniel, Rosalie and Phillip sat next to each other on one side of a long table. An empty chair was positioned on the opposite side for the applicants who waited in chairs placed in a line outside the interviewing room. Those who arrived first were at the head of the line, followed by those who came after. Today they were mostly male applicants applying for the jobs that were predominantly in the mechanical maintenance section; however a few female candidates also waited, confident that big companies these days chose on merit and not gender alone.

As the interviews got underway, Daniel flicked through the folios in front of him, watching as Rosalie and Phillip asked the standard questions of the applicants for the maintenance crew. The workers chosen for the six positions at the main workshop section would work at what was known as the main camp. Daniel and his team worked quite a distance away from this busy central point, dealing with the finer and more specialised components of maintenance and workshop mechanics.

The huge work sheds that the mining company leased from him were on his property and within walking distance to his house, and although he wasn't employed directly by the mines, instead working through long-term contracts and leases with Seelo, his workers were. The three chosen today to work with him would have him as their boss, but be paid by Seelo.

These arrangements had been established in the earlier days and allowed him the security and money that came with the development of the high-earning mining camps, but let him run his own business the way he wanted. This way he was also able to keep a distance from the stress and politics that went with the work sheds in the main camp. The contracts had run successfully for years and the managerial staff of Seelo had come to value his opinion and local advice, particularly in the area of hiring staff to work and live in such a remote area.

Today he was looking for two mechanics for his own workshop and also wanting to ensure that the office worker for the main camp was someone who was going to stay and add some quality. The last young woman hadn't worked out, and he knew the boss lady at the office was getting irate with the inefficiencies and slackness of some of the previous employees. He also needed a reliable courier driver, perhaps a middle-aged person who was going to be trustworthy and get the parts to him as soon as they came off the plane. The last driver had always been confused and sometimes lost deliveries between the town and workshop.

Daniel had become suspicious of the young driver when parts just disappeared into thin air, or as the locals liked to say, fell off the back of the truck. He started to investigate and supervise the deliveries more closely, annoyed that both time and money were being wasted. The problem was solved when the driver flew back home on his week off last month and just never returned.

★ ★ ★

This morning the interviews flowed smoothly, and Rosalie commented on how they would be finished early if this pace continued. Both she and Phillip, although making sure the applicants were put at ease to begin with, left no time in asking the hard questions, and often Daniel thought how both of them could be quite intimidating, leaving no doubt for those sitting opposite as to who was in charge of the choices.

So far the applicants had been of a high quality, and he already had his eye on two young men for the two positions at his plant. Daniel flicked through the paperwork in front of him, leaning forward to talk to Phillip. 'There's some fabulous young people applying for these positions. Those two fellas who've flown down from Gladstone for the interview stand out. They both come highly recommended.'

Phillip agreed. 'There's definitely another six in there to fill the other positions also. It's a shame that none of the female applicants fit what we're looking for.'

Rosalie added, 'There's only a handful left to interview, and you know we have to have a female in there somewhere. Remember the quotas.' She went to the door to show the next applicant in.

Daniel flicked through his folders again. 'Surely there will be some women chasing the office job. It's well paid.' He looked up as Rosalie intro-duced the next applicant.

'This is Phillip Bellow, the manager of our staffing section here at Seelo Mines, and this is Daniel Smith, owner at our specialised mainte-nance division and boss of our ground staff in that area. Gentleman, this is Jessica Bailey.'

Daniel watched as Phillip stood and gently shook the hand of the very nervous young woman who appeared to have a firm self-assured grip and a friendly smile. More importantly, she looked straight into Phillip's eyes and spoke confidently and clearly. 'I am pleased to meet you, Mr Bellow. Thank you so much for your time today.'

Her reaction to Daniel was a little different, and they all watched her face turn crimson as she hesitantly reached over and shook Daniel's hand, sitting down quickly as he greeted her.

Phillip watched her curiously as she placed her manila folder on the table. There was something about her that he couldn't quite put his finger on. She appeared professional, however she wasn't dressed in the usual formal office attire.

Her dress was old and a little faded, but it sat well, and she had such a lovely face. He looked closer: no make-up, just a natural beauty with dark, brooding eyes. He decided he liked the way she looked and spoke, even if it was a little different from the usual.

Rosalie was also assessing the way the young woman entered the room and greeted Phillip. *She carries herself well*, she thought. *She's polite and trying to be confident, but, goodness me, those shoes — she can hardly walk in them.* The older woman tried to put her at ease. 'Sit down, Jessica. You look a little nervous, so have a drink of water first and just relax.'

Rosalie, much like Phillip, carried a soft spot for some of these younger applicants who obviously came from lower socio-economic areas.

She could pick them straight away — nervous, missing that polished, confident stance, and lacking the highly groomed look and well-practiced words that many of the other applicants displayed. Part of her HR job that she loved the most was to go and visit the local high schools and talk to kids about how to land that perfect job, how to go for what they wanted and show confidence; to get up and keep trying no matter what sort of background they came from.

Daniel, meanwhile, hadn't taken his eyes off Jessica as she sat down ever so carefully in the seat opposite him. The morning had been busy and he'd completely forgotten about the young woman who had been on her way to an interview when he'd tried to help her. Now he recalled the sharp words that had flowed so smoothly from her lips as she branded him a pervert. Not only was he shocked at the polite, articulate language she was using now, but he was also surprised at the difference in tone that Rosalie used towards the nervous woman on the other side of the table.

Rosalie asked in a calm, friendly manner, 'Jessica, what particular job are you interested in applying for? Because there are a few different ones listed here.'

Jessica took a deep breath, attempting to compose herself, trying hard to get over the shock that the man she had abused and not even thanked this morning was now sitting opposite her. A manager, an interviewer who would decide if she was the right person for her dream job. She should just get up and walk out the door now. *What a stuff-up*, she thought as she replied. 'I'd like to apply for the courier role you have advertised. That's my first choice, although I also have the experience and capabilities for the office job.' She took a deep breath, relieved that her words were finally out.

Daniel's next words shocked both Rosalie and Phillip. He hadn't added too much to the previous interviews, just the standard questions, leaving both of them to ask the hard questions, probing, trying to put the applicant on the spot, attempting to determine just how badly each one wanted the position. 'Miss Bailey, I noticed that you're walking a bit strangely. Is there something wrong with your feet, or your shoes?'

He looked straight at her and watched her eyes spark as she looked directly back at him, and spoke in an eloquent voice. 'I'll be perfectly honest, Mr Smith — I purchased some new shoes, and yes you're right, they've given me terrible blisters and I can hardly walk in them.'

Rosalie laughed out loud. 'You men, you have no idea how we women suffer just to try and look our best. Jessica, slip them off while you sit here; no one can see under the table anyway. I feel for you. I've been in the same position myself and there's nothing worse. See me after the interview and I'll give you some of my band-aids. That will get you home in one piece.'

Jessica relaxed a little, the kind words putting her at ease. Rosalie frowned at Daniel, looking over her glasses at him as she spoke, 'Now, gentlemen, let's continue with some *business* questions. Phillip, perhaps you'd like to start.'

Phillip watched the young woman's face and observed that she directed all her eye contact and answers toward himself and Rosalie, avoiding looking Daniel's way at all. But applicants usually were more at ease with the relaxed manner of Daniel, who had leant back comfortably in his chair, his arms crossed in front of him.

Phillip was always envious of the rugged, casual look of the older man seated beside him. As much as he tried to keep up the gym visits and personal training sessions, he could never match the physique of someone who was naturally well muscled and toned from the years of heavy yard work and lifting. He'd once asked Daniel how he kept his body looking so fit. Daniel had laughed and told him that they didn't worry about that too much where he came from. It was all about working hard during the day and eating what was healthy and filled him up.

Phillip turned his attention back to the folio in front of him that detailed Jessica's work experience and school results. He asked some easier questions about her experience and then questioned her, 'Jessica, you haven't given us any referee numbers that we can contact about your past work history. The plant nursery you worked for when you first left school, you were there for just over two years. Surely there's someone you worked with who could give us a character reference.'

'Um, I have . . . um I have a letter here.' Jessica fumbled with the papers in front of her, pulling out a single creased sheet of paper. 'The owners were an older couple. Jake passed away,

26

and the nursery had to be sold. His wife Ellen and I tried to keep it going, but she was in her seventies and it just didn't work. This reference is one she wrote for me. I don't know where she is now. She moved away, I think maybe into a retirement home. I'm sorry, but this is all I have from that job.' She passed the reference across to Phillip, who looked closely at the beautifully hand-written calligraphic writing, so typical he thought, of someone from that era.

'She speaks highly of you. You need to have some photocopies of this made for future résumés.' He passed it over to Rosalie, who read it with a smile.

'We were very close,' Jessica opened up a little. 'They were the best employers I ever worked for, both of them. They treated me well and even let me live in a small cabin on the property. Jake helped me get my driver's license and then I did all the deliveries and runs for them. He told me the experience in driving would help with jobs later on.'

'This next job, the cleaning work, three years at the same place. That must have been hard work. Tell us a little about what duties you performed while you were there.' Rosalie spoke kindly to Jessica, who answered the questions carefully.

'There were a few of us who worked for JT Cleaning. We did commercial buildings, new houses and apartments. I worked a lot inside the buildings, scrubbing, mopping, using industrial vacuum cleaners, scraping concrete and paint and cleaning up after the tradesmen left. I also used to clean up outside the buildings, carting off all the bricks, concrete, tiles, you know all the rubbish that's left behind.'

Daniel decided it was time to intervene. 'You haven't written down a referee connected to this job either. After three years, there should be someone we can contact?'

Jessica looked straight at him, her voice shaky. 'No, there isn't.'

Rosalie broke the awkward silence. 'We don't intend sounding critical, but you also don't state why you left this job. I'm getting the feeling that you didn't leave on good terms.'

Sitting up straighter, Jessica went to speak, however her nerves were becoming uncontrollable. An overwhelming impulse to collect up her papers and walk out of the room ran through her mind.

Sensing her angst, Phillip leaned forward, smiling as he spoke. 'Sometimes, we as a team are not so much interested in what an applicant has done in previous jobs, but in what they have to offer us today and what it is that they are aiming for in the future. We all started off at the bottom of the ladder at one stage or another, and everyone has had different experiences in their lives. Tell us, and I want you to be honest with us, because at the moment we don't have a lot to go on otherwise. Why do you wish to work for us? Why do you want this particular job? Take a sip of water, take your time.'

Taking a long drink of water with hands that were now shaking uncontrollably, Jessica decided it was all or nothing. After all, what did she have to lose?

# 5

'I haven't always had the best run of luck with jobs in the past. The nursery job was probably the best, because Ellen and Jake were lovely people and I worked hard for them because they treated me well. I'd have worked for them for nothing; they were such caring, honest people. Now I just want a decent job that I can settle down in and be treated well. Cleaning, lifting, driving, sorting, whatever you want, you name it and I'll give it a go. Reliability and pride in my job are my strongest points, and I don't ever take days off.'

Jessica paused for a moment, her eyes moving from Rosalie to Phillip and back again. 'You said you want the truth. The reason I left the cleaning job was because the boss had loose hands, and after three years I was sick of avoiding his advances. I left before it got any worse. There was no one to talk to about what was happening, so I figured I'd just resign. He wasn't happy being left down one worker and he didn't pay me for the last week of work. I didn't think he would be a good name to put down as a referee. I've worked in loads of other odd jobs, but nothing that was permanent or long enough to really get to know anyone who could say much about me. So many jobs that I've worked in have been temporary. I guess I just want a break, an opportunity to prove myself. I'm a hard worker and I just need someone to give me a go.'

Phillip replied, 'I can't speak for Daniel, but both Rosalie and I have had experiences as juniors where we've worked for sleazy bosses. It doesn't just happen to females.'

Rosalie looked at the two men before talking to Jessica. 'It was rampant back in my day. I used to spend most of my day avoiding a particular boss. God, I can still remember his sordid comments. Well, thank goodness workers don't have to put up with that rubbish anymore. There are a wide range of protocols and work ethic procedures in place. Seelo Mining and Daniel's workshop have a strict code of conduct, and those who breach it find themselves in serious trouble.' Rosalie continued, 'Thank you for letting us in a little on your work experiences. If you were to be successful, you realise it's a three weeks on, one week off schedule with the option of fly in and fly out for most of these jobs. A couple of them have different schedules with weekends off, but they all require you to live out in the area. How would you go being separated from your parents or perhaps a partner?'

'I never knew my father, and my mother died when I was young. I also don't have a partner. So it wouldn't bother me at all.'

There was another awkward silence, and although the three interviewers wanted to ask more details about her childhood, no one felt the right to ask further questions in that direction.

Daniel broke the silence, his face cynical, unlike the other two. 'I just have a couple of questions here about your school results. History was always my favourite subject at school. These senior results show a result of A for history in year eleven and twelve. I'm curious, did you do ancient or modern history? It doesn't say here.'

There was a small pause before Jessica replied, 'I studied it just recently when I was in senior, so I think it would be modern history. I loved learning about the pyramids, Egypt, you know all the Roman ruins, places you can visit in the modern world.'

Sweat was starting to run down the insides of Jessica's arms and she hoped that dark spots weren't showing under her arms. Phillip closed the folder in front of him. 'I think we have nearly finished. Do either of you have any further questions?'

Rosalie stood up. 'Any more questions, Daniel?'

'No, that's all.' He stretched out his legs, unused to the long stint of sitting at a desk.

'Do you have any questions for us, Jessica?'

'Um, I do have a couple. I talked to an older gentleman while I was waiting outside. He said he worked for your company for a number of years previously and that I should ask you if I was to get the job whether I had to live at the main camp. He said there is another little area a bit further out where he and a few of the others live. If I was successful, could I live at the smaller area?'

Rosalie looked surprised. 'The main camp is set up with everything you need, particularly for younger workers, as there are lots of opportunities for social interaction. There's a gym there, a pool to cool off in, meals three times a day, plus a small shop with everything you need. If you lived out at the smaller camp, you'd be very isolated. Would that be right, Daniel? You know the area better than we do.'

'That little camp, and I'm guessing it was Hoppy you were talking to, is in a dusty, isolated area, and only a few of the older male crew live there. There's nothing there, just a shower and a toilet block plus a few old vans.'

'It would suit me better, and if I am successful I'd prefer to live in the smaller camp.'

Phillip answered, 'We will take it into consideration. Thank you for being open with us today and we'll be in touch by tomorrow afternoon, one way or the other. If you were to be successful, when could you start?'

'I could start as soon as you want me to. Thank you so much for your time.'

Rosalie talked to Jessica as she headed for the door, taking into account her strange walk, as if she was backing out the door, keeping her front to the three of them.

The door closed quietly behind her.

# 6

Clinking cups and saucers heralded the arrival of lunch. A trolley filled with sandwiches and coffees along with plates of cut-up fruit was provided for the three interviewers. Phillip spoke to the young man who had brought the lunch in. 'There're only a few applicants left waiting outside, Bud. Could you please make sure that they get the same as us? They're probably starving, waiting out there all morning.' Phillip touched the young man on the arm as he spoke, the connection between the two of them immediately apparent to both Rosalie and Daniel, who looked at each other as the young man left the room. Phillip followed him out and when he returned, Rosalie and Daniel both smiled at him but didn't speak.

'What?' Phillip said as he sat down next to them.

'Phillip, is there something you're not telling us?' Rosalie raised her eyebrows at the younger man as she passed the sandwiches and coffees around to the other two.

'Ok, ok, you just don't miss anything, Rosalie. Bud and I are a couple. We've been dating for a couple of months now.'

Daniel smiled broadly before asking, 'How did that get past you Rosalie? You're normally pretty quick picking up on the relationships in the company, and here's one you missed right under your nose.'

'I did have an idea. I was just waiting for Phillip to tell me before I pried.'

'It never stopped you before.' Phillip was flushed, his face alight, happy at sharing his news.

'I do love a good romance. So, how about you, Daniel?' Rosalie asked. 'What have you been up to? Any new interests?' Rosalie was aware of the casual flings Daniel had when he came to town, however she often wished that he'd meet someone special. He deserved to be happy. She knew there had been heartaches in the past, so she usually didn't ask too much about his personal life.

'No, there's nothing on the romance scene for me. I've dated a few times, and I must remember I have an appointment with Miriam downstairs for drinks this afternoon before I fly out. But they're just dates. No sparks, no fireworks. Not like loverboy over here.'

Friendly banter flowed back and forth, the three of them enjoying the break and catching up on what had been happening since Daniel's last visit to head office.

Rosalie looked at her watch. 'Right, before we go onto these last three, I just want to have a quick chat about the applicants we've already interviewed. Daniel, do you have a list of recommendations?' Phillip and Rosalie both pushed their lists over to Daniel, who perused the names for the six positions at the main camp.

He nodded, ticking the names on his list. 'We're pretty well on par with those names. The young guy, Troy, from Gladstone, I'd rather have him out with me though. I can see myself working well with him; he's methodical and relatively quiet. I also think this young man, Gus, he'd be my other choice for my depot. That leaves the other six you have on the list here for the main camp. As usual, we've chosen the same names.'

'Agreed. I love it when that happens. They're pretty clear-cut choices.' Phillip opened up another folder and continued speaking. 'Now, so far the only applicant for the courier job is the young woman we just interviewed. There's a few more waiting outside, however their driving records are terrible, and nothing in their résumés is standing out to me. In fact, all of them are riddled with spelling errors.'

'They've only got to drive back and forth. They don't have to write articles for the newspaper. I'm not that concerned about the spelling in their résumés,' Daniel said as he stood up and stretched, the hours of sitting starting to have an effect on his body. 'I think you should just scratch that last applicant off the list. She's dishonest, plus she interviewed terribly, and it's never a positive choice when there are no referees. I'm not interested in her for the courier job, and I don't think she has the skills for the office job.'

'I think she was fairly honest with us. Perhaps the report card was a bit dodgy, but who hasn't inflated marks or told little white lies to get a job they want,' Rosalie said, looking at Daniel. 'I lied to get my first job here many years ago. I told the boss I had intermediate computer skills. I had only learnt the week before when a friend of

35

mine taught me how to control a mouse and type on a computer. That was the extent of my computer skills, an uncontrollable hand and the cursor moving wildly around the computer screen as I typed up my resume for Seelo Mining.'

Daniel was adamant. 'I don't want her working with me. I get the feeling that she's hiding something. She skimmed over the questions, plus look at how many different jobs she's worked in. If you're going to employ her, put her in the office. The ladies over there will sort her out quick smart.'

Legs swinging, Phillip sat on the desk, listening to the conversation between the other two. 'Don't forget, we need a quota of females and so far we haven't picked one. Also, Daniel, the next applicant is probably the pick for the office job. He's perfect, experienced and professional, and wants to work out in a small community. He's, um, actually a friend of mine; well actually, he's Bud's friend.'

'Well, that's all right. I don't mind allocating the office job to Bud's friend if he has the best skills, but let's re-advertise the courier job. I don't think that last woman we interviewed is the right person.'

'I liked her.' Phillip sat back down. 'She's had a hard life, you can tell. Rough around the edges, but she has grit, and I bet she has a heart of gold.'

Rosalie added, 'I also liked her. She spoke beautifully. In fact, I have such a positive feeling about her that I'd be prepared to be her mentor. I can set up regular coaching sessions with her, perhaps when she flies back in, or I've done it before over Skype. I know with a bit of help she could go a long way. She's smart, streetwise perhaps, but there's something about her. An unusual quality. I'm rarely wrong, you know, Daniel.'

'Oh, she's articulate. I'm sure she wouldn't have any difficulty expressing her opinion. If you think she's so good, why don't you give her a job here?' Daniel waved his hands around the room, worried that he was being outnumbered.

The young woman's application had so many holes in it. Not only had she answered the history question incorrectly, but also it was obvious to him that the report card was not genuine. Senior subjects usually numbered five or six, but the report card that she presented to them today listed eight subjects for both Year 11 and 12. All with an A or B next to them. He had wanted to ask her, with such high academic marks, why she hadn't considered going to university. There were too many lies, and there was also the other side of her he had observed outside the lift.

During the interview, she used an entirely different voice than the one he had heard when she directed her abuse at him. He was amused at how easily both Rosalie and Phillip were fooled by the sweet and well-spoken woman. This time he was sure they were both wrong, and he'd need to remind them of that fact when this young woman only lasted a month or even less. When they needed to replace her, the choice would have to be made over the phone, because he had no intention of coming back in so soon. The trips into the city didn't suit, and he was getting restless with the sitting and the hustle and bustle of those around him.

Rosalie walked to the door to get the final applicants, her voice adamant as she added, 'She wouldn't last a second in here; she'd probably take someone out in the first hour. She'll be okay out with you, and I feel that the tougher sort of environment will suit her. You'll see, Daniel. I'll even place a bet on it. Twelve months and see who is right.'

'What's the bet, Rosalie? Actually, I'll name it. Whoever is right shouts the other and, of course, Phillip and Bud to the best restaurant in Brisbane once the year is up.'

'You're on. Start saving your pennies.'

# 7

The next few applicants did nothing to impress the interviewers, and they pushed through them quickly, asking the usual questions, flicking through their résumés and informing them that they would be contacted in the next two days as to the outcome of the interview. Bud's friend Jeffery was second last to be interviewed and provided a welcome upbeat relief after the mono-toned and negative answers from the previous two applicants. He was perfect for the office job, enthusiastic with exceptional people and office skills, leaving them in no doubt that he'd fit in well with the ladies who ran one of the site offices. He was also delighted that he wouldn't have to wear the regular fluorescent work gear but could dress up each day and be comfortable in an air-conditioned site office. Phillip was beaming as he shook Jeffery's hand, the two of them laughing and chatting amicably as they both left the room.

'I hope he goes okay out there,' Daniel whispered to Rosalie. 'It can be a pretty blokey environment, although he will be mainly up with the ladies in the office.'

'I'm sure he'll be fine. Perhaps you could keep an eye on how he's going. He is a good friend of Phillip's, and he does come with great credentials.'

Both of them looked up as the last applicant

for the day followed Phillip into the room. Daniel jumped up to greet him. 'Hoppy, my old mate. How are you? You're looking great.'

'Pleased to see you, Mr Daniel.' The older man smiled broadly at Daniel before turning to Rosalie and politely nodding his head. 'Good afternoon Mrs Rosalie, and thank you so much for considering me for the storeman job. I have my résumé and papers all ready.'

They all sat down together, Phillip asking Hoppy some questions about what he'd been up to and how his sister was doing. After a while the three of them questioned him about the hours he'd prefer, what days he wanted to work, and decided on his rate of pay. Hoppy was formal throughout the interview and acted surprised when they informed him at the end that he had been selected for the job and that he could start whenever he was ready. 'Thank you all so much,' he said. 'You're a great team and no doubt you have interviewed some good applicants today. If I could just put my two bobs worth in, though. Do you mind?'

Rosalie said, 'Go ahead, Hoppy. We all of course value any input you have.'

Hoppy continued, 'Well, there was a young woman you interviewed quite a while before me. Brown hair, a real pretty little thing. I wanted to tell you something about her.'

Daniel leant forward, smiling. *Here we go,* he thought. *This will be interesting.* He raised his eyebrows at Rosalie and Phillip as if to say *I told you so.*

Rosalie was intrigued. 'You know, Reg, Phillip

and I were both taken with that particular young woman, but Daniel's not keen. So your information may be valuable to us.'

'Well, I'll tell you something. When you first arrive at these interview days, it's a bit of a competition to see who can get let in first and be at the front of the line. I guess they all figure that you guys are fresh and more interested in the morning, and that if you're near the end of the line, you may have already decided on who you want.'

'We know it's not the perfect way to establish the order, but we also just think we should let it run its course. I guess it's first in first served.' Rosalie looked over her glasses at Hoppy. 'Go on.'

'Well, that little lady obviously arrived early and was sat, I'd say, probably second at the front. When I arrived, which was, um a bit late, I realised that I'd lost one of the joining screws out of this old prosthetic — ' He tapped his leg. ' — and the bottom part was coming away from the top. I started telling one of the guys sitting in front of me what had happened. I was a bit loud and I'd say that most of them waiting would've heard me because they all turned around to see what was going on. But you know what it's like. It's a competitive world out there, and not one of those buggers wanted to get out of their chair to help because they might lose their spot.' Hoppy was winding up. He loved telling a story.

'You'd already called the first person in and I think the woman was up to come in next. Instead, she came down to ask me what had happened, and when I explained, she asked me how she could help. Ended up, she backtracked all the way back down through the lift, across the entryway, you know with the flash white tiles, that's where you come into the building.'

Phillip was getting a little impatient at the long story and wanted to hear what had happened. 'We know where you mean, Hoppy.'

'Well, she walked out to where I said to her it might have fallen off, because I did feel it jig around a bit there. That is, right out on the pavement when I hopped out of the taxi. You'd never believe it; she said it was like finding gold. That pin or screw thing was just lying there in the gutter, right where I'd told her where I got out of the cab. She brought it back up to me, and together we put it back in, and ... ' Hoppy pulled up the leg of his trouser, revealing an old-looking prosthetic that nevertheless seemed to do the job for him. He slapped the leg hard. 'Good as gold, look at that. I reckon it would have cost a fortune if she hadn't found it for me because they're all specially made, not just your usual old screw. I just thought you might like that story because it's not often these days that young people will go so far out of their way to help an old bugger like me. That's why she was right near the end of the line, and also ... ' He stopped for a breath. ' ... she was having a bit of trouble with her shoes as well. I think all that walking gave her blisters on her blisters. Anyway, she's a lovely young woman. I hope you're considering her, as she looks like she needs a job, because her dress was also broken.'

Rosalie and Phillip laughed loudly, both looking at Daniel, who threw his hands in the air. 'Ok, you two, I lose. Bloody employ her as the courier. But when the shit hits the fan, don't say I didn't tell you so.'

# 8

Interview days were always long, and Daniel was glad that the day was over. He did, however, always find it valuable to be present for the selection process, just to get that extra information that often came out in the interview. He was pleased with the two young guys selected for his workshop, and knew that Phillip's friend Jefferey would be well and truly capable in the office job. His annoyance at the selection of the young woman for the courier position was further exacerbated when he observed her again later that afternoon.

★　★　★

Miriam made sure that she was waiting and ready to go when Daniel finished the interviews for the day. She watched him, thinking how handsome he was as he made his way over to the front desk.

'You're right on schedule,' she said as she emerged from behind the counter, her hair and makeup pristine, like the white tiles and polished tables that surrounded her. It amazed Daniel how perfectly she was dressed, her shiny black court shoes with pinpoint high heels clicking across the tiles, her arm quickly finding its way through his own as they walked across the foyer together. She talked how she walked, efficiently confidently, he thought to himself as she continued, 'I thought we'd go to a small café down the road for a quick bite and drink, so that you can wind down and relax. After that you have a couple of hours before your flight, so we'll have plenty of time to rest back at my apartment before I drive you to the airport. Does that sound okay?'

'That sounds good, Miriam. You lead and I'll follow. Definitely up for the food and dying for a cold beer. Are you still in the same apartment?'

'Same place, yes. You can't beat it, city views and close to the centre and the airport, plus it's walking distance from here.' Chatting endlessly, she guided Daniel along the busy streets towards a small café that was starting to fill with workers looking for a peaceful corner to sit after a day at work. Small rooms with chunky wooden tables and chairs allowed those who wanted some privacy to sit away from the crowded centre, while other tables and chairs were positioned next to the large windows that looked out onto the street.

Miriam chose a room with just enough space for the two of them. *Very close and intimate,* thought Daniel. She was not wasting any time this afternoon, and he knew she'd be watching the clock to ensure she left enough time for 'relaxing' back at her apartment. Although Daniel had to admit that the woman sitting opposite him was stunning, and he did enjoy spending time with her, there was unfortunately no spark. Once he left he rarely thought about her, and he'd have been just as happy to have wandered around the city for a while, grabbing something quick to eat before making his own way to the airport.

Miriam, however, had the schedule worked out, and she was going to make sure they stuck to it. After asking Daniel what he wanted, she beckoned impatiently to the waiter, who wandered over casually. 'Two beers and the house special pizza, and could you make sure the beers come out straight away.' She folded up the menus, handing them briskly back to the waiter, who filled up their glasses with water before heading back to the kitchen. 'Some of these waiters are so slow,' Miriam said. 'If he's not up to scratch, this guy, I'm going to put in a complaint. How hard can it be? I mean it's not rocket science. But you watch, I bet he'll mix something up.'

'You're pretty harsh, Miriam. I think he's probably doing his best, and he has a trainee badge on so he will be a bit slower. He's just making sure he gets it right.'

'No, there's no excuses. I tell you I'd love to be a boss somewhere; I wouldn't put up with anything because there's no room for errors or slowness. Probably similar to your interviews today. I mean really, some of those applicants who presented at the front desk. I wouldn't employ them to clean out the toilets. One guy who came through had a wooden leg. I've seen him before. I could see the stump bit under his trouser leg and some of the others were scraggy, rude, no makeup, and their clothes . . . ' She rolled her eyes. 'Seriously, who'd employ them? And then they wonder why they can't get a job.'

Thankfully the beers arrived and Daniel didn't have to listen to her views on the applicants she had welcomed today. Steering her off the subject, he moved the topic to a lighter conversation, recalling some of the funny incidents that occurred in the small town of Gowrie, finding that once Miriam stopped talking about work she was actually pleasant company.

A large pizza was placed in front of them and the flowing beer left them feeling relaxed. Behind Miriam, the narrow doorway allowed Daniel a glimpse of other patrons who came and went from the popular café, and he watched the city workers chatting to each other, enjoying the food and drink. Interesting, he thought, how the pace slowed a little in the afternoon as patrons wound down and enjoyed the space in between work and the journey home.

A young couple squeezed into a small space near the large windows on the other side of the room and he realised that one of them was the same woman who was going to be employed as his courier driver.

Ensuring that he didn't arouse the attention of Miriam, he watched as the couple sat down, the young woman sliding over to where her companion was sitting, oblivious that she was being observed by her future boss. The cold weather had got the better of her, and she pulled her worn coat over the floral dress, holding it firmly around herself as if she was still freezing. *What a bloody liar*, he thought, watching as the young man with her reached across and rubbed her arms trying to warm her up. No partner, she'd told them. How many of her other stories had been lies?

The young man with her had a rough appearance, with unkempt hair and dirty-looking clothes that hung loosely on his gaunt body. He appeared to be agitated, unable to sit still, and kept looking from Jessica to the people walking along the street outside the window where they sat.

Miriam stood up to go to the bathroom, allowing Daniel an even better opportunity to watch his newest employee. Coffee arrived for the couple, and it seemed like the young man downed it all in one go. Although Daniel couldn't hear what he was saying, he could see that he talked non-stop, arguing with her, fidgeting with the salt and pepper shakers, tapping a spoon on the table, leaning back and forward, all the while scanning the room as if he was looking for someone. Jessica kept patting his hands as if she was trying to calm him down. At one stage he leant over, reaching into her bag, refusing to let it go as she tried to pull it back from him.

It was obvious that they were arguing and Daniel leaned back in his seat, angry that he'd allowed Phillip and Rosalie to choose this woman for a position that was so vital to the everyday running of his workshop.

The tensions between the two appeared to escalate, and the young man now stood over Jessica, his face close to hers, his hand still firmly on her bag. Grasping at his hand, she moved it away from her bag before reaching in and taking

48

out her wallet. Daniel could see that she was angry, but was also trying to keep the disruption to a minimum, probably aware that she was in a crowded city café full of customers; some nearby patrons were already annoyed at the interruption to their early evening drinks.

She pushed some money into the young man's hand; he appeared to be unhappy with the amount she had given him. He said something that Daniel couldn't hear before scrunching the notes up and pushing them down into his pocket. Still standing over her, he leaned down and talked directly into her face. Daniel could vaguely lip-read her reply. 'Take it all,' she said, before handing over what appeared to be everything that was left in her wallet. The young man bent down and gave her a quick hug, adding the last of her money to the other notes in his pocket before walking out the door of the café and onto the street without a backward glance.

Jessica sat upright, her fists clenched, nodding politely to the waiter who had also observed the altercation and had come over to ask if she was okay. She assured him she was fine and continued to finish the last of her coffee, turning away from anyone who sat in the café, observing the people walking past the window. Daniel was unable to see if she was angry or perhaps upset, although her shoulders slumped and she appeared smaller and defeated. She was still sitting in the same position when Daniel and Miriam left. Miriam had paid for the pizza and beers before she returned to Daniel. 'Sorry to take so long,' she said. 'Are you ready to go?'

'You shouldn't have paid. I was going to shout. I'm a bit old-fashioned like that.'

'You can pay next time you're in town.' She snuggled into him as she linked her arm through his, both stepping out of the café, Miriam guiding him back down the street towards her inner-city apartment. Daniel wondered if Jessica had seen him when they walked directly past her window.

# 9

The week following the phone call to say she had been successful in gaining the courier's job had passed in a flash for Jess. There was paperwork to complete, police checks, health assessments and more forms to fill in, followed by a fitting for uniforms and a two-day induction course in the city. The work readiness program had kept her busy and not allowed her much time to think about what she was about to undertake. Goodbyes with Johnno had been difficult, although she needed to remind herself that he had been the one who pushed her into applying for the job, assuring her that they'd see each other when she flew back each month.

This was her chance, a break from past hardships, and no matter how much she wanted to be with him, she knew deep down that this was an opportunity for her to get somewhere in life. Waiting for him to get his act together was never going to work; it was up to her, and she gritted her teeth, telling herself she could make it happen. She clenched the armrest as the ascending plane banked steeply, clearing the distance and pointing in the direction of the Western Queensland plains.

'It'll straighten up in a minute; they always do this when they leave the city. Just take a few deep breaths.' A young man sitting beside her smiled politely, looking across her so that he could see out her small window as the plane seemed to fly completely on its side.

'I've never been on a plane before. I just thought it would fly straight.' Her voice was shaky, and he noticed the paleness in her face, her knuckles white as they gripped the armrests between them.

'You get used to it. They often leave Brisbane like this. My name's Jefferey. I'm the new office person for the main camp.' He leant over and offered Jessica his hand.

She gave him half a smile and shook his hand, amused at the energy and excitement that he showed as the plane evened out, passing over the last of the city centre, increasing height as it flew over the urban sprawl that now seemed so far below. Jefferey's voice was excited. 'Oh my god, I'm so thrilled just to escape the city and see a bit of the outback. Maybe there'll be cowboys to meet. How about you, um, what was your name, lovely?'

'Jessica.'

'How about this, Miss never-been-on-a-plane-before Jessica — isn't this exciting?'

'I guess so. Wow, we're so high up. The clouds are around us.'

Jeffery laughed loudly, amused at the astonished look on her face. 'You can let go of the armrest now. You won't fall out of the sky. Where are you working?' he asked. 'Maybe we'll be together.'

'I'm going to be a courier. They'll give me a ute and I'll pick up mostly mechanical parts from wherever they say and then drop them out to a workshop about thirty kilometres out of town. I think I also have to deliver to the main camp.'

'Sounds great, although I thought you might be in the office with me. I think it's all females who work there. Hopefully we'll all get on. I usually find I get on better with the ladies than most of the fellas.'

'Are you gay?' Jessica turned towards Jeffery, her dark brown eyes looking straight at him.

'Goodness me, you're up front. People don't usually just come straight out and ask that. But the answer is yes.'

'You look like Ricky Martin.'

'Oh my god, I love you. We're going to be best friends. We definitely need snacks, they should be about to serve them. See, they're bringing them around.'

'I'll be fine, thanks. I'm not hungry.'

Jefferey was quick at reading people, and as soon as he looked into her brooding eyes, he knew there was a complex background to the skinny woman who sat nervously next to him, her knuckles white from her grip on the armrests.

He patted her hand. 'You can let go now. It'd be great if you could relax just a little, and the food and drinks are free, the company sorts all that out.' He nodded at the waiting flight attendant. 'Sandwiches and orange juice for both, thanks.'

Before long Jessica could feel the plane starting to descend and she turned to Jefferey, who had chatted to her excitedly all the way,

53

even prompting some laughter from her with his stories of nightclubs and past relationships that had usually ended in tears and disaster.

'How's that, what a quick trip,' he said. 'Look, we're starting the descent.' They both peered out of the window, Jeffery pointing to some of the structures below. 'You can get an idea of the countryside. Dusty and dry, that's what it looks like.' He scrunched his face up as they both looked down at the miles and miles of endless brown flat ground, broken only occasionally with a scattering of green shrubs.

Off to one side, they saw clusters of buildings organised in neat rows, larger tin roofs and smaller buildings positioned next to them.

Jeffery's voice was excited. 'Look, there's a swimming pool. That must be the main camp, and you can just see the mine further there in the distance. Maybe we'll get huts next to each other!'

'I'm not living in the main camp,' Jessica said. 'I asked to live out at the small caravan park. They're only a few vans there.'

'Why did you do that? The social aspect will be way better at the main camp. Can you change it?'

'I don't want to change it. I prefer it that way.'

Jeffery felt a barrier come up, and he knew better than to keep asking questions. 'No worries. We'll have to make sure we catch up, though.'

Although she was usually wary of new people, Jessica had warmed towards her chatty co-worker, and she smiled back at him, once again clenching the armrests as the plane levelled out, its tyres winding squeakily downwards before unravelling and grinding across the bumpy runway.

★ ★ ★

The two newcomers made their way off the plane together, the blast of hot, dusty air that greeted them causing them to stop in their tracks and look at each other.

'Shit, who opened the oven door?' Jeffery said as he put his bag down on the ground, freeing his hands so he could adjust his collar and hair. 'First impressions have to be good, right?'

Other workers trickled out from the plane, the new employees in their regular clothes standing out in the bevy of fluorescent yellow and navy work gear of the workers returning to their shifts. Jessica and Jeffery followed the other recruits over towards a minibus, the driver jumping down to greet them. 'I love this guy already, what a body. How gorgeous is he?' Jeffery whispered in Jessica's ear as they neared the van.

★ ★ ★

Daniel stood in the dust, welcoming the new arrivals. The workers for the main workshop were already standing in a group and each shook Daniel's hand heartily, exchanging banter as they jumped up into the bus. *All typical lads*, Daniel thought to himself. *Full of gusto and confidence. Let's hope it stays that way.*

Too often he'd observed the consequences of fly-in, fly-out lifestyles, particularly on young blokes. It all sounded and looked so appealing: grinning young workers, smiling in glossy mining brochures and websites. However, the reality of living out in the middle of nowhere, working fourteen-hour shifts and longer, as well as being a long way away from family and partners, often had a terrible effect on workers.

Troy and Gus, the two workers chosen for Daniel's camp, were quieter than the others and shook hands, nodding politely before taking their seats. The last two waiting to board the bus now stood in front of him. He looked down into a pair of intense brown eyes before firmly shaking his new courier's hand. They both looked hard at each other before Jessica, without speaking, took her seat on the bus.

Daniel smiled broadly as the last of the new crew stood in front of him. 'Ah, the amazing Jeffery. Welcome, buddy. It's good to see you again. How was the flight?'

'Great, Daniel. I'm excited to finally be here. I just can't wait to meet the ladies and get into the swing of things.'

'You'll have to come out home and have a look at the setup we have out there. I'll keep in contact with you and get you out for a beer and meal. Make sure you ring me if you need anything or have any questions. Those ladies in the office want someone who's going to work well and fit in, most of all someone who will stay.'

'That'll be me. Keen as mustard, and I love the offer to come and visit. Thanks.'

'All on board.' Daniel looked back at them all,

Jeffery sitting next to Jessica, who was staring out the window, as usual not making eye contact with anyone else around her. He'd keep a close watch on her, regardless of what Hoppy had said, or what Rosalie and Phillip thought of her. He was good at sensing trouble, and he had a feeling that with her, sooner or later it would arise. His voice was loud above the noise of the bus. 'Welcome to Gowrie. Welcome to Seelo Mine.'

# 10

Bitumen roads led the minibus and its occupants away from the small airport. Dust flew up as the vehicle turned off onto a small dirt patch before stopping outside a weathered sign that said *East Bend Caravan Park*. Some of the letters were missing from the sign and it hung from one bit of chain instead of two, lopsided, much like the rest of the run-down park. 'Christ, don't tell me this is it,' one of the guys in the back of the van yelled out.

'No, our new courier has elected to live here rather than at the main camp, so Jessica, if you'd like to grab your stuff, this is it,' Daniel said, watching her in the rear-view mirror.

'Don't forget to come and see me,' Jeffery said as he helped her out with her bag. He gave her a quick peck on the cheek. 'Ring me if you need to.' He looked concerned and gazed warily around the park, which at least seemed to have a concrete amenities block and office.

Daniel raised his eyes as Jess thanked him. She spoke quietly, her eyes down, and he shook his head as she jumped down from the bus, a cloud of brown dust flying up around her as her boots hit the ground. How the hell was she going to lift machinery and heavy parts? Daniel thought. She was tiny, and the tight jeans and t-shirt as well as her riding boots looked about the size that a kid normally wore.

Jeffery sat behind Daniel, chatting to him as the bus continued out to the main camp. 'Why does she want to live there?' Jeffery asked.

'Not sure, and if I had my way she wouldn't be allowed to. But Phillip is a bit soft sometimes, too kind-hearted. It won't work, I can tell you right now. It's rugged living out here and that's why they have the main camp with the extra comforts that make the workers' lives a bit easier. It's rough living at the van park, and usually only a few old fellas who don't like the crowds live there. It should've been closed down years ago.'

One of the young guys a few rows back spoke up, 'She's not very friendly, that chick. She is hot, though. I asked her out for a drink after the induction. She ignored me to start with, and then when I got, well maybe I was a bit persistent, she let loose, mouth like a sewer!'

'She has a partner,' Troy said. 'I saw her with him a couple of times. He was with her outside the building before the induction, and he waited there for her in the afternoons. That might be why she wasn't interested.'

Daniel listened keenly, the information backing up his own observations. Another one of the young guys started telling a funny story about his attempts at meeting women and everyone was soon laughing. The subject quickly changed to what they'd heard about the food, the money they were going to make, and the jobs they were looking forward to starting. Jeffery sat quietly, staring at the dusty paddocks, amazed at the amount of traffic that used the road connecting

59

the mine and the small town.

'The town must have boomed with all this mining,' Gus said to Daniel.

'Well it did to start, particularly with so many workers coming in to do the infrastructure set-up and the commencement of the mining. The trouble is, and it's the same with a lot of these small towns, most of the workers are like you guys, FIFO, fly-in and fly-out. It's great for the workers and the mines, but you don't spend any money in town. Most of your time is spent working, and then just some time for eating and resting, sleeping until the next shift starts. It all grew so quickly. The money is great now, but you know what, it will slow, and then what will be left for the towns? Houses and rent are expensive. If you're local you can't afford to buy in.'

'It's much the same in Gladstone,' Troy added in, 'and the whole town has changed, well it's become a city. Trouble is, none of us can afford to buy there unless we come out here and make a shitload of money. To tell you the truth, I'd rather have stayed in Gladstone because I love the beach, the fishing — well what's left of it, and all of my family and my girlfriend, they're all there.'

Daniel looked in the rear-view mirror at Troy, reminding himself to keep an eye on these newest recruits. Mental health issues were rife amongst the workers, and only last year a young fella had taken his own life. Drugs and alcohol were also a problem, and the mining companies were starting to experience a whole new set of issues with these isolated mines and the workers who gave up everything to make their fortune.

'This is it,' Daniel said as the bus pulled up outside the administration building. The new employees filed off the bus and Daniel led them in the direction of the office block for their latest induction and introduction to their new life in the mines. He smiled broadly, pleased at the selection of new workers. 'Seeya, fellas, and take care. Gus, Troy, I'll be seeing you tomorrow. The manager here will fill you in on times and places, so just go with the others, and then tomorrow you'll be making your way out to my workshop and picking the courier driver up on the way. Jeffery, if you come with me, I'll take you down to the office where you'll be working before I pick up my ute and head back out.'

A path led to the back of the admin block and Daniel opened the door into Jeffery's new workplace. A chorus of 'Welcome' boomed out across the room, and they looked up to a bevy of colourful streamers and balloons greeting the newest office worker.

# 11

Rosalie didn't waste any time checking how the newest recruits had settled in. Daniel answered her questions over the phone, enjoying her excitement when he told her that the office staff had made a big fuss over their new worker, Jeffery. 'They baked a cake, decorated the office with balloons and streamers, and basically just completely fussed over him. He was in his element, a grin from ear to ear. He definitely has no trouble making friends. The others are all settled in as well.'

'And how did your friend Jessica go?'

'She's your protégé, not mine. Yep, I dropped her off at the old van park; she doesn't talk much. I still think you've made a mistake, firstly employing her and secondly letting her live out there. There's nothing there for her and it's rough living; a city woman like that she'll be lucky to last a week without the luxuries of home.'

Rosalie was still adamant. 'I've told her if she doesn't like living there, she can move into the main camp at any time. And just wait, Daniel. I know she's going to work out in that job. She followed everything correctly at the induction. She's sharp and intelligent. Perhaps she doesn't mix so well, but that will come.'

'Hmmph,' was the only reply. 'Well, Rosalie, I'll let you go. I can tell you, it's good to be back here. I can only cop that city rush for short periods of time.'

'We love it when you visit, Daniel. Perhaps Phillip and I will make a visit out your way later this year. That could be fun.'

'I'll hold you to that, Rosalie. Looking forward to it.'

The phone call ended and Daniel enjoyed the solitude as he drove the final stretch before entering into the gates of his property. The farm stretched out across five hundred acres, small in comparison to most properties out this way, but perfect for what he wanted. The homestead perched upon the highest parcel of land, its lengthy verandas providing shade from the relentless outback Queensland heat. Not far from it were the massive worksheds that housed the equipment and machinery making up the bulk of Daniel's business. Fenced paddocks further to the back of the house held a few cattle that picked at the sparse grass poking through the loose, dusty soil. Most of the fenced property was leased out for cattle, the remaining sectors near to the house and sheds often used to store equipment waiting to be fixed.

Pulling up next to the few steps leading to the front of the house, Daniel looked up to the roof and gutters that he knew needed repairs. There was always something to fix on these old houses, he thought. He had a never-ending list: painting, replacing handrails, re-nailing or renewing boards. It was endless and ongoing, yet he loved the homestead. It was the original house on the property and the front veranda offered a relaxed sitting area, ideal for watching the sunset across the vast endless paddocks.

A flock of galahs' squawky calls echoed across the plains, and he looked down towards the only hint of green that lined a distant western fence-line. Beyond that fence was his favourite part, the reason that the property continued to exist and operate as a small cattle agistment. Standing on the veranda, his hands resting on the railings, Daniel looked towards the distant line of trees marking the run of the Black River.

For years now it had been a parched, sandy riverbed with occasional tufts of grass growing where water once flowed. Low-leaning river gums, their long, thin leaves weeping towards the riverbed, provided a cool shady area in the arid environment. The river had been barren for years, and the trees appeared drained, with a stressed look to them. Sand stretched across the wide indentation, often ending up in whirly winds that ripped up and down, picking up loose material and depositing it on the dusty banks of the river.

*Rain*, Daniel thought. *It has to come soon.* He looked out across the parched earth towards the horizon. The ground rippled with a haze of wavy mirages, dust whirling as the wind swept it up, throwing it against the tin sheds, their corrugated roofs glimmering in the heat. A metal windmill, its head held high, creaked and clanged as a dry wind crossed through its blades. It was dusty and it was dry, but he loved it — the isolation, the beauty of the Australian outback, and the huge open paddocks that stretched in every direction.

Sometimes it would be nice to have someone

to share it with. After all, he was only thirty-four, no kids to fuss over and no wife to keep him company. He'd tried that once — engagement, a wedding, a beautiful wife; it was everything he'd ever wanted. But it ended in disaster, heartache, and a hefty settlement through which he'd only just managed to hang onto his business and property. The rest of the investments he had accumulated over the years had gone her way, along with the house in town, the new car, and the expensive furniture that he had never wanted anyway. He was relieved to see the back of it all, and in the end accepted that Helen was gone, gone for good, never to return; not that he'd have her back anyway. Lying was not high on his forgive list, and no amount of apologising had been enough for him to take her back. Now he had his daily routines, the business was successful, the house the way he wanted it, and things were in their particular spot, just how he liked everything to be. Bachelor life suited him fine.

# 12

Jess would have struggled to explain how she felt when the minibus dropped her off at her new home. Standing outside the entry to the park, she gazed out across the property in front of her. Gates that no longer hung on hinges leant against rotted out fence posts, permanently open, propped up amidst the long grass. Not a blade of green grass, instead spindly brown spears that intermittently pushed through the dust. Everything seemed brown. The roofs of the sheds and vans were brown. The plants struggling to keep their heads up in the gardens were brown, as were the bottles lying scattered to the side of the path and the plastic chairs scattered around a fire pit. Even the sheets flapping on the clothesline had a brown tinge to them. The only signs of colour were the fluorescent shirts and trousers hanging stiffly on a long piece of thick wire strung between two wooden posts; wooden posts that leant dangerously to one side, threatening to drop clothes and an assortment of other washing into the dust beneath.

Taking a deep breath, Jessica surveyed her surroundings. There was hardly any movement, only a screen door flapped against an open entry into one of the long vans further down the row. There were ten vans all up that she could see from where she stood, all in much the same condition — old, faded, and some patched with a variety of materials that added to the dilapidated look and feel of the entire park. The office block was adjacent to the amenities, both concrete buildings painted brown, the difference discernible only by small signs that designated their purposes.

It wasn't often that she allowed her emotions to bubble to the surface, but today, at this moment in time, as the sound of the bus faded into the distance, the reality of where she was sank in. This van park was going to be her home. If she could just keep her head down and work hard, if things would just go right for once, this was where she could stay. She could call it her own. For a moment the load lightened from her shoulders, and for once she felt like there was something ahead, a place to settle into and a future with a purpose.

She instantly loved this first introduction to the dusty outback and her heart thumped excitedly, the scene in front of her so different from what she was used to. A loud voice broke through her thoughts and she looked up.

'You must be the city woman. He told us you'd be 'ere today.'

Jessica was greeted by a woman who appeared to be in her late sixties carrying a large laundry basket full of work clothes, freshly washed. She swung the washing basket onto her hip so as to have a free hand to shake Jessica's with. 'I can't put anything down in this rotten dirt. I'd 'ave to wash 'em all again. Pleased to meet you, and the name's Myrtle. You must be Jessica.'

'Pleased to meet you, Myrtle. They just dropped me off at the gate. I was hoping someone knew I was coming.'

'Ah that mining mob. They're well organised, and so they should be, all the money they make. Of course, we knew you were coming, my love. We have everything ready for you. Not so sure why a young slip of a thing like you wants to live 'ere, though. But then again, each to their own.'

'Thank you. It looks all right.'

'It ain't fancy but it's clean as a whistle, and if you pay me extra, I'll do your laundry for you. You won't get cleaner toilets and showers anywhere, and being the only lady living here, you get the female block all to yourself. You gotta watch those fellas, though, because I'm sure they use them sometimes. Never mind, they're a good bunch 'ere. You'll find they mind their own business, and just want to be on their lonesome most of the time.'

Myrtle, who was a very large lady, wore a billowing tent-like dress that came to just above her knees. The sturdiest, broadest calf muscles that Jess had ever seen poked out from under her dress, her feet pushed into extra-large riding boots that stood solidly apart on the sun-baked ground. Myrtle placed the basket down on a block of concrete, beckoning for Jessica to follow so she could show her the caravan that was to become her home.

'All I ask is that you ring me when you're not going to be 'ere. There's a book up in the office, and you have to either write in there or let me know. You buggers fly in and out all over the

68

place, and I hear your shifts are organised by Daniel's workshop. I need to know when you're going and coming. Otherwise, I'll worry bout ya. Got me?'

'I'll make sure I do that.'

The vans were set out neatly so each occupant had space and privacy. 'Yours is the seventh one along. The others at the end are vacant at the moment. When you get your ute from the boss, you can park it here.' She pointed to a well-worn spot adjacent to the van. 'That fire pit in the middle there, you'll find the fellas like to sit around that at night. Sometimes they cook their dinner there together and maybe have a few drinks. You'll find them pretty quiet on the whole. Mostly off to bed early, ready to start the shift the next day.'

Myrtle opened the screen door of the van. 'See, freshly oiled yesterday.' She swung it back and forth to demonstrate the lack of squeakiness. 'And you could eat off the floor.' Her finger ran over the shelf that was lined with blue and cream mugs, cups, plates and saucers. Glassware and bowls were displayed on other shelves, and Myrtle took great joy in opening the cupboards to show Jessica the range of wares that filled every available space in the kitchen.

'Wow, I didn't expect all new things.' Jessica's eyes were wide, and Myrtle noticed the young woman's astonished look as she ran her hand over the bed. 'The doona cover, it's beautiful. The pillowslips and sheets match. Everything's so lovely.'

'They're not a bad size, these vans. They look

69

like shit from the outside, but they're air-conditioned, and Seelo always makes sure they fit 'em out to look good inside. Now the fridge and pantry are stocked for you to begin with, but when ya need extra, you can let me know, or there's a small grocery in the main street of town. I'm going to leave ya to it now. I believe Daniel is sending the other two new workers out here early tomorrow morning to pick you up and take you out to the workshop. He'll show you the run of the place.'

'Thank you so much, Myrtle.' Jessica was still running her hand over the bed cover. The bright colours and crisp newness left her feeling like she'd come to the best place in the world.

'Oh, and also — see that box there? That has all your uniforms, all washed and ironed. Let us know if the sizes are okay. If not, we'll work it out. That HR lady, Rosalie, she's usually spot on with the fitouts. It's the regular old yellow, orange and blue trousers, shorts and shirts. Leave ya to it. I'm always around if ya need me. I gotta get this washing out before it dries in the basket. The heat out here will suck the moisture out of everything,' Myrtle said as she patted the leathery skin on her arms.

Jessica sat for a long while after Myrtle had left, running her hands over the sheets and covers, gazing in amazement at her new home. Freshly laundered towels were folded neatly, along with soaps, shampoos and a basket of other bathroom extras. She picked up a towel, rubbing the fabric across her cheeks, shocked that towels could be so soft and thick.

Placing them neatly on one of the bedside tables, she surveyed the entire van. It was large and roomy, a compact kitchen with just a small cooker and fridge, a table that had bench seats on both sides, and a tiny television mounted on the wall. 'Oh my god.' She laughed out loud, flopping onto the bed. If she lay back on the pillows, she could watch the TV. Luxury, absolute luxury. And to top it off, at the rear of the bed behind the curtains she could see through a window that looked straight out onto the paddocks beyond.

The sight of the motionless brown cattle and the swirling dust reminded her of where she was and that she needed to be prepared to begin work the following day. It was a rare feeling to be so excited for something good to be happening in her life. Most of all to be in a place that was just hers, where no one else could intrude, with her own belongings, the thick, soft towels, and the most amazing doona she had ever seen. She had finally found home.

# 13

Excitement about both the job and her new home had broken Jessica's sleep into small patches that first night, and in the morning she lay awake long before the alarm clock sounded. Sitting on the metal steps of the van, she wrapped her hands around a steaming cup of coffee, watching the sun as it threw the first warm rays of light across the dusty paddocks behind the van park. Flocks of galahs heralded the new day and a mob of kangaroos formed a line as they bounded across the dusty terrain, their movements continuous and effortless as they easily cleared the barbed-wire fence on the eastern boundary. A red glow covered the earth, and the early-morning light threw its crimson colours across everything in its path.

Unfamiliar emotions overwhelmed her and tears welled as she looked out across the vastness of the outback. Rays of light filtered across the brown of the earth, illuminating the dry grasses that sprang up in small clumps across the yards. The sky wrapped around the vastness of the earth, and she looked up into the never-ending darkness, the last of the stars fading into the dark blue of the sky as the new light of day filled the surroundings.

A vehicle sounded in the distance, and Jessica straightened her stiff uniform down, retying one of the laces on new work boots before gathering the backpack with what she needed for the day. A dust cloud travelled along the road in front of the park and soon a work vehicle stood in front of her van, two enthusiastic faces peering out at her. She nodded at Gus and Troy as she stepped down and walked towards them, her unblemished boots quickly covered in the brown dust that coated everything in its path.

'Morning, Jessica,' Gus said. 'Daniel asked us to pick you up so you can travel with us to the workshop. Once we get there, I think he'll have your vehicle ready so he can show you around.'

'Thanks,' she said nervously as she hauled herself up into the rear seat of the dual cab ute, realising that new jobs could be daunting, that everything and everyone was going to be unfamiliar, and that she needed to step up and be confident.

'You look a bit different in your uniform. How's the van park?' Troy spoke quietly, politely, wanting to break the ice, both boys unsure of how to approach someone who had previously been unfriendly.

'It's lovely, thanks.' She couldn't help herself and the words tumbled out. It was, after all, very exciting. 'It has new crockery and brand-new sheets and towels. It also has a TV.'

The boys looked at each other, amused at her enthusiasm. 'That's great,' Troy said. 'The main camp's pretty good too. There're rows and rows of huts right next to each other, but it's okay.'

'Thanks for picking me up, I wasn't sure who was coming to get me.'

'Daniel is busy this morning and he wanted us

to all arrive together.' Gus sounded a bit nervous. 'I hope I go okay. He makes me a bit edgy. You know what it's like when someone watches you do your job; well sometimes you stuff up. Also, I think he'll be a strict boss to work for and I'm not sure I'd want to get on the wrong side of him.'

Troy slowed down for some cattle crossing the road. 'Yeah, he won't put up with any shit. You can tell. I've worked for tough bosses before. The thing is not to complain about anything and just do everything the way he asks. They say he's the best in the industry for this type of work, so I reckon he'll be great to learn from. I just want to nail this job. Maybe we can have each other's backs. You know, look out for each other.'

'That'd be good.' Gus sounded relieved. 'I'm glad we're out here and not at the main depot. Sometimes at smaller places it's a bit easier. I get a bit lost sometimes, you know; unsure of how I'm going.'

'How about you, Jessica?' Troy said, looking back at her in the rear-view mirror.

'Of course, I'll look out for you both. I want to do well too. This job means everything to me. We can help each other out.' She'd surprised herself again. Most of her life had been spent just trying to keep her head above water. Sometimes she had felt like she was slowly drowning, like there was a massive lead weight dragging her down to the bottom of the ocean. It would be nice to have some support. God knew she was already on the wrong side of her new boss, so she might need all the help she could get.

'Here we are,' Troy said as he steered the car in through the gates. The three of them looked out across the vast paddocks, the sun now throwing its heat at them. Jessica suddenly felt sick. Her hands were shaking and she closed her eyes, telling herself to be calm. She could do this. All she was required to do was drive, pick up parcels, and deliver them back to these sheds and some other workshops.

'You've gone pale,' Troy said as he passed her a water bottle. 'Have a drink. You'll be fine; remember it's just a job. We'll all be okay, it's just the nerves that get you to start with.'

'Let's go.' Gus opened the back door for Jessica, waiting patiently as she tried to get her legs to function. 'It's just a job, remember.' He smiled nervously and winked at her. In return, he received a glimmer of a smile as she hopped out of the ute.

Daniel stood up near the shed, watching the three of them. He'd liked the look of the two young fellas at the interviews and had been pleased watching them yesterday, noting that they were quieter and a bit more serious than the other six. They would be hard workers, and he was looking forward to training and teaching them the many aspects of the maintenance section. One of his managers was waiting up at the sheds, ready to start showing them around and to ensure they were comfortable and happy with everything so far. His day, well part of it, entailed showing his new courier the ropes and teaching her the intricacies of what might appear to be an easy job. So much depended on her following safety requirements, as well as delivering quickly and accurately.

Daniel watched Jessica walking towards him, looking completely different now in her new cargo work shorts and fluoro shirt. Once again, that first thought returned — *She's just a skinny kid*. Not even the bulk of the new work clothes could hide her tiny frame, and he wondered how on earth Rosalie thought she was ever going to be strong enough to lift many of the parcels that she'd be delivering. Shaking his head, he walked towards the new recruits, trying hard to be friendly and welcoming to all three.

Jessica noticed Daniel shaking his head, so she immediately straightened up, feeling a rising antagonism at his negative attitude. She walked with purpose, holding her hand out first for him to shake, looking with determination straight into those piercing blue eyes.

'Good morning, Jessica,' he said, his eyebrows raised in surprise, reading the look that she was giving him. A look that said, 'Just try me, go on, have a go, I'm ready for anything.' He shook her hand firmly before turning to the two boys, who looked keen and eager to start the day.

'Righto, let's go,' Daniel said. 'Come into the office and we'll get you all started.'

# 14

Jessica listened intently, only once or twice asking questions as Daniel drove her around the various sites from where she would pick up or deliver parts. He spent a considerable amount of time going over the safety requirements of driving on bush roads, the perils of the abundant wildlife that wandered on and off the road, and how to drive defensively where the bulk of the traffic consisted of road trains and other huge mining vehicles. Road trains, she discovered, were not actually trains, but rather trucks that stretched forever, often blanketing the ute in a cloud of dust as they passed. 'Don't sit behind them when they kick up the dust because it's like driving blindfolded. You're on a tight schedule delivering parts, particularly the bulk of it that will be to my workshop. But just remember, safety always comes first.' He turned towards her. 'Got it?'

She looked out the window on her side, answering in a firm voice, 'Got it. Safety comes first.'

It was over three hours later before they began to make their way back to the workshop. Daniel hadn't offered for her to drive and she didn't like to ask, determined to keep her head low and just do what she was told.

'Now, any complaints or issues, you see me; or if you don't want to do that, you ring Rosalie.

She's going to keep in regular contact with you.' He leant against the side of the ute, watching her as she stood like a school kid in front of him, skinny little legs poking out of the knee-length work shorts, new boots already dusty and a work shirt that looked just a little too big for her. 'Make sure you always wear sunglasses when you're driving. The glare is constant out here, and you need to make sure you've got a decent pair.'

She looked down at her feet, her wavy brown hair soft around her face, big brown eyes only glancing up at him for a second as he added, 'You do have some, don't you?'

'I'll get some. I'll make sure I get them as soon as I can.'

He leant into the glovebox of a nearby truck. 'Here's a pair of mine you can use. They're old, but they're still good. They'll do at least until you can buy some yourself. Right, spare keys are in the glove box, and I'll see you here in the morning with the first delivery. The instructions for tomorrow are written on the clipboard on the front seat. Don't forget what I've told you today.'

'Thank you.'

He watched her get into the ute, surprised at how quiet she was today, with only a few questions and just lots of nodding and listening as he went through everything she needed to know. It annoyed him that she didn't always look him in the eye when they spoke, like she had something to hide. He could usually tell a lot about the new workers, which was the reason Rosalie and Phillip ensured that he came into the city for the interviews.

The two young fellas were nervous but keen, and he was confident in their ability. But this new woman, he would give her a month, if that. It wouldn't take her long to find something to complain about; the novelty would soon wear off and he was ready for the arguments, because he was not going to put up with any nonsense from her.

Too often young ones picked up these jobs because of the good money, and plenty of them were making their fortunes out in the remote areas where the mines were booming. But it wasn't easy work: the shifts were long, the heat was often unbearable, and being away from family and partners sometimes wore them down. Walking towards the huge sheds to meet with Gus and Troy, he wondered how long she would last.

# 15

Steering carefully and slowly, Jessica drove the work ute in through the entry to the van park. She had gone into town to pick up a few things and then dropped in some more paperwork at the main camp as Daniel had requested.

Jeffery had been ecstatic to see her and showed her around the office, pointing out his desk and introducing her to the other ladies. 'They're just fabulous and I love them already. They've already shown me so many of the procedures and I just know I'm going to enjoy the work. Life here seems so different from in the city, so much more relaxed and friendly. How are you going?' Jeffery slowed down a little, aware that Jessica was quiet and had hardly spoken.

'Fine, thanks, Jeffery. I'm about to go back. I just needed to drop off this paperwork. I'll be okay, and the caravan is great. It has a TV and new linen, and even the cups and plates are new and all match.'

Jeffery had felt protective towards Jessica from the moment he'd met her, although he knew that she'd hate to think that she needed anyone to look after her. But there was something about her. He wanted to give her a cuddle and tell her to chill out. 'How about I come out to your place on Friday after work,' he said. 'I finish at five and I'll bring some beers and something for dinner.'

'That'd be nice. I'd better go.' She left hurriedly, confused at her response to Jeffery's invitation. What was she doing? What was she thinking, agreeing to a stranger coming to her van for dinner? She hadn't had many friends over the years, and those she'd been friendly with hadn't hung around when the going got tough. It was better to go her own way, to stick with Johnno and not trust anyone, because sooner or later people turned on you. They criticised and judged, rarely actually wanting to help. Jeffery had attached himself to her, obviously deciding that he wanted to be her friend. Strangely enough, she had warmed to him. The fact that he was gay immediately eliminated the worry that he wanted anything more than friendship. It'd be nice to hang out with him. She wasn't doing anything wrong, and he made her laugh.

\* \* \*

The next few weeks were a settling-in period and Jessica worked hard, carefully following the instructions given, focusing intently while trying to get used to driving on wide open roads that stretched out endlessly, all the while making sure that parcels were delivered as they should be and on time.

Hoppy had come to see her and wasted no time introducing her to the other five permanent occupants of the van park. At night, the men gathered in chairs around the fire. Hoppy liked to cook for them all, and during the week, he

81

insisted that Jessica join them. Tonight she'd brought her folding chair, a plate and some cutlery so she could join in and indulge in what Hoppy promised her would be the best stew she'd ever eaten.

'Hello, Jessica. Come and meet the fellas.' Hoppy welcomed her warmly, moving over, making way for her to enter into the circle of men seated around the fire. 'This here is Charlie.' He pointed at a huge scruffy miner who Jessica guessed looked a lot older than he actually was. Although his face was mostly covered by a thick dark beard, years in the outback sun had taken a toll on his skin, the hard work of mustering and bull riding wreaking havoc with his bones, causing him to walk with a strange gait, his back slightly bent. Hoppy continued, 'He lives in van number one.'

Charlie leant over to shake her hand, talking slowly, his drawl gravelly. 'I saw you loading out at the mechanics' shed today. You keep going, you'll get stronger. There's always ways to get heavy stuff up onto that ute. I'm gonna call you Miss Geronimo.' Jess smiled at him as he passed her a drink. 'I've always hauled heavy gear throughout my working life. Used to be as fit as a Mallee bull. These days, though, you're not allowed to lift like we used to. You got all sorts of equipment to help you now.'

Hoppy interrupted, 'Blind Freddy can see you don't do too much lifting these days, Charlie.' He prodded Charlie's stomach with a stick, causing the burly truck driver to laugh loudly.

'That's why the truck job suits me fine. Sitting

on my arse all day. So what if my gut's getting bigger and bigger. I say it's a sign of contentment. Got no woman to try and impress, so really, who gives a shit?'

From that day on, he always called Jessica Miss Geronimo. Although Charlie liked to be the one talking, preferring the others to do the listening, Jess perceived that he was a decent fella who just liked living by himself. Charlie had let them all know. 'Not living at the main camp. That fancy shithole is not my thing, full of wowsers. Don't like that amount of people, and besides half of them full of bullshit anyway.'

Next to Charlie in van two lived another truck driver, Thommo, who also told Jessica that he could never live anywhere else. 'Me and Hoppy, we've been together since day dot. Wherever he goes, so do I, well except when he goes into the city to stay with his sister. You never get me in there, all that traffic and people rushing around.'

'You just don't fit into any of your city clothes anymore, that's your problem. That's why he doesn't come in with me,' Hoppy said, laughing, as they all looked at Thommo's huge stomach.

'I know, I know. I can hardly see my toes these days. One day I'll get fit again. I used to be famous, you know,' Thommo said. 'I was a boxer.'

'Let's not bore the young lady to death straight away now,' Charlie growled. 'We've heard it all before.'

Jake and Edward, who lived in three and four, were in their sixties, one of them nearly as short as Jessica, the other tall. Edward's gangly frame could fill a doorway and he needed to bend his head over to enter the vans. Both their vans still wore the previous year's Christmas lights entwined around their antennas, and every night a colourful 'Merry Christmas' flashed sporadically from the top of the van. 'Gives it a festive feel,' Jake said.

The two men worked on the stop and go signs, spending long hours standing, designating when the huge trucks and other equipment could make their way across the highway and rail tracks that were the lifeline for everyone and everything at Seelo Mining. 'Bloody hot, dusty job, but we wouldn't change it for quids, would we, Eddie?' Jake said.

'The name's Edward, if you don't mind. It's a beaut job. I agree with you, Jake. We get to see everyone and everything coming and going.'

Jake and Edward were quiet men and Jessica had the feeling that they were living remote to escape something or someone. 'No one will bother you out here, miss,' Jake said. 'As long as you go about your work and do what you're supposed to, you can keep away from all the other stuff that might be back in a past life.'

All the men in the first four vans were friendly, and apart from sometimes sharing the evening meal together around the fire and a few quiet beers, they pretty much kept to themselves. Up at sunrise to go to work and then back home late, time for a clean-up, dinner and then to sleep, ready for the next day.

Cedric, however, in van five was a different kettle of fish altogether. The wiry tanned man, who told Jessica he was thirty-eight, worked in the storerooms and lived out at the van park, because as he said, 'Get myself into too much bloody trouble up at the main park. Yeah, I tried that for a while. Too many whingers and upstart city mongrels. Dob you in for anything. I liked to bring the women in from town sometimes; you know plenty of them up here making good money their way. Well, that didn't go down well, along with the fact that I also like a few drinks and yeah, all right, sometimes a smoke.' He winked at Jessica, who got the gist of the 'smoke' comment. 'Stingy bastards, dobbed me in, nearly got me the sack over just a little bit of dope. That's why I came back out here to the park. Gotta behave myself real good, don't I, Hoppy? Fair dinkum, these boring old farts out here keep me well under control. Don't you worry, Joelene, I'll leave you alone. I gets on it sometimes, but I just like to have a song and a dance.' Cedric did a little jig in the dust, waving his hands like a ballet dancer in Hoppy's face.

'Her name is Jessica, Cedric. And you just watch yourself. You're bloody ten years older than what you say.' Hoppy turned to Jessica. 'Just keep out of his way on his week off, because he goes on a bender.'

'She won't know what that is, you dumb shit.' Cedric was moving with his arms by his side now, imitating an Irish dancer. 'Just call me Eileen. Do you dance, Janet?'

'It's Jessica,' Hoppy said as he waved him away, all of them laughing at the energy of Cedric, who constantly had a cigarette hanging from his mouth.

'Don't worry,' Charlie added in. 'He goes away on the weeks he has off. Home to his little town near here, well it's five hundred kilometres away, but we call that close.'

'Got a tribe of kids, I have, Janet,' Cedric said. 'They live with the missus, they do. I don't.'

'She kicked you out years ago,' Edward joined in the banter.

'Cedric's scared of her, Jessica. He shits his pants as soon as she yells at him,' Jake added in, all of them laughing at the serious look on Cedric's face.

'She's a mean bitch, that woman,' Cedric said, his eyes flitting each way as if his wife was hiding in the darkness, listening in. 'She's only about your size, mind you, but man, she don't take any nonsense. She says jump, I jump. Everything I go to do, she wants me to do it different, always changing everything on me. I spend my time off out there with the kids. They're great, all getting big now, but they love their old dad. They're all shit scared of her as well. Ah well, just gotta stay out at the shed when I'm there. She lets me sleep there; it's down her backyard. Have to smuggle the grog in, though. Last time out there I took off like a bride's nightie, cause she found my stash and smashed every bottle.'

Jessica sat quietly, loving the chatter and jokes between the men, who were all living at the park for different reasons. None of them asked her why she chose to live here. It was like they already knew she wanted her space, or just that they minded their own business. That's what she liked about them. They didn't ask a lot of

86

questions about where she'd come from or what she'd done. Living at the van park was going to suit her nicely.

# 16

Over the next few months, Jessica became more confident and relaxed around the men, and Hoppy always made sure to include her. Some nights he would ask her to cook for them. 'What fancy-pantzy meal are we having tonight?' Cedric asked as he jigged around, stirring up the dust in front of the fire.

Edward yelled at him, 'Sit still, you stupid old bastard; you're as mad as a cut snake.'

Jake added in, 'What've you got, ants in your pants?'

'At least I can still move, not like Charlie over here. Soon he won't be able to see his toes!'

'I can't see them now, you drongo. It's called being bloody content. Leave me alone. I'm looking forward to this special meal.'

Jessica had cooked up a stir-fry for them. Fresh vegetables were hard to find, and she'd eventually conceded that she'd have to be satisfied with the frozen variety; the fresh ones cost too much, and she just didn't have the money for it. The steak, however, she had splurged on, and hopefully it would make up for the lack of fresh veggies. She knew the men wouldn't be happy unless there was meat in their meal. This was the one dish she could make that she knew would go a long way.

Years ago she'd cooked it continually, pilfering the ingredients, waiting outside fruit shops and markets for shopkeepers to discard their spoiled or excess vegetables. Tonight, though, the ingredients were all purchased, the added spices borrowed from Hoppy, giving the meal an aroma that wafted across the van park. As Jess looked around at the men who were all silent because they were so busy eating, she felt an overwhelming sense of déjà vu.

How many times had she sat around a fire in an abandoned warehouse, or under a bridge sharing food with others, all different ages, but all with their own story to tell? Tonight, though, there was something missing, an enormous gap, and her chest tightened as she thought of Johnno. They'd always sat side by side, and she'd made sure he had enough to eat, pretending that she was full, giving him the last of whatever it was they had cooked up.

Over the previous months, she'd flown back to the city a couple of times on her days off and spent the week with him. He was still keen and supportive for her to be working at the mines, reassuring her that he was doing fine. Of course he said he was missing her, but the money she sent him each week was seeing him through. 'You're keeping me alive, Jess. I love you for that,' he'd told her. She visualised his pinched face, always begging, pleading for money, twisting her emotions until she gave in. She missed him like crazy, but her work and now the people who were her friends made her feel happy, like she was worth something. Last time she had seen Johnno, he'd told her he was going down to Sydney for a while with some mates.

'Could be for a couple of months, maybe more,' he had said as he gave her a hug. 'C'mon, Jess. I'm letting you do your thing for a while, now it's your turn to let me break free a little.'

'That's all good, Johnno.' She had been angry with him. 'But who do you think's paying for all of this? All of my money seems to be going to you at the moment.'

'I know, I know.' He had put on a cajoling voice. 'Once I'm in Sydney, I'm gonna get a job. The guys I'm going with reckon it's easy, and they know how to make some quick money.' Jessica screwed up her face. 'It's honest money, Jessie. I'll keep out of trouble.'

There was no option but to let him go. How was she supposed to stop him? It had been she who had broken away, and he had supported her going. Was it to let her get ahead, or was it purely about the money and the fact that she could support him while she was being well paid?

'Penny for your thoughts.' Thommo broke the quietness, the only sounds the noise of the cutlery as it scratched across the surface of the now empty plates.

'I gotta lick my plate. Man, that was the best meal ever. Did your mum teach you to make that?' Edward said as he stood up to see if there was any more left in the pot.

'I wasn't brought up by my mum, and I didn't know my dad. I was a foster kid.' Jessica stared out into the blackness of the paddocks around them. Sometimes she just wanted to blurt it out, to get it all off her chest. She liked all these men. They were kind and she felt a camaraderie, a friendship that she hadn't experienced before. It was the same with Jeffery. Every Friday night without fail he'd arrive at the van with pizza and beer for them both. Afterwards, they'd join the others around the fire, the men all chatting and laughing, Jessica mainly listening. If Cedric was there, he and Jeffery would keep them all amused, Myrtle sometimes banging the door up at the office, yelling out at them to keep the noise down because she was trying to watch the soapies she had taped during the day.

Many times Jessica wanted to join into the conversation, to add in the details of some of the things she'd dealt with over the years. As they all became familiar with each other, often the men told stories of hardship and heartbreak, broken marriages, the fight with the bottle, deaths of loved ones, and kids they never saw. Often her mouth opened, but then her mind stopped her. The issue with sharing was to do with trust, or lack of it. Sooner or later everyone moved on, and one of them would tell someone else, and then people would talk about her, judge her for her background and not for herself. Nothing ever stayed the same, and it was better to keep it all in. Sometimes her chest felt heavy, the burden of previous years overwhelming. But still she didn't add to the conversation.

It was the same when she met up with Troy and Gus. If her visit to the workshop coincided with lunchtime, she'd sit out the back with the two workers, both of them around the same age as herself. She liked the two boys. They always encouraged her, treating her as an equal from the first day they had all started. The boys liked to talk about their girlfriends and families back in their home towns, and she loved listening to the stories of where they went and what they did on their holidays. She never said anything, but listened empathetically as they talked about the fact that they were struggling because they didn't see their girlfriends much. Similarly, she was missing Johnno, and it was only because she had been kept busy that she had been able to push aside the pangs of separation whenever she thought of him.

★ ★ ★

Jessica, Troy and Gus all got on fabulously, and after ten months in their new jobs had all passed their probationary period. Daniel signed off on their paperwork and rang through to let Rosalie know that everything was in order. 'So, it sounds like they're all going well, Daniel. I can tell you're more than happy with the two boys. Are they both liking the living arrangements and the lifestyle?'

'Yes, they're working out great. I talk to them regularly. I mean we all work together every day, so I feel like I've got to know them both. Their work ethic is exceptional, nothing is left to chance, and both are perfectionists, which is how it needs to be in this business.'

'And how's our Jessica?' Rosalie asked, a hint of sarcasm evident in her voice.

'She's okay, I guess. She's passed everything for the probationary time, and there haven't been any major mistakes. Everything is delivered on time, she doesn't ask too many questions, and just does what she's supposed to.'

'You were worried about her size with the lifting, with heavy things. How's that going?'

'She's been inventive with trollies and manual lifting equipment. I don't know how, but she seems to manage it all okay. Thommo down at the van park tells me he's been doing some training with her, strengthening her muscles.'

'Thommo? Isn't he fairly overweight? Is that the truck driver with the huge stomach?'

Daniel chuckled. 'Both Thommo and Charlie look like that. They tell me it's a sign of contentment. Thommo used to be a professional boxer in his day, though, so he knows the training requirements to build up strength. Maybe it's been helping her with work, who knows.'

'Well, don't you ask her about it, Daniel?'

'I figure you talk to her regularly. You're her mentor. Besides, she and I don't communicate that well. We've just never hit it off. I can't stand the fact that she hardly ever looks me in the eye, plus she rarely talks to me, well really only about work-related issues.'

'Did you ever think of talking to her, maybe getting her to open up a little bit? She communicates with me fine, and we have long conversations about work, where she lives and what she thinks of being out in that horrible dusty town that you love so much.'

'And what does she say? Is she sick of it yet? Perhaps the van park is a bit primitive for her?'

'On the contrary. She loves the environment

out there. She talks about the colours of the dirt, the sunsets and the noises that the birds make in the morning and the evening. Sounds dusty and dry to me, but each to their own I guess. Also she's coping fine with the distance from home, just in case you're wondering. I know you like to keep a good handle on that aspect of your workers' needs.'

'Look, Rosalie, you keep an eye on her. She doesn't talk to me at all. I'm keeping a good check on the other two. I'll leave Jessica to you. To tell you the truth, I can tell she doesn't like me, not that that worries me. As long as she works well.'

'She probably doesn't like you because you obviously haven't developed a rapport with her at all. She's a lovely woman.'

'Ha,' Daniel laughed. 'You sound like Hoppy. They all love her down there at the van park. She's fitted in perfectly. The camp of misfits, as Hoppy refers to it. He reckons she doesn't talk much about home, though.'

'I know she's had it rough,' Rosalie said. 'That's about all I ever get out of her. Anyway, it sounds like she's doing brilliantly. Wouldn't you agree? You have no complaints, and she's done everything just right.'

'She's doing okay at the moment, so let's just leave it at that.'

★　★　★

A few weeks after Daniel had spoken to Rosalie, he was surprised to see Jessica waiting in his

94

office doorway. Usually when she delivered for him, she just dropped the items off and picked up the next worksheet, ready for the following directions. Sometimes she would look around for Gus and Troy and the three of them would sit and eat together on their lunchtime break.

Now she shuffled her feet nervously, waiting for him to finish the phone call he was on. 'Could I see you for a moment, please?' Her dark broody eyes looked through long eyelashes, and he noticed that her face, arms and legs were tanned from the time spent in the sun, in between deliveries and pickups.

'Sure. Come in, take a seat.'

'I um, I don't know if it's my place to say anything, but you did say when I started, to come to you first and then Rosalie if needed.'

'Yep.' *Here we go*, thought Daniel. *I wonder what complaint she has.* 'That's right,' he said sternly.

'Well, I don't want to cause any trouble for no one.'

'Anyone,' Daniel corrected her, watching her eyes glint angrily, her shoulders straighten.

'I don't want to cause trouble for anyone,' she said, emphasising the *anyone* and saying it slowly as a small child might. 'But Gus is not travelling very well. You may already know that, and I don't want him to know I said anything, but he's not good.'

'What do you mean by not good?' Daniel's face showed concern and he leant forward, taking her comments seriously.

'He's down a lot. I know he acts all cheery and

says everything is great, and he loves the work and living here. But underneath all that, things aren't right, and he's getting near rock bottom. I think he might be thinking of harming himself.'

'That's a fairly serious comment to make. What makes you think that? Has he said something to you?'

'No, I can just tell.'

'How?'

'Because I've seen it before. I only talk to him over lunch and I know. You need to work it out for him because he's not coping with living here and being away from everyone.'

'Are you sure he hasn't said anything to you? I mean, that's a big statement to make without him saying anything.' He looked straight at her. 'I want the truth.'

'I've told you the truth,' she spoke as she stood up. 'Like I said, I don't want him to get into trouble or lose his job, but if you don't do anything about it, I'll ring Rosalie. It's my week off starting today, so could you please tell me if I need to do that?'

'No, no, of course not. You don't need to ring Rosalie. I'll take care of it, but I'm surprised because I regularly check on both Troy and Gus. I always ask both of them how things are and if I can help them with anything. I'm pretty good at picking up on those sorts of problems.' He realised straight away that he had put himself right in, by pronouncing that he always checked on the two boys, but never once had he asked her if she was travelling okay. Standing up, he called after her as she left the office. 'I'll check.

96

Thank you.' He watched until she disappeared out through the doorway of the shed, the sound of her ute starting up, moving him into action.

# 17

After a week's break, Jessica had been shocked when she returned to the workshop to find Troy working alone. She had spent her time off at the van park figuring there wasn't any reason to go back to the city. Johnno, who she hadn't heard from lately, was probably still down in Sydney, and apart from him there wasn't any reason to return. Troy had also been on his fly-out week at the same time, and she looked down through the workshop, peering around the odd assortment of equipment that found its way here to be fixed. Troy was working on a massive piece of machinery, the tyres three times the height of Jessica.

He looked up as she approached. 'Hi, Jessica. Did you have a good week off?'

'Yes I did, thanks. I didn't do a lot, just bummed around. I did some training with Thommo, Hoppy gave me some cooking lessons, and the rest of the time I just chilled out and read some books. How about you?'

'Yeah, I flew out. Spent the week mainly with the girlfriend, caught up with me mum and dad, had a few drinks, the usual. Great to see everyone again. You know, I just get settled in and then it's time to come back again. Oh well, I guess my bank account is looking good. Penny and I want to buy a house one day.'

'It's a good way to make some big money,

these jobs.' Jessica was looking around for Gus.

'I guess you're stashing it away as well,' Troy said. 'You must save a lot not going home on your week off. I go through a heap on drinks and eating out. Anyway all good, back in the swing of things now, though.'

'Is Gus out the back?' she asked.

'No — you wouldn't believe it, but Daniel said he's not coming back. I think he got sacked. Daniel said he'd fill me in at smoko time. He sounded a bit serious about it all. Maybe Gus just didn't want to do it anymore. Strange, though, because he told me he liked the job, plus he'd bought a new car and a boat. He'd taken out hefty loans for both of them, so I don't know how he's going to pay them off now. I thought he'd stay, the same as me.' Jessica felt sick at his last words. 'I don't know why, but there's something funny gone on. I've got a strange feeling that he got the sack. I'm not sure what he did wrong, though.' Troy's last words were directed at Jessica's back as she strode quickly through the shed towards Daniel's office. This time, she didn't wait politely at the door but rather barged in, standing opposite to where he was sitting behind his desk, talking on the phone.

'You bastard, you told me he wouldn't get in trouble. Troy said he thinks you sacked him. I fucking knew I shouldn't have said anything to you.'

Daniel spoke quickly to the other person on the end of the phone. 'I'll ring you back — talk to you soon, mate.' He looked up at Jessica, her eyes sparking, the foul language flowing, her

99

vitriol directed squarely at him while he stood silently waiting for her to finish. A few more choice words and accusations flowed easily from her mouth and Daniel took some deep breaths, eyes narrowing, his anger rising as the words 'trust' and 'lies' were flung around the room.

'Ok, that's enough.' His voice was deep and very direct, and he glared angrily straight at her. 'How about you sit down and take a breath. It's taken a while, but here we have the real Jessica again, not the polite young lady everyone else thinks you are.'

'Why did you fucking sack him?'

'I asked you — actually, now I'm telling you — to sit down. I'll not talk to you while you're ranting and swearing at me.' He sat down himself, annoying her even further with his calm demeanour and the casual way he rearranged things on his desk, waiting for her to sit opposite him. She remained standing, so he repeated his directions. 'I will not explain anything to you until you sit down. Can I just remind you that I am the boss, and the reason I've asked you to sit down is so I can talk to you rationally and calmly, without any of the previous hysterics. No, stop,' he said, holding up his hand signalling for her to be quiet. He realised she was about to let loose with more abuse and he watched as she tried to gain control of her anger. 'Thank you. Now let's be calm, please.'

Jessica sat opposite, every muscle in her body clenched. She was not in the habit of backing down from anyone and she certainly wasn't afraid of the man on the other side of the desk, even though he was very stern and serious as he waited for her to sit down. Over the last ten months he'd hardly spoken or taken any notice of her, unless it was to give her instructions for work that needed to be done. She'd made sure to tread lightly around him, ensuring jobs were completed to perfection, always going the extra mile and doing work before she was asked. Not once in all that time had he ever praised her, or even said she was doing okay. Not once did he ask how she was going, or if there was anything she needed. She had just about had enough, and this was the final straw: she had trusted him and obviously he'd used the information to get rid of Gus.

'Right, are you calm now?' He watched her as she bit her lip, probably to stop herself continuing with her tirade. Her face was bright red, and she looked as if she wanted to hit something. 'Why are you so feisty? How about listening to people for a change and letting them explain what's going on.' He waited for a reply, but there was nothing, only her steely stare straight into his eyes. 'All right, now listen carefully and remember what I'm telling you is confidential. I'm only telling you because you started the ball rolling. First of all, tell me, what made you think Gus was really near the edge?' He waited. 'I need you to talk to me. It's important, because I missed signs that I should have picked up on.' Still she glared at him, taking deep breaths, trying to get her temper under control.

'Okay, let's approach this differently. First of

all, Gus hasn't been sacked. He's actually been admitted to Gladstone hospital and is under surveillance in the mental health unit, getting help from every specialist that we can get him access to. His family and his girlfriend are with him and he has lots of support. He won't be coming back to work out here, though. I've talked to some friends I have in Gladstone and once he's feeling better, there will be a similar job to this one waiting for him to start there in town and close to where he lives. They're a good company. The pay's a bit less but they'll keep an eye on him. I think though that once he gets this extra help and he's back near his family, he'll be fine. Apparently it's been building up. He started out doing well, but lately he hasn't been able to cope with the isolation and separation from his family and friends.'

Jessica's eyes were wide and the redness faded from her face. 'Is he all right? Please tell me he didn't hurt himself?' Daniel thought he saw tears in her eyes, but he knew better. A tough nut. It was like she'd seen it all before.

'Firstly, I want to know how you knew he was so close to the edge. I look out for those types of problems. We've experienced too many suicides in the mining industry lately, all good young kids who just couldn't cope, and nobody ever picks up on how serious it is until it's too late. Did he say something to you?'

'He never said anything directly about wanting to hurt himself. But he was lonely, I could see it in his eyes. He kept saying everything was okay, but I could tell it wasn't. You could just feel it.

102

Last time I saw him, I knew he was going to do something bad to himself. He never said anything; I can just tell those sorts of things.'

'You mean like ESP.'

'No, I don't believe in that shit, um I mean rubbish. No, I guess I've just been around a lot of people with a lot of different problems. Did he hurt himself?'

'No. When you came to see me, I thought I'd leave it until the next day and talk to him just before he flew out.' Daniel didn't tell Jessica that he'd kept hearing her words over and over in his head, and so had driven in especially to check on Gus before he'd originally been going to. He was angry with himself that he hadn't picked up on the problem earlier, and the state that he had found the young worker in had left him shaken. It was good to talk to someone about it and he wanted to fill Jessica in on what had happened.

'That night, I went to his room over at the main camp. He didn't want to let me in at first, but I talked and talked until he unlocked the door. He was a mess.' Jessica could tell that Daniel was still affected by the encounter with Gus. 'He said he couldn't cope anymore and wanted to end it all. We sat and talked for hours and it was as if he'd been waiting for someone to come, like he was crying out for help. I asked him directly if he wanted to end his life, and he told me that he had it all planned; then he showed me the pills. Once he'd told me how low he really was, it was like he gave in, all the fight went out of him. He didn't even put up an argument when I said I was calling the

103

ambulance, and I guess things just went from there. They had him in at the clinic and with the flying doctor's within a couple of hours. I've rung his parents every day since, and they're extremely grateful to you for alerting me. Once things calm down a bit, they want to come and meet you, or to have you come and stay at Gladstone with them on a week off.'

'Oh, I couldn't do that. I didn't do anything. I just knew he was close to the edge.' She stood up, looking down at her feet. 'Thank you.' The words were forced out, but at least Daniel thought she was acknowledging what had happened.

'No, thank *you*, Jessica. If you hadn't come and talked to me, that kid wouldn't be here today.' Daniel pulled an envelope out of his top drawer. 'He sent this here for you. It's a letter. I guess I did mention to him that you had suggested that he was hitting rock bottom.'

Jessica took the letter from him, a puzzled look on her face. 'He wrote a letter to me?'

*Why does she look so confused?* he thought to himself. *It's like she's surprised that I've recognised what she's done.* 'Yeah, it's a pretty big thing, you know. He said you three made a pact when you arrived to look after each other.'

She nodded, taking the letter from him. 'I'd better go or I'll be late for the next delivery. I'm relieved that he's okay.'

Daniel stood next to her. 'I'll give you some leniency with time today. Just today, mind you.'

The barrier went up again as she turned and walked out, talking as she went. 'There's no need, I'll get it all done.'

104

# 18

Life and work continued as normal for the next few months. Daniel had over the previous year returned a few times to Brisbane for more interviewing sessions, and now once again felt obliged to comply with Rosalie and Phillip and fly back to the city. They needed to recruit a new worker to replace Gus, plus they wanted Daniel to assist with selecting workers for the other maintenance sections. Miriam had been waiting for him, making sure her work schedule fitted around his interview times and flights in and out.

As usual, they had made their way back to her apartment, Miriam ensuring there was plenty of time in between dinner and his flight out. 'Do you think about me sometimes, Daniel? Just sometimes?' she asked him.

'Do I think about you? Well, I'm thinking about you now. I've been thinking about you for the last two hours.' He avoided the question, instead running his hands over her naked body as she straddled him, her pouting lips coming closer to his as he pulled her head towards him. 'I'm definitely thinking of you now,' he said before kissing her, his hands running over the back of her legs, making her squirm.

'You haven't answered me. Do you ever think of me, even once after you leave here?'

'Why? Do you think of me?'

'I do. I miss you, and I look forward to when you're in town. Maybe I want more from our relationship than I have previously. I think I want to see you more regularly.'

'Miriam, when we started meeting like this, you told me you never wanted anything serious. All you wanted was some fun together, with no strings attached.' He sat up in bed. 'I'm telling you now, and I'll be completely honest with you. I don't want more than that.'

Miriam also sat up, pulling the sheet around her body. 'I think that if I didn't chase you, you wouldn't even bother with me. I never hear from you in between visits.'

'You always said that you didn't want more, that you wouldn't be able to deal with anything else.'

'Well, maybe now I do.' She ran her hand over his back.

Daniel stood up, picked up his clothes and headed to the bathroom. When he came out, she was still sitting on the bed waiting for him to reply. He spoke slowly, 'I'm sorry, but I can't do this any longer. It has no meaning for me, and I can't pretend it does.'

'Don't go, Daniel. I'm sorry. We can keep it just the way it is. I'd rather you sometimes than not at all.'

Daniel grabbed the rest of his belongings and headed for the door. 'Sorry, Miriam. We need to be honest with each other. Whatever it was, it's over.' He didn't look back, and once he had closed the door behind him a weight lifted from his shoulders. Now the decision had been made.

It had always been more one-sided from her direction, and he often wished he could just sneak in and out of the city without her knowing.

Making his way out of the busy streets, he grabbed a quick coffee at the airport before sleeping most of the way back in the plane. Another sigh of relief, and that lovely feeling that he was back home enveloped him as he picked up the ute from the airport carpark and began the long drive home.

★ ★ ★

The next morning he woke refreshed and was pleased to be able to slip back into his routine and schedule. He had become a creature of habit and liked to do the same things at the same time each day. This morning was no different. Waking at six, he squeezed three oranges, drinking the juice immediately before it lost any of its vitamin C. While the bacon and eggs were cooking, he made sure the jug was on the boil and the plate and cup ready for serving. Washing-up water, always the same heat, was run into the sink and once this was complete, he'd sit down and enjoy his breakfast. The cup for his tea had to be of a particular size and couldn't be the smaller cup that he preferred for coffee. The washing up was completed, and the table wiped before he flicked the iron on ready to run over his work gear. Once this was done, he'd have strictly a maximum five-minute shower, always ensuring that the bath mat was laid out over the edge of the bathtub afterwards, the towel back on the hanger and the window opened to let any steam out. Surveying the bathroom before he left, he ensured that it was tidy and ready for the next time he used it.

Now he was ready for the day. It was the same each morning, and he consoled himself with the thought that it was not because he was getting older, or a perfectionist because he only had himself to think of. No, rather it was because this was the best way for things to be done. He liked the order and routine, and it kept the house tidy so that he could put his hand on anything that he needed, and everything stayed in its place.

Today was Saturday, though, so he didn't need to iron his work gear, instead just quickly press a pair of jeans and a shirt. There were some items from Rosalie to hand in at the office, plus he wanted to visit one of his sisters who lived in town. Standing on the veranda, he surveyed the paddocks and the few cattle picking at the sparse grass in the home area. It was dusty and dry because there hadn't been any rain for as long as he could remember. It had to come sooner or later, and surely this rainy season they'd get something. Even just a bit of a drizzle was better than nothing at all. Heading for town, he looked at the same scene in every direction. Nothing different, just the endless dry ground and sun shimmering into the distance.

The sun was low in the sky by the time Daniel completed his deliveries for Rosalie and spent time with his sister and her family. The final thing he needed to do was to drop off a parcel at the van park.

Myrtle was happy to see Daniel. He usually bought her something to eat when he dropped in. 'Hiya, Myrtle. Just a small package here, plus I've got a surprise for you in that bag there.'

They stood and chatted for a while, both of them locals, born and bred in the area. Myrtle's husband had passed away a few years ago, and she'd nursed him until the end. Deciding to stay on and run the park had been an easy decision for her. After all, as she said, where else was she going to go? Plus it kept her busy.

'You going down to see the boys? They're all around the fire as usual,' she said as she stood in the entrance, her solid body clad in a floral tent-like dress.

'I will. I'll just drive down a bit further for a quick chat.'

Darkness drifted in, and Daniel's headlights shone on the group, who as usual were seated around a fire pit, a large cast-iron hot plate off to one side, perfect for cooking and heating water.

'That looks like Daniel's ute.' Hoppy stood up, excited at the prospect of someone else joining their group.

'Mr Good-looking,' Jeffery said with a laugh.

'Mr Grumpy, you mean.' Jessica looked down into her glass, Thommo raising his eyes at her comment as a couple of the men stood up to greet Daniel.

'G'day. I just needed to drop a parcel in to Myrtle, so I thought I'd come and say hello.' Daniel shook the men's hands and nodded at

Jessica, a look of surprise on his face to see her seated around the fire with the group.

'Have a seat, stay for dinner and some drinks.' Hoppy was excited to see him. 'It's a special night. Miss Jessica has cooked her famous stir-fry for us. There's plenty there, hey, Jess?'

Jessica nodded, her unsmiling face looking up into Daniel's. 'Plenty there.' She noticed how different he looked out of his work clothes. Jeans that fitted firmly showed off a fit well-proportioned body, the navy shirt accentuating his blue eyes. Short sleeves fitted firmly around his upper arms, and she watched him as he squatted in the dirt next to the fire, his face highlighted by the glow of the flames. *What a shame his looks don't go with his personality,* she thought to herself, *because Jeffery is right, he is handsome.* She studied his face, noting his chiselled chin. He was tanned, always neat and tidy, with a rugged bush face, full of character.

She noticed that the men from the country had a different look about them than their city counterparts. Long hours spent in the sun as well as hard physical work gave them a rough but handsome look. Even the older men were interesting to look at, their weathered faces lined and craggy, yet full of character. She loved the way that the creases around their eyes crinkled when they laughed or told a story. That was the other thing; they were full of stories. Tales that she'd never heard before: adventures with cattle, wild pigs, crazy people, living in isolated places with dust, flies, horses and cattle. Lengthy stories about droughts, lost fortunes, places they'd been, wild experiences, so unlike anything she had ever experienced.

So many nights she had watched and listened as the sparks from the fire spiralled into the dusty air, which would be filled with the crackling of the dry wood burning as one after the other they talked. Tales of heartache, love found and then lost, losing money, drinking their lives away, it seemed to go on and on. Sometimes after one of them recounted a difficult time in their life, there would be silence after they ended. Often there was nothing left to say, nothing that could fix what had happened, just the warm feeling that they had all listened and cared about what each other had been through.

Charlie in van one had only ever had one son. 'Stevo was his name,' he told them. 'A beaut kid, rough and tumble, loved the horses and most of all his motorbike. He was the apple of his mother's eye, just a beaut kid. When he was a teenager, he got sick. Just like the flu it was, you know what kids are like, they pick up colds and viruses. We didn't think much of it, but it lingered. The doctor in town sent us into the city for tests. And you know what, just like that, he had cancer. Riding a motorbike and chasing the women one day, and the next day given twelve months to live. There was nothing they could do for him. Tried a bit of chemo, but nothing was going to work. We brought him home to die.'

Charlie got all choked up that night, and you could have heard a pin drop around the fire. No one knew what to say. 'I stopped the rodeos when he got sick, and that's why I never went back. I didn't have the heart for it after we lost him. Nothing meant much after that.' Jessica got up and made Charlie a strong cup of tea, pouring it from the boiling billy and putting an extra teaspoon of sugar in for him. 'The wife didn't hang around much after that; we had nothing to say to each other.' Taking the cup of tea, he nodded. 'Thanks, Miss Geronimo. Anyway that's a long time ago now. You know, you never get over it, though. Not a day goes past that I don't think about him. You know what it's like, Thommo. You can't explain it to anyone.'

Thommo nodded. He had also lost a child, a three-year-old son, drowned in a dam on a neighbouring property. 'You're right, not a day goes past that you don't think about it. All the 'what ifs'. Rosemary, that's my missus, she was never the same after the drowning. I guess she blamed herself and I blamed myself. We're lucky that we have four others who have all grown up into great kids, well adults now actually.' He turned to Jessica. 'Hoppy's godfather to two of them. Him and I've been mates for a long time. My missus thinks he's the bee's knees.'

Jake from van four was the quietest out of all the men. 'That's why it suits me standing on the road holding a sign all day. I don't have to make a lot of conversation if I don't want to.'

Cedric butted in, 'You wouldn't believe it, Jess, but Jake used to be quite the ladies' man.'

'What do you mean, used to? I still have plenty of company when I go out for my week. I had a wife once, you know. Thank god I ain't got her anymore. Just couldn't do a bloody thing right by her. Didn't matter what I did, it was never good enough or done the right way. She pecked and pecked me until there was nothing left. I'm a patient man, but there's only so much you can take.'

'What about you Eddie?' Hoppy loved to tease the lanky road worker who so easily took the bait.

'Edward's the name, thanks. It's not so hard to remember.'

'Sorry, Eddie. Tell Jess your story.'

'Well, once,' he said, trying to use his posh voice, 'my wife and I had it all — the big house in town, overseas travel, always everything first-class. We couldn't have kids, so there was always plenty of money. We owned shares, property investments, even a valuable art collection. But, yes well, oh dear, we made a few bad business investments, and meanwhile Shirley, that's my wife, well she'd developed a gambling addiction. We lost everything except each other. After a long while, she finally listened to me, and we got her some help. She does well now. She's worked in a good job in the hardware shop near where we live for the last five years, and I've made some big money out here. We're fine these days. We've still got each other and no more gambling problems.'

Cedric also had his own sorrowful story to tell. His battle was with the bottle. 'It ate me up for years. Never there for the kids, and the wife ended up hating me. It was like I was two different people, one when I was drunk and a different one when I was sober. Gets you in the end, Jessica. Don't ever get addicted to anything. Look at me, twenty years later and still on occasion fighting the demons with the grog. I have to really watch myself, because I like working and you gotta be sober to work. As for these mongrel things,' he said, as he flicked a cigarette into the fire, 'they never let go of you.'

Hoppy always listened carefully and added gentle advice, continually looking after everyone. Although, Jessica thought, just like all the others, he had also survived plenty of tough times. His father had worked as an underground miner, and after surviving being trapped in a tunnel, was never the same again. 'It was like something went missing in his head. You know he was a good father before all that happened, but after the accident, it was like there were devils in his head,' Cedric said.

'One night he overturned the entire kitchen table. All the plates, cups, the meal my mother just served up, well it all went flying. Then he went for her. There were nine of us kids, and I was third eldest. I remember hanging off his arm, because after he swung at her, he went for my older brother. We all tried to stick up for her. She was an amazing woman. All those years she put up with his demons.' He paused, looking for a long while into the fire before continuing. 'She died young. I'm not sure even to this day what she died of. I left home straight after. I was only fourteen. My father brought in a new woman straight away. It was like she was waiting in the wings. I reckon he was seeing her when my mother was in the hospital for all those months.

That new woman, the younger ones suffered under her rule, aye. Sometimes I catch up with them, but they're scattered all over Australia now. Yeah, there's a few I still see.'

'What happened to your leg, Hoppy?' Jessica had always been curious about what had happened but had never been sure about asking.

'When I was in my twenties, I got a blood poisoning thing in my leg. They couldn't do nothing to save it, well not back then anyway. So they just cut it off. Righto, they said, you'll be apples. At least you still got the other one. No bloody sympathy for anything back then, Miss Jessica. You just got on and did what you could. And look at me, I do just fine, sitting around here today with all of you. I got a good job, some money in the bank, and look at the food we get to eat. Wouldn't be anywhere else or change if for quids. Remember that,' he said, pointing at Jeffery and Jessica. 'No use whinging about anything, because you just gotta get on with it, which you two seem to do all right.'

Tonight they were all here together, sitting around the fire, happy in their own way, all surviving, all working in one way or another and fairly content with their lot in life. Now, Jessica's boss, who was always curt and direct with her, and who she imagined had never experienced any such hardships in his life, was standing around the fire, possibly about to share a drink and eat a meal that she had cooked.

'So you're staying? Get another plate out, Edward.' Hoppy dragged a chair over for Daniel.

'No thanks, Hoppy. I'll only stay for a

moment, just a quick hello.'

Thommo stood up, his bulging stomach glowing in the firelight. 'What, you got somewhere better to go than here with us, someone to meet?'

'No, I don't, but I shouldn't stay.'

'Why not? Don't you like our food? You got better plans?' Edward added.

Daniel seemed to think for a moment. 'You know what, actually I don't have anything to do. I will stay. Set another place at the fire for me.' To Jessica's dismay, he sat down two chairs away from her, in between Jeffery and Cedric.

'How often are you out here, Jeffery? I'd have thought you'd get decent food out at the main camp.' Daniel accepted a beer from Jeffery, who as usual was immaculately dressed, as if he were going out on the town for the night.

'Friday night is usually my regular night. I always come out to have pizza and beers with Jess, but sometimes like tonight I'll drive out so I can see everyone while they're all here together. It's good when our schedules match up because it's no good having a late night before work. Although those ladies in the office love to fuss over me if I'm a bit off colour.' He laughed and took a big swig from his beer. 'Don't worry, I never drive back in. Jess usually puts me up, cooks me a big breakfast, and then sends me on my way.'

Daniel was pleased to see how well the other men accepted Jeffery. People could sometimes be homophobic, and he'd worried about how Jeffery would find the company out in these parts. It was, in fact, an odd assortment of friends seated around the fire. Not only the oddities and eccen-tricities that he knew came with the older guys, but the fact that they'd accepted and become good friends with Jeffery, not to mention his little courier driver who sat quietly, rarely speaking.

Charlie piped up, 'Miss Geronimo, you are unusually quiet tonight. Cat got your tongue, or are you dreaming about the next meal you'll cook up for us gentry?'

'Sorry, uh, no, Charlie. I was just thinking.'

'She's not always this quiet, Daniel,' Cedric said as he got up to stoke the fire. 'I know why she's quiet. She's still getting over the other night.'

Jessica chuckled softly, unable to contain her laughter.

Cedric patted her on the head. 'This little miss, she'll make a grand line dancer one day.'

'That looked more like Irish dancing than line dancing to me,' Thommo quipped, resting his beer on his stomach, his feet doing an imitation of dancing in the dust.

'That's about how much he moves.' Cedric pointed with the burning end of a stick to Thommo's shoes.

Thommo sat up straighter, his face coming alive, eyes sparkling as he looked towards Daniel. 'These two bloody kids.' He pointed at Cedric and Jessica. 'Well, Cedric thought he'd teach Jess how to dance. Cedric tanked to the eyeballs and Jessica, well she only needs a couple of vinos, look at the size of her. Well the two of them, not sure how they didn't both end up in the fire. The rest of us, well Edward fell backwards off his

117

chair, laughing. Laughing so much, you never seen the like. My poor little belly.' He rubbed his hands gently over his huge round stomach. 'It ached for days. These bloody two idiots, heel and toe, heel and toe, together now. Jake was playing the drums and Hoppy found his cassette player and got some Irish music playing. You've never seen anything like it. Fire in the background. You'd think they'd let both of them out of the loony bin.'

'You lot are a bunch of old codgers.' Cedric did a little jig in the dirt. 'Jessica's only a baby, and I'm just a spring chicken. We need to let our hair down sometimes, hey, Jessica?' He winked at her, and she smiled in reply. 'We can't just sit around like you old farts. Just you wait. We're practising for our Christmas pantomime. We'll get you to come to it, Daniel. Wait until you see the show Jess and I have got planned. Jeffery, you don't know it yet, but you're going to be the baby Jesus in our play.'

'Holy dooley, I can hardly wait. Let me know when the rehearsals are,' Jeffery said.

The banter and laughter of the group carried on, and it was nearly midnight when Daniel stood up to leave. 'All good, Hoppy. I've only drunk two beers. I'll take it easy. Goodnight, all. Thanks for the food and company. I really enjoyed the night. It's great to have a good laugh.'

'Ah, Cedric will do that to you every time,' Hoppy said as he walked Daniel to his car, the others packing up what they needed to go away.

'Night, all,' Jessica said. 'It's all right, Jeffery

— stay here with me, because you're not driving home.

'Thanks Jess, you're a gem.'

Jessica had long ago worked out that it was okay to let Jeffery sleep with her in the big double bed. Often they'd lie together, him on his side of the mattress and her on hers, chatting late into the night. 'When did you know you were different, Jeffery? I hope that's not too personal, but when did you know you were gay?'

'I always knew, even as a little kid, that I was different. I mean I just didn't go for all the other things that other boys liked. You know like playing sport, or even playing with cars. I know it sounds a cliché, but I really liked the Barbie dolls my sister played with. I just wanted to dress them in the best outfits, and I used to get so annoyed with her when she didn't match their clothes up in the best possible way. Once I was at high school, I really knew then. I guess once you're a teenager the boys start talking about the women, you know their bodies, what they want to do to them. I just didn't have those thoughts. I'm just not sexually attracted to women. I mean I love women, like I love you as my friend, but there's not that sexual attraction that there is for men.'

'You make a lovely best friend, Jeffery. I hope you meet someone cool one day and find your happy place.'

'Thanks, Jess. You're a great friend, too. I've always had women as my best friends. I love you lots.'

'Thanks, Jeffery. That means a lot to me.'

119

Jessica lay still, unable to sleep, thinking over the night's events for a long time after she heard Jeffery snoring softly beside her. It was nice to have someone next to her at night again, and she felt peaceful, content, as she recalled the conversation that night. Outside, stillness filled the air and nothing moved as the dry heat of the summer poured over the earth that was becoming drier and more barren by the day.

# 19

A new boy had been employed to replace Gus. Troy introduced him to Jessica as she trolleyed heavy parts from the ute to the middle of the workshop. She could feel the sweat running down her neck and back, and she remembered how hot it had been this time last year. This was her second summer and the heat was taking its toll. 'Don't forget to keep the water up,' Hoppy reminded her every time he saw her. 'And try and stay out of the sun, find the shade. It's bloody hot, even for those of us who're used to it. It's like it's building up. I can feel it in my bones. I reckon we might get a wet season yet.'

'Hi, Jess. This is William.' Troy helped her manoeuvre the large piece of equipment onto the floor of the shed.

'Yep, already met him. Thanks, Troy, I appreciate your help. I'll catch up with you some other time.' The dirty look she threw William's way was not lost on him, and he smirked back at her.

She had encountered William at a recent workplace safety day held at the main office. He'd followed her at morning tea break and questioned her about who she was and what she did. 'I guess I'll be catching up with you a lot, seeing you come out to where I'm working,' he said. 'I'm free, so maybe you'd like to hook up with me. You know I could keep you company at night, warm that pretty arse of yours.'

Speaking quietly so no one else could hear, Jessica leaned in closer to him, finding it hard to believe that he had just pinched her on the arse. 'Touch me again, you bastard, and you'll be dead meat.' Her eyes drilled into his. 'Fuck off, and don't come near me again.' With that she walked away, not giving him a chance for further discussion or comeback.

Jeffery, who was helping to run the course, came over to her at the next break. 'Did that new guy insult you?'

'It's okay, I sorted him. You're wanted out the front again. You're doing such a good job, Jeffery, and you're actually making this one interesting.' They both looked over to where William was busy talking to some of the other guys from the main work shed. Looking over, he raised his eyebrows when he saw Jessica and Jeffery together. 'Watch out for him, he's got a bad vibe to him,' Jeffery muttered. 'I've had a few run-ins with him. Christ, he's only been here a week and he's already getting on the wrong side of people.'

Neither of them thought any more about the incident, although Jessica noticed that William always let Daniel know how efficient he was at his new job. He big-noted himself all the time, telling everyone how good he was and how fast he worked. He had also tried to get her into trouble a few times, complaining to Daniel that she hadn't left drop-offs in the right position.

The week had started off badly for Jessica, and the last thing she needed was Daniel using that stern voice to remind her about the location of drop-offs, making her feel like she was a kid back at school being told what to do. She had nodded compliantly, knowing full well that the delivery had been left in the correct place, but what was the use of arguing? A couple of days later, when she arrived with a ute-load full of deliveries, Daniel came out and asked her to come to his office and see him after she finished. Meetings with the boss always made her nervous, and he didn't look happy, his tone far from friendly as she entered and sat down.

'I'll get straight to the point,' he spoke sternly. 'Did you notice in the last delivery yesterday that only half of the parts for the new machine were there?'

'Were they the small boxes with the red writing on the outside? If so, I delivered twelve of them.'

'You only delivered six.'

'I delivered twelve.'

'Do you realise how much those parts are worth?'

'I wouldn't have a clue. I imagine like all the specialised parts that I deliver here, they'd be worth quite a lot of money.'

'They're worth thousands of dollars each, and there are six of them missing. Do you have any explanation for how you picked twelve of them up from the airport but only six arrived here?'

'I delivered twelve. I double-checked them before I left.'

'There were a lot of parts that you delivered yesterday. You made three runs out here. Are you sure you're thinking of the correct parts? Are you positive there were twelve?'

Jessica could feel herself becoming irate. She knew one hundred percent that she had delivered twelve of those parts to the workshop yesterday. Her voice became louder and she stood up, speaking through clenched teeth and reminding herself not to use the f-word. 'I delivered twelve.'

'How about when you come back tomorrow, you come in here and have another chat with me and see if you can remember anything else about those parts. Like I said, they're worth a lot of money, and there's no way that six of them can just go missing. No one has seen them here, and with Troy away at the moment, William said he counted them, and there were only six delivered.'

Tears filled her eyes the moment she turned away from his desk. It took a lot to upset her, and over the years she had learned to toughen up and take things on the chin. To be accused of stealing, after all the hard work and effort she'd put in over the last year or more, was just about the limit. She'd also been in trouble earlier in the week after arriving over an hour late with a delivery that was urgent. Daniel had not been happy. 'Is there a reason this has taken an hour longer than what it should have? I rang the depot to see what time you left because we were standing around here waiting for it. Christ, these things have to come out on time.' He had been furious, his eyes flashing angrily as she stood there with nothing to say.

And now today, she wiped the tears away with the back of her hand, telling herself not to lose it.

The noise of her mobile phone ringing broke her thoughts and she answered, her voice still shaky from the confrontation with Daniel. It was Jeffery. 'Are you ok, Jess? You sound terrible.'

'Yeah, I'll be all right. Actually, you don't sound great yourself.'

'I'm going through a bit of a bad patch. Can I come out to your place tonight? I need to talk to you.'

'Sure, I'd enjoy the company. I'm just finishing up for the day, so whenever you're ready. See you soon.'

She looked forward to when Jeffery visited, enjoying the fact that sometimes they'd talk for hours, while other times they'd just sit together quietly, watching a movie or listening to music. Today, though, he sounded upset. Had his week been as bad as hers?

Sometimes when she was a bit down, she'd try and ring Johnno, but he rarely answered his phone and lately didn't return her calls or messages. Over the last year, he'd moved around a fair bit and was hanging around some different fellas that she didn't know that well. When they had first decided that she'd move out and work in the mining industry, they had agreed it would be for a year. However, once the money started flowing in, Johnno suggested that she should stay on. She liked her job, and at least she was sleeping in the same place every night, not moving around like they had always done. 'It'd be good if you could find some work too,' Jessica had tried to talk to him last time she'd flown back home. 'I'd like to save some of this money

I'm making, but it always seems to go mostly to helping you out.'

'You know what it's like, Jess. I've got mates scratching at me for cash. I owe a few people favours, and I've gotta keep the supply coming in.'

Johnno was always addicted to something. It had started off with cigarettes, alcohol and weed, progressing quickly to the harder drugs that were expensive but gave him what he wanted. 'Just this week, Jess,' he pleaded with her. 'I just need this next hit, and then I'll stop for a while.' But she knew it never ended — he was always looking for the next best thing, chasing another high, living with those who were after the same.

Going to the mines had been an escape from him. It hadn't been easy leaving, and even harder knowing that she wouldn't be there to pick him up, to look after him, to drag him out of one place after the next, to make sure he didn't die right there on the streets. So many times she'd tried to resist giving him money, pleading with him to dry out, to keep away from the mongrels that kept dangling every new drug on the market under his nose. Nothing was ever easy, though, not for him and not for her.

Life had always been on the move. They had lived in dirty squats and abandoned houses for years, and Jess had watched Johnno get skinnier and sicker. She'd always managed to find casual jobs where she could bring in enough money for their food and always, of course, money for his habits. She stayed with him because she loved him. She didn't love the way they lived or the

126

habits he had, but she loved him, and until the day she won the job at Seelo Mining, she had never thought that she'd leave him. Now she had her own place to live, great people in the van park who had become like her family, and the most important thing of all, a best friend, Jeffery. Sure, her boss hated her, and the work often involved heavy lifting and hot conditions, but she loved the area where she lived and worked. Most importantly, for the first time there was a sense of pride, achievement in a job well done, pleasure in being able to help the men at the van park sometimes, and happiness and a sense of freedom at night when they all sat around and talked and laughed.

Last time she'd seen Johnno, he had been heading up north and didn't seem to care that he might not see her for a while. 'Just got a new gig travelling up north, making a few deliveries for a fella. Sort of like what you do.'

'My deliveries are legal. You're going to get yourself into all sorts of trouble.'

'No, Jess, it's all good. Only thing is, I need some money, you know to pay for the petrol and food on the way up. I don't get the payment until I do the delivery.'

Johnno had persisted, pleaded and started to get angry with her. As usual, she had given in and agreed. 'This is it, Johnno; I can't do this anymore. I need to start saving for us together, you know, to buy things in the future.'

'Ah, live for the day, Jess. You're only young once.'

Just like so many times before she had

transferred the money, knowing full well that he'd spend it on drugs. The situation had worsened in the last couple of months, and she was suspicious that he was using something else other than what he'd been on previously. The anger that he often showed towards her now was a whole new thing. He had always pleaded and begged but never been as aggressive as now. She promised herself that this was it. This would be the last time she would give him money. The people he was moving around with were a different crowd, and she didn't care what any of them were on; it was all the same to her. She hated all of it.

How many friends had she and Johnno watched die from the drugs, one way or another? Overdoses, suicides, she'd seen it all. Well, she decided, there would be no more money transfers. She was about to turn twenty-three and wanted desperately to start saving the money she was earning. Who knew, perhaps even one day she could save up and get a house, just a little cottage somewhere, where she and Johnno could live. He'd be clean of his habits and get a job, and she'd feed him all the good food she'd learnt how to cook, maybe even fatten him up.

As she pulled into the driveway of the van park, she thought about where Johnno was now and what he was doing. Her thoughts were cut short as she pulled up next to her van, looking straight through the window at Jeffery, who was sitting waiting for her on the step. It was going to be a long night. He had a bottle of wine under his arm and another one in his hand that he was already drinking from. Well, she had things to vent about also. He stood to greet her, both of them hugging for a long time before heading inside.

# 20

A week's break had been just what Jessica needed, and she spent the time cleaning out the van and helping Myrtle around the park, once again having no reason to fly back home. The other men came and went, and she enjoyed the time spent with them around the fire or sharing a cup of tea. One of them often knocked on her door to see if she was free for a cuppa. They had become her family and she'd grown used to all their idiosyncrasies.

If she spoke to Edward like he was someone very important, she could get him chatting, and sooner or later he'd pop back with the latest book or travel magazine he was reading. 'You know, I would not loan these to just anyone,' he'd say. 'It's only because I know you appreciate them and treat them like gold. See my name there, it's in the front of every one of them so that you don't forget who they belong to. Also, if you don't mind, I don't like the pages bent back. Here, the wife sent this down for you. It's a bookmark with your name on it.' He handed Jessica a glossy cardboard bookmark that did indeed have her name written on it.

'I'd never turn the pages back, but thank your wife for the bookmark. I love it, and I've never owned one before, so I'll treasure this. Thank you, Edward.'

Charlie, on the other hand, was easily

persuaded with sweet biscuits. A couple of Monte Carlos and a strong cup of tea and she could ask him anything. Anything, of course, to do with the outback, rodeos, cattle or mustering. Question after question, it didn't seem to matter; if she could keep the biscuits coming, she could find out the history of the region, the surrounding area and everyone who'd ever lived in or around it. He was like a walking encyclopaedia and Jessica loved to get him talking, fascinated with the hardships and lives of the people who had pioneered the area.

★ ★ ★

Charlie had happened to run into Daniel in town the Sunday before Jessica was due to start back on her shift. 'G'day, Daniel. What's going on with the cattle they're running out on your place?' Charlie asked, starting up a lengthy conversation, taking in cattle prices, trucks, the drought and the mining industry.

'You're looking well, Charlie. The job must be agreeing with you.'

'I feel good now. Mind you, I suppose you heard what happened a couple of weeks ago?'

'No, I didn't hear any stories. I'm usually the last to know anything.'

'I'm surprised Miss Geronimo didn't fill you in.' Daniel looked confused as Charlie continued. 'Sorry, boss. You know Miss Jessica — the little pocket rocket, that's the other name the boys give her.'

Daniel scrunched his eyes up a little, unsure of

131

what Charlie was telling him. 'She must have told you, because she'd have been late for her delivery. Tuesday it was, not last week but the week before. She dropped a parcel off to Myrtle and noticed me slouched in me chair outside the van. Bundled me in the ute and took me to the medical centre. I told her not to wait, but she wouldn't leave me until they saw to me. Looked after me like me own family would and never left my side. They kept me in hospital overnight, and she came up again that night to check on me. No wonder I was in pain, bloody gallstones playing up. I'd passed out with the pain twice. They're gonna take em out next week, so I hope I don't get another attack before then. Anyway, I'm sure she's told you.'

'She did not tell me anything. I asked her why she wasn't on time but she didn't say anything. Why the hell didn't she tell me that she was helping you? I wouldn't have minded at all, but she just didn't say anything when I asked her why she was late. Bloody hell, I gave her a bit of a hard time about it too, although there have been a couple of other incidents also.'

'You know, you want to give her a bit of credit, Daniel. She's a bloody hard worker and I don't think she's had an easy life. She never says nothing when we all talk about the shit that's happened to us in the past. She listens and is very empathetic about all of our woes, but you know she's never really told us much about herself. I've got a good hunch that her life hasn't been all rosy before she came out here.'

Daniel was still irritated and confused. 'Shit, I

can't believe she didn't tell me why she was late. Thanks, Charlie; I'll have a chat with her when she comes in next. You look after yourself and let us know if you need anything.'

'Call in for a feed again. We got a great bunch out there, and that Jeffery comes out a lot. God, between him and Cedric, there's always a load of laughs.'

As they shook hands, Daniel's mind ticked over. 'I might just do that.'

# 21

It was Tuesday before Jessica made a delivery out to Daniel's workshop. The temperature had reached over forty degrees, and her feet dragged as she carted the delivery into the designated corner of the shed. William watched her struggle with the heavy piece of equipment as she carefully manoeuvred it off the trolley, placing it gently on the ground.

Leaning against the tyre of a huge dump truck, he called out to her, lewd comments that at first she just ignored. His next comments alluded to Jeffery and Jeffery's sexual prefer- ences. As she turned around to face him, all she heard was something about how perhaps Jeffery might be bisexual and that was why he and Jessica made a good pair. She felt her patience and temper snap and before she knew it she had grabbed the nearest thing she could see, a piece of metal piping.

Her voice was loud as she came closer to him. 'You fucking piece of shit. What the fuck do you know about anything! You say one more thing to Jeffery or anyone else about him, and you're going to wake up in the morning minus your tiny little dick.' The venom flew forth from her mouth like a waterfall that just kept spilling over. Jeffery had been distraught last week, all due to comments and gossip spread by the filthy piece of shit standing sullen-faced in front of her now.

Even though William was a good head taller than she was and had a solid build, the anger and force of her words had taken him by surprise, and he backed away from her, his hands shielding his face. 'You wouldn't dare, you dog,' he said, his voice a bit shaky.

With that Jessica flew for him, the bar held high, ready to bring it down on whatever part of his body she could make contact with. But she suddenly felt it ripped out of her hands by someone behind her. William smirked when he spoke. 'You're fucking crazy. The boss is behind you now, and I hope he heard everything you just said, because you're a crazy dog-faced bitch.'

Daniel snatched the metal bar from Jessica and now grabbed her tightly by her other arm, standing in between her and William. 'Calm down. What the hell is going on here?'

'She's nuts, man. She was going to hit me with that. If you hadn't come out, she'd have cracked it over my skull.'

'You're fucking lucky I didn't, you piece of shit,' Jessica continued to abuse William as she tried to pull her arm free of Daniel's tight grip.

Daniel noticed that her body was shaking, and from the look on her face, he knew he wasn't going to get any sense out of her. 'Calm down,' he spoke to her, looking around for Troy, who was sitting out the back having his lunch. He yelled out loudly to him, 'Troy, get your arse out here now. Take Jessica out the back and sit with her while I try and work out what the hell's going on.'

Troy had jumped up and taken the situation in

quickly — a smirking William, Daniel holding Jessica's arm as if holding her back, her face wild almost like there was fire coming out of her eyes. One look said it all. She was furious and badly wanted to get into William over something. Troy guided her out the back of the shed and made her sit down, trying to get her to stop shaking and to tell him what the hell was going on.

'What's the use, Troy? Look how he's talking to William. That piece of scum will just make up bullshit anyway, and the boss will believe him. It doesn't matter, I just wish I'd hit him.'

Troy sat with her, reminding her that they were supposed to look after each other. Look how she'd picked up on Gus, practically saving his life. 'I want you to go from the start and tell me everything.' He waited until she looked up at him before speaking again. 'I've got your back, Jess. We started together. I reckon I can help. I've been wondering about a few things that are going on here at the moment. Talk to me, will you, and tell me what's been happening.'

The two of them were in deep conversation so Daniel kept his distance, watching them from inside the shed. He decided not to interrupt. Jessica wasn't going to talk to him, anyway; there was no rapport between them, and besides it looked like Troy might have calmed her down. As for William, he'd sent him home early. Daniel had caught part of the conversation to do with Jeffery, and he hoped that Troy was getting the full story on what the hell was going on. What a spitfire. Bloody hell, he'd felt the strength in her arms when he held her, stopping her from taking to William even after he'd taken the metal bar from her. He'd also seen the look on William's face, and it hadn't mattered that the young fella was bigger and stronger. Her attitude and stance were enough to obviously scare the shit out of him. Chuckling to himself, he kept seeing the vision of a petite young woman scaring the pants off a much larger, robust, tough-looking mechanic. He made himself a strong coffee, shaking his head at the events of the morning. Christ, there hadn't been a dull moment here lately.

All things aside, he had a hunch that soon he'd be looking for a new mechanic, because for once he was on her side. She hadn't given a shit what anyone thought; she was going to stick up for her friend. He could hardly wait to hear the full story.

Jessica's ute had not long gone when Troy knocked on his door. 'Got it all sorted for me, Troy?' Daniel asked, laughing and beckoning for the young man to sit down.

'I will need to sit,' Troy said. 'Because it's a bit of a long story, and I've got my own information to add. I think you'll be very interested in all of it.'

# 22

The next time Jessica made a delivery out to the workshop, she felt sick, nerves swirling in her stomach as she pulled up sharply in the dirt, the dust kicking up from under the tyres. Perhaps she could just deliver and not run into Daniel or William. Drop the goods and disappear again. It would all be so simple. However, as soon as she opened the door, Daniel emerged, walking straight over towards her.

'Could I see you for a moment, please?' he asked abruptly before disappearing back into his office.

'Shit,' she muttered under her breath, feeling her legs shaking, the anxiety making her chest tighten, forcing her to take short breaths.

Daniel watched her sit down, her clothes dusty and dirty, a smear of grease or something on her forehead. He had noticed the other day that she was no longer as skinny as when she first started working for him and had actually put on some weight; her arms and legs were still slender but showed obvious muscles that hadn't been there before. Her skin was tanned with a lovely healthy glow, those darks eyes still as brooding as ever as she looked down at the ground where she sat.

'I'll cut to the chase,' he said. 'You won't have to worry about running into William again because he's been laid off, from here and from Seelo Mining. Troy filled me in on the harassment that you and particularly Jeffery have been going through, and William has signed written statements that detail most of what he said to Jeffery. The documents have been confirmed and countersigned by Jeffery. I have the ones here that relate to the incidents that occurred between William and yourself. After we finish, you can take them and read over them carefully. I want you to add anything else that may have been omitted from his statements. The issues with Jeffery were enough to get him sacked, however we wish to do the right thing for you also, because it's very obvious that he made inappropriate comments and gestures to you.'

'Oh.'

Daniel continued, 'Troy also revealed some other information that was useful, like details about the tools that have gone missing since William started working here. Those and the other six boxes of parts have now been retrieved from William's quarters, and there will be police charges laid against him in relation to those thefts.'

'Geez.'

'Is that all you have to say?'

'Wow.'

'Now there are a number of communication problems, workplace issues that you and I need to talk about. I have a list here of rules that you haven't followed very well. You need to read over this list carefully, which I have noted down and will give you at the end of this meeting, and then you will need to amend some of your work practices.'

Jessica's face turned from incredulous to a cranky, unhappy look, instantly conveying to Daniel, 'I'm listening, but I'm not really hearing you.'

'Firstly, and I impressed this to you, both at your interview and during your time here, you need to be honest with me. If I ask you something about what's going on, or why you're late, you need to be truthful and tell me the facts without exaggeration.'

'When have I ever exaggerated?' Her eyes looked straight into Daniel's, and he gave her an equally angry look in return.

'I didn't say you did. Now the second thing is, you cannot assault anyone, no matter what the reason is. If you'd reported the incidents of harassment that were occurring both to yourself and Jeffery, this wouldn't have got to the point that it did. You were clearly told that from the start. Next time you must report any incidents of harassment, either physical or verbal. Try and remember that you are a female working in a male-dominated workforce. Seelo Mining has a ratio it has to meet with local, indigenous and female workers. They don't want issues with sexual harassment or the like. We don't want anyone to be bullied or put under stress from other workers. Am I clear?'

'Yep. Is that it?'

'Thank you. As long as you go by the rules and tell the truth, we'll all be fine.' He stood to see her out, her eyes never leaving his, as if in defiance, as if to say, what are you going to do about it? He could nearly hear her silent words

140

in his head. Daniel tried to use his kindest voice, 'Jessica, I am sorry that I insinuated that you may not have delivered the correct number of parts. It's just they are worth a lot of money, and over the years so many of our workers have given in to the temptation of easy money to be made.'

'Yeah, well I'm not one of them.' She had the final say, he thought, as the door slammed loudly behind her as she left his office.

# 23

All the men were back at the van park this week and they'd made sure to organise who was cooking on what night. It had become standard routine for them to take turns in preparing a meal that everyone could share. Tonight it was Cedric's turn, and he was making what he called wallaby stew. 'It doesn't really have wallaby in it, does it?' Jessica asked as she held a piece of meat up to the firelight, dubious about what type of meat she was eating.

'Just you eat it and tell me what you think.' Cedric turned to Jeffery, and out of the side of his mouth so Jessica couldn't hear him, he muttered, 'You don't think I'd go to the bloody butcher and pay money for meat. Not when there's plenty of those hoppy bastards out there eating the only shreds of grass left.'

A lot of the conversation as usual centred around the drought, how long it had gone on and how the farmers in the area were coping. Jake loved to talk about the weather. 'It affects everyone,' he said, 'the shops in town, the schools, every business there is, except perhaps the mining companies. They just keep kicking along.' Jake had always lived in the area and was an expert in the weather patterns and the history of droughts and floods in the district. 'The farmers will just hang in there; there's not much they can do but keep plodding along, or droving their cattle where there's some good feed, which ain't anywhere even remotely close by at the moment.'

'The cattle are dying out there and the waters have run out even in the most reliable creeks.' Edward quoted a poem: 'We'll all be ruined, said Hanrahan.'

'What?' Jessica looked up, smiling at Edward, who often loved to flower his conversation with quotes.

'Haven't you ever heard that poem?' Edward said. 'What did you learn at school? I don't know, you young people. How about Dorothy McKellar, do you know that poem? That's the one everyone should be able to quote.'

'I've never heard it, Edward. Can you recite it?'

Edward looked over the top of his glasses at Jessica. 'Is the pope Catholic? Of course, I can recite it.' He stood up straight, pushing his glasses back up his nose, shoulders back and started in a dramatic voice: 'I love a sunburnt country, a land of sweeping plains.'

Jessica was listening intently, the eloquent language of Edward coupled with the stirring words of the poem, a background to the flickering of the fire. She looked up at the sky, always amazed by the brightness of the million stars that filled the darkness, stretching down to the horizon. Edward finished the poem, and they all stood up and applauded him. His voice became emotional towards the end and everyone admired the passion that he put into the recital. 'You know we live in the best country in the

143

world and there's great pride in being Australian,' Edward said as he sat down. Jessica thanked him and promised herself that she would get a poetry book out from the town library and read up on Australian poetry. Perhaps she'd surprise Edward and learn some off by heart.

Hoppy was serving up the wallaby stew and now there was silence as they all appreciated the tasty stew, full of rich meat and vegies. Hoppy spoke in between mouthfuls, 'Eat up, Miss Jessica. We have managed to fatten you just a little since you arrived.'

'Oh, was that your plan, Hoppy?'

'Well, you looked like you was half starved when you first came. You gotta eat, woman, especially with that work you do. You'll burn it all off. I don't think you'll have to worry about getting fat, or getting a big gut like some people.' Hoppy looked over towards Charlie, who was going back for his third plate of wallaby stew.

'Good to see you like it, Charlie.' Cedric dished out the last of it, all of them commenting on how hearty and tasty it was.

'You can make that again for us,' Jeffery said as he collected the plates and cutlery, ready for the washing up which someone always volunteered to do. Tonight it was Jeffery's turn and he asked, 'Boil that billy for me, Jake, will you please? I'm going to need a lot of hot water to clean this up.'

Talk resumed as they all sat back around the fire and relaxed. Charlie continued where Edward left off about being a proud Australian. 'You know, it is a lucky country, but there're a lot of

144

country people that do it extremely tough. Look at what the drought has done to so many of them over the years. It can be a shitty tough life out here. Those city people, they need to come out here and look for themselves. All of them with their comfortable lives, living in their big flash houses and always plenty of money to spend.'

Jessica looked up, her voice soft. 'You know, Charlie, there're a lot of city people who do it really tough also. It's not just country people who can have a shit life.'

Charlie continued, 'That's garbage. I never seen anyone doing it tough when I've been in there. They all seem to have plenty of money and don't care less about what happens to the poor old country folk.'

'Well, you've obviously never been to a lot of the places where I've lived over the years,' Jessica said. 'Life can be very hard in the city also. If you don't have money, there's nowhere to live, jobs aren't always that easy to get, and in winter it's not great if you don't have a warm place to stay.'

The men were quiet and looked at each other, not quite sure where the conversation was headed. Charlie turned to Jessica. 'What's your story, Miss Geronimo? What do you know about doing it tough?'

Jessica took a deep breath and looked at Jeffery, who she had talked to about some aspects of her life before she came out to the mines. She poked the fire with a stick looking straight into the red embers. 'I lived on the streets for years, through winter and summers, in dodgy abandoned houses, deserted factories and even sometimes

145

in huge drains or under bridges. You just sort of find places where you can keep a bit safe, and warm and dry. There were always a few of us who stuck together, and sometimes I'd get a bit of work, but not enough to pay for rent, food and clothing.' She stopped, realising that it was the first time she'd ever revealed the details of her past life to the men who she now considered as family. 'It used to be a bit like this at night, especially in winter. We'd try and have a little fire, maybe in a park, always well away from other people. And — ' She looked across at Charlie. ' — there were many, many people who I met who lived in terrible situations. Men and women the same age as all of you are, their lives ruined, families estranged, kids that disowned them.'

'What made them different from us, do you think?' Edward was listening, drawn in by her description of the life she once led.

'They suffered from all sorts of things that just didn't allow them to lead a normal life. Look at all of you. Sure you've all experienced hard times in the past, but you're all still leading a fairly good life. You say so yourselves. The major difference is that you all work, you hold down a job and are respected in the field you're in. Sure sometimes you might go off the track a little.' She looked at Cedric. 'You know, like you say, on a bender. But the street people I've lived with are on constant benders. They're alcoholics, drug addicts, gamblers, all with problems that stop them leading any sort of normal life. So many of them suffer mental health issues, they're in and

146

out of hospital. They try and look after themselves but they either end up back in the psychiatric ward or the lock-up.'

'Why did you end up on the street?' Hoppy was affected by her story, and his voice sounded sad.

'Mum looked after me until I was about ten. I can remember her only a bit and I only have a few photos of her. She didn't have any other family. I'm not sure what happened to them, but after she died, children's services told me there was no next of kin, and that the only family my mum ever knew was her own mother, and she was dead too. So there was no one.'

'What did she die of?' Thommo spoke quietly from the other side of the fire.

'Heroin overdose; she was a drug addict. After that, there was a run of foster families that I was with. None of them really worked out, and at thirteen I was sent to a community house for kids who couldn't be placed anywhere. There were carers who came and went, but they didn't check up on us much, so I guess I just did what I wanted. Not long after, I ran away and started living on the streets. There were some of us who roamed around together, watching out for each other and sharing what we could. It was a shit life, and once I got old enough I got a job at a nursery owned by a lovely old couple. I worked hard for them and they let me live on site. It was good timing and I always think that they saved me, it was definitely a good turning point for me. That's how I got my driver's license and experience in driving. After that, I had a cleaning job that didn't work out, and then not much else happened until I got this job.'

'Where you ever on the drugs?' Jeffery too was intrigued.

'No, never! I hate drugs. More than anything else in this world, I hate the drugs. The trouble was, the others who I lived with always sponged off me for money, so I never got ahead. I could never seem to save enough money to rent somewhere and have a decent lifestyle. It's hard when you don't have someone else to help you. Just even one person. I guess I found that person firstly when Rosalie at head office helped me out, and now I have Jeffery, plus all of you around me. It's the best feeling in the world.'

'Someone pour that woman some wine.' Cedric's eyes were full of tears and his voice was shaky as he grabbed a glass and beckoned for the bottle that Thommo tried to hide from him. 'That's a sad, sad story, missy, but look where you are now. From now on you can only go forward, save your money and make your own life. You know all of us are always around to help you out; you just sing out because we're your family now.'

'Thanks, Cedric. That means a lot to me. You all do. I'm sorry I talked so much, but I've never told anyone except Jeffery anything about my past life.'

'Jesus, you've sat there for over a year and listened to all our stories of woe; we're glad you shared it with us.' Cedric raised his glass and clinked it against Jessica's.

She had shared some stories with them, but

she'd only skimmed the surface and purposely left out any mention of Johnno. It was just all too hard to explain. Anyway, she hadn't heard from him since she stopped making payments to him. She'd wait a couple of months and see if he contacted her. If not, she could fly out on her time off and try to track him down. He usually wasn't that hard to find. Perhaps he'd managed to get some honest work for once, or maybe he was off drugs. What if, what if, what if? She had been over it so many times before.

# 24

That month, there was a shift in the weather conditions and people around town started to look skywards. Hoppy came to see her for a cuppa and he sat on the doorstep of her caravan, sipping a strong cup of tea and munching on the biscuits that she bought especially for him. 'These pillow biscuits have gotta be good for you,' Hoppy said. 'It says they've got fruit in them.' He squinted at the packet, trying to read the fine print that told him what the ingredients were.

'Of course they're good for you. Here, look, I'm going to have two. I've got a lot of work coming up this next week and I need to keep my strength up.' Jessica munched on the biscuits as she sat on a small stool next to Hoppy.

'See those clouds to the north, Miss Jessica? Well, they reckon we're going to get a heap of rain. Those cyclones that built up to the north of Australia each summer, well usually . . . ' He paused as he munched on another biscuit. 'They cross the coast, you know, somewhere up around Cairns, sometimes down as far as Gladstone, but usually in that central coast area. We've been dealt some doozies over the years, and the biggest one ever hit Darwin in nineteen seventy-four. I remember it well because I was in the hospital getting my leg operated on. Razed Darwin to the ground, and people that lived there had no homes after it passed through. Nowhere to go. They flew a whole lot of them down to the coastal towns, you know gave them somewhere to live until they could rebuild. There's been some other big cyclones; sometimes they've crossed the coast a bit lower down. Most of those coastal towns and cities have copped it at one stage or another.'

'But how does that affect us out here?' Jessica asked.

'Well after they cross the coast as a cyclone, they usually head inland, and that's where they dump all the rain. They weaken into a low, not so much damaging wind left in them and they run out of puff, but the rain they bring is what we depend on because it'll keep us going for a long time afterwards.'

'It hasn't rained properly since I've been here. Just a couple of spits or a quick shower. Only indents in the dust, like tiny spots. I'd like to see it rain properly.'

'Well I think it will be sooner rather than later, and just you wait, once it starts, it often keeps up for days, even weeks. Living here in the van can be a pain in the arse then, because there's no real cover in between anything and this dust here.' He nodded his head towards the dirt. 'Well, you ain't never seen mud until you see what water does to this fine stuff. Just you wait.' He looked towards the sky. 'It's not far off.'

Hoppy had been right, and Jessica watched the reports on television at night, following the path of a cyclone as it threatened the northern part of Queensland. This cyclone was named Edward, much to their own Edward's pleasure, who took great delight ensuring that Jessica knew exactly the course it was travelling and where he predicted it would cross the coast.

'You know they used to only give them ladies' names,' he said. 'Reckoned that they were unpredictable, just like a woman. See here.' He showed Jessica a page out of the newspaper. 'Look how it changes course all the time and can't make its mind up. Down, then out, and then down and across. You watch, it'll follow the coastline, and I reckon it'll cross near Townsville somewhere.' He pointed to a tiny dot on the map, a little settlement south of the larger city. 'Yep, I reckon that's where it will cross, right there. And then you'll see once it crosses the coast. It'll head exactly southwest, more west than south, and guess who'll be in line for all the rain, then?'

Jessica looked at the map, following the direction where Edward, who now regarded himself as an authority on cyclones, was pointing. 'That's right where we are,' she said.

'Yep, just wait and see. That's where I reckon it will cross, and then the rain will come directly our way.'

'But the cyclone is a long way north of Townsville and steering right in towards the coastline, so what makes you sure that it will cross there?'

'I just know these things. And look here.' He pointed to the article in the paper again. 'Right on its tail there's another one, they've called it Matilda. That's what they do now, one female and then the next one a male. The feminists jumped up and down about the sexism in the naming, so now they have to use both male and female names for the cyclones.'

'Are you sure that's why, Edward?'

'I'm positive.' He scrunched up his face, disgruntled that Jessica would question his cyclone knowledge. 'And they only ever use distinguished names. You know — solid, strong, notable names. Hence Cyclone Edward.'

Edward had been spot on about where the cyclone would cross, and before long the city of Townsville along with the smaller towns to the south were battening down, ready for the big blow. In Gowrie, the tension was growing as townspeople and farmers anticipated the much-awaited rain that would most likely come their way. Jessica waited too, excited to see the difference that rain would bring to the landscape. She'd only ever seen the place dusty and dry, and she had become used to the sight of crows picking at the skeletal remains of kangaroos and cows which fell prey to the never-ending drought.

That same week she heard from Johnno, who pleaded that he'd lost his phone and with it her number, only finding it written down recently on a bit of paper. He begged her to fly home on her next break and said that he missed her terribly and desperately wanted to see her. Some friends of his were letting him stay in a shed in their backyard for a couple of weeks so they'd have somewhere to sleep and could catch up. It had been a long time since he'd seen her. He'd made a bit of money, so perhaps they could even have a couple of meals out.

He sounded sincere, like he was truly missing her. In fact, she thought Johnno sounded normal, as if he was sober and not high or drunk. But she was suspicious. She'd been down this road before with him. Perhaps he was missing her and did genuinely want to see her, but she was getting more and more entrenched in life and work here, and had to admit to herself that she really wanted to fly back to the city. Just like so many times before, though, the overriding desire to be together with Johnno tugged at her and she smiled at the thought of meeting up with him.

Johnno as usual was persistent, reminding her that they fitted together, they'd stayed together through thick and thin, her flights were free, and he really wasn't asking for too much. Before she knew it, she agreed and quickly booked her flights home for the following Friday. Trying to push the thoughts of the trip to see Johnno to the back of her mind, she concentrated instead on the upcoming week. It was going to be extremely busy and the job charts were piling up. By the end of the week she'd be exhausted, because she'd be lucky to come up for breath in between so many urgent deliveries.

The rain fell in patches on Tuesday and Wednesday, and the town was full of chatter about the heavy falls that tiny places to the north of them were receiving. By Thursday, the dust turned to mud and those in low-lying areas brought in sandbags, getting ready for the water that would come from the rain occurring upstream. The town had survived floods in previous years and a levee built only ten years earlier promised to save the centre from any real flooding. Still, people out in the country never took anything for granted: they'd seen how unpredictable the weather patterns could be, and so just as Hoppy had advised, Jessica took some precautions such as storing some extra food and water.

It was difficult to maintain the usual speed of the deliveries in the rain. The tracks and roads were all very different with water over them, and thank goodness she'd gained extra driving skills before having to navigate the potholes and gullies that started to form in the dirt tracks.

By Friday morning, the rain was so heavy that her clothes were drenched in the short time she took to check her load and get into her ute. The other men had all left before her, and she looked around the deserted park, the fire pit now a muddy overflowing pond and the yard a continuous stretch of shallow murky water.

Throwing her travel bag into the ute, Jess quickly jumped in, the sound of the torrential rain on the roof of the vehicle deafening. In her mind she went over what she'd packed, because this afternoon after the deliveries were finished she was heading straight for the airport. Her flight was booked back to the city and Johnno left just after three o'clock, so hopefully she might even finish earlier. If she did, at least she could wait in the dryness of the airport sheds and hopefully stay awake.

It had been one of the busiest weeks she had

experienced, and her arms and legs ached from the lifting and rushing around, her entire body drained. She wanted to curl up and sleep for a week, however at the moment she needed to concentrate hard. Staring through the noisy windscreen wipers, she memorised the pickups and deliveries, focusing on avoiding the potholes that had deepened and widened overnight.

Soon there was only one delivery left, and Jessica checked the particular item that was to be taken to Daniel's workshop. It was highlighted on the work program, identifying it as a high priority, same-day delivery. This part would ensure that a job could be completed and sent off, as quickly as the workshop could turn it around.

Often she'd ring ahead and leave a message that she was on her way; at least then he'd know that it was coming and have everything else ready to go. Pulling over to the side of the road, she tried to find her phone. Outside, the drenching rain continued, and Jessica peered through the windscreen hoping that it wouldn't get any heavier until she had delivered this last item. She searched through her bags and looked all through the ute to no avail. She vaguely remembered her phone sitting on the kitchen table back at the van. *Damn*, she thought. *I don't remember picking it up. I've left it there. That means I'll have to go back to the van park before I fly out.*

Looking at the clock in the car, she worked out that there would still be plenty of time to fit that in, even with the wet driving conditions. It was going to be a slow and steady trip because she could only see a short distance in front of her, the windscreen wipers rolling back and forth steadily, allowing her only blurring glimpses of the road ahead. Once she turned off the main road and headed to Daniel's property, she felt more at ease. There were three properties before his and she was soon past them, with only a small section left to go before she turned and went over the grid at the entrance to his property.

Peering up closely to the windscreen, she looked ahead, knowing that there was still a bridge over the river to cross. It was a narrow, high, one-lane bridge and she always took it slowly, rattling over the thick rickety timber that formed the base over the usually dusty gully. A car's headlights shone around the corner coming up behind her, and she guessed that it might be one of the men from the main camp coming out to pick up the piece of machinery that she had the part for. Troy would be waiting to fit it out and then he'd also be flying out this afternoon for his week off.

Slowing the ute down, she tried to see if there was water in the gully, however the driving rain and the leaves that flew against her windscreen made it increasingly difficult to see past the bonnet of the car. It wasn't until she was on the bridge that she realised that the brown swirling water was actually racing over the bridge, pushing sticks and debris across in front of her vehicle. Hands clenching the steering wheel tightly she contemplated reversing back off the bridge, but she was worried about going off the side. Besides, the machinery part for the workshop was really important, and it'd only take her a short while to drop it off and then drive back out. Hopefully the water level wouldn't change that much in an hour or so.

Putting her foot down, she pushed the car forward, ensuring that she kept her cool as the force of the water pushed the car towards one side of the bridge. It wasn't until the car cleared the bridge and climbed the steep road on the other side of the gully that she realised she'd been holding her breath. Putting her foot down, she picked up a bit of speed and checked the clock. This would need to be a quick delivery if she was to get back across that bridge.

Surprisingly, she noticed that the headlights that had been behind her had not followed across the bridge. They were probably having a look around before coming across. Country people wouldn't worry about a bit of water, she thought. They didn't seem to stress about too much at all. She decided not to mention to Troy that she'd been worried about the bridge. He was a country boy at heart and would probably just think she was being a nervous city woman. And as for Daniel, he rarely came out when she delivered parts and she hadn't talked to him since their last discussion, when she'd taken great pleasure in slamming the door in his office.

Pulling up outside the workshop, the ute's headlights flashed against the tin walls and she looked skywards, watching the water pouring from the roof onto the muddy quagmire below.

Annoyingly, the massive doors weren't open like they normally were, meaning that she couldn't drive into the shed. Of all times, why hadn't they left them open for her? Perhaps they were worried that the rain would blow in that way.

There was a light on in the office, so she beeped the horn, cranky that no one was ready for her delivery. She needed to be back out of here and over that bridge in time to pick up her phone and fly out this afternoon. Beeping loudly again, she peered through the blur of the rain, relieved when she finally saw someone at the window of the office. Slowly the massive roller door opened in front of her. Driving in, she was surprised that all the lights were off in the shed and that Troy's ute wasn't parked in its usual spot. In fact, there didn't seem to be anyone in the shed ready to work on the machine that she had the part for.

As the ute came to a halt, she could finally see out of the front windscreen. Daniel was striding towards her and as usual, she thought, whenever he had to communicate with her, he looked angry. The fluoro orange and navy shorts and work shirt that she wore were still wet from the drenching she'd received earlier. Pushing her wet hair back from her face, she looked up, straight into a furious set of blue eyes.

'What the hell do you think you're doing?' Daniel's voice was loud and angry.

'Good afternoon to you also. I have the part here that you requested as urgent. I'll just get it out for you.' She turned towards the back of the ute, ready to unload her delivery.

Daniel stood in front of her, blocking the way. 'I've been ringing you since six o'clock this morning. I'm not sure if you're ignoring my calls or what the hell you've been doing, but in case you haven't noticed, the roads are flooded.'

'Yesterday you said the delivery was urgent.'

'That doesn't mean that you risk your life to deliver it. For Christ's sake, George from up the road rang me to say he'd tried to stop you crossing the bridge. He said he flashed his lights and chased you until you started to cross the river. He also said that you were extremely lucky you didn't get washed over the edge.'

'I didn't realise he was trying to get me to stop. I thought it was one of the mine workers coming out to fix up the machinery.'

'I rang Troy and the other new fella here the same time I rang and then messaged you this morning and told everyone not to come in. There's no way you can drive around in this sort of weather. Once it starts flooding, the roads are too dangerous, and as for the point of crossing flooded bridges — ' His eyes sparked angrily. ' — people die from doing stupid things like that out here.'

'I must have left before you rang.' She looked down at the ground. 'I left my mobile back at the van.'

'Shit, what's the rule with the phones and driving safety issues out these ways? It's supposed to be on you and always charged.'

Jessica had nothing to say, knowing that it was a golden rule to have a phone with her at all times. The roads were isolated out these ways, and it was a safety requirement in the case of breakdowns or emergencies.

'I need to get this part off and go back across the bridge. I'm flying out to the city this afternoon,' she said firmly.

'Don't you get it? The whole place is flooded! There won't be any flights coming or going for a week. Everywhere in between the town and those low hills out to the west will be under.'

'Well it hasn't rained since I've been here. I just thought — '

Daniel didn't let her finish. 'You thought what, that you'd just drive anyway, cross a flooded river, and now think you can just drive out again?' He grabbed her arm as she glared angrily at him and attempted to get back into the ute. His free hand snatched the keys out of the ignition, and he pulled her away from the open door of the vehicle. 'You aren't going anywhere. I'll not be responsible for one dead stubborn woman who has no idea about what happens when a blown-out cyclone drops heavy rain for two days.'

Pulling her arm away from his grasp, she stood firmly in front of him. 'Well, give me directions as to how I can drive out another way. There must be another road that goes from here to town.'

'I hate to break it to you, but you're stuck here. There isn't another way out, and there won't be for some time. I've stored up supplies to last for weeks because I need to stay to look after the place. The house and sheds are built on higher ground, so they don't flood, but I'm telling you right now everything else around here will go under. This place will be an island in the middle of a lake in about two hours.'

'What about the town?'

'They built a levee that hopefully will work. It stops the flows that come down from further upstream. You'll see the van park, the mines, the camps and all the town are protected, so they should stay relatively flood free.'

'I need to get back.' She was starting to feel stressed, not only about the fact that she appeared to be stuck here with her boss who disliked her intensely, but also that Johnno was expecting her. She was supposed to be flying back to him tonight.

'Can you listen to me for a moment and get it through your head? There's no way out. The river comes up quickly and the water over the bridge will have risen even higher by now. Maybe in a couple of days they might chopper you out, but at the moment, no one needs to put their life at risk just to rescue you when you're safe here.'

A phone rang in the office and Daniel, taking her keys to the ute with him, ran to answer it. She followed hesitantly, unsure of what to do next as she listened to him on the phone. It was Hoppy, and she could hear his voice, relieved and happy that she was safe and sound. 'Yep, pass it on to Myrtle for me please, Hoppy, and ring Jeffery, because I've been on the phone to him also trying to track her down. Yeah, yeah, she's fine, just a bit wet, but she's okay. Crossed the bloody river in flood, though; she's lucky she wasn't swept off.'

Jessica couldn't hear what Hoppy said next, but Daniel replied more kindly, 'I will. I know,

Hoppy, but bloody hell, you know the rules. I know . . . yep, yep. She'll be here with me. Don't worry I won't let her go anywhere.' Daniel listened for a while to Hoppy before talking. 'I'll tell her, don't worry. Take care of everyone there, won't you? There's nothing else to do except bunker down until it's all over. Yes, yes, of course I will. Yes, Hoppy, we'll talk soon, and thanks again.'

Daniel hung up, turning to find Jessica standing in the doorway looking at him. 'Hoppy said don't you dare try and go anywhere. All the roads are cut into town and one car has already been washed off one of the smaller bridges towards the north. It's just one of those things. You have to stay put.'

Jessica just stared at him, her eyes wide. She had nothing to say.

The phone rang again, and he watched her slump into the nearest chair, her hands rubbing her legs as she tried to bring some warmth back to them. She listened to him talking on the phone and noticed how agitated he was as he paced angrily around the office, eventually finding an old towel that he passed to her.

Finally the conversation came to an end and Daniel turned to her, his voice only slightly calmer. 'That was Mervin; he's an old Aboriginal fella. Him and his wife live down on the river bend in an old hut. At the moment, though, they're stuck in town. No one is getting in or out now.' He ran his hand through his hair, exasperated at the events taking place. 'He wants me to drive down to his hut and get some papers and money he has stashed there. I need to get down there before the whole lot goes under.'

Jessica had picked up on more of the conversation that took place between the two men, but decided not to ask too many questions at the moment. 'I could hear the conversation. Will it be flooded now, the road to their house?'

'No, the road out there runs along the ridge, but I'm not sure where the water will be up to in their hut. I told him I'd have a look for him, though.'

She stared blankly at him as he added, 'You're coming with me. I'm not leaving you here, because you have a nasty habit of not doing what you're told. Grab your bag and get into the ute. Hurry up and we'll try and get out there before the water gets any higher. It's only about ten kilometres down the road.'

For once, Jessica just did as she was told. Obviously, there was no way to get back into town and she could see he was in a hurry, so she thought better of arguing the point that she preferred to stay in the warm office.

The ute slued across the road, pounding rain coming at them horizontally as Daniel followed a narrow, winding track that led them down towards a further reach of the river. Mervin's hut was just visible through the relentless rain, and from where they parked high up on the ridge, they could see that the water was starting to enter it. Further down near the river, an old tin shed was already half inundated with fast-flowing water. 'Just wait here,' Daniel said. 'He's told me exactly where to find what he wants. It

164

will only take a minute.'

Daniel jumped out of the ute, and before long he came back with a couple of tins and some other items that he had packed into boxes. He threw them all into the back and then went back for some more belongings before walking down to the river to have a quick look at the flooded shed. By the time he returned to the ute his coat was drenched, the water running off his hat as he threw it at Jess's feet.

She turned to him as he sat back in the driver's seat. 'Do you want me to help you? Is there more stuff that we can save for them?'

'To be honest, that's about it. I've got everything he wanted plus extra. They don't have a lot of personal belongings, just a few special things that I've been able to grab. Time to head back, because that water is rising fast and we don't want to get stuck out here ourselves.'

'Can't you find the dog?'

He turned to her. 'How do you know about the dog?'

'I was listening to your conversation on the phone. I could hear parts of what he said. I clearly heard him ask you to check on his dog Betsy and her pups.'

Daniel spoke as he started the engine, 'He said if Betsy was still around, which he didn't think she would be, to try and bring them all back in. I've looked down near the shed, and she's not there. You'd see her because it's an open shed, plus she'd be barking. She's a red cattle dog and I can tell you she barks and barks when someone comes. It's quiet down there. She's either taken off, or I hate to say it, but she may have been swept away, because she's a pretty old dog.' He peered through the windscreen, grabbing a rag to wipe the inside of the glass.

'So where are the pups?'

'Mervin said to look for the old dog, and if she wasn't there to forget about it. The pups can't survive if she isn't around; they're only a week old, plus they've probably been swept away. I looked and the shed's flooded.' He started to drive slowly up the ridge concentrating on the sheets of rain that seemed to be getting heavier. 'What the hell!' he yelled, turning around to see Jessica flinging open the door of the ute before stomping through the thick mud towards the flooded shed.

★   ★   ★

The rain pounded on Jessica's face, making it nearly impossible to see what was in front of her. Before long, she could make out the frame and roof of what had been an old timber shed, a few pieces of corrugated iron still holding tightly to the roof beams, as parts of the slat walls continued to be plucked away by the swirling torrents of muddy river water now flowing freely through the middle of it. She stood still, looking frantically into the murkiness at what was left of the structure, just visible in the driving rain.

Above the roar of the river and the pelting rain, she could hear whimpering, occasionally rising to a yelping noise, coming from the highest part of the shed wall. Wading into the

166

water, she ignored Daniel, who was now sliding down the bank behind her, yelling at her to get back into the car. Once she stepped into the water and was under the few pieces of tin that remained on the roof, she could make out a wide wooden shelf that jutted out from the main wall. A wooden ramp that once led up to it was now broken in half, the bottom section washed away. Squinting into the shadows, she was sure she could see something on the shelf, and there were definitely sharp little yelps coming from that area.

Daniel was just behind her now and yelled so loudly that she could hear him above the noise of the water. 'Leave them. He told me to leave them if they were here. They won't live without the mother; they're too young. For fuck's sake, get back into the ute. Mervin doesn't want them.'

Jessica turned and glared furiously at him before wading deeper into the water, climbing onto some beams that had fallen and were stuck up against the walls. She hung onto them, falling a couple of times into the water, the timber beams saturated and slippery. Clambering up, she finally reached the spot where she could see something. Lying in a huddle, yelping, crying out for their mother were the puppies, four of them together, their tiny bodies wet and shivering. Looking back down, she realised the only way to save them was to pass them down to Daniel, who was standing in knee-deep water, unable to reach her and stop what she was doing.

'There's four and I can get them,' she yelled out to him, her voice just audible above the roar of the river and the pounding of the rain.

He knew that it didn't seem to matter how much he yelled at her or tried to get her to come back, she was determined to save the pups. His voice was exasperated. 'Pass them to me, hurry up, the water is rising by the minute.'

She hesitated, and he yelled at her again, his voice deep and demanding, startling her into action as he waded into the water, standing just below where she was. 'I'll put them in my pockets. I won't drop them.'

Reaching up she picked up the first tiny puppy, passing it down into his hands. Three more pups were passed the same way before she started to look around for the others. Mervin had specifically said there were eight pups. They must be further along the beam, perhaps in the furthest darkest corner of the shed.

Daniel had moved back into the shallower water, expecting Jess to follow and be right behind him. She heard him yell out to her and she hesitated as the beam she was standing on started to move with the water. Jumping outwards, away from the deeper water below her, she stumbled, landing in swirling water up to her waist. Part of the shed knocked up against her, and she tried to push forward to get back into the shallower parts where she'd first entered. The water was rising fast, though, and where it had once been up to her knees it was now up to her hips, the current pulling her with it as she tried to move her body back towards the bank.

Daniel came down closer to where she was and reached out, his face frantic as he watched the unfolding scene in front of him. The shed moved slowly off its base, as if in slow motion, in readiness to join the swirling muddy water.

'Grab my hand,' he yelled, his worried face looking down at her as she reached up, his strong arms pulling her into the shallow water before he dragged her up onto the muddy bank. His grip was firm and his hands hurt her arms as he pulled her upwards.

Jessica tried to get her breath, speaking between gasps. 'The others are further on the shelf. I could just see them. There are four more of them there.'

A loud cracking noise made them both turn and look back towards the shed. Daniel's vice-like grip on her arm tightened even more as they both watched the shed and everything in it move slowly away from its foundations. The timber structure splintered as it smashed against a large tree that had also joined the swirling water, moving along quickly, picking up speed before much of it descended under the water.

Daniel looked down at her, his voice uneven. 'You're bloody lucky that you're not going with that. Jesus, that's twice today you've nearly been dragged into the river.' Seering eyes revealed his anger although Jessica could also see he looked shocked, and she realised just how close she'd come to being washed away with the shed.

'You're hurting my arm.' She tried to wrench away from him but there was no way he was letting go, and he dragged her along behind him as they both plunged through the mud back to the ute.

Opening the door for her, he made sure she

was seated before grabbing his hat and putting it on her lap. One by one he lifted four quivering, whimpering puppies into it. Jessica was shaking. The reality of how quickly the river had risen in such a short time, as well as the feeling of the strength of it as it tried to take her with it overwhelming, and she did not speak again until they reached the workshop.

Daniel, however, remained silent only for the time that it took them to get back up along the ridge and safely onto the higher track home. 'That's it; you're fucking crazy. I told you to leave them there. Mervin said not to take them if the old dog wasn't there. You don't risk your life for any animal. You came so close to being swept away. I just can't fucking believe that you did that.' He had gone on and on, berating her continuously as he steered through the mud and rain. Jessica had never seen him so angry or swear so much, every word directed straight at her.

The ute pulled up not outside the workshop where she thought it would, but instead right next to the front steps of his house. Daniel turned the ignition off and shook his head, looking at the pups and then at her. His voice was calmer. 'Why did you risk your life like that? You could have drowned.'

'They would have all died.' She tried to stop her teeth from chattering, her legs from shaking.

'Mervin told me to drown them if she wasn't there. They need their mother's milk to survive. The dog obviously realised the flood was coming and moved them up onto that shelf via the ramp.

170

You could see half of it had already washed away. She's too old to have brought them up to higher ground, otherwise she'd have probably done that.'

'Surely there's something we can give them. I'll look after them; we can't just let them die. Betsy probably drowned trying to put them up higher.'

'You nearly bloody drowned attempting to save them.' He put his large hand into the hat and picked up three of them together, looking at them closely before passing them to her. The last pup lay lifeless in the bottom of the hat. 'This one didn't make it. Probably died of the cold or shock.'

'Are you sure?'

'Can you just listen to me for once?' He picked it up gently, showing her briefly. 'It isn't breathing. I didn't think it looked good when I put it in with the others. Don't be surprised if the others die, either. They've been without the warmth of their mother; they're only new still.'

'I don't want them to die. They've been through so much.'

'I know they have. Now listen to me. I'm going to leave this little one here in the hat. I'll come out later and find somewhere to bury it. We need to get these others warm, so wrap them up in this shirt here and don't muck around, just straight up the stairs and in through that front door. I'll be right behind you. Is this your bag here? I'll bring it up.'

Moving around the outside of the ute, he quickly opened the door for her, grabbing her

171

bag and following her up the stairs into the dryness of the house. The door shut firmly behind him, blocking out the noise of the rain and wind. What a day, he thought, and now there was not only one dead pup to bury and probably three more by the morning, but also an extremely stubborn, wilful and argumentative woman to keep him company, for god knew how long.

# 25

The warmth of the old wood stove in the kitchen greeted Jessica as she carried the bundle of pups into the house. Trying to warm not only herself but also the shivering pups, she crouched down in front of the fire. Daniel tossed her bag on the floor and disappeared, returning with a bundle of old rags and a cane washing basket. He made a small nest out of the rags and then vanished again, this time bringing a hot water bottle filled with steaming hot water. 'Tuck them in the rags and I'll put this underneath. At least that will give them a bit of warmth. I had the wood stove on because I thought sooner or later I'd need to dry something out. I didn't figure on it being a litter of pups.'

Jessica's hands were shaking so much that she had trouble lifting the pups, leaving the littlest one to last, holding it for just a bit longer, trying to bring some warmth from her hands into its little limp body.

'It's hardly moving, this little one. What can we do?'

'We can only help them with what we have here,' Daniel said. 'That one was the second smallest one after the one that died. It's going to be a miracle if you can save it.' She looked at him and he could see she was upset. 'But we'll try. We'll give it a good shot. You're shaking — you need to get dry first before we do anything.'

173

'I'm fine. What can I do with them next? What are we going to feed them?'

Daniel stood up from where he was crouched in front of the fire and spoke gruffly. 'Firstly, pick up your bag. I'm guessing that you had it ready for your flight out. Come with me.' She looked up at him and he could see she didn't want to leave them. 'Yes, now they'll be okay. I want you to have a shower and warm up. Get out of those wet clothes. While you're doing that, I'll have a look in the storeroom. I'm pretty sure there's some powdered milk out there. I always have emergency supplies just in case I get cut off.'

Following him down the hallway, she pestered him with questions. 'Will it work? Will that be okay for them to drink? Do you think they'll be all right?'

'I'm not sure. It's the best we can do at the moment and the nearest thing I'd have here to their mother's milk. The milk in the fridge might be a bit strong. I think the powder stuff may be a bit better and we can dilute it down. Next door have a pet goat, but there's no getting to that at the moment because they're the other side of the river.'

He pointed to a bedroom. 'Dump your stuff in here. It's the spare bedroom. My sister and her family often stay there when they come to visit, and she put clean sheets on before she left last time.' He pulled a towel out of a cupboard. 'Shower's down there on the left. Warm up, get changed, and then we'll work out how we're going to get this liquid into their stomachs.'

By the time Jessica returned to the kitchen,

Daniel had mixed and warmed the powdered milk and was searching through cupboards, looking for a first aid kit. 'Got it. I thought there was an eye dropper in here. We'll use it to try and feed them with.'

Jessica sat on a chair, now dressed in clean jeans and a t-shirt. The shower had warmed her up, although she was still shaky, her hands having difficulty working the small dropper and milk. Daniel showed her how to open the mouth of the smallest pup, pushing the drops of milk into its tiny mouth. 'Why aren't they opening their eyes?' She looked worried, watching most of the milk spill back out of their mouths and run onto the rags they were wrapped in.

'They don't open their eyes until after they're about two weeks old. They're the same as kittens. Haven't you ever seen them when they're this little?'

She shook her head and tried to steady her hands.

'I'll leave you to it for a minute. I want to get out of these wet clothes and have a shower, and then I'll make you something to eat. Have you eaten today at all?' She didn't answer him and he muttered something under his breath. 'No, I thought not. Just keep going, get what you can into that little, one and then do the other two. I won't be long.'

The smallest pup was having difficulty swallowing the milk and even though Jessica persevered, she was unsure just how much made it down its throat. Placing the pup back in the basket, she picked up the next one that was just a

175

bit bigger. It squirmed as she held it and moved its tiny head upwards, pushing at the dropper, searching for milk. The two larger pups fed similarly and most of the milk went into their mouths. Still feeding the last pup when Daniel returned, she held it up for him to see how fat its stomach was. 'These two have sucked on the dropper; they're hungry, and I think they've drunk quite a bit. I'm not sure if they should have more. Do you know how much we should give them?'

'Not really. We'll just have to try and work it out.'

He picked up the little one and handed it to her to try and feed again. Her voice was shaky as she told Daniel, 'I've called her Rosie. She won't suck like the other ones do, though. I don't think there's much going down.'

'She's a lot smaller than the other two, so she might only take a little bit at a time.' Daniel wished that Jessica hadn't named the pup because he was doubtful it was going to live. Watching her continuing to persevere, he noticed how pale she was and that her hands were still shaking. 'You've had a pretty full-on day. How about you leave them be for a while and we'll have something to eat. That sounds like the phone ringing — what do you want to bet it'll be Hoppy checking up on you.'

Sure enough, the men at the caravan park were concerned as to how she was, and all of them wanted to talk to her about the dangers of crossing flooded waters. 'I have discussed that with her.' Daniel was trying to talk on the phone and make sandwiches at the same time.

'You mean you yelled at me,' Jessica muttered, just loud enough for Daniel to hear.

'Yes, Thommo, she's fine. Although she's risked life and limb to rescue three of Mervin's pups from the old shack down on the river.' He listened to Thommo. 'I know, I know, don't blame me. I tried to stop her, but as usual I'm the last person she'll listen to. Now we're trying to use an eye dropper and milk powder to keep them alive because they're only just over a week old.'

Cedric must have grabbed the phone next and he demanded to speak to Jessica. 'How are you going, love?' Daniel could hardly hear her replies. She sounded very quiet and subdued for once. Cedric continued talking, berating her for going into the water, both in a car and then to rescue dogs of all things. 'Just this once, Jessica, you need to follow directions. Natural disasters out this way are a lot different from what you have in the city. Things change quickly, as I'm sure you've seen today.'

Daniel couldn't hear what she asked Cedric next because she took the phone and turned away from him, talking very softly. Handing the phone back to him, she went back to the pups, picking up Rosie again to try and get just a few drops into her mouth.

Cedric said to Daniel, 'She's worried you're going to sack her, because she drove the work ute through the water. Can you just be nice to her? She's really shaken up. I can hear it in her voice.'

'Of course, Cedric. Yep, it's all good. Listen, I'm going to go; we both need something to eat. It's been one hell of a day. At least you guys are all okay there and we're all good here. Plenty of food, and this place should stay high and dry.' Daniel talked to Cedric for a bit longer, asking him how everyone was coping with the flooding. When he got off the phone, he finished making them both something to eat, determined to make sure that Jessica ate something.

They sat silently at the kitchen table, both hungry and munching on the sandwiches that Daniel had made. Jessica hadn't taken her eyes off the basket where the three pups were curled up together. They were sleeping, two of them with their bellies bulging, all of them occasionally twitching or snuggling in closer to the others. 'That's how they'll keep warm, pushing in together like that,' Daniel said. 'Between their body warmth, the hot water bottle under them and the heat from the stove, we should be able to keep them warm.'

'How often should I feed them?' Jessica asked as she devoured two huge sandwiches.

Daniel, who was in the process of making her more to eat, turned and looked at the pups. 'I think to keep them alive at this stage, we'd better feed them every couple of hours. If we take turns during the night, at least then we'll both get some sleep. I can set an alarm.'

'I don't mind doing all the feeds.'

'You look like you're ready to fall asleep. You know it's nearly seven o'clock. I'm not sure where the afternoon went, but I reckon if you went to lie down, you'd be out like a light. Go, go to bed. Make yourself at home in that room, and if you need anything at all, just help yourself. There's plenty of food here in the fridge and cupboards. I'll keep the fire going all night for the stove, and then you just need to pour that kettle into the milk powder and get as much food into the pups as you can. I think if they survive the night they'll probably be okay. I'm not so sure about that little one, though, so don't get attached to it.'

For once, Jessica did what she was told. She was exhausted, both after the busy week and then the turmoil of the day. The sandwiches filled her up and she had stopped shaking, but her body felt like lead and all she wanted to do was shut her eyes, curl up in a ball and go to sleep.

Daniel's voice was reassuring. 'I'll stay up late. I always do anyway, so I'll do the next few feeds. After that, I'll give you the alarm and you can do the next feed. Once you've done that, set the alarm for another three hours and put it in my doorway. I'll get up and do the next one.'

'Thanks,' she said, taking one last look at the pups before dragging herself into the spare bedroom, changing quickly and collapsing onto the bed. She was asleep before her head even hit the pillow.

# 26

Rain continued to fall solidly, and Daniel put on a heavy raincoat before driving cautiously over the muddy ground towards the main shed. The car lights beamed across the rain-drenched ground and he used a strong torch, shining it upwards across the top of the massive shed, checking that everything was where it should be. Moving quickly from the ute to the office door, he shook the water from his raincoat before darting inside, deafened by the thunder of the rain on the metal roof.

The roof and walls didn't appear to have any leaks, and Daniel checked the equipment as he moved across the huge workshop. Thank goodness he'd spent the money and built something strong and sturdy to endure whatever the weather threw at them. Everything appeared to be intact and he breathed a sigh of relief. There was a lot of money tied up in machinery, tools and equipment held here and he'd sleep easier knowing that everything was high and dry.

Driving around the outside of the building, he watched the water as it ran in rivers from the roof, moving along the drains that he'd built years earlier. The drains had always remained dry, never used, due to the years of drought, but now they were serving their purpose as they steered away the bulk of the water down the slopes to the larger drains below. Once the water drained from the higher spots, it would flow down, joining the already flooded paddocks below.

Shining his torch down the hill from where he stood, Daniel looked at the paddocks that were now one entire lake, stretching out as far as the light allowed him to see. It would be an interesting sight in the morning to check where the water was and how wide and deep the river had become. He knew that there was much more water to come, both from the dark clouds that had travelled inland from the sea and also from the river flow that brought the rain down from further north. It was going to be one hell of a flood. Turning for home, he looked at his watch, ensuring that he was going to be ready for the next lot of feeding.

He couldn't remember a time when he'd been so angry with anyone as he had been with Jessica today. Firstly, the frustration when he hadn't been able to warn her not to deliver the parts. She was his responsibility, and therefore the reason he insisted, and always reminded all of them, that rule number one was always to have your phone charged and on you.

Secondly, that she had driven across a flooded bridge, risking being washed off, the chances of drowning in a submerged vehicle highly likely. The last event was the final straw, and he had totally lost it. It took a lot for someone to make him swear, particularly when there were females present, but he had found the words the only way to express his anger and anxiety at the stupidity of going into a flooded shed to try and find puppies that Mervin specifically asked him not to worry about. She'd been extremely lucky, and for a moment he'd admired her courage — or was it just plain naivety? *So bloody stubborn*, he thought. *God knows what she'll be like if that little pup dies*. Because he could see she was already attached to it.

★　★　★

The pups started yelping right on schedule for feeding, and Daniel warmed up the mixture and begun the tedious task of trying to get the milk into their tiny stomachs. With every feed, the larger two pups seemed to get hungrier and more boisterous. They pushed and pulled at the dropper as he repeatedly filled it up and dropped the milk into their tiny mouths. It was as if they were getting fatter each time they fed, and they both fell back to sleep quickly after each feed. The smaller one that Jessica named Rosie hadn't improved much. Her little body was limp, and Daniel held her head up, trying to push the milk down her throat. He glanced up at the clock and saw that it was just after two o'clock in the morning.

Jessica's voice startled him and he looked up as he put the pup back into the basket. She still looked tired, and he noticed big dark rings under her eyes. 'I've fed them twice,' he said. 'Those bigger two are feeding well, but your little one here, she's not doing so good.'

'Can I make myself a coffee? I think I'll sit up for a while and see if I can get a bit more into her.'

'Sure, sure. I'm going to get some sleep. Everything's there, just help yourself.'

Jessica sat warming her hands on the coffee mug, watching the pups as they slept together, the little one uncomfortable and twitching more than the other two. She wrapped it up in a clean rag and held it up close in front of her. 'C'mon, Rosie, you can do it. Just take a little milk.' She put the pup up tight next to her shirt, feeling the warmth of its tiny body against her own. At least they kept warm when there were three of them and Daniel had kept the water bottle heated that was under them.

Rosie snuggled in, and she could feel its tiny heartbeat next to her own. She picked up the dropper, attempting to push some drops of milk into its mouth, smiling when she thought that some had been swallowed.

She was still sitting there feeding the pup drop by drop when Daniel got up in the morning. 'Have you been asleep and then back up again? Don't tell me you've been there since I went to bed.'

'I might go to bed now, just for a few hours. The other two need feeding in an hour or so, and I think I may have got a few drops into Rosie — just a few, though. She's still limp and hardly moves, but I can't keep my eyes open any longer. Can you look after her?'

'I will. Now go back to bed. Don't stress.' He looked at her worried face. 'I'll concentrate on her. We'll get something into her. Hopefully she'll turn the corner today.'

# 27

Rosie hadn't improved when Jessica returned to the kitchen around nine o'clock that morning. The rain continued to pelt down and she tried to look out the window to see what was going on outside. Lakes of water covered the ground, but luckily around the house and sheds it was only shallow, quickly running off down the slopes into the paddocks. Further out, though, she knew it'd be a different story, and going from what she'd seen yesterday, she realised that they were surrounded by a sea of murky water.

Daniel was on the phone and had just started talking to someone. It was Mervin, and he put the phone on speaker so that Jessica could also hear. 'You got those things out for me, Mr Daniel? You manage to get them all, boss?'

'We did, Mervin, plus I collected anything else I could see in the house that you might want. The water was lapping through the house, so it would all be well under by now. I got the tins though and all the documents, plus some small bits of furniture and clothing. I couldn't see anything else there.'

'That's all good. The missus, she says thanks. Don't suppose Betsy was still there, she being pretty old.'

'I'm sorry, Mervin, but she wasn't anywhere to be found, and that shed was half under when we got there. We actually watched it break off the

184

bank and wash down the river.'

'What, the whole shed? She's gone?'

'Yep, wasn't much left of it when we got there. Don't worry, Mervin. I'll get you a better shed and we can see how the house goes. Whatever happens, we'll fix it up so you and Dora have got somewhere good to live down there. Maybe it should all be higher up.'

'Thank you, boss. You always been good to me and Dora. Looking after us and all. We like it there on the riverbank. It's our home. Now we are stuck in town for god knows how long. Lucky Dora has Aunty Doris in here. She got plenty room for us and lots of other cousins staying here also. Aunty Doris, she nearly one hundred and she is mighty happy.'

'She's happy that you're all there. It's a wonder she's got the room for you all.' Daniel smiled, thinking of how small Doris's house was.

'She reckons, when else does she ever get to see all her family all together like that, all under her roof? She plenty happy. She don't want water to go down coz she wants us all to stay here.'

Daniel laughed, knowing full well how the Aboriginal families loved sharing everything and being together. He could imagine the old lady fussing around them all, happy that they were all stuck there with no way out, all under her roof. 'There's one more thing, Mervin. I have Jessica with me. She's our courier driver. She's actually stuck out here with me for the present.' He started to tell Mervin about how she'd driven out to the shed across the flooded river. 'Drove out and over the bridge that was well under.' Daniel

185

watched her trying to feed the pup. 'Well anyway, Mervin, that's another story.'

'I already heard that from Hoppy. He say that she drove right across the flooded river. He was all upset about it, saying she could have been washed away, and that he should have talked to her about all that, you know river crossings and floods. He said she a city woman and not used to those things.'

'News travels fast in these parts.' Daniel raised his eyebrows and looked over at Jessica who was listening but not looking up. 'Well out at your place she waded into the shed and picked up four of those pups of yours. One died in the ute on the way back, but she's got the other three here and we're trying to keep them alive on powdered milk. Your old dog Betsy, well it looks like she'd walked up that plank to that middle floor, you know the shelf bit in the shed. Well I reckon she's put them up high, like she knew the flood was coming. The other four were further along but Jess couldn't get them. She just got out in time and the whole shed washed away.'

'Jeez, I wasn't really that bothered with them. That Betsy was so old I didn't really think she'd live anyway. That woman shouldn't have gone into the water for just some pups. She could have been washed away herself. She's that skinny courier. I've seen her around town delivering stuff. She always give me smile and a wave when I see her. What she do that for, now you gotta get rid of them, otherwise you gonna have to feed them every couple of hours. It's worse than looking after a baby. Plus they'll only be half-breed cattle dogs. I think she mated with a bitsa over at my cousin's place. They'll only be bitsas, not purebred like Betsy was. I gonna miss that dog, I had her for long time.'

'Well Jess is sitting here now trying to feed the surviving three. Two of them are taking the powdered milk pretty good and they already have fat tummies, but there's a little one and she's not looking too good. She doesn't seem to want the milk and her body is limp.'

'You got some honey there, boss? You get that honey, or something sugary into that little one, plus the milk. Maybe you save it. If not, that's only two left to feed.'

'Thanks, Mervin. We'll try that. You have a good time in town there.'

'I don't know 'bout that, coz these women here, they talk, talk, talk. Talk your head off, and there's nowhere to go. It's pouring rain and I have to go and sit in the dunny for a while to get away from them. Their chatter starting to hurt my head. We talk to you again soon, boss. Let me know how those pups go, but if they all die, well it's meant to be.'

Jessica was standing next to Daniel, the tiny pup wrapped up as she held it closely up next to her. She looked at Daniel. 'She's just getting weaker and weaker. I can feel it.'

He tried to give her a reassuring look, but deep down he thought they were probably fighting a losing cause. 'Let's try the honey. I think it's our last chance.' He grabbed a jar out of the cupboard and they mixed it in with the warm milk to put in the dropper.

187

Jessica held the still puppy close to her and started pushing the honeyed milk down inside her mouth. 'She does gulp a little bit when she's up next to me, like she's making an effort.'

'It's your heartbeat. She thinks it's her mother's. Often with kittens or pups, when you wean them and take them away from their mother, you put an old clock in the basket with them. They think the ticking is their mother's heartbeat and they don't yelp or cry out as much at night.'

'Oh, I could feel her heart before. I didn't think that she'd be feeling mine.'

'Sure, she'd feel it. So maybe that's a good way to feed her.' He handed her the dropper. This time, Rosie took a bit more interest in the milk, and they both smiled as they watched the liquid go down her throat instead of spilling back out onto the rags as it had been previously. A comfy lounge chair was placed in front of the stove and Jessica leaned back, her legs tucked in beside her, the pup sprawled out across her chest as she continued to put drop by drop into her mouth. Daniel went to and fro, cleaning up in the kitchen, going in and out, making sure each time that everything was warm and ready for the next feed. At one stage he placed a cup of tea and biscuits next to Jessica, who apart from thanking him, hardly spoke.

At lunchtime when he came back to check on them again, he found Jessica asleep and the pup now looking a little more relaxed, also asleep, sprawled out across her chest. Mixing up some more powder, he made sure the other two greedy pups were fed. By now they fully understood what was at the end of the dropper, and with the added honey nearly pushed it out of his hands as he fed them. Gently prising Rosie from Jessica, he picked the pup up and placed it in the middle of the other two, who now with full bellies were sprawled out like they were drunk, the three of them nestling in together. *Everyone asleep*, he thought. *This is the most peace I've had in two days.*

# 28

The rest of the day passed much the same, and Jessica only left the kitchen once when Daniel asked her to come out onto the veranda and look at the lake that now encircled them. Dark clouds still hung low and the air was cool, rain still falling heavily, adding to the already flooded plains surrounding them. 'Can you see down there where the river is?' Daniel pointed to an area west of the house. 'You can't see the fences anymore because they're covered in water, but look down there — see that moving brown sludge? That's the river you drove through yesterday.'

'But it's up so far. How does it get that high? The banks are higher than twice the height of this house.'

'That's exactly right. Once that river fills up — and it's done so due to the rain upstream, plus the torrential falls here in the last day — it has nowhere to go, so it spills over the banks. Think about how flat the paddocks and plains are around here. This house and the workshop are the only buildings on high ground. This is probably a once-in-fifty-years flood. Ten years ago that levee around the town was built, because five years before that, most of it was inundated with water from flooding that was much less than this. I've been checking with my sister on the phone. She lives in town, and she told me that the levees there are holding it all back. It's creeping up the levee walls, but they're pretty confident that they'll hold.'

'What happens to all the cattle?'

'There's not much you can do about them once it floods. A lot of the farmers predicted this coming and will have moved them to higher ground. Sometimes, though, the properties are so large you just can't track where they all are. They will naturally look for a hummock or a piece of high ground just like all the other wildlife does. I went over to the workshop this morning and saw probably about ten snakes. They're all looking for higher ground.'

Looking at the scene before her, Jessica was in awe of how the dry and dusty roads that she'd driven over since she arrived over a year ago no longer existed. The arid earth with its faint specks of dried grass and an occasional straggly half-dead tree were now covered in water, any trees now forced out of the ground and washed away with anything else that stood in the water's path.

'I learnt a poem. Edward taught me. It's called 'My Country' and it talks about the flooding rain and the greatness of this brown country.'

'Dorothy McKellar. I love a sunburnt country, a land of sweeping plains, of ragged mountain ranges, of droughts and flooding rains.'

'You know it?' Jessica looked surprised.

'Of course I know it. Every kid in Australia learns that poem at school. It epitomises what it means to live in this country. It's about times like this. This is outback Australia. This is what

191

happens out here, and we stick with it because we love it. You're seeing it all through new eyes.' He turned towards her. 'What do you think of it, our country out here, drought to flood?'

'I love it. I loved it from the very first day I flew into town and was dropped off at the van park. Everything is brown, the sky is huge, the stars are so bright, and the paddocks just stretch forever. Every time I drive out here I'm amazed at what I see: the endless paddocks, the dry riverbed, the windy track I follow, even things like this old style of house. I'd never seen anything like it or even imagined that something like this ever existed. Hoppy, Jeffery and the others at the van park have become my family, and I love how most people don't judge you out here, they just take you for who you are.' She stopped for a moment to think. 'Now I'm not so sure. These last few days I can see that the countryside changes quickly, that it can be dangerous to live out here.' She looked at Daniel. 'Yet I feel safer here than when I'm in the city.'

Daniel was surprised. He'd never heard her talk for so long, or reveal her true thoughts about how she felt. The yelping of hungry pups broke the silence, and they both turned at the same time to restart the feeding cycle. Daniel took the two bigger pups and fed them quickly before picking up Rosie and passing her to Jessica. 'I thought she might come on a bit better after getting that liquid into her this morning. But apart from her tummy looking a bit fatter, she doesn't seem to have much life in her.' The puppy lay limp in Jessica's hand. 'You keep trying. I'm going to get us some dinner ready; we may need some sustenance to get us through the night.'

'Do you think she's going to die?' Jessica's voice was small and quiet.

'Just keep going. You're doing a good job. She's still alive isn't she?'

Outside, the rain continued to fall, the river rose higher, and darkness fell upon a land filled to the brim with muddy brown water. Inside the house, high and dry on the hill, two of the pups slept, their tummies full, their bodies warm from each other and the hot water bottle beneath them. Jessica continued to feed Rosie throughout the night until Daniel appeared to do the next feed. Unable to keep her eyes open, Jessica dragged herself out of the comfortable chair. 'I think she's getting weaker, because she won't take the milk anymore. She's all floppy and doesn't move much. I'm sorry, I just can't keep awake any longer.'

'It's fine. I've had a good sleep and I'm wide awake. I'll feed the other two and then make sure she keeps going.' He made himself a cup of coffee, watching the three pups as they all slept together, snuggled up in the rags. Rosie's tummy looked full and she slept along with the others. *Perhaps I'll leave them for a while,* he thought. He remembered his sister telling him never to wake a sleeping baby and not to pick them up until they cried. He was going to heed her advice because the pups did indeed look peaceful all together for once.

Weak light filtered in through the kitchen window, a tiny short break in the dark clouds allowing a brief sliver of the morning light to shine in through the window. Pushing himself upright, Daniel stretched out his stiff limbs, the comfy couch in front of the fire not so comfortable for his long legs and arms. Shaking his head, he tried to work out what the noise was and then remembered that he was in charge and supposed to have fed the pups throughout the night. Sitting upright instantly, his eyes flitted around to make sure no one knew that he'd fallen asleep on his shift. He looked over at the basket.

Three puppies pushed their heads upwards, all of them yelping and squirming around in the basket, searching for the sweet milk that came in a dropper. He boiled the jug quickly to make up the mixture, ensuring that he picked Rosie up first to feed. Although her tummy did not look as fat this morning, she moved around just like the others did and before long was swallowing the mixture, her little head pushing against the dropper searching for more. Refilling the dropper for the fourth time, he watched as her stomach started to fill and her desire for the milk diminished a little. The other two fed vigorously and he placed them all together in the basket, breathing a sigh of relief. In between cups of tea and toast, Daniel fed the pups twice more before Jessica surfaced.

'I can't believe I slept for so long,' she said as

she looked up at the clock on the kitchen wall. 'You should have woken me. I don't think I've ever slept in that late.'

Daniel was excited. 'It's probably all catching up with you, busy week and then all this happening on top of it. Have a look at them.'

All three once again were pushing their heads upwards, trying to move around the basket, pushing up against each other, searching for the sweet milk they knew came from above.

Jessica's face lit up. 'She's moving around. Has she been feeding?'

'She has. Pick her up. You can feed her this time. She has the makings of being the pushiest out of the three of them.

'She's taking it just the same as the others do. Look at her sucking so hard on the dropper. Do you think she'll be okay now?'

'I'd say so. Once they turn the corner, they're normally all right. Now the fun begins, because they're going to want to be fed all the time. They'll be making up for lost time.'

# 29

The pups kept Jessica busy through the day, and she now also ensured the basket was kept clean and the rags thrown out when they became messy.

'You know, I don't normally let dogs inside the house,' Daniel said. 'This is a one-off, and once we're sure they're okay they'll need to be kept down in the laundry, otherwise they'll stink the kitchen out.'

Daniel spent most of the day putting his raincoat on and taking it off as he travelled between the workshop and the house, checking everything constantly, watching as the waters continued to rise. Towns further to the south and north were inundated, and he'd been on the phone a large part of the day, checking in with friends and workmates. Late in the afternoon, he returned to find everything tidied and sorted in the kitchen, the puppies thankfully fast asleep. Making himself a cup of coffee, he offered to show Jessica through the house.

'I'm not sure how long you're going to be stuck here, because the river is still rising. Besides, I'm going to need you to help look after those pups. Looking after three of them is going to be full on for the next week or so. I'd say nothing much is going to be working or operating around here for the next week at least. The mines have shut down and everyone is just hunkered down until the rain stops and the water recedes.'

'Oh, will it be that long?' She wanted to ask what would happen to the pups, but he'd walked off down the hallway into what he explained to her was the lounge area.

The house was over eighty years old and had been the family home of Daniel's parents and grandparents before that. 'The property was ten times as big back then, but we sold most of it off. I didn't want to go into farming, so I trained as a mechanic instead. I bought this section with the old house from Mum and Dad so they could move into town.'

'So you grew up in this house?'

'I did. That room you're in used to sleep my younger brother and myself. The other room past yours was where both my sisters slept, and the room I'm in was the main bedroom. If you look in the corner of your room just past the windows, on the floor you can see where my brother and I scratched our names into the floorboards, and the year 1980. I think I remember getting a belting for that. My brother probably didn't because he was the youngest and usually blamed me.' Daniel smiled as he showed her through the lounge, the light dim as the greyness outside darkened the interior.

'What a lovely room.' She looked around as he flicked the light on. 'The furniture matches the house.'

'It's the old original furniture. Thank goodness my sister stored it for me, because my ex-wife wanted the whole lot burnt. I love it.' He ran his hand over a timber sideboard, the wood matching the other pieces in the room. 'It's Silky Oak, an Australian timber that was used a lot in the early days.'

'How pretty the colour is, and the way the lines run like waves across it. This bookcase is much the same.' She peered up, looking at the old books that lined a very tall bookcase that took up nearly one entire wall. Running her hand across the spines of the books near to her eye level, she stopped and read some of the titles, tilting her head to one side to make out what each one said. 'You have a lot of books on history here.'

'I do. I have a lot of books on ancient history.' She didn't turn around, the memory of the question she'd been asked at the initial job interview still fresh in her memory.

'Jess, what grade did you go to at school?' Daniel stood near the window, looking outside at the never-ending rain.

'What do you mean?'

He turned to look at her as she continued to scan the books. 'What year level did you go to for your schooling? When did you leave?'

Wiggling a book out from its allotted space, she opened its pages, scanning the words inside. 'I went to grade eight; actually, I only completed year seven because I only attended about three weeks of year eight. Then I left, and I never went to school again.' She turned around, her eyes flashing. 'Is that what you wanted to know? I know you picked up on that in the interview because obviously I didn't know the difference

198

between modern and ancient history. That's because I never did either of them. I just like reading about history and things that happened thousands of years ago. I thought because I read about it now, it would be called modern history.' She placed the book back in its space, ensuring it was lined up with the others. 'I'm going to check on the pups.'

Focusing on dropping the milk into the pups' mouths, Jessica tried to push the conversation to the back of her mind. Daniel obviously knew all along that most of what she presented at the interview was false — the report card, the merit awards from school, the glowing senior certificate. It was all forged, and he had always known. What an idiot she'd been to let Johnno and his mate talk her into falsifying records in order to get the job. But she had so desperately wanted it.

Johnno had pushed her to apply so that she could support him and his variety of habits, and it had been worth a try. It just might offer a fresh start, a new life, somewhere far away from what she'd always known. And it had. She loved living in the country, the people, and especially her job. Now she was not so sure what was going to happen because she had forged documents and falsified official reports.

Daniel appeared with a bottle of red wine in his hand. 'We are going to have a special dinner. There's not much else we can do this afternoon, so you can look after those pups in front of the woodstove and I'm going to cook up a storm on it. We're going to celebrate Rosy coming good with this bottle of red.'

Once the pups were fed and nestled up asleep together, their tummies full, Jess asked Daniel if she could help him. With the rain pelting down outside, there was nothing for it but to find something to do inside. The television hadn't worked for months and the internet and phone were working only intermittently. Not that any of that bothered Jessica that much; she usually preferred other interests to keep her busy. Daniel directed her to the different cupboards and drawers and soon the table was set, ready for their celebratory feast. She watched him move around the kitchen, clanging dishes and saucepans, passing her glasses and cutlery for the table.

Leaving him in the kitchen for a while, she found her way to the lounge, drawn back to the collection of books that lined the wall. She loved books, but rarely had the opportunity to read the many different types she now discovered there were. This bookcase was home to many reference books, large hard-covered ones that were heavy when she lifted them down, their pages filled not only with words but also glossy photographs and prints. She'd have to write the names of some of these down and try and borrow them from the town library. Daniel's voice broke her daydreaming and she quickly returned to the kitchen, the smell of delicious food wafting through the doorway to greet her.

Soon they were sitting down to a sumptuous meal of rib fillet steak with mouth-watering roast vegetables. 'This old stove is a gem. I don't use it that often because I usually use the modern one there.' Daniel pointed to the other conventional oven. 'But I just happened to stoke it up, because sooner or later we'll have to do washing and it's a great place to dry clothes in front of. There's lots of dry firewood out in the laundry, so we should have enough to keep us going.'

They sat opposite each other, Jessica as usual with a voracious appetite, cleaning up her plate and waiting to be offered seconds. 'God you can eat. I'm not sure where you put it, but it's great to see someone enjoy my cooking,' Daniel said.

'It's delicious. The steak is really tender and I just love the vegies roasted.' She took a big gulp of the red wine, enjoying the blend of food and drink, the warmth of the kitchen stove and the pounding noise of the rain outside.

Daniel was relaxed and enjoying the fact that someone actually appreciated his cooking. He even told himself to stop being so pedantic and forget about the fact that she was sitting in his spot at the table and that she used the tea towel instead of the hand towel to wipe her hands on after washing up. *Just let it be for once*, he told himself. *Don't spoil a special moment.*

They sat chatting after they finished eating, the red wine relaxing Jessica and making her talk more than usual. 'I was looking at some of your books. There are two called *The First Australians*. The photos inside them are incredible, and just the bit I read said that Aboriginal Australians have been here for over sixty thousand years. I never knew that.'

The red wine was going down nicely and Daniel leant back in his chair, relaxed and enjoying the company. 'They are very well researched books and yes, the photos in them are unique. I often get them down and just flick through the photos. I read them both years ago, but I love looking through them again. There are some photos from the early nineteen hundreds that were taken not far from here. Take them to bed with you if you want. There's a reading lamp attached to the headboard.' He filled both their glasses again. 'Do you know much about the true history of the Aboriginal people?'

'No, I don't know anything at all. Not a thing.'

'Well, those books are probably a good place to start. Tell me — ' He leaned forward, his hands and arms now resting on the table in front of him. ' — why you left school at such a young age? It's pretty rare these days for a kid not to finish high school.'

She took a big sip of wine, enjoying the warmth of it on her throat. 'I got into a lot of trouble, and they asked me to leave.'

'And what sort of trouble were you in?'

'Fighting.'

'Fighting? Like with your fists? That's probably not very lady-like.' He raised his eyebrows, trying to keep a serious face.

'I never picked on anyone. I wasn't a bully or anything like that. I just used to have to stick up for myself or sometimes someone else, and then my mouth would just shoot off. I have a bit of a temper.' She looked up at him as he laughed out loud. 'And then before I knew it, I'd be in the thick of it. I was always smaller but I could hold my own.'

'What about your parents? What did they do

about you getting into so much trouble?'

'I told you at my interview, I never knew my dad, and my mum died when I was young. By the time I got to high school, I'd been with three different foster carers. None of them worked out, so I just walked out of school, out of where I was supposed to live, and that was that.'

'So that part of what you said at the interview wasn't a lie.'

Jessica sat upright, her eyes glaring. 'The only thing I lied about was my schooling, the report card and all that. I never normally lie, but I wanted this job and I knew I'd never get it if I told you all I'd left school in year seven. I wouldn't have even been accepted for an interview.'

'Okay, okay, calm down. I'm just trying to work out what the hell happened to you that you needed to leave school in year seven and then be — where? Where did you live?'

She took another big gulp of wine. 'I lived on the streets. I've always lived on the streets until I came out here to work. It hasn't been the greatest time, but I survived, and now I just want to keep working. I like my job; I work hard and do my best.'

'Holy hell, are you telling me that at the age of thirteen you looked after yourself? No permanent home to live in? Didn't the authorities come looking for you? You were still a kid.'

'There was always a big group of us; we were all different age groups, but mainly from fourteen up to about seventeen. The DOCS — that stands for Department of Children's Services — would catch up with us sooner or later, but then they'd just take us in for a week or two to one of those halfway houses. There were supposed to be carers there to look after us, but you could just come and go as you wanted and no one checked who was going to school or what your story was. There are just too many kids for them to keep a check on in the city. There are homeless people everywhere, living in places you wouldn't even dream of.'

'I've never spoken to anyone who's lived on the streets. You've done well to get to where you are. That's a tough gig, especially for a young woman.'

'I got by. But I'm not going back there, ever. I want to save some money up, and one day I'll buy myself a little house somewhere. Then I'll always have a home; no one will be able to take it.'

Daniel was dumbfounded. Of course, she'd always come across as rough around the edges, and her temper and language matched up with the lifestyle she had been exposed to. But she was fairly quick at learning, and had worked hard and honestly over the time she'd been with the company. It had just been the lying he'd picked up on at the interview. He'd always known that most of the paperwork was forged, but now it was a bit easier to understand the reason why. They sat silently, neither knowing what to say next. Daniel spoke first.

'Thank you for being honest with me. I know that you don't probably share that information with many people. Do Hoppy and the others know much about what you've been through?'

She looked down at her glass. 'It's strange; I don't usually talk about it. The others only know bits and pieces. There's too much to go into. Jeffery and I talk a lot. He has his own struggles, well actually most people do. We've all got our issues to work out or put behind us.'

The loud yelping of three clamouring, hungry puppies brought them both back to the moment, and they laughed out loud at the insistence and demanding noises coming from the basket. 'You do the feeding and I'll clean up,' Daniel said. 'These pups are worse than babies.' He smiled at Jessica as she passed her plate and glass over, before heading to the stove to get the mixture ready.

Jessica spoke to the pups, 'Three little pigs, they are. Here you go, Rosie first.' And with that, the feeding process started over again.

# 30

An early phone call the next morning from Daniel's sister Liz filled them in on the condition of the flooding and the rainfall. Daniel repeated it to Jessica as they shared their breakfast together, once again sitting opposite each other at the kitchen table. 'Liz says that there're two more days of heavy rain and then it should start to ease off. The levees are holding up, and most places in town are okay, as is your van park. I'm going to go over to the workshop to try and sort out some paperwork, make a few phone calls and tidy up a bit. If you like, you could do some washing for both of us. The machine is down the back laundry room, and there's two fold-out drying racks. Just use what you can and we'll try and dry it in front of the fire. All our work gear can go in one load, and then you can work out the other.' He noticed that she mainly wore jeans and a t-shirt, the small bag he had brought in only seeming to carry a few clothes. 'It didn't seem like you had many clothes in your bag. Weren't you supposed to go for the week?'

'I travel light. Besides, I don't have a lot of clothes. I only go to work and hang around the van park.'

'Right, well if you could do the washing for us both and then have a good look at the books? Have a relaxing day, because there's just not much else we can do.'

Jessica did have a lovely relaxing day, and when Daniel returned, she was lying with Rosie, who was fast asleep across her chest, a large book in front of her, both curled up in the comfy chair in front of the fire.

Jumping up when she saw Daniel, she sounded surprised. 'I didn't think you'd be back so soon. Sorry, but I have all my clothes draped over the chairs and racks.'

Daniel chuckled at the variety of clothes drying in front of the fire. 'I have seen underwear before you know,' he said with a laugh, watching her frantically pulling down her underwear that was hanging on the racks in front of where he was standing. 'When it rains like this, you just have to dry everything wherever you can. It's okay, at least we'll have dry clothes for the rest of the week.'

# 31

The next day the sky lightened somewhat, however the rain continued, and Jessica found herself missing the routine of work and the ability to walk around outside. Daniel had just returned from the workshop for lunch and she placed some sandwiches in front of him. 'Just as well you stock up for these sorts of events. It's a bit strange not to be able just to drive into town and get supplies.'

Munching on the sandwiches, he replied, 'That's why we have storerooms, freezers and generators. You just never know when you get cut off or when you're going to need extra. I didn't count on having an extra mouth to feed, either.' He turned his chair around to face her as she sat on the chair in front of the fire, watching as Rosie pushed at the dropper. 'I think it's time we moved them down to the laundry. It won't be long before they start to move around and it'll be easier to contain them in there.'

Together they moved the pups, cleaning out the area before making a cosy bed for the three of them to sleep in. The two bigger ones settled in straight away and seemed content with the new arrangements, however Rosie squirmed and wriggled around, howling and crying, pushing her nose up into the air as if searching for Jess.

'Mervin won't be happy with you. You've spoilt

her, and she wants human contact all the time,' Daniel said.

'It's just so hard not to pick her up. She likes to be next to me.'

Daniel pretended he didn't know that she was bringing the pup into her bed at night, and that night he kept silent as the fat little Rosy rested on Jess's lap. She'd found a stack of old board games at the bottom of the bookcase and insisted that he teach her how to play Chinese checkers. After he'd beaten her several times, they moved onto Scrabble, and he needed to think hard to eventually beat her, although she'd insisted some of the words he used were names and shouldn't add to his points.

For a while he felt like he was a kid again. Many times, his family had sat around this very table and played games well into the night. Having a younger person in the house made him realise that perhaps he had become a bit staid in his ways. The last few nights had been fun, full of friendly arguments as he tried to explain to Jess that yes, it was imperative that the bathroom be kept exactly how he was used to it. He told her that he thought there must have been a duck in there after she used the bathroom, and he showed her how he expected it to be kept after she'd showered. She rolled her eyes and asked him how old he was. 'That's how people get when they get old,' she said, laughing and flicking water onto the tiled floor just to annoy him.

Last night he'd found another bottle of red wine, covered in dust and stashed away in a corner cupboard. Sharing it over their dinner, they both became a bit tipsy and Daniel spent the night recalling the many funny stories that had happened over the years. With one younger brother and two sisters, there were plenty of amusing tales for him to tell.

Jess added in with some stories of her own. Incidents that had happened around the campfire back at the van park and exaggerated stories that Edward or Jake had embellished, thinking she believed anything they said. The funny nights dancing with Cedric, who she said fully believed that he was good enough to join *Riverdance* and tour the world. She giggled when she recalled some of the funny incidents and realised that she was enjoying Daniel's company. After so many months of not being able to communicate with him at all, she now found that surprisingly, she was talking to him about all sorts of things.

'Time for bed,' he said, draining the last of his glass. 'I'm thinking we may be able to get over to the workshop in the morning. The rain is supposed to be easing up a bit, so I might get you to come over with me. There're plenty of parts that need sorting out. I could use a hand, and we could make sure it's all ready for when the boys come back to work.'

\* \* \*

The next morning when he came out to the kitchen, the table was set ready for their breakfast, and Jessica was already sitting at the table eating her toast. A large book she was reading was splayed out on the table in front of her.

'You look like you've been up for a while, also like you're ready for work.' He noted her neatly ironed work shorts and shirt. 'Thanks for ironing mine also. It's great when they just appear all clean and pressed like that.'

'Morning. Hang on, I'll put this book away. Here, I have your breakfast ready to go. Oh, the ironing and washing, it's only done because I have so much spare time. Housework is normally not my thing.'

'I appreciate it,' said Daniel. 'Thanks. I'm guessing you've already fixed those pups. We'll come back during the day to feed them. They're still looking for milk every few hours, so I'll find out from Mervin when we can start giving them something else.'

Jessica hopped up to put her dishes in the sink. 'Um, what happens when the flood is gone and I go back to the van park? What happens to the pups? Because that park is strictly no animals, and I know Myrtle is not flexible about her rules.'

'I know. I've also been trying to work that out. I'm not sure when Mervin will get back up home. If he were here, we'd just give them back to him, but I doubt he'll be back that quick. We'll have to find them somewhere to live first. I can't feed them all the time once I'm working; maybe you could stay here another week, at least until we work out where Mervin is going to be?'

'Another week would be good, because they're

still only tiny. They'd be over three weeks old then.' Jessica hated the thought of parting with them but knew that Mervin would want them, particularly after losing the mother. 'As long as you don't mind me being here. I'd just work my schedule out around their feeds. I could do it easily, and then I'd be here for the night feeds also.'

'All solved, then. You'd better use my phone today and let Hoppy and the others know. It's highly likely that the roads might be open in the next couple of days, so they'll be expecting you back. I'll give Mervin a ring tomorrow and see where they're going to go.'

Both of them enjoyed getting back in and doing some work. The shed was still surrounded by a muddy lake of water and the rain continued to fall, however nowhere near as heavily as it had been. Daniel had plenty of jobs for Jessica to do and she found herself enjoying being kept busy throughout the day. The next three days passed in the same way, Jessica always up first, cleaning completed, ironed work clothes for both of them, breakfast ready, and three pups fed and their area cleaned up.

The only problem was Rosy, who whined and howled as soon as she heard Jessica come back to the house. At night the chubby pup nestled against Jess as they sat in the chair in front of the fire together. Daniel sat at the kitchen table, the two of them talking to each other, going over the work for the next day or discussing the situation with the flooding.

The river levels dropped considerably, and

tomorrow they were going to drive down and check out the bridge. Jessica was not looking forward to being able to access the outside world, or for that matter, she thought, the outside world being able to access her. Whilst she was at Daniel's place, it was as if she was in a bubble. The pups took up most of her time and she enjoyed keeping busy washing, ironing and even doing some cleaning around the house.

Spending time with Daniel was fun and she felt comfortable in his company now, so different from how she had felt before. The other major factor was that Johnno had no way of contacting her, and therefore for the very first time in many years she was able to switch off. There was no sinking feeling about the obligation to give in to his demands, and no worrying about when he was going to call her next. A heavy weight had been temporarily lifted from her shoulders.

Daniel also was feeling that something quite special was coming to an end. It had been great to share stories and laugh together, eat, drink and even play kids' games with someone who made him feel young again. He had become used to Jess's underwear drying in his kitchen, sitting on the opposite side of the table to where he usually sat, and things not being exactly where they were supposed to be. It was pretty special to come out in the morning and look at a very attractive young lady whose huge brown eyes no longer spat fire but looked straight at him as she listened and showed interest in his life. Another week would be nice, but then life would go back to normal. As to what would happen to the pups, well that was up to Mervin and what he wanted to do with them.

# 32

The river level dropped quickly, and the landscape was littered with debris as the receding water hurried to travel on to the next floodplain or town. Pieces of timber, rusty tin, a dead cow, and huge logs were amongst other debris caught up in the branches of trees or scattered across the plains. The bridge was still intact, but debris blocked the pipes underneath, causing the water to still run over the top of it. Daniel talked to his nearest neighbour as Jess sat in the car, observing the landscape around her. It was hard to believe that it had all been completely underwater, and she looked up at the high riverbanks, finding it hard to comprehend how much water had actually flowed down through the gully.

'They're going to unblock the bridge, and then we should be able to get out tomorrow,' Daniel said as he started to drive back along the boggy track.

'I can't believe how thick the mud is,' Jess said as she passed him his phone, the ringing sound a pleasant reminder for her that she hadn't had to contend with any calls herself.

It was Mervin, and he was very excited. 'Hello, boss. Yep, yep, we still in town, but they're starting to move out though. Lots of roads them opening up, so all should be good. My cousin Benny, well he's gone to work over in the west, you know Western Australia. He went last year. Well he rung me and said he want me to have his big caravan. He say Doris and I can live in it. He don't want it no more.'

'That's great, Mervin. Do you want to put it on the same spot where you were before? I'm thinking maybe just a bit higher up.'

'Yeah, all good. It's a bloody big van. They had the whole family live in it, so plenty big for us two. My uncle said he'll tow it in for us soon as the water goes. Will that be all right, boss? We'll just go a bit higher up and then maybe build one humpy down lower, where we just sit some-times.'

Jessica was listening keenly, waiting for him to ask about the pups. Daniel eventually brought the matter up. 'Mervin, those three pups are all going well now, and Jess is going to stay here for another week to help me feed them, but then we think they'll be ready to go back to you.'

'You telling me they all alive? That skinny woman, she keep feeding them? She must have done a real good job, coz I thought you said they probably die.'

'I'm not sure how one of them lived. Actually, the honey did the trick; you know you told us to use honey? We can look after them until you want them, but they need feeding every few hours at the moment. I think they're still catching up.'

'I don't want three of the buggers. The missus here is listening.' Daniel could hear Doris yelling in the background. 'She say we only take one, and she the boss, so yep, we only take one. You keep one or give it to that woman, what's her name?'

'Jess.'

'Yeah, all good. You have one, and we take one and maybe find a home for the other one. Someone will take it. I gotta go coz this mob are getting plenty restless. These women all starting to bitch and fight. All too cooped up, too many kids here, maybe twenty. All need to go home now. We see you soon, boss.' Before Daniel could answer him, he hung up.

Excitement was written all over Jessica's face. 'He wants you to have one of the pups. I heard him. He said you or I could keep one.'

'He did say that, but you're not allowed pets where you live.'

The car pulled up outside the house and Jessica sat staring straight ahead, neither of them speaking until they were back inside.

'Well, I'm here for another week. After that, maybe I could rent a little house in town or somewhere where I can keep a dog.'

'The rents are way too high in town, and besides, the deal with the company is for the van park or the main camp; they won't subsidise a house with a yard, not for a single person.'

'Would you consider keeping her here, if I can't find any other way around it? I can't bear to part with her. At least if she were here, I could pick her up on my days off, and I'm out here nearly every day with deliveries. I'd come and feed her before work and pay for her food and play with her.'

Daniel knew that he was stuck in a hard place.

He hadn't owned a dog since his ex-wife left. It had been a fluffy little house dog and thankfully she'd taken it with her. Rosie was already attached to Jess and her to it, and after all, she'd saved the three of them. He had to admit he too was attached to the yelping bundles of fur that were all starting to develop different personalities.

'How about you give me some time to think about it. I want to get cleaned up and have a good dinner tonight. There's one more bottle of red left to get through. Tomorrow we'll get back into work and there'll be lots to catch up on. How about we talk about it when we're having dinner?'

\* \* \*

Daniel noticed that Jess was going out of her way to make sure everything was ready for dinner, and she hovered in the kitchen, reminding him that all the pups were fed, the area cleaned, and was there anything she could do to help him?

'There's no use trying to butter me up so you can persuade me to keep Rosie here,' Daniel said, giving her a firm look, watching as she cleaned the benches and table. He took the broom out of her hands and put it back against the wall.

'What?' She looked at him wide-eyed, pushing strands of wavy brown hair behind her ears.

'I know what you're doing. You're trying to make everything nice, no work for me, everyone happy so that I'll agree to keep one of the pups.'

'No, I just want to help, that's all.' She smiled at him, and he shook his head, laughing. 'Sit down and pour us both a glass of wine. I'm going to serve this up.

The dinner was delicious as usual, roast beef and vegetables, done in the tastiest sauce that he told her was a secret recipe passed down through the generations. Jessica was impressed, and cleaned up her plate, looking for any leftovers. 'You're lucky you can cook. Who taught you?' she asked, spooning the last of the vegetables onto their plates.

'I guess my dad always liked to cook, on weekends or special events. He and Mum often used to cook together. She'd put on her classical music, and they'd drink wine and create something special to feed us all. When there were big family gatherings, my grandmother loved to cook for everyone also. She used to make the most delicious cakes and slices. I can cook a lot of the dishes they used to make, but I can't make the sweet things. Grandma was the best at that.'

He sat back, swirling the red wine in his glass. 'Grandma and Pop are still alive. They live in a little house in town. They're both in their nineties and don't move around that much anymore, but their minds are clear as anything. I see them most weeks.' He realised he was talking a lot and that Jessica was listening keenly but not adding anything to the conversation. 'You look a bit perplexed, Jess.' It was more of a question than a statement.

'It must be lovely having not only your parents live near you, but to have grandparents you can

219

visit too. I can't imagine what that'd be like.'

'Sorry, I guess you haven't had any of that growing up.'

'Or now,' she added. 'It's all good, though. I do all right.' She hurriedly got up and started clearing the table, signalling that she didn't want to get into a discussion about it. 'Thanks for the meal; it's the best one you've cooked.'

'It was all right, wasn't it. I'm glad you enjoyed it.' He changed the subject. 'Now let's cut to the chase. What's going to happen with these pups? We only have a week to decide what to do with them.'

She came and sat back down. 'I can't think of anything at the moment apart from maybe renting somewhere in town. Even if it takes a large part of my wage, it'd be worth it. I want to keep Rosie.'

'I know you do, but a change in accommodation isn't an option with this job. I mean workwise you answer to me, but the bottom line is, Seelo employs you. That's who pays for everything, and I think you were pretty lucky that they've let you live out at the van park.'

She really didn't have any more solutions and sat waiting, watching his face because she could see there was more he was going to say. Living under the same roof as Daniel over the last week, she'd come to know many of his traits and the different ways that he approached problems. Waiting for him to speak, she watched the way he twirled his glass, his blue eyes as always looking straight into hers, like he could read what was going on in her mind.

She found it unsettling when he looked at her like he was at the moment. It wasn't that she was intimidated by him. It was just a strange feeling, like he had some sort of say in her life, just a tiny bit of control over the direction she was headed in. That feeling was often the reason why she completely lost control of her temper when he tried to tell her what not and what to do. Like the day he yelled at her for driving over the bridge and then later tried to stop her rescuing the pups. He needed to realise that even though she was ten years younger than he was, and he was her boss, that she was her own person, and no one would tell her what to do. She'd learnt that lesson a long time ago, and that was the reason she'd survived and come out uninjured, but most of all not become addicted to alcohol or drugs. Now that her life had taken such a positive turn with the mining job, she was even more determined to never to let anyone or anything rule her life. She'd make her own decisions.

Tonight, though, her steely determination was fading. There weren't any solutions for her to keep Rosie as long as she remained working in the mines, not unless she could get into a share house or a cheap rental in town. The van park suited her perfectly, especially now that she had such a great bunch of friends around her, but it would be out of the question to have a pup there with her. She knew that she was going to have to look to Daniel for help with this one.

For so long she'd put up with his abrupt responses to her in the workplace, making sure to go the extra mile with jobs and ensure everything was done just as he wanted. But the animosity had always been there under the surface, because he'd known all along that she'd lied. He'd seen the real her, recognised it from the start, both in the tattered dress with the busted zip and then with the forged documents and blatant lies she'd presented at the interview.

Sometimes he still scared her a little; his stern looks, followed by sharp words, directed at something she'd done or said. However the last week, once she'd been up front and admitted to the lies she'd told at the interview, she had thrown caution to the wind. The pretence that she often displayed, to meet what she considered were his employer expectations, was all becoming too much, and she'd decided that if he didn't approve of her the way she was, well it was too bad. Surely by now her work ethic and record of quality work over the last year would stand her in good stead if he decided to reveal her lies.

Now she waited for him to talk, her sweetest smile thrown his way as she asked him if he wanted anything more to eat or drink.

'Don't give me that little smile. I know that you aren't normally so sweet and co-operative. It's a shame, Jess, but after this week I've come to know the real you.'

She fired up instantly, her eyes sparking as she sat upright in her chair opposite him. 'What the hell is that supposed to mean?'

Laughing out loud, he leant over, looking straight at her. 'At least I feel now that you're being honest with me. It always irked me that you'd lied and got away with it. But, well, you know what? I admire your approach. It worked. Rosalie and Phillip knew also, but they could see something in you that day of the interview. I didn't back then, but now I see it also. You're going to keep on the straight with this job, you're good at it, and probably the best courier driver I've ever employed. There's always room to learn other areas of this business, and I think you can do whatever you want. Your life is headed in the right direction, and from what you've told me, I think you deserve some breaks in your life.'

Jessica looked down, pretending to rub some dirt off the table, her eyes unable to meet his. 'Take it, Jess. It's not very often I give out praise, as you well know. You're a bloody good worker, and you know what, you're good company as well.'

She finally looked up. 'Thank you. That means a lot to me.' She paused. 'Especially coming from you.'

Raising his eyebrows at her last words, he changed the topic to talk about what really needed to be discussed. 'Now, I may have a solution for the pups, but I'm not sure if you'll agree to it.'

'I don't have many options.'

'It's just an idea, but I'm prepared to fix that yard fence up so that it's dog-proof, and keep the red male pup for myself.'

'Oh.'

'And,' he continued as she looked up at him, 'I'd suggest that Rosie stays here also. She'd be your dog, but the two of them can keep each other company. On weeks off, or whenever you want, you take her; but other times, like when we're both at work, the two of them can be here together to keep each other company. It should work as long as you let me know when you're taking her. What do you think?'

A lump formed in Jess's throat, and she tried to breathe evenly and remain calm. Her voice was uneven as she answered, 'I don't know what to say. That's so generous that you'd do that. I'll pay for her food and vet's bills or anything else.'

'I'm not worried about that, but you'll need to train her. I'll work with Red, so I can help you train Rosie if you like at the same time. I haven't had a dog here in years, and I wouldn't mind one. They'll be company at night, so I don't mind having them both. The other one, that's the biggest red one, she can go to Mervin. He said he wanted a female. That little blue one, well, I guess she's yours if you think the idea is all right.'

'All right? I think it's amazing, and I'm a bit overcome that you'd do that for me.'

'I'm not a complete bastard, you know.' He laughed, feeling content and happy about his solution. 'If you could just stay for the next week so we can look after them until Mervin comes back, and by then they should all be feeding by themselves. After that, it'll be easy. I think having Red here will keep Rosie a bit calmer, and hopefully she won't whine at night when you're not here.'

'Thanks so much, Daniel. Wait until I tell Hoppy and the others. I can't believe that I'll actually have my own dog.'

Daniel laughed as he replied, 'They'll all laugh. They'll think I've gone soft in the head.'

# 33

Everything moved quickly once the floods receded and the bridge that linked them to the outside world was cleared of debris. They had both been kept busy organising the workshop and rebuilding much of the fence that ran around the house. Daniel asked Hoppy and Cedric out for dinner one night so they could catch up with everyone's news. The other men were all away on their time off, and Jessica was happy that at least two of them were able to come out and see her new pup.

The four of them sat around the table, munching into her tasty stir-fry, Hoppy and Cedric with many questions and stories to tell about the floods and events that went with it. Hoppy, as usual, was as upfront as ever. 'So, Miss Jessica, you survived staying with your boss. He wasn't too grumpy?'

'Now, now, Hoppy, let's not get too personal. Jess and I got on just fine after a few initial mishaps. Isn't that right, Jess?' He gave her a stern look, daring her to say differently.

'I survived, Hoppy.' She giggled and gave him a hug; a week away from her old friends reinforced exactly how much they all meant to her.

'I bet he can't do the Irish jig like I can.' Cedric was relaxed and calm. A week disconnected from the outside world suited him fine, and he only became fidgety when Daniel asked him about his upcoming visit to his family. Cedric's voice became serious. 'I know, I know I said I wouldn't stay with her. You know the missus, but she's been quite friendly to me over the phone. Wants me to come and stay for my annual holidays, even said we could take the kids and go somewhere together.'

Hoppy chuckled. 'Maybe she wants to rekindle the flame. You know, perhaps she just can't resist you anymore. She's gonna put the hard word on you.'

'Jesus, don't make me nervous with ideas like that. That woman still scares me to death. She did tell me, though, that she thought I was looking good, and that she wishes I'd cleaned myself up years ago.'

'Maybe you need a woman to point you in the right direction and change your habits,' Daniel said.

Cedric rolled his eyes. 'Jesus, that's the trouble with women. Not you, Miss Geronimo, but that wife of mine. She just loves to try and change everything.' Cedric pointed at Jess, his eyes wide, eyebrows lifted. 'You know that a woman put Mount Everest where it is, don't you, Miss Geronimo?'

'What?' Jess laughed, watching Cedric become more animated.

He stood up to prove his point. 'Of course it was a woman who put it there, because if it had been a man, a bloody woman would have moved it!'

They all laughed. Jessica loving the friendship

and familiarity that they shared, and the feeling that she was in a really good place. She was getting along with and actually liked her boss, work was going to resume tomorrow, Cedric and Hoppy had come out to see her, and best of all, she now for the first time ever had her own dog. Moments like this had been extremely rare over the years, and she soaked it in, smiling at Daniel when he winked at her as Cedric told another crude joke. Life felt good, and she closed her eyes, trying to capture just this one moment in time, storing it away with only just a few other special times. This night she'd remember for a very long time to come.

# 34

Slowly but surely the mines reopened and the workers returned to their jobs. Shops in town restocked, and the locals flocked in to socialise and replenish their food supplies. Jessica was busier than ever as she worked through the backlog of deliveries, observing the changes in the landscape as she drove around. Green flecks of grass started to poke through the thickness of dried-up mud, new shoots appeared on trees that had previously appeared dead, and the creeks and river pushed their water under bridges that were still littered with debris and trees.

It was a strange feeling when she eventually left Daniel's, and she thought back over the events of the past weeks as she cleaned out the room that she'd stayed in, collecting her belongings to take back to the van. Daniel carried her bag out for her before picking up both Red and Rosie to wave her off. Mervin was more than happy for Daniel and Jessica to have a pup each, and couldn't believe the healthy-looking pups that greeted them when he and Doris pulled up, towing the long van that was to be their new home.

'What you think, boss?' Mervin dipped his hat to Jessica, showing both her and Daniel through the van. 'Not bad, aye? Doris and I will be happy living in there. Plenty of room when the family come and stay with us. I gonna build a little house thing for this here pup.' He looked at the largest of the three pups, already settled in, sitting on Doris's lap in the front seat of the car.

'This gonna be real good one, this one,' said Doris. 'I can tell. These red ones always the best watch dogs, those blue ones though they being extra smart. You done plenty good to save them. Not sure you should 'ave gone in that water, but anyways they 'ere now, so all of them 'ave got a home. You make sure not to spoil that little blue pup. Hurry up Mervin, Joanie and Dawnie coming to visit in an hour. I gotta set the kettle up and have the tea and biscuits ready.'

'What?' Mervin yelled from where he stood with Daniel. 'You organise visitors already, woman? Haven't you talked with that one mob enough for the last couple of weeks?'

'Just hurry up, Mervin,' Doris yelled out the window, impatient to get the van placed and settled. Daniel and Jessica watched as the couple pulled away, their new home bouncing behind them across the rough road out to the riverbank.

'They don't want for much, do they?' Jessica recognised the simplicity in which the couple liked to live and how happy they were with their new van, which would be placed above the riverbank, providing them with a temporary place to live until a new hut was built.

'They're just happy as long as they can be in that spot close to where they were before. They've always lived there, and my grandparents can tell all sorts of stories about Mervin's family who always camped there along that river. They've come and gone as they want over the years, and there have been a series of sheds and humpies down there, all eventually washing away with one of the floods we've had in the past. How are you going reading those books, *The First Australians*?'

'I started reading the first one, but I've been a bit busy.'

'Take it with you. I know you'll look after it. I've already read them, so take it, because it will give you accurate information on the real history.'

Each night she read a chapter of the book, amazed at how the first Australians had lived. Often she was too tired to read, however, and instead flicked through the photos in the book, the old black and white ones giving her an insight into the original people of the area.

Life back at the van park returned to normal, and Jeffery came over for dinner a couple of times, all of them sitting around the fire once again: Cedric swearing and telling his jokes and Hoppy fussing over everyone, making sure they were well fed. Edward continued to spout his knowledge about floods and the weather, and Jake would add in, often trying to correct what he considered Edward had exaggerated. Charlie was relentless in admonishing her about driving through floodwaters and now decided to give her and Jeffery little tips about driving in all sorts of conditions. As usual, there was plenty of chatter, Jake butting in telling Charlie that they'd heard enough about his driving expertise and could Edward please stop lecturing about the weather patterns. It was all getting too much for him.

'Anyway,' Jake piped up again, 'I think we'd better check on how Thommo is going again tomorrow.

He's not going to be happy about getting regular tests done.'

'Well, he was supposed to get a check-up months ago.' Hoppy was unhappy because Thommo had been carted off to the hospital just after the flood waters went down, after putting off having a check-up over a year ago.

'See, nothing's changed, Miss Geronimo,' Charlie said as he passed Jessica a piping-hot cup of tea. 'Nothing ever changes. It's all the same — just work, no women, well except for Cedric now. He's got one hot on his tail. Work, eat, drink, and more work. All the same.'

'I like that it stays the same.' Jessica sat next to Jeffery, who she could see had something he wanted to tell her. 'I like the way it is.'

One by one the men drifted off to their vans, ready to take up the next shift in the morning. Soon only Jeffery and Jessica remained the fire flickering low, as the two friends sat talking to each other.

'What is it, Jeffery? Come on, I know you've got something to tell me. I can tell by the look on your face.'

Jeffery looked up at the stars, then back to Jess before talking, 'Well, while you were away, I met someone.'

'You met someone here, in Gowrie?'

He put his arm around her. 'Yes, I have. Because everything was shut out at the mine, I spent a day in town. It's a shame you weren't here. Actually, I did lunch, had a pedicure, and went for a haircut.'

'Go on, go on, don't keep me waiting.'

'Well, you know Sally down at the hairdresser's? She has a brother, a gorgeous brother who just happens to be a hairdresser also and has returned to work in town.'

'Wow, a hairdresser.'

'He's gorgeous. Great body, smart, funny, and around the same age as me.'

'And?'

'Well he cut my hair, and we hit it off straight away. I've just spent the most fabulous week with him. I'm only here tonight because he had a work function to attend. We've spent every evening together, and we can talk for hours. Honestly, Jess, we're on the same wavelength, and we just get on like a house on fire. I think I'm in love.'

Jeffery's face was flushed, and Jessica could see that he was smitten. 'That's great, Jeffery. I hope it all works out for you. When do I get to meet him?'

'You'll have to make time in between Rosie and work to come out for dinner with us, or perhaps go in and get a haircut. You'll love him. I've already told him about you, and he's keen to meet you also.'

She knew it wasn't easy for Jeffery to meet someone, particularly in a small town, and she hoped that everything worked out for both of them. Feeling unusually lonely, she waved him off, the lights of the other vans all turned off already, everyone sleeping ready for the next day. Her thoughts turned to Johnno, and she reached for her phone, trying again to ring him. There had been several missed calls on her phone when she'd finally returned after being flooded in at Daniel's. However, the numerous times she'd tried to call him had been fruitless, and she'd given up in the end, knowing that sooner or later he'd contact her. At the moment, she tried to push him to the back of her mind. On the one hand, she was enjoying a small window of time without any dramas from him intruding on her life, but on the other there was a nagging worry that persisted, as she wondered what he was doing.

She knew they were growing further and further apart, and that, as had often been the case over the years, he only contacted her when he needed money. Lately she'd been having some very strange feelings about him, and the thoughts often stopped her in her tracks as she went about her work. Yesterday she had felt panicked and couldn't think straight, having to stop and calm herself down before continuing with what she was doing. Something was not right with Johnno, and she could feel it, but at the moment there was no way of contacting him, so she'd have to wait until he phoned her. Their relationship had worked this way for the last couple of years, and at the moment perhaps it was for the best.

# 35

The situation with the pups worked well, better than Jessica or Daniel had anticipated. Afternoons were usually free for Jess, so she spent the time in the yard, training and playing with both the pups. Daniel's pup Red was a lot bigger and had a much blockier, squarer face than the finer, shorter Rosie. Both of them had white paws and white tips on their tails. Although they were only six weeks old, Jess had already taught them how to sit and stay and to lie down when they were told.

'I can't believe how quickly they learn something, and they don't forget. When I come the next time, they remember it straight away.'

'Yeah, cattle dogs are smart, that's why they use them on the properties. I'm not sure about that Rosie, though. I think you've spoilt her.'

'Why do you think she's spoilt?' Jess cuddled the pup up against her, rubbing her face into Rosie's soft fur.

'At night, she whimpers until I let her in. I only leave them in for an hour or so when I'm watching television, then once I put them out she's happy. She just needs that extra time inside. I think she looks for you.'

'It's good they've got each other during the day, because they're always playing together,' said Jess.

'They haven't been a problem, and I must say

I like having them both here. They're company.'

Both pups sat together, waiting to be fed. Their tails wagged incessantly across the floor, and they looked expectantly up at Daniel and Jess. 'I'll feed them and then I'll have to go,' Jess said. 'It's another big day tomorrow. I think I'm out here a couple of times, so I'll time my lunch here. Troy wants to come and have a look at them, so we'll both be over here together, if that's okay.'

'Of course it is. I'm just glad to see it all working out.'

Jessica hated leaving Rosie at night, but she knew there was no alternative and that Daniel would look after her. Besides, it was good the smaller pup was with Red; they both snuggled in together at night, keeping each other company, and there hadn't been too much yelping to keep Daniel awake. She wasn't sure how it would work out in the future, but she needed to do as Daniel said and just take each day as it came. 'Things always work out in the end,' he told her. 'She's your pup, but she's just staying with me. At the moment, it's the best we can do.'

Work was extra-busy that week, as she had anticipated, and on Thursday afternoon she went back to the van, cleaned up and fell asleep on the bed. A knocking noise on her screen door woke her, and she sat up wondering who it could be. The men usually called out, and Myrtle always whistled whenever she walked around, so you always knew when she was coming. Opening the screen door, she was surprised to see Daniel standing there, still in his work gear. He must

236

have needed to drive into town for something, she thought, or perhaps he needed some gear picked up.

'Hello, have I forgotten something? Jess said as she tried to flatten her hair, her hands telling her that it was sticking up everywhere from the deep sleep she'd fallen into. 'I'm charging my phone at the moment, so if you tried to ring, I'm sorry, it might have been flat.'

'Hi, Jess. No, I haven't been trying to ring. Looks like I woke you up. It's been a big week at work. I know we've been flat out also.'

She was standing in the doorway, still surprised as to the purpose of his visit. 'Did you want to come in, or were you after Hoppy or one of the others?'

'No, actually I came to talk to you.' From the doorway, she could see Hoppy and Charlie sitting on their doorsteps looking her way. Daniel looked up at her as he spoke. 'Are you busy on Saturday?'

'No, it's a day off, but I can do something for you if you need. I don't have anything planned. Did you want a special run done?'

'Would you like to go out to Ferry Gorge with me? I'd like to take you out there. It's a nice drive and there are some interesting things to see.'

'Sure. Do we need to pick something big up? Did you want me to take my ute or your truck?'

'We're not picking anything up, Jess. I'm asking you to have a day out with me, you know, like a date.'

She could feel her face turning bright red.

'You want to take me out on a date? I'm confused. Are you sure?'

'I'm sure, but if you're not, you don't have to say yes. I'm asking you if you'd like to go. Just give me a simple yes or no.'

She stammered, folding her arms, not sure which way to look or what to do. Behind Daniel, she could see Hoppy and Charlie still looking her way. 'Do those two know anything about this? They seem awfully interested in what's going on.'

'I may have run the idea past Hoppy just to check what he thought. Just a yes or no, it's just a date.'

'Well, I guess, yeah sure, I, maybe, well, yes, I'd like to do that. That would be nice, thank you.'

Daniel breathed an audible sigh of relief, his eyes not leaving hers as he told her to be ready by seven, and no she didn't need to bring anything as he'd pick her up and have everything organised. 'See you at seven,' he said, smiling as he walked back to his car. He gave Hoppy and Charlie a wave before driving off, a cloud of dust following him out of the driveway.

Jessica sat stunned on the steps of the van, watching the speck of dust fade into the distance. Where had that come from? Not in her wildest dreams had she ever thought that he'd ask her on a date. She looked up to see Hoppy and Charlie grinning mischievously at her as they walked towards her.

'Hope you said yes, Miss Geronimo. He did check first, and we told him we thought it was a good idea,' Charlie said.

'I can't believe he asked you two first. I'm a bit shocked, and besides I've never been out on a date before.'

'Well, this will be a first then, won't it.' Hoppy gave her the biggest grin and squeezed her arm. 'Don't be so shocked. You're a lovely young woman. I'm surprised more fellas here aren't around chasing you.'

'Geez, Hoppy, I am a bit, because in one of the last conversations I had with Daniel, he said I reminded him of the wild kittens with the mother cat down the back end of the workshop. He showed me them to explain what he meant. As soon as you get close to them, they spit and go crazy, and when he tried to grab one, it dug its claws in, scratched him and drew blood.'

'Well, you've had to learn how to stick up for yourself over the years. I can't say I blame you for firing up with Daniel, because we know him and he's bloody stubborn. No wonder you two have had some run-ins.'

Jessica still looked confused and was now also starting to get a bit nervous about it all. 'Why does he want to take me out?'

'Bloody hell, obviously because he thinks you're a bit all right,' Charlie said. 'You've spent some time together, and he's enjoyed your company. He checked with us because he wanted to know if we thought he was too old to ask you out.'

'And what did you say?'

Hoppy laughed before he spoke. 'Nope, all fine and dandy with us. That's not that much of an age difference; you are after all twenty-three, old enough to make your own decisions.'

'I've been making my own decisions since I was ten,' Jess mumbled to herself as she returned inside and shut the door behind her. She needed some peace and quiet, a strong cup of coffee, and some time to think over what she'd just agreed to. A phone call to Jeffery straight away was her first priority, to get some advice — and what the hell was she going to wear? Her wardrobe was very limited, and she hadn't spent any money on herself since arriving, making do with whatever clothes she already owned and relying on the uniforms supplied to wear every day. Picking up the phone, she nervously called his number. 'Jeffery, I need help.'

'God, Jessica, you sound distraught. What's wrong?'

'I need to talk to you and get advice. I've been asked on a date.'

Jeffery replied, his voice excited, 'Who's the lucky guy?'

There was a gap of silence before she replied, 'Daniel, as in Daniel my boss. I need some advice on what to wear because I've never been on a date before.'

'Darling, I'm in the car right now as we speak.' She could hear the car start up. 'This is serious business. I'm on my way to your place immediately.' He stressed the 'immediately' and she knew he loved the drama of such an interesting piece of news. 'Hang up and I'll be there in a jiff. We need to get some sort of wardrobe thing happening for you. Sit tight.'

# 36

Jeffery was elated that Daniel had asked her on a date. 'Of course he should ask you; he's come to know the real Jessica and has fallen for you. Besides that, he's absolutely gorgeous! Yes, yes, pull all those shirts out and give me a look.' A few pieces of clothing were scattered on the bed, Jeffery grimacing at the scarcity and quality of what she owned. 'Fine, fine, the jeans will be okay, and thank goodness you let me talk you into buying those boots. The bottom half will be okay, but really, Jessica, those blouses — they look like they're out of the op shops.'

'They are. I've worn them for years. I always thought they were okay.'

'They're threadbare. Tell you what, meet me in town tomorrow at lunch and we'll go to the only decent clothes shop on the main street, Dimity's. It sells some gorgeous blouses. There's a beautiful one in the window at the moment. I've been looking at it myself, but it will look great on you, and tucked in with those jeans and boots, we should have you looking fabulous. Leave your hair out also. It's nice out. No, don't tie it up.'

The two of them laughed and talked until Hoppy called them both out to share dinner with Jeffery, the others all off working, or on their time off. Jessica felt much more at ease now that the clothes were half worked out, and she kept reminding herself it was just a date.

Waving Jeffery off later that night, she returned to the van, still confused as to why Daniel would ask her out. She knew that there were quite a few women in town who were keen on him, and Jeffery sometimes repeated the gossip to her that flowed back and forth at the hairdresser's.

'The women love to talk about him. They say he doesn't bother with the women from here. Some of them say they've tried but never get anywhere. The talk is that he's got a woman in the city and apparently she works for the company. You should hear what they say about that. You know what the local women are like.'

Jessica hadn't taken much notice of the gossip at the time, but now she thought about what Jeffery had told her and wondered if Daniel did have a girlfriend in the city. Not that it mattered, she told herself. It was just an outing, most likely a picnic, because Hoppy and Charlie had told her that there wasn't much where he was taking her.

'Nice view,' Hoppy said, 'and you'll enjoy the drive, especially after this rain. It'll be pretty out that way.'

★   ★   ★

She was ready at seven, and just as Hoppy had told her to do, she waited until Daniel knocked on her door. 'Don't be looking too eager, now. Let him come to you.'

'Christ, Hoppy, it's just one date. I think you're getting a bit carried away.'

242

'You never know, because stranger things have happened. I've seen it all before.'

Jess was glad she'd followed Jeffery's fashion advice, because Daniel arrived looking handsome and well dressed, a blue shirt tucked neatly into his jeans, topped by a thick leather belt sporting a chunky silver buckle. His rugged face was freshly shaved, and he smiled, trying to put her at ease as he picked up on her nervousness.

'You look lovely, Jess. Is that a new shirt?'

'It is. Jeffery took me shopping yesterday during my lunch break.'

'Well he, well both of you, have good taste. The dark colours in the pattern complement your eyes.'

Lost for words, Jess didn't reply, entirely unused to anyone, let alone a very handsome man who also happened to be her boss, complimenting her on both how she looked and her eyes.

Hoppy was right, and the countryside where Daniel took her for that first date was different to the places around town. Daniel's ute bumped along the track he was following and the dust turned from brown to red. In the distance, she should see red hills rising from the flat earth where green shoots of grass had started to poke through the surface.

The day had been perfect, and Daniel was pleased with how everything worked out. It had been a long time since he'd been on a date, and last night he'd spent hours preparing a picnic for the day, ensuring that there was cold wine and plenty of food to eat. He loved watching Jess's face as they drove out through the changing landscape, her eyes moving everywhere as she questioned him about the hills, the river they followed out, and the use of the land this far from town.

As they neared a clump of hills, she marvelled at the whiteness of the gums, their delicate green leaves dripping down, stark against the background of the red dirt. They walked up into the hills and Daniel showed her where the water had flowed down during the floods, to a waterhole that he said was a gathering point for the local indigenous people for hundreds if not thousands of years. Lastly, what he'd really brought her to see, the caves and overhanging rock ledges that were adorned with drawings done by the Aboriginal people who once lived in the area.

Together they followed the stories detailed in them, trying to work out the different symbols and characters depicted on the rock walls. Jessica was fascinated, and he'd eventually persuaded her to leave, promising to bring her back again one day. He wanted to allow time to drive to a point where they could eat lunch and get a view of the entire area.

The view from the top of the hill Daniel drove to took in the entire plain that stretched out in front of them. A long way in the distance, the tiny town of Gowrie was just visible on the horizon, the road they had travelled along earlier in the day a squiggling snakelike etching in the earth. Daniel heard the emotion in Jess's voice as she spoke. 'This is incredible. I never knew all of this was out here, and it's just so beautiful.'

'It's pretty amazing,' he said as he set the

lunch out in front of them. 'I never get sick of it. Wait another couple of weeks and then you'll start to see things green up again. It just keeps changing all the time, what with the seasons and the weather.'

The food disappeared fast and they washed it down with the chilled wine. Relaxing comfortably in the fold-up chairs that Daniel had brought for them to sit in, Jessica couldn't stop looking at the view in front of her. She plied him with questions, wanting to know everything, both about the history of the area and the people who lived here today. They talked for hours before packing up, the sun starting to slide down the western side of the sky, the light changing, a dusty orange hue soon throwing its golden colours across the earth. 'Time to go,' Daniel said. 'I hope you've enjoyed seeing all this. There are plenty of other fabulous places to visit, but this one is my favourite, so I wanted to share it with you.'

'Thanks. This is such an incredible place,' she said, getting into the ute as he opened the door for her. 'It's been a special day, and I appreciate all the effort you've gone to with the food. I won't be able to sleep tonight. I'll be thinking about everything I've seen; all the beautiful colours of the countryside.'

The ute bumped over the track back towards town and the van park, Jessica and Daniel continuing to talk the entire way home, often both of them laughing together at one of Daniel's stories.

As they pulled into the park, they could see a

few of the men seated around the fire, all of them turning to watch as Daniel drove Jessica up to the door of her van.

'Nothing's sacred here, is it,' Daniel muttered. 'Look at Charlie looking at his watch. I told them I'd be back before dark. Jesus, it's like they're checking up on me.'

Jessica laughed and waved at the men before walking with Daniel up to her door. 'Thanks for such a lovely day, Daniel. It was special.'

He touched her on the arm softly. 'It was pretty special for me also. I haven't enjoyed myself like that for a long while. Make sure you still come out tomorrow to the pups. I'll be doing some work around the house, so drive out whenever you want.'

'I will, thanks.' She gave him a smile. 'I'll see you in the morning.' She watched him give the men a quick wave before driving off. She also gave them a wave, calling out goodnight before shutting the door behind her.

# 37

There were a few more dates after that first one, each time Daniel asking her if she was free and then picking her up and dropping her off at the end of the day. They visited beautiful spots along the river and found a gorge where cliffs soared high above, dwarfing them both as they stood gazing up. Vertical rock walls loomed above them, their impenetrable solidness broken intermittently by the green foliage of small plants hanging precariously, their roots clinging onto small cracks that zigzagged across their surface. Daniel followed dusty backtracks that took them to nearby sleepy towns, where they ate hamburgers and sat on old wooden railway seats, watching the locals walk up and down, the old men sitting and chatting on the bench seats outside the local pub.

She went shopping with Jeffery again to find another shirt and let him talk her into buying a beautiful floral dress as well as some cute little sandals. 'You just never know where he'll ask you to go next. Women have to be prepared for the unexpected.' Jeffery was enjoying seeing her being spoilt and wanted her to look her best, but as he told her, 'Not that you need much. You'd look good in a hessian bag.'

'I have no idea about clothes, make-up or shoes. I've only ever owned a few items growing up and just made do with whatever I was given.'

Thank goodness for Jeffery's intervention, because Friday night Daniel wanted to take her to an outdoor concert that was being held down on the riverbank, just outside of town. He'd rung to ask if she'd like to go. 'There's a band coming in from out of town, and you just bring a blanket, sit on the banks and listen to the music. I'll get the food ready and pick you up around six, if you'd like to go.'

'I'd love to,' she said, pleased that she'd let Jeffery talk her into buying the new dress and sandals. The dress had a tiny flower print on it and hugged her figure nicely, coming to just above her knee, little flat sandals finishing off the outfit perfectly. A hairclip she'd bought in town last week pulled up one side of her hair, the soft wavy curls now reaching down below her shoulders.

She could tell from the look on Daniel's face when she opened the door that he was impressed. For a while he didn't say anything, but just stood there looking at her. When he finally spoke, he fell over his words. 'Wow, I mean wow, I mean . . . you look fabulous. Is that a Jeffery choice?'

'It is.' She giggled, not sure who was getting the most enjoyment out of the purchasing of her new clothes, her or Jeffery.

'Well, it's suits you perfectly.' He nearly added that it reminded him of the dress she wore on that very first day he'd met her in the lift, only this was new and showed off her figure even more than the one with the broken zipper.

The night was magical and they sat together on a blanket, listening to a variety of musicians singing country and blues music. Jessica soaked in the atmosphere, the lyrics washing over her. She was overcome with the sight of so many people being together, all sitting side by side in an area that was a bit like a natural amphitheatre. When she lay back on the blanket, she could feel Daniel's arm next to hers and they both looked up at the sky that was naturally decorated with thousands of bright twinkling stars.

Quite a few people said hello to Daniel, a few of the local women taking a second look at Jessica, trying to place who she was. As they were walking back to the car, a couple came up behind them, the woman twisting her arms in through Daniel's, squeezing him hard, her cheek against his shoulder.

'Belle,' he said as he gave her a warm hug and peck on the cheek. 'Where did you spring from? I didn't recognise you without the kids hanging off you. G'day, Tyson. How are you both?'

'A few people told us you were here . . . and with a friend.' The woman called Belle smiled at Jess and then turned back to Daniel. 'Are you going to introduce us?'

'Jess, this is my sister Belle and her husband Tyson.'

Jess nodded at them both, feeling Belle's eyes on her as she looked from Daniel to Jess and back again.

'They normally have a tribe of kids with them,' Daniel said. 'Who let you two out tonight?'

'Mum and Dad have the kids. It's just so good to come out by ourselves. I feel nearly human again.'

'Plus,' Tyson added, 'she's drunk a bottle of wine. That's what happens when you let her loose for the night.'

Belle giggled and swayed a little as she walked beside them. 'So how come we haven't met Jess before?' she said, raising her eyebrows, pushing her face up close to Daniel's.

'You need to go home. You're going to feel like crap tomorrow, and you'll still have to get up early and pick up the kids.'

'Nice to meet you, Jess,' Tyson said as he steered Belle towards their car, holding her arm so that she didn't fall over.

'Bye, guys. Don't behave yourselves.' Belle fell over her words, giggling loudly, holding on tight to Tyson, who was shaking his head, pulling funny faces at Daniel behind Belle's back.

'She's going to be sad and sorry tomorrow because she gets terrible hangovers,' Daniel said to Jess. 'Plus she'll have to look after the kids; they have four of them. What a great first impression you have of my youngest sister.'

'How old is she? She doesn't look much older than me.'

Daniel thought for a moment. 'She must be about twenty-eight because Liz is thirty, Ben the youngest will be twenty-six this year, and Jeez, I'll be thirty-four. I still feel like I'm twenty-one.' He looked at her. 'You're only a baby at twenty-three.'

'I'm twenty-four this year. Besides, age means nothing.' She watched him as he unlocked her car door, thinking how before she knew him well she'd always thought of him as much older, particularly when he lectured her or talked to her in his boss role, giving her instructions or telling her how to change the way she was doing something. Now that she knew him better, she didn't think anything of his age. It was irrelevant. He was just Daniel.

Leaning against the car, she looked up at the stars, always so much brighter out here than in the city. Daniel unlocked the door and stood in front of her, watching her gaze upwards. She looked down and straight into his eyes as he bent his head down towards hers. Warm hands touched her face, and his lips brushed softly against hers as he kissed her, short soft kisses that took her breath away. His mouth closed gently over hers and this time he kissed her for a long time, their bodies pressing against each other as she felt herself kissing him passionately in return, his hands at the back of her head, those piercing blue eyes looking straight into hers. Closing her eyes, she felt his kisses on her face, before once again their lips met, the feel of him next to her sending sensations through her body.

Finally Daniel spoke. 'I couldn't help myself. I've wanted to kiss those lips for weeks, and they're just as soft and warm as I thought they'd be.' He lifted her chin up, her eyes looking up into his as he kissed her forehead and her cheeks before finding her mouth again. 'You look so beautiful in that dress. You've really got under my skin, Jess, and I can't stop thinking about you.'

'I'm a little surprised, you know.' She could

hardly get her words out. 'For so long, you didn't like me, and everything I did was wrong. And now you're kissing me.'

'I know; I've surprised myself. You bring out feelings that I'd forgotten existed.' She hung onto his arms, strong arms that were wrapped tightly around her, squeezing her gently.

Looking up at him she, smiled. 'I like your kisses and I don't want this night to ever end.' She touched his arm, her small hands warm against his skin. His mouth closed over hers again, and she lost all sense of time and place as his lips pressed down on hers. They stood holding each other, Daniel pulling her in towards him, her head nestling into his chest, a feeling of warmth and passion sweeping over both of them.

'I need to get you home. It's been one hell of a night.' Daniel finally pulled away from where they both still stood, neither one wanting the moment to end. Jessica ran her fingers over her lips, wanting the feeling to remain, the tenderness of his lips on hers. 'You have a very dreamy look on your face, Jess.'

'You think my face looks dreamy? I'm in shock. I'm tingling from my head down to my toes.'

He chuckled. 'I'm going to take you home. I'll be dreaming about your lips for the rest of the night.'

Daniel kissed her again outside her van, opening the door before giving her a final hug. 'Thanks, I'll see you soon,' was the only thing she could think of to say. Her head was whirling, and the implications of the night kept her awake, her mind going over everything Daniel had said to her, the feeling of his lips on hers, his hands in her hair and the feel of his skin under her hands.

'Good night, Daniel,' she spoke out loud to an empty van, the sound of his ute a faint noise now in the distance.

# 38

When she woke the next morning, she lay for a long time looking up at the ceiling of the van, her mind going over the night before. How would Daniel react to her today? He'd be busy at the workshop for most of the day, and she was supposed to be heading out to his place to spend time with Rosie. Perhaps he'd regret the way he'd held her and kissed her the night before. How would he react when she saw him next?

A million questions whirred around in her head. How had she allowed herself to be drawn into a closeness with someone whom she had earlier despised, and who also happened to be her boss? There hadn't been any romantic notions in her head when she'd stayed with him during the floods. She'd enjoyed being there with him, although there'd been a few disputes, and she'd fired up because she thought he'd been having a go at her. Sometimes he could be intimidating, especially when he was so serious about things or trying to show her why something should be done the way he suggested. She'd learnt, though, how to lighten his mood, and after a while had thrown caution to the wind, allowing herself for the first time in a long while just to be herself.

Since a very young age, she'd needed to think and act like an adult, shouldering huge responsibilities and making all the decisions about where she was headed, who she would live with and where the next lot of money and food was coming from. The job at Seelo gave her the freedom of living by herself, a steady income, and most of all friends of her own. Sure they were a motley crew, all of them at the van park much older than herself, and all with their individual, quirky personalities. Jeffery had become a close friend, and she loved the fact that he'd ring her at all odd times to tell her something that was just gossip or a funny story. She'd never had a close friend before, and Jeffery filled that gap with his energy and enthusiasm for her and life in the tiny country town.

Pangs of guilt hit her as she let her mind drift where she'd been trying to stop it going. Johnno. She closed her eyes, wanting to block all thoughts of him out: his addictions, the whining and pleading, and the never-ending dramas that were associated with being near him. Determined not to let anything spoil the night before, she told herself that she'd deal with Johnno whenever they next talked. Perhaps he'd also moved on and was happy to have no contact. Pushing the persistent thoughts of him from her mind, she readied herself for a day with the two boisterous pups, excited but a little bit nervous at also seeing Daniel. It was going to be an interesting day.

Daniel watched her car drive in as he moved around the workshop, some of the other mechanics already working on the huge pieces of machinery that needed to be finished today and moved back out to the mine. He kept himself busy, giving her some time to play with the pups and clean the laundry out where Rosie and Red both slept.

He also had lain awake for a long time last night, the softness of her lips under his and the feel of her slender body pressed up against him going back and forth in his mind. The fitted dress she'd worn last night had been the last straw, and the vision of her bare back in the lift so long ago came flooding back to him. There was something unique about her from that very first time she had abused him, flashing angry eyes and foul language showing him that she was not someone to mess with. The lying, however, hadn't impressed him, and he'd failed to see how a female was going to be able to handle the job that she'd won. Jess had, however, proven herself, making very few mistakes, often finding practical ways to move heavy things around, and ensuring that everything was delivered correctly and on time.

Not long before the floods, he started to notice that she'd filled out, and although her body was slender still, the shapes and curves were still apparent, even under the stiffness of the work shorts and shirts. The day she'd taken to William, he'd felt the strength in her arms and noticed that her body was becoming fit-looking, tanned, and, he had to admit, very sexy.

Over the past year at work, he'd left it all to Rosalie to mentor Jess through meetings over the phone, knowing that the older woman was checking in on her, and that she'd let him know if there were any problems. His tolerance for Jess had grown, and Hoppy and the others continually let him know that they all loved having her as part of their crew, and that he needed to lighten up and stop giving her such a hard time. He'd told them that he treated her the same as any other employee and certainly wasn't going to start doing any favours for her just because they all thought she was lovely and doted on her.

The morning of the floods he had nearly gone crazy trying to phone her, hoping like anything that she'd use common sense and not driven out. He'd forgotten that she was a city woman and didn't know much about how floods worked out this way, having no concept about the dangers and swiftness of rising rivers and the power of even shallow water running across a rickety bridge. It was obvious from the earlier rainfall and the forecasts from upstream that morning that the river was flooding, and he had felt nauseous when her ute pulled into the work-shop, the vehicle barely visible in the torrential rain. As usual, she'd given him a mouthful, both then and later on when she once again went completely against what he told her to do and instead rescued the pups.

Funny how things work out, though, he thought, because the time she was forced to spend with him allowed him to see what she was really like. When he'd put her on the spot about her schooling, she'd been honest, and he felt something lift, a change in the way he thought about her and the way they communicated.

Over the two weeks that she stayed with him,

he enjoyed himself more than he had in a very long time. Having her as an extra in the house made him realise that he'd developed routines and structure in his life that had in fact turned him into thinking a lot like a much older person, and not like the thirty-four years that he was.

When he was with her, he felt young again, and the responsibilities of work and the hurts of the past lifted from his shoulders. He could just enjoy being out, socialising and showing someone who shared his love of the countryside the sights nearby. Best of all was the feeling of her next to him, holding and kissing her, feelings aroused in a way that had been missing from his life for many years.

Driving over to the house for the morning tea break, he ran his hand through his hair, trying to flatten it down a little, attempting to look at least a bit respectable even in work clothes that were already showing signs of grease and dirt. He could see her running around the yard with the pups, both of them chasing her, barking and jumping up and down when they caught up with her.

Red and Rosie stopped in their tracks when they heard his car; Rosie, as usual, growling and putting on her most fierce bark before realising it was Daniel's ute pulling up in front of the house. Both dogs left Jess and bolted around the front, sitting obediently on the doorstep of the house, waiting for Daniel to approach. It had taken only a couple of weeks to train them not to rush vehicles as they drove in. Both pups liked to bite at the moving wheels of anything that came into the yard, and Daniel and Jess trained them to sit and wait, not to jump up on the car doors and to keep away from the wheels. Red and Rosie were familiar with most of the vehicles that came and went, however if anyone else drove in, they were quick to bark incessantly. Rosie always fired up the most, her fur standing on end, tail stiff out behind her as she showed whoever it was that she was on guard.

'She's a good watchdog,' Daniel had told Jess. 'Well they both are, but you watch Red. He's going to be the one who'll not bark as much, but if someone puts their hand out or walks near, he'll just quietly go for them. Rosie's a lot more showy and aggressive. See how she goes crazy when a car pulls up. She barks and carries on, then growls and won't let anyone she doesn't know on the veranda. Red just stares at them, and they know that he won't let them even set foot on the stairs until I come out.'

'It's funny how they're so different, yet they were trained the same,' Jess said.

'They're just like people, really. Look at my siblings and myself — we're all very different individuals. Rosie reminds me of you, guarded yet feisty, and will bite your arm off if you come too close.'

'Well, in that case, Red reminds me of you.' Jess had been washing both the pups when Daniel decided to compare her to the ferocious little Rosie. She added, 'Just sits and observes, doesn't say much, and then just goes in for the kill.'

Daniel laughed. 'They say dogs and their

259

owners are often the same. Perhaps that's correct.'

He thought of the comparisons they'd described that day as he walked towards the steps where Jess was standing cuddling Rosie. Daniel leaned down with one hand on the railing, the other tickling the pup under her chin. 'Morning, beautiful,' he said, looking at Jess.

'Are you talking to Rosie or me?' She laughed, smiling as Daniel bent over and kissed her on the lips. Rosie tilted her head to the side, looking up at both of them as she nestled in Jess's arms.

'I just wanted to make sure that last night was real, and that your lips are really that sweet.' He laughed. 'I think you're blushing. I don't think I've ever seen you embarrassed.' He kissed her again, his hand around her waist. 'God, if I wasn't filthy in these work clothes, I'd hold you and kiss you until you couldn't breathe.'

Jess could hardly speak, her head was spinning, and her legs felt weak. Rosie barked sharply at Daniel and licked Jess's neck. They both laughed, and Daniel, his arm still around her waist, guided her inside, nearly tripping over Red, who always managed to get tangled under his feet. Daniel looked at his watch. 'I can only stay for about half an hour because it's flat out over there. I just thought I'd sneak back here for a bit, to make sure last night was real.'

'I'm glad you did. I feel a bit the same.'

Jess felt a little uncomfortable with the changes in the relationship, however Daniel soon made her laugh and before long he was telling her all about what the two pups had been up to.

Rosie kept stealing his socks and burying them in the loose dirt, and Red had taken a liking to his work boots, choosing to sleep with his nose always buried in one of them.

The time flew past, and he gave her a quick kiss before heading back to the workshop, trying to keep his mind focused on work and the job underway at the moment. 'I'll be in touch with you soon. I'll either ring or drop in.'

★ ★ ★

It was hard for her to think straight over the next couple of weeks. Work, as usual, was busy, and most afternoons she either went out to Daniel's to be with Rosie or came straight back to the van and cleaned up. Often she fell into an exhausted sleep until teatime, when Hoppy or one of the others saved her from having sandwiches for dinner again. Some nights she'd cook for all of them, organising well ahead of time, making sure she had all the ingredients and dishing them up a hearty meal, always full of vegetables and meat. Jeffery came out to visit less and less as he spent more time with his new love, the hairdresser, a relationship that Jess approved of. She'd met Dylan quite a few times and thought how well the two of them got on. She missed Jeffery being around as much but knew he'd fit her in when he had time.

Outings with Daniel consumed much of her spare time, and she loved hearing his ute driving in, knowing that he'd have somewhere organised for them to go, usually taking a picnic lunch so they could sprawl out in the shade somewhere, talk and be near to each other. So far he had only kissed her, holding her closely, his hands often rubbing up and down her arms, his leg sometimes thrown across her body as they lay on the rug. She was glad that he wasn't rushing into anything, because all of these feelings were new and she didn't want to think ahead, rather just enjoy the moment for what it was. Daniel told her that he had strong feelings for her and thought about her constantly. She took a bit longer to reveal how she felt, not used to talking about emotions. One day after lying together, kissing passionately, she'd whispered to him that she loved being with him, and she also thought about him all the time.

Daniel knew he was taking things slowly, but he wanted it that way, giving them both time to get used to the change in their relationship. Everything seemed to be just moving along nicely. He loved surprising her, taking her to see the different sights in the area, while other times they'd sit in the kitchen and talk for hours, afterwards going outside to play with the pups in the yard.

★　★　★

Daniel smiled to himself as he drove out towards the van park. It was late, and Jess wouldn't be expecting him this afternoon because the plan was for him to pick her up in the morning, another surprise date. She'd pestered him to tell her where they were going, but he'd been obstinate and told her she needed to wait. It was the start of her week off, and Daniel had planned a special lunch at a town a bit further away than where they'd previously been. This afternoon, though, he knew she'd probably just be resting in the cool after a busy day at work.

As he drove up the road that led to the park, he remembered that all the men were on shift or out of town. It would be nice to visit Jess, just a quick pizza and beer before he went home, picking her up again early in the morning. The aroma of the pizza filled the cab of the ute and he grinned at the thought of how surprised she'd be.

# 39

The van park appeared deserted, and not even Myrtle came out with her usual wave as Daniel drove up and parked near Jess's van. Strange, he thought. He didn't recognise the green car that was parked near the fire pit next to Thommo's van. He walked over to it, thinking that it had seen better days: paint scratched off it, dings in various places, and one front light smashed in. The inside of the car was full of various items and the back piled up with clothes and blankets. *Looks suspicious*, he thought, wondering who Thommo's mate was. It was unusual to see old vehicles around these parts; most people drove utes or four-wheel drives.

The smell of the pizza he was carrying caught his attention and he started walking towards Jess's van. As he got closer, he began to hear voices and soon realised that they were coming from inside her van. Placing the pizza and beers down on the outside table, he lifted his hand to knock on the door, however the raised voices inside stopped him in his tracks.

A man's voice that he didn't recognise spoke angrily. 'You said you'd send more money, yet you haven't fucking sent any for months. How the fuck am I supposed to live?'

'I can't keep giving you all my money, Johnno. I just can't keep doing it forever.'

'You said you'd always love me, that we'd

always be together. What the fuck has changed?'

Jess's voice was loud but calm. 'Nothing has changed. You know the two of us are the most important thing. I love you just the same as ever and you mean the world to me, but I can't give you all my money.'

Daniel felt sick, the bile rising in his throat, listening in shock as the man repeated himself. 'It was my idea for you to come out here. We said it wouldn't split us up, now I've had to come out here to contact you. What the fuck's going on?'

'I've tried constantly to ring you. The floods cut me off for ages, and you know I don't ever forget you. I think about you every day. It's what I wanted to work here for, so we could have something together one day.'

The man's voice started whining, wheedling. 'You know I need you, Jess. I can't live without your help, and it's got me bad this time. I just need you to help me out.'

'I will, Johnno, I will, but I'm only going to give you a little bit, and you have to leave. No one here can know that you've been here. I've got to try and keep this job, for both of us, so that one day I can get somewhere nice to live and then we'll be together again.'

Daniel had heard enough, his gut churning as he turned to walk away. He stopped as the voices inside became louder, the man's voice increasingly aggressive. 'You reckon you love me? Then give me what you've got. You owe me. There's new stuff coming, and I need more money. You fucking say we're attached and I mean everything to you, so give it to me now.'

Jess's voice sounded panicky. 'We are always attached, Johnno, but shit, you're hurting me. What's the matter with you?'

Daniel heard Jess scream and the sound of something inside the van crashing, the flimsy walls moving with the impact of an object or someone being thrown around. Instincts kicked in, and Daniel pushed Jess's declaration of love for whoever was in the van to the back of his mind. He threw open the van door and barged in, his body filling the doorway as he quickly took in the situation.

Jess was sprawled out on the floor, her body squashed up against the cupboards. She was trying to sit up, and was holding her arm, blood coming from her leg and head, a dazed shocked look on her face. A scruffy, filthy-looking man who was obviously Johnno was standing over her, yelling, still demanding she give him whatever money she had. 'I know you've got it hidden here. I need it Jess, fucking give it to me.'

Daniel grabbed Johnno from behind and dragged him back to the doorway, throwing him out, the landing on the hard ground outside taking the air out of his scrawny body. He lay still as he attempted to get his breath, the bulky figure of Daniel looming above him. Before he could move, Daniel threw him over on his side, twisted both arms behind his back and pushed his face hard into the dust. Myrtle yelled out from up near the office, but Daniel couldn't hear what she said, instead concentrating on holding the twisting body beneath him, also aware that Jess had come up behind both of them.

'Are you fucking mad? Let him go,' she yelled, and started hitting him on the back with her fist. 'You're going to kill him, let him go.' She was shouting loudly, abusive language spilling easily out of her mouth as her temper kicked in. Daniel turned around to face her, refusing to let go of both arms of the man below him, but wanting to look at her to remind him that this was the same person he'd come to visit, to surprise with pizza and beers.

Jess thumped Daniel on the back harder, making him clench the man's arms tighter, trying to contain the anger that he was feeling towards her. He noticed she was only using one hand, the other arm limp beside her body. Rage was written on her face, and he shook his head, the harsh look he gave her stopping her in her tracks. 'Let him go, please, Daniel. Myrtle's called the police. Fucking let him go.' She stared hard, her face angry, tears of rage welling in her eyes before spilling over and running down her cheeks.

Johnno remained silent and still, and Daniel, who still held him tightly, wondered if he had actually knocked him out. He was relieved to see the flashing lights of the police car as it rushed towards where they were, the headlights lighting up Johnno's body on the ground. Dave, the local policeman, stepped out of the car and spoke to Daniel, his offsider taking over holding Johnno.

'Myrtle called us a while ago. She's got that bad knee and couldn't get up to see what was happening, but she didn't like the look of the car when it pulled in. We've been keeping an eye on this little green car and its occupant for a while. He's been camped down the riverbed. Looks like a whole lot of trouble to me.'

Dave turned around to see Jess still standing, holding one arm, some blood running down her face. Daniel could see a good-sized cut on her leg and her arm hung limp at her side. He took one last look at her, his blue eyes staring hard, an icy glare straight into her shocked eyes, before he turned away. 'I'll leave you to it, Dave; I've got better things to be doing at the moment. I'll check on Myrtle before I go.'

'Right, let's sort out this mess.' Dave sat Jess down on the step of the van. 'We're going to need you to come in also, Jess. I think there's a lot more here going on than what we already know.'

'What do you know?' Jess said, her voice still angry as she tried to wipe the blood from her face.

'We already know that this here is Johnno, he's on parole, and has a record of drug and minor theft-related charges against him. We've been running some checks on him and were looking for him when Myrtle rang. This is a small town, and you can't just float in and out.' Dave gave Johnno a nudge with his foot. 'And think no one is gonna notice. People look out for each other around here, and we ain't got room for any druggos in this town.'

'He hasn't done anything wrong, Dave. Can't you just let him go?'

Dave looked at her harshly, shaking his head. 'Jess, I know you're a good worker and keep your

268

nose clean, but you and I, we need to have a long conversation. I think there's a whole lot of information that you may need to fill me in on. Now both of you, get in the car.'

# 40

Daniel didn't sleep that night, and instead watched the sun come up, only nodding off in the chair on the veranda when the first warmth of the morning sun soothed him to sleep. When he woke, it was mid-morning and the events of the night before flooded back. He lay still, going over what he'd observed and heard, recalling the day of the interview in the city when he first met Jess.

Johnno, who he'd encountered yesterday, was the same scruffy guy he'd observed with her in the café late that afternoon of the interviews. They'd been a couple then, and he vaguely remembered that they'd argued over something that day. Yesterday he'd repeatedly heard her declare her love for him. 'I'll always love you, we're attached,' she'd said to Johnno. He had clearly heard it. The entire time she'd been sending him money, supporting his addiction, and always that plan to have something together later on.

She'd fed Daniel lies. His head spun, and he wondered if she had a split personality, because she'd fooled him, sucked him in completely and eventually won him over. Thank God he'd found out before going in any deeper with her.

The pups jumped up on him, catapulting his thoughts back to the present. Red pushed against his leg with her nose and Rosie growled at him, pulling on his sock with her sharp little teeth. He pushed her away with his boot, feeling angry, gutted, and then also guilty when the sulky pup slunk away, unused to any rough treatment. What the hell was he going to do with her dog? There was no way she was taking it back to the city or wherever she planned on going.

He found it hard to think straight, and his mind kept flitting back to the fact that Jess had been thrown across the floor. She'd been hurt, and he could tell that her arm had been badly injured. How could someone with such a bad temper let that scumbag treat her like shit and throw her around? Why hadn't she flared up at Johnno, defended herself like he knew she was capable of?

He knew that it was often the case. He'd heard about women who put up with domestic violence because they were in love with a man, even if he left them with black eyes and broken bones. Well, he'd seen it all for himself this time. Thank goodness he had, because he'd never have believed it if someone had told him. Shaking his head, he tried to gain some sanity, some reasonable thinking in his mind. *Just another shit stage in my life*, he thought. *Something else I need to push far behind me.* He picked up Rosie and she licked his face, already forgetting the rough boot from before. *Guess it's just you two and me now*, he thought, picking them both up and taking them to the kitchen for a feed.

# 41

Two days had passed since the incident at Jess's van, and Daniel felt like he was just dragging himself out of bed every morning, going through the motions, with nothing having much meaning to him. He knew he was cranky and lacking patience at work. Everyone seemed to steer clear of him, and at night he busied himself with the routines of cleaning up, dinner and then sleep.

Rosie somehow sensed that something was amiss and woke him at night, howling at the laundry door until he let her in. Both pups slept on the floor beside his bed, curled up neatly together, Rosie whimpering occasionally throughout the night.

On the third day, he decided that he was going to check on Jess. This was her week off, and even though he'd decided he was not going to have anything to do with her again, he couldn't seem to get the sight of her limp arm and cuts on her leg and head out of his mind.

The park was deserted and there was no sign of the turmoil that had taken place earlier that week. Myrtle was in the hospital for a week with her knee, and the other men were still off on shift or leave. Daniel walked up to Jess's van and knocked loudly on the door. He thought that he heard a noise from the inside as he approached, however his knocking was to no avail, and when he tried the handle it was locked. The work ute was parked next to the van, a sign that she was home. Calling out, he knocked loudly again, sensing that she was actually inside and not answering him. Silence wrapped around the park and he realised that even if she was inside, she was not going to come out.

He decided to call in and see Dave, curious as to what the outcome had been. As long as she hadn't been charged with anything, she could continue at work; that was if she intended staying on. They'd just have to keep their distance from each other and return to strictly work terms.

Dave slapped Daniel on the back, beckoning him into his office and pulling out a chair for him to sit down in. 'How're you going, buddy? Thanks for your help the other day. You didn't leave much for us to do.'

'Actually, that's what I've come to see you about. What was the outcome for everyone?'

'Jesus, it's a long story, and you know a lot of it's confidential. I'm sure you'd know most of it anyway. We all know that you and Jess had become an item. I was a bit surprised when you just took off the other day.'

Daniel sat quietly, waiting for Dave to talk again.

'I spoke to her in here for a long time. That woman's got quite a story behind her, but it's a shame about him. Jesus, you know about this new drug? It's epidemic in some parts. Ice, it sends them crazy. Jess said that he's never been violent with her before; she said he'd never normally hurt a fly, that he's a really quiet, lovely

273

guy who just happens to have been addicted to one thing or another for a lot of years.'

'So where is he now? Did you lay charges?'

'Well, it was sort of a tricky one because she definitely didn't want to lay any charges for assault or anything. He didn't have any drugs on him, and we searched the car and camp and couldn't find anything either. The thing is, he's broken his parole order: he's not supposed to be too far away from Brisbane. So we've let him drive back. I wasn't sure that he'd make it back in that heap of shit car or not. Jess gave him enough cash for fuel and food, and we told him to report to his parole office within three days. I've been in contact with them this morning actually, and he'd just checked back in with them. His parole officer said the same thing as what I found when I spent some time with him — he's a nice young fella.'

Daniel was annoyed, and Dave could hear it when he spoke. His words were sarcastic. 'Lovely, a nice young fella who just happens to be a drug addict and likes to throw women around. Shit, Dave, I'm surprised you didn't ask him over for dinner.'

'You know what, Daniel? Not all of these kids have had the breaks that we did. A lot of them are good deep down. It's just once those drugs get hold of them, well it's a vicious cycle. That's why he hits her up for money all the time. You know, he thinks the world of her. She's all he's got.'

Daniel felt the bile rising in his throat. How the hell had he been so fooled by her? All those special moments. When he'd held her, he'd thought he'd seen something in her eyes, like she truly cared for him.

'She's a liar, Dave, and I feel like an idiot. I'd fallen for her, and all along this was going on, and she hadn't told me anything about it. Thank god I found out now. I've nearly made a real fool of myself again.'

Dave stopped tapping his pencil and leant across the desk from Daniel. The two men had gone to school together, spent their teenage years getting into trouble, and had always been good mates. Dave had watched Daniel go through the separation and divorce, years of single life following, knowing that his friend no longer trusted people like he once had. Some of that youthful, fun-loving personality disappeared with the divorce and settlement, and Dave always hoped that one day Daniel would once again find what he was looking for. Talk around town was that Daniel and Jess were dating, and Dave had hoped that the young woman who he often saw around town doing courier work was someone who Daniel could be happy with.

Dave leant forward, his tone confused. 'Mate, don't you think you're being a bit harsh? I mean she obviously didn't want you to know at the moment, but maybe she was going to tell you at some stage.'

'At some stage!' Daniel stood up, furious now as he began to really think about how Jess had lied to him. 'I didn't even know this guy existed, let alone that they were both tied up in the drug scene.'

'I talked to her for hours, Daniel, and she's one hell of a nice woman. I think you're making a wrong decision if you're going to ditch her because of him. And also, she's never touched drugs, she's not involved at all, and they both impressed that on me. It's always just been him that's had the problem, not her.'

'Well, you know what, Dave, none of it's my problem anyway, because there's nothing left between us. I could never trust her again. She's lied to me. All the times I went out with her and yet she supported a partner out of town. That's it for me, mate. Women, I'm over all of them. They're all bloody liars.' Daniel started to turn towards the door.

Dave called out to him, 'Well, you know what, mate? You can't choose your family. I've got a brother who I'm not particularly proud of, similar problems. But it's the same thing — blood is thicker than water. You can't just always ditch family because of drugs or other issues.'

'That's family, Dave. This is her choice. This guy was with her before she came out here. I saw him the day I first interviewed her; they were all over each other then.'

Dave stood up, choosing his words carefully. 'They're extremely close for siblings, Daniel. I guess it comes from them looking after each other since they were little kids. She still mothers him. I could see it just from the time I spent talking to both of them, and contrary to what you witnessed the other day, they care a hell of a lot for each other.'

Daniel was looking strangely at Dave. 'I've lost

you a little bit. Did you say siblings?'

'Well, who did you think he was? That's her brother; you did know, didn't you?'

The realisation of what Daniel had surmised hit Dave, and he shook his head, starting to smile as a look of panic crossed Daniel's now reddened face. The policeman threw his pen in the air. 'My god, you thought Johnno was her boyfriend? You're a bloody idiot, Dan. That's her twin brother!'

Daniel went pale. 'Shit, I've made a huge mistake.' He looked directly at Dave before striding quickly out of the office, the policeman following, but unable to keep up as Daniel leapt into his car, shaking his head, and giving a quick wave before speeding off up the road.

# 42

This time, Daniel only knocked a few times before banging loudly on the van door. 'I know you're in there, Jess, and I can tell you right now if you don't open this door it won't matter, because I'll smash it down. I need to talk to you and I will break this door down to get in. Now open it!'

'Go away,' her small voice sounded from the inside, and he breathed a sigh of relief just to know that she was all right and inside the van.

'Open it now. You know me and I will break it. There's no one here to stop me. Open the door!'

'I don't want to talk to you, and I don't want to see you.'

'Open it. You have three seconds.'

He waited, expecting a torrent of abuse to be hurled at him, but there was only silence from the inside of the van. Slowly the door opened, the interior of the van dark, her face just visible as she moved back from the doorway. 'Go away, I don't want to talk to you or see you.'

Daniel got his hand around the edge of the door and flung it back, pushing his way into the van, surprised at the dimness inside. Jess had always been proud of her van and usually the curtains were tied back, the bed made and everything neat and orderly. Today dishes were stacked up in the sink, pulled curtains let only a sliver of light in, and the bed was unmade. He pulled open the nearest curtain, letting some light in before turning to her, his body blocking her way out in case she decided to try and leave. 'Sit down; I want to talk to you. I came to see earlier to check if you were all right.'

She said nothing, just stared blankly at him, large dark rings under her eye, her left arm up in a sling, as she stood in front of him.

'Sit down, Jess,' he said, propelling her to the bench seat beside the table, noting some other bruises that were on her other arm. 'You and I need to talk.' Sitting down next to her, he turned slightly so he was looking at her, his body blocking her from moving from where she was sitting.

She looked down, still not speaking.

'Jess, look at me. We need to talk. Why didn't you tell me that you had a brother? To me it just looked and sounded like he was your boyfriend. I can't believe you never mentioned him.'

Her voice was barely audible. 'It doesn't matter now anyway. I want you to leave.'

'Can't you see how it looked to me? I heard you say you loved him. What was I supposed to think? You've never mentioned him to me. I've only just found out talking to Dave that he's your brother.'

'Great confidentiality.'

'At least I know what's going on now. It explains so much — where your money goes, why you go back home sometimes and not others. Why haven't you talked to me about this?'

'What for? It's not anyone's business. It's just me and Johnno. It always has been, and that's how it needs to stay.'

'You can't ruin your life because of him. From what Dave said, your brother, apart from the fact that he wants your money all the time, also wants you to have your own life.'

'Well, so what? It'll never be, because this is what always happens. He gets in deep with drugs and deals and it comes back on me. If I don't help him out, he'll end up murdered or in jail.' She finally looked up at Daniel. 'It's always been the same.'

'You know, Jess, when two people are a couple like we are, they share everything. They help each other out and take on each other's problems. If you'd just told me, perhaps we could have worked something out. At least you could talk to me about it.'

'I don't want to go out with you anymore,' she said, her eyes looking straight into his. 'It's no use. Anything good never lasts, so there's no use drawing it out. Please go.' The tears were running down her face, and she used her free hand to wipe them away. 'Please leave. I can't do it anymore. I don't want to see you.'

'No, no, that's not how it works. You can't just walk away from me. I've fallen for you, Jess, and I don't care about what your background is or who your family are. I'm not sure how you feel about me, but until I can work that out, I'm not letting you go anywhere.'

He passed her a tissue, feeling himself starting to get upset from watching her trying to control her tears. 'Now listen to me. I'm only going to say this once, and you will — ' He made sure she was looking at him. ' — you will do as I say.' He was finding it increasingly hard not just to take her in his arms and hold her close, however he wanted to make sure how she felt about him. 'We're going to pack your bag. You need to bring enough for the week because I'm talking you out to my place. I know you have the week off work and there's no one here at all to help you or look after you.' He held up his hand as she began to talk, his voice steady as he continued. 'There's no use saying anything, because I'm not interested. You'll come with me and stay until you're feeling better. You're going to need some extra time off work until everything heals.'

'I'm okay here. I can look after myself. Please just go. I've told you I don't want to see you or anyone.'

But Daniel had already located a bag and was starting to look for items she'd need. He spoke slowly. 'I'll go through these drawers and pull out clothes if you don't. You don't need to talk about us, and we won't be together like we were, you just need to come and stay where there are people around you until you're okay. I'll be at work most of the time anyway during the day and you can look after the dogs.'

'Please go.' Jess's eyes pleaded with him and she stood up, watching as Daniel pulled clothes out of her drawers and placed them in the bag.

'Right, grab your toothbrush and things out of the bathroom.' He moved aside so she could enter the tiny en-suite at the back of the van. Jess moved slowly, gathering up a few personal items from the bathroom, and Daniel felt an

281

overwhelming protectiveness towards her. Knowing, though, that if he said the wrong words or tried to comfort her, she was more than likely to either fire up or completely refuse to come with him.

'Is there anything else you need?' he said as he kept her moving, guiding her gently towards the door, down the steps of the van and into the front seat of the ute. He tossed her bag into the ute, surprised that she'd followed his instructions, although he noted the lost, resigned look on her face, almost like she'd given up on everything, like nothing mattered. Unused to this side of her personality, he almost wished that she'd instead yelled and fought with him. The foul language and abuse were easier to deal with than this silent, beaten attitude that she was presenting.

The trip out to the property passed in silence, Daniel figuring that it was better just to give her some space, only speaking as they neared the house to let her know that she was to stay until he said otherwise, and as usual just to make herself at home. The spare bedroom was hers, and with him at work during the day, she'd have the house to herself. He kept talking to her, not asking any questions, just letting her know how it was going to be. Watching her walk slowly up towards the house, he decided to take it all calmly and carry on, just like it had been when she stayed during the floods.

Rosie and Red jumped up and ran around Jess as she walked slowly across the veranda, her only response a quick pat of both before she entered the house, closing the door quietly behind her.

# 43

Daniel tried on a couple of occasions over the next few days to get Jess to talk about what had happened, but she cut him off each time, telling him she didn't want to. Each time she walked away from him, ending the conversation, leaving him frustrated and unsure of how to get her to open up. During the day he was busy at work and left her alone, eating his lunch over at the workshop, confiding in Troy that he was at a loss as to how to get through to her.

'She's a hard nut to crack,' Troy said as he sat out the back of the shed with Daniel, going over what had happened. 'You know she still keeps in touch with Gus. She sometimes rings him and checks he's okay. But all this time she's never told him or me about this brother. Must be pretty heavy shit that he's into. I guess that's why she never said anything.'

'I just feel like I'm going to lose her. I can feel her heading in the other direction, like she's going to totally block herself off from me. It's like I got too close to the real her.'

Troy felt sorry for Daniel and tried to sound positive. 'You know, she was like a different person when she was spending time with you. As if she was just young and having fun for once. I think if you're patient, she'll come around. Don't give up. The two of you are great together. You make a nice couple.'

'There's no way I'll give up on her,' Daniel said. 'You don't think I'm too old for her, though? I mean you're around the same age as her, what do you think? I am ten years older.'

'No way. She might only be my age, but you need to remember she's experienced a lot in life and dealt with situations that you and I will probably never have to deal with. Besides,' he laughed at Daniel, 'you're not that much older than we are. No way, man. Don't think like that. Just hang in there and she'll come around. Use your charm.'

They both laughed, Daniel feeling lightened by talking to someone else, particularly someone who was more the same age as Jess. He recalled the conversation that night as the two of them sat eating dinner, Jess having cooked up her tasty stir-fried chicken. 'Delicious as usual.' Daniel got up to get seconds for both of them, choosing the right moment to tell her his plans for the rest of the week. 'Jeez, there'll be no leftovers, so tasty as usual. I think this is the best one yet.'

Jess smiled a little, eyes down, sipping slowly at the wine he poured for her.

'Tomorrow you'll need to be up early and I'll drive you into town. You have a doctor's appointment at nine, and then if you want to pick up anything else from the van, we can call in there before we come back here. I've told the fellas I'll be back before lunch.' She looked up at him, blinking, still chewing her dinner, her mouth full. Luckily, he thought, so she couldn't immediately speak back to him. Daniel continued, 'I'm thinking with that arm the way it is, you won't be able to work or drive until next week, which will be okay. You've got sick leave that will cover you, so you'll still get paid. I wanted to ask you if you'd stay here for the week after, because I have to go to Brisbane for three, maybe four days. I need you to stay and look after the dogs. Troy and the boys will be working at the shed every day so there'll be someone around if you need anything. Would you be all right here at night by yourself?'

'Of course I'd be okay. Why wouldn't I be?'

'So that's all right?'

'Yes, except I don't need to go to the doctor. I can look after myself.'

'It's not a question. The appointment is at nine, just be ready.'

'I don't need to go to the doctor's; everything is fine.'

'You don't have a choice, Jess. You'll need the paperwork for time off, plus your arm is not right. I've seen you several times holding it. It's not healed yet, and I'd say those stitches in your leg need to come out also, don't you think?'

Jess ran her hand over the cut that had been stitched on her leg. 'I can take them out myself. I've done it before.'

Daniel laughed. 'That's what we have doctors for. Just be ready at nine, and don't touch those stitches because it doesn't look fully healed yet. Thank goodness that cut on your head is okay. So you don't mind staying a bit longer?'

'I'd rather be at work and back at the van, but you need me to look after Rosie and Red.' Jess hopped up, cutting the conversation short.

'Good night; I'm going to bed.'

Daniel sat for a long time at the table after she'd left, his mind ticking, going over everything that had happened, thinking ahead to his trip to Brisbane.

The next morning she was ready early, and Daniel was pleased that at least some of the colour had come back into her face, the dark circles no longer under her eyes. Much to her annoyance, he walked into the doctor's surgery with her, sitting outside in the waiting room until she returned. The sling had disappeared, and a small bandage was over the cut on her leg, the stitches removed by the doctor who followed Jess out to where Daniel waited. Daniel stretched out his hand, shaking it with the doctor. 'Good to see you, Thomas. Looks like you've sorted Jess out.'

'Well, I figured she was going to take the stitches out herself if I didn't, so we came to an agreement, and I took them out probably a day or two early. The arm is on the mend and she needs an extra week off work, but then no heavy lifting for a few weeks after that. Her head has also healed nicely.'

'Um, what happened to patient confidentiality?' Jess said as she stood next to Daniel, her good arm holding up her other arm.

'Thomas and I went to school together, so we've known each other since we were kids. How are Jenny and the kids? What are you up to, about number five by now?'

'Yep, you've got a good memory, Dan. Five under ten, three women and two boys, all keeping Jen and me on our toes. Three of them are at school now and the other two are still at home. Life's good, still living in the same place. Mum and dad are still up the road.'

'You do a good job, Thomas, and we're lucky to have you stay in the town. Thanks for looking after Jess; she's had a few things going on lately.'

'Um, I am standing right here,' Jess said. 'You're talking about me like I'm not here.'

Thomas laughed and patted her on the shoulder. 'Surrender now, Jessica. I don't think he's going to give up easily. I've known Daniel for a long time, and he's the most stubborn man I know. We've had a few conversations earlier this week, and you need to rest up and have that extra week off work.'

Shaking hands, the two men said their goodbyes, Daniel following Jess, who had walked out and was already getting into the ute, slamming the door behind her.

'You can't talk to my doctor about me or tell me how to run my life. I look after myself.' She turned angrily towards him as he started the ute. 'I can't believe you keep organising my life.'

'Well at the moment I think someone needs to point you in the right direction.'

'What the fuck would you know about what direction I'm headed in? There *is* no direction. I just want to put one foot in front of the other and keep my head down.'

'Okay, okay, calm down. You're yelling. You just seem like you needed some time out after what happened. Before you know it, you'll be back at work and things will be a bit more back to normal. As Thomas said, though, you need to rest that arm, otherwise you'll be back to square one.'

There was no reply as Jess stared angrily out of the window, her mind in turmoil, hating the feeling that she wasn't in control, the fact that she couldn't drive, leaving her with no option at the moment but to let Daniel get her from one place to the other. The trouble was, she had to admit to herself, she liked staying at his place. The days were all to herself, and at night, even though she didn't feel like talking, he was always there. They ate their meals together and cleaned up the kitchen while he continually chatted, even if he didn't get much of a response back. It was the same now as they drove back out to the property. Daniel didn't talk much, but every now and then he'd point out something to her, ask her a question or tell her something about what was happening at work. By the time they'd driven in through the gates, she felt calmer, her annoyance at his interference pushed to the back of her mind as she enjoyed the familiarity of pulling up in front of the wide steps of the house, the two dogs bounding down the steps to greet them both.

# 44

The sun was low in the sky and Jess sat on a chair in the remaining shade, the two pups rolling and playing near her feet. She loved the sunsets and was always amazed at the way the colours played across the different shades of the ground and trees, throwing a golden haze over everything she could see. For the first time in a while she felt relaxed, the scene in front of her uplifting, the sight of the hazy golden hues across the land making her feel happy.

'I thought you'd like a beer. It's a good afternoon for one.' Daniel handed her an open cold beer, sitting down on a chair across the small table from where she sat.

'Thanks.'

They sat silently, watching the sun as it dipped down below the small trees that lined the riverbank far to the west. 'Beer okay?' Daniel said.

'Yes, thanks. It's nice and cold.'

'Can I ask you a question, Jess?'

'Depends.'

'How come your brother Johnno went so far off the rails, yet you always managed to stay on the straight and narrow?'

Jess was surprised at the directness of his question and took a few more sips of her beer before answering. 'He was always in trouble, right from when he was little. He was always in the thick of everything.'

'I thought you were the one with the bad temper.'

She smiled. 'I always had a shocking temper, right from when I was little. But Johnno . . . ' She shook her head. ' . . . he used to bottle it up, all the hurt, all his feelings, and then he'd take it out in different ways. Sometimes he'd destroy things that belonged to the families that fostered us. He'd cut their curtains up, destroy parts under the bonnets of their cars, steal jewellery and sell it, whatever he could think of to annoy them, he'd do it. Sooner or later they'd work out that it was Johnno doing all the bad stuff, and they'd move us on. Some of the families tried to get me to stay, but Johnno and I made a pact that we wouldn't be separated, so on we'd go to the next family.'

She took a long drink from her beer. 'And then I'd just get settled in again, school, my own bedroom sometimes, and occasionally nice foster carers. And then . . . ' She looked out at the horizon, the sky losing its lightness as it turned to the darkest blue. 'Well then, it would all happen again. Anything that was good for a while, it always ended. Nothing ever lasted. The last family we were with, I was about thirteen. They tried hard, they worked with Johnno, got him into playing sport, took him to camps, supported him, and were so good to me. By then, though, he'd started getting in with the wrong kids at school and on the streets. He was smoking and drinking, and started to use drugs. I pleaded with him, tried everything to keep him straight, but he was intent on self-destruction.' Jess looked down at her feet. 'I just couldn't help him. He started bringing knives home and threatened the other kids in the family. You know, they were the actual kids of the parents who were trying to help us out. Children's Services would come out and then there'd be meeting after meeting, social workers, doctors, they tried everything. But the family had no choice; they just couldn't let him stay. They said it was endangering their family.'

Daniel brought her another beer. It was like once she started talking she just couldn't stop, and he only spoke a few words, waiting for her to continue. 'You can't blame them, I guess. That's pretty scary once someone brings knives into your home.'

'They were good people and they begged me to keep living with them. The mum talked and talked to me, but there was no way I was going to stay without him. That was the last family that we lived with. After that, Children's Services tried to set us up in these halfway houses where carers were supposed to be there day and night. They were crappy places, and no one ever checked that we went to school.'

Daniel was shocked. 'Bloody hell, you were only so young. I just can't imagine what it must have been like.'

Jess looked out across the paddocks as flocks of cockatoos descended noisily into the trees out further. 'It was shit. I can tell you right now, there was nothing good about any of it. Not the halfway houses or the other places we lived at.

And what was even worse was being completely homeless. Cold in winter, trying to find food to eat, and most of all finding places to stay that were safe.

'There was a group of us, all young, and we'd stick together, trying to keep away from the areas where we knew there was always trouble. We tried to keep our distance from any sort of authority, you know like Children's Services or the police. Looking back, I realise how very young we were. Really we were just little kids, but I spent the entire time trying to keep Johnno out of trouble. Once I got a bit older, I'd sometimes pick up some work, although it was a bit hard because we didn't have any fixed address and I didn't exactly have any decent clothes to wear.'

'But the two of you managed to stay together?'

'Well we did for most of the time, but Johnno started to get in with some of the other groups that were living in different parts of the city. They were older kids and some adults that he became friends with.' Jess's voice became shaky and she struggled to speak. 'He wanted us to go live in the squats. He took me there one night, areas near the middle of the city, abandoned warehouses full of old mattresses and filthy rubbish. I mean, where we'd lived with the other kids hadn't been great, but these places were the pits, and the people there . . . ' She stopped and took another long drink from her beer. 'They were either drug addicts or mentally ill. I couldn't get out of there fast enough, and I begged him not to hang around them; told him that he was just going to get himself deeper into squalor. By now he was addicted to the drugs, and he wanted to be with the others. They could get him some drug runs, do a bit of dealing, and that would feed his habit.'

'So what happened? Did he go?'

'He did. He was okay with me staying where we were, but he needed the others more than me. I guess that was the first time we separated. I'd seen an ad in one of the local papers for a worker at a nursery further out of town, and that was the job I ended up working in for the next few years. Jake and Ellen were just the kindest old couple, and I loved working with the plants and doing their deliveries. They helped me convert one of the unused sheds into a living area and let me use their old outside toilet and shower block as my own. I used to eat with them at night, and I guess they were the closest thing I ever got to having my own family.'

'What happened to Johnno?' Daniel was intrigued and brought out another couple of drinks for them both, wanting her to continue with her story.

'We used to meet every week. I'd get one day off a week, and I'd meet him somewhere in town, usually in a park, you know somewhere quiet where we could sit and talk. I'd always bring food to eat and some extra for him to take with him. And, as usual, I'd give him most of the money I was earning, which wasn't a lot because Jake and Ellen were paying me in food and a place to live. He'd always wheedle more out of me than what I'd intended giving him, because by now he was heavily involved in the drug scene. He always needed to pay someone to get them off his back, or he'd want to buy the next hit to keep him going. It stayed like that until I was nearly twenty and then Jake died, and like I told you before, Ellen ended up in a nursing home. Once again I had nowhere to go and no money to my name.'

'Is that when you did the cleaning job?'

'I did. I worked for that slimy boss for over two years. The only good thing about it was that we cleaned new houses or empty apartments, so I always made sure that I left a window a bit open so I could sneak back in at night and have somewhere safe and warm to sleep. I tried to keep mainly to myself, but occasionally I'd meet up with a couple of the kids I used to live with when I was younger.'

'Where did you keep your belongings, you know all your stuff?'

'I hardly owned anything. I could pretty well carry it in one backpack. I did keep some stuff hidden out at the nursery. The whole place had been sold and just left to more or less rot, waiting for the developers to move in. I left a bag there with some clothes and blankets and sometimes I'd go back there and stay and collect some of my things.'

'Jess, that's a pretty tough life. I'm amazed that you survived and didn't get dragged into what Johnno was doing.'

'I was always determined that I was never going to touch drugs, but I've always needed to be with him. Johnno doesn't seem to remember

294

much from when we were little, but I have vivid memories of my mum and the drugs that eventually killed her.'

'How old were you when she died?'

Jess was nervously picking at the label on the beer bottle, memories flooding in as she thought back. 'I would have been nearly thirteen. They'd taken us off her quite a while before she died. She used to get me to help her mix the drugs, even to hold the needles before she put them in. We were all living in squalor. There was never any food, and I remember being so hungry and Johnno crying a lot. I think the school alerted the police, and I remember a policeman and policewoman coming to the door one day and taking Johnno and me away. Our mum was in such a drugged state that she didn't even realise they were taking us. I think I was only about ten that first time they took us. After that it was a back and forth process, you know, temporary foster care, then back with her, and then the police would come again, and then we'd end up with someone else looking after us.'

'Did you ever see your mum when you were with foster carers?'

Jess let out a false laugh. 'We were supposed to. I remember one stint. We were with this one family for over six months. The mum's name was Sally, and I was probably about twelve. The arrangement was that Sally would take us to this park nearby, and mum would meet us there and spend the morning with us. Sally was kind to both of us, and she always used to buy me nice dresses and do my hair. I liked her, and she

295

looked after Johnno, always trying to help him work things out. She had a lot of patience, and I remember her trying to talk to him and get him out of the habit of going through her bins when she wasn't looking.'

'He was stealing stuff out of the bins?'

'He used to get the food scraps out of the bin and hide them in our room, just in case he was hungry later. She tried to teach him that she'd always have proper food for us, and that we'd never be hungry while we lived there. But he'd lived hungry for all those years, and it was a bit of a natural instinct.'

'That's so tragic. You were both just little kids.'

'Sally used to make up these amazing picnic lunches to take to the park so we could meet Mum. I'd hear her on the phone organising it all with Children's Services: what time, where we'd be, all the arrangements. The very first time Mum came, we had a great morning. Sally went to the shops nearby and left us alone with her. The three of us sat on the picnic rug and ate all this yummy food that Sally had made. Johnno was so happy; I can still see his little face. He doted on Mum and all he wanted was to be with her. He still says he'd rather have lived with her and her drug addiction than been in foster care.'

'So how often did you meet her in the park?'

Jess looked out across the darkness of the paddocks, the last light of the sun slipping below the horizon. 'We were supposed to see her every weekend, but she missed the second one, so Sally said they'd reorganise and made it every second weekend. Johnno and I would get dressed up and help Sally pack the lunch, then she'd pile us into the car, and we'd get to the park and wait.' Jess stopped, and she was glad it was dark so that Daniel couldn't see the tears rolling down her cheeks. 'We did that every fortnight for probably the next three or four months. Sally never let us down; she'd organise the visit, prepare the food and make sure we were there early. Mum never came, she never came again after that first time. We'd sit in the park sometimes until it was nearly dark and then Sally would make us get in the car and take us back to her house. Johnno wouldn't speak for days, and then he'd let loose at school. He'd go nuts, beating other kids up, throwing chairs at the teachers, or generally just hitting or taking out his anger on anything he could find.'

Daniel spoke quietly; he could tell that Jess was crying. 'That's heartbreaking, Jess. How did you deal with all of that?'

'I just kept plodding along until someone at school would say the wrong thing or do something to Johnno, and then I'd also lose the plot. I'd end up in fights, abusing teachers, throwing chairs and whatever I could lay my hands on. And then it all became too much, and I just started walking out of school. Both of us did. One of us would walk past the room where the other was in class, and we'd both just get up and walk out. Out through the gates, sometimes running if someone spotted us.

'We'd spend the day in a park, or somewhere where there was no one else to bother us. Johnno was starting to steal food and other stuff from the shops, so then the police would come looking for him during the lunch hour. After a while, the school couldn't deal with us any longer, and it all just became overwhelming for Sally. I was a few weeks into year eight when both of us walked out of school and out of Sally's life, never to return to either. That's when they put us in the halfway houses, and not long after that, we were told that Mum died of a drug overdose.'

Jess was wiping the tears from her face with the back of her arm, trying to make sure Daniel couldn't see. They sat silently, Daniel finally breaking the quiet. 'I don't know how either of you survived, and it explains a lot why Johnno is the way he is. It'd be pretty rare to come through all of that unscathed.'

'I know. I think I was lucky that I was a stubborn kid and wouldn't let anyone push me around. The other big factor was that I didn't go into the city with Johnno. Those places he lived were the bottom of the barrel. I don't think many kids come out of there in one piece, not physically or mentally. I always needed to feel safe, and I was lucky with Jake and Ellen taking me in like they did. Sometimes you just need that one break, or just someone to help you. Those years let me grow up and get a taste of working and being independent. That's why the job here was always so important to me, not only was I with such great people at the park, Hoppy, Thommo and the others, but I also had Jeffery as my friend. To make it even better, I love my job. I love the work that I do.'

'And you know what? You do a bloody good job,' Daniel said. 'Everyone always remarks on it.

298

It's rare to find someone who's so reliable and can think on their feet. Apart from, of course, when it's in relation to flooding.' Daniel picked up the empty beer bottles, a half-moon rising in the sky throwing enough light for him to see Jess's face. 'So many things make so much sense now, Jess. I just wish you'd shared all this with me before it turned the way it did.' He looked at her pensive, dark eyes holding his stare, full of sadness and memories.

He could hardly hear her as she spoke. 'I've never shared this with anyone. Even Jeffery only knows parts of it.' She stood up. 'I'm glad it was you I shared all of that with. You're a good listener.'

Daniel walked back up into the house, Jess following him as he talked. 'I think we should have something to eat, because some of us have work tomorrow.' He turned a light on inside, both of them heading for the kitchen.

'After all that talking, I think I do need food, something to soak up the beers.'

They laughed, both of them drained emotionally from the conversation, but also a feeling that a weight had been lifted. Jess felt the lightness of sharing her problems with someone else, and Daniel was pleased that she'd finally opened up and revealed some of the events of her past. So many issues that had followed her and impacted on the way she looked at life today. He knew that tonight's conversation had given them a lot to think about.

# 45

The next morning, they were up and about early, the kitchen soon filled with the noise and aroma of breakfast being cooked. 'How come you wear your work uniform when you're going to head office?' Jess looked him up and down, his uniform neatly pressed, boots shiny and clean.

Daniel ran his hands over his shirt, flattening it down, moving his collar around. 'Rosalie and Phillip say that it puts the applicants at ease, that they can relate better to someone in work clothes rather than formal office attire.'

Jess sat down, plates full of bacon and eggs in front of both of them. 'You certainly didn't put me at ease, work clothes or no work clothes.'

Daniel raised his eyebrows. 'Well I didn't expect to be fixing zippers on half-naked young ladies in the lifts before an interview,' he said as he looked at her, enjoying watching her relaxed and smiling.

'Anyway, you look good. You should be nice to those nervous applicants sitting in front of you trying to impress.'

'Thank you, Jess. I'll take that as a compliment, and I will try to be as nice as I can.' He looked at his watch. 'Righto, I need to get a move on because the plane leaves in an hour. Now are you sure you're going to be all right here by yourself?'

'Well I'll be lucky to get any time for myself.

You seem to have organised company for me each night. Cedric rang me and said him and Thommo are coming out tonight, Jeffery's coming the night after, and Troy said he'll check on me during the day and that he'll be over for lunch. I think I might be okay.'

'Good, I just wanted to make sure. I mean you're out here by yourself.' He picked up his bag and keys. 'Okay, Jess, I'm going. I'll see you when I get back.'

She stood awkwardly, not sure how to say goodbye, but Daniel made it easier, throwing a cheeky wink her way before opening the front door and making his way to the ute. 'See you in a few days.'

# 46

The following days passed quickly for Jess. Daniel messaged every day to check everything was going okay, and then rang one night to let her know he'd be held up for an extra two days. 'There're just a couple of things I need to sort out while I'm here, so I'll be another two days. Will you be okay?'

'Everything is fine; I haven't had that much time to myself because everyone keeps popping in to see if I'm all right. Even your friend Doctor Thomas rang to check on me. I'm going to enjoy tomorrow. I don't think anyone is coming to visit, so I'll wash the dogs and spend the day with them.'

'I's great that you're spending time with them, because they needed some extra attention.'

Jess thought that he sounded a bit different. 'Are you okay? You sound a bit unhappy.'

'It's just the city, Jess. I'm not big on it and I'll feel better when I'm back at home.'

The two of them talked, Jess filling him in on what the dogs had been up to and the news from Cedric, who along with Hoppy had been out for dinner the night before. 'Cedric is going to move back out with his family; his wife wants him to go back home.'

'That has been a long-running saga, believe me, but maybe now he's cleaned his act up a bit, perhaps it'll work out. She's a pretty straight shooter, you know; she won't put up with any rot from him. It'll be an interesting time to watch.'

They continued chatting, Daniel eventually concluding that it was after midnight and he was supposed to have an early start in the morning. 'I'll see you when I get back. Look after yourself.'

'I will. Good night, Daniel.'

# 47

The day for Daniel to arrive home had come around quickly, and Rosie and Red both sat on the top step, the noise of their incessant barking bringing Jess out of the house. She tried to quiet the dogs, who were both excited, jumping around and barking loudly as he carried his bag up the stairs. Bending down, he patted both of them.

'It's great to be home. It's good to see you, Jess.'

Trying to calm the dogs, she smiled at him. 'I'll put the jug on.'

Daniel followed her into the kitchen, stopping in the doorway before throwing his bag on the floor. 'The place looks different. You've changed some things around.'

'I hope you didn't mind. I dusted and rearranged a bit. Just in here and the lounge. I had heaps of spare time so I thought I'd do some cleaning for you.' She followed him through to the lounge, watching as he looked around, noting the changes. Jess asked him, 'Do you like it?'

He laughed. 'Wow, I don't believe it's the same room. There's so much more light in here. It looks great.'

'I just moved things around a bit and got rid of the dust. You had the cupboard in front of the window blocking most of the light.'

Daniel walked to the window. 'Jeez, you've even cleaned the glass. I can see out of it. The

304

furniture looks great, and you've polished it.'

Jess sounded pleased. 'I've had fun. You know, you've got some lovely pieces of furniture. I didn't go into the bedrooms or anything, but I cleaned a lot in the kitchen. You might have trouble finding things in the cupboards out there.'

'Come and make me a cup of tea. I need to sit down and look at my new house.' He smiled at her, thinking how good it was to be home. 'I should leave you here in charge more often.'

Daniel sat on one of the high bench chairs, his boots resting on the lower rails on the stool, watching Jess as she made him a cup of tea. She wore the floral dress she'd often had on when they'd gone out, and her wavy hair was pinned up on one side, strands escaping the clip and falling softly onto her face. She brought the cup over to him and put it down on the bench, standing in front of him, her eyes meeting his as she spoke.

'I missed you. It was quiet here at night. I missed talking to you.'

Daniel took a sip from his tea, noticing that she stayed standing directly in front of him. 'You had visitors every night,' he said. 'You can't have missed me too much.' His eyes locked with hers and he smiled as she tried to push her hair back behind the clip, her words coming out slowly, nervously.

'I did a lot of thinking while you were away.'

'Did you?' He raised his eyebrows, sitting up straighter on the stool. 'And what did you think about?'

'I thought about how I felt when I told you I

didn't want to go out with you anymore. All the reasons why I didn't want to chance something that was good being ruined. I went over and over it in my mind.'

'You know, Jess, sometimes good things do last.'

She took a big breath and looked him straight in the eye. 'I wondered if we could maybe start going out again, you know on dates like we used to.'

'Really?' He leant forward, his face coming close to hers. 'Well, you'd have to give me a reason why you might want to do that. I seem to remember you telling me that you didn't want anything to do with me, and you wanted me to leave you alone.'

'You know the reason.'

'I want to hear it from you. I'm not interested in short-term relationships, so if you want us to go out, you're going to have to convince me that you're not going to change your mind again. I think I've made it pretty clear how I feel about you.' He casually sipped his cup of tea, leaning back on the stool waiting for her answer.

It took a while for her to reply. 'You know I'm not good at this. Sometimes it's hard for me to put how I feel into words.'

'Keep talking, Jess. I'm listening.'

She moved closer to him and took a deep breath, her hand resting on his arm, her body in between his legs. 'I realise now that I have feelings for you. Well, I've always had feelings for you, but I thought I could live my own life and not be involved with you. But I can't.' Daniel looked down straight into her eyes as she continued. 'I want to be with you, spend time with you, and I want you to hold me like you did before.'

Putting his cup of tea down on the bench, he wrapped his arm around her waist, pulling her in closely towards him. 'My God, I've been waiting for you to say something like that. I need to know, Jess, before we come back together, if your feelings for me are the same as mine are for you, because if we start this up again, you have to be honest with me about everything, and not run off when things get too difficult.'

'I will talk to you about my problems next time. I just can't promise not to fly off the handle, though. I've always been the same. I'm not sure I can change that overnight.'

He laughed, running his hands through her hair. 'I don't want you to change that. I'm as stubborn as you are feisty, so I'm sure we're going to have our fair share of disagreements. The main thing is that when problems come up it doesn't mean the relationship is over, it just means that it gets tricky for a while, and then we sort it out. Like I said before, I'm not in this for the short term.'

'I still have a fear of it all ending, though. I'm not sure how I change those feelings.'

'You have to trust me. Believe in the fact that I won't walk out, that this time the person you want to be with wants to be with you just as much. We just need to start over, and sometimes you need to listen to me. I have been around a bit longer, and just sometimes, I can help you with all sorts of problems. I'm just asking you to have faith, to trust me.'

She nodded, and Daniel could tell that even though she'd opened up and finally admitted her feelings, there was still some hesitancy in believing that good things could last. Both of his arms wrapped around her and he ran his hands over her back, feeling the smoothness of the cotton dress that clung neatly to her body. His lips pressed down on hers and her arms wrapped around him, her firm body pressed up against him as she responded passionately to his long kisses.

'My God your lips are sweet,' Daniel said as he pulled her in closer, Jess loving the feel of her body up next to his and the way his hands caressed her back.

The dogs barked outside but they ignored the noise, neither of them wanting the moment to end. 'That sounds like someone is here,' Jess finally said as she looked up, her head snuggled into his chest, not wanting him to let go of her.

'Damn.' He looked out through the nearby window. 'Shit, that's my sister Belle's car. Great timing.' He stood up, giving Jess one final tender kiss just as two small children ran in through the kitchen door.

'Mum, Mum, there's a woman in Uncle Daniel's kitchen,' the tallest boy yelled back to Daniel's sister Belle, who was not far behind them.

'And, and . . . mum, they were kissing.' A younger boy, holding a plastic toy in his hand, jumped up and down before running towards

Daniel, who managed to untwine himself from Jess before reaching out and picking the small boy up, tossing him in the air.

Belle stopped instantly, surveying the situation, taking in Jess, who was attempting to straighten her hair and appear composed while Daniel tried to calm the excited gibberish of the two boys.

'Well, good morning. Surprise, surprise.' Belle giggled. 'Sorry, I didn't mean to interrupt anything. Don't let me stop you.' She placed a box of fruit on the kitchen table, stretching out her hand to Jess. 'Hi, I'm Daniel's younger sister Belle. Pleased to meet you.'

Jess was flustered and shook Belle's hand, watching the boys, both of them now climbing over Daniel, their small arms wrapped tightly around his neck. Daniel gave them long hugs before placing them back down on the ground. 'You've already met Jess, on the night of the concert. Oh you probably don't remember.' He raised his eyebrows.

'You're so funny, Daniel,' Belle said, landing a cheeky kiss on his cheek. 'Mum wanted me to drop this fruit off to you. I didn't realise that you'd be busy.' She raised her eyebrows, reaching over to turn on the jug. 'Christ, you've moved stuff around. Unbelievable. That jug has been in the same place for ten years. Where the hell is it now?'

'Sit down and I'll make it for you,' he said, pulling out chairs for the boys and Belle. 'This is Jess. Jess, meet Robert and Thomas.'

'Are you Uncle Daniel's girlfriend? Because it

309

looked like you were kissing him.' Thomas stood in front of Jess, all fours years of him looking her up and down.

Jess smiled, not sure what to say, totally unused to being around small children.

'She is my girlfriend and yes we were kissing, so no more questions. If you sit there nicely, Jess might get you both a drink of cordial.' He gave the stunned Jess a squeeze on the arm, prompting her into action.

The two boys' eyes lit up as she placed huge glasses full to the brim of sweet cordial in front of them, Thomas promptly picking up the glass and spilling it down the front of his shirt. Daniel retrieved the two glasses, pouring half of the cordial down the sink before returning them to the boys. 'Jess is not used to rowdy little boys.' He turned to her. 'Don't give them more than half, they'll just spill it. They're messy little critters.'

Belle sat down and passed the boys a biscuit each from a plate that Daniel had placed on the table. She turned to Jess, who was leaning against the kitchen bench. 'So, Jess, do you work at the mine? I can't believe Daniel hasn't brought you out home to meet everyone.'

'I'm a courier driver. I deliver to the mines, although most work goes to the workshops. Well, mainly this one out here.'

'Oh right.' Belle passed the boys another biscuit, moving the glasses of cordial away from the edge of the table, her eyes moving from the two boys to Jess. 'Wow, you're not the one who rescued the pups, are you? Daniel told us how

Rosie and Red came to be here, he just didn't elaborate on the rescuer.' She gave Daniel a solid stare.

Both boys jumped up at the mention of the dogs. 'Can we see the pups? Please, Mum, can we go outside and see Rosie and Red?'

Daniel placed a cup of tea in front of his sister. 'I've just made your mum a cup of tea, so give her a minute to sit. Maybe if you ask Jess she might take you out, but watch those two dogs don't knock you to the ground; they're getting big.'

Two sets of bright blue eyes turned towards Jess, who looked firstly at Daniel. He was nodding at her, encouraging her to take the boys outside. 'I'll take you out if you like,' she said, glad to make a retreat from the kitchen. She was unsure what to say to Daniel's sister, who seemed friendly enough, but was obviously not happy that she hadn't been filled in about the developing relationship.

The door shut behind Jess and the boys, and a calm silence filled the kitchen. 'Thanks, Daniel. It's rare to get a break these days, even just a few quiet minutes is a special treat,' Belle said.

'They're full-on, those two.' He laughed as he peered out through the window. 'Jess won't know what to do with them. I don't think she's ever had anything to do with little kids.'

'She's very pretty, but um, one question — how old is she? Because she looks like she's about eighteen.' Belle looked at him over the top of her cup, eyebrows raised, her blue eyes much the same as Daniel's, questioning.

311

'She's twenty-three, nearly twenty-four. I admit she's a lot younger than me, but she's not had an easy life, and besides I'm a young thirty-four. The age difference doesn't worry either of us.'

'That's not much younger than me, but I can tell you right now she looks a lot younger.' Belle had that self-righteous look on her face that she always got when she thought she knew more than Daniel.

'Do you know what, I can tell you right now, she is twenty-three and the age difference doesn't matter, so you can get that pious look off your face because it's not any of your business anyway.'

'Jesus, Daniel, calm down. I'm just curious, that's all.' Pouring herself some more tea, she questioned him further. 'You sound like you're serious about this relationship.'

'Look, it's early days.' He sat down next to Belle. 'But I haven't felt this way for a long time.'

'Wow.' She squeezed his arm, her eyes sparkling at the hint of a good romance in the making. 'Well, I hope for both of you that it works out. You deserve someone nice.' They both looked up as the two boys, followed by Jess, came back into the kitchen. Thomas was covered in dust, and Robert was holding both his boots in his hands.

'Jess can make them both sit and shake hands,' Thomas said as he clambered up onto Daniel's lap.

Robert, who was the older of the two, gave his mother his dusty boots, trying also to fit onto

Daniel's lap. 'Jess can make them stop jumping up on us and she just tells them to stop. Jess can make them stop, Uncle Daniel, better than you can.' He reached over, picking up three biscuits from the plate. Daniel leant over to take two from him, placing them back on the plate. 'One at a time. Just choose one biscuit at a time. Sounds like Jess has won a couple of friends,' Daniel said, watching her as she stood in the doorway, unsure of where to sit. 'Come and sit down, Jess. You survived the two of them?'

'They love the pups, but Rosie gets a bit rough, and she dug her sharp little teeth into both of them a couple of times.' Jess sat down on the other side of the table from where Daniel and Belle were sitting.

'You know,' Thomas started speaking with his mouth full, both Belle and Daniel stopping him, telling him to wait. He chewed vigorously, swallowing dramatically before opening his mouth wide to show that he'd finished the biscuit.

'Lovely, Thomas. Okay, now you can talk.' Belle sipped her tea, smiling at Jess as both boys tried to speak at once. 'Robert, Thomas was speaking first. Let him finish what he was saying.'

'You know,' Thomas started again, 'I'm three and Robert is four and next year Robert's going to go to school, and at school they have chickens and if you're good you get to take them home and . . . '

Robert sat up straighter, a plate almost knocked from the table as he reached over for his drink, looking at Jess, both boys vying for her attention. 'I'm the biggest and Thomas is the second one and he's not going to school but I am, and I'm going to bring the chickens home, not Thomas. I'm going to get the chickens to bring home.'

The boys were boisterous and talked excitedly, both of them trying to tell Jess all about school and the chickens. Her eyes moved from one to the other, trying to keep up with the conversation, smiling and nodding with each extra piece of information they came up with.

Belle stood up, collecting up the plates and cups, placing them all in the sink. 'Righto, you two,' she said, 'that's enough. Jess knows all about you now, and I'm sure she won't forget all the things you've told her. It's time we made a move.' Daniel put both boys down on the ground, dusting off their clothes and holding out Robert's boots for him to put on.

'Nice to meet you, Jess,' Belle said. 'Daniel, don't forget, Saturday after next at ten, and make sure you bring Jess with you.'

Thomas and Robert jumped up and down excitedly. 'It's Lea's birthday. She's going to be two and there's going to be a cake.' Thomas grabbed Jess's hand and was pulling hard on it.

Belle asked, 'Are you busy Saturday week, Jess? Lea is the boys' younger sister, and there's a family gathering at our house.'

Jess looked at the two small boys. 'You must have a busy life.'

'I do. There are four of them. Mind you, these two are probably the most energetic. Baby Sarah and Lea are at home with Tyson. It's pretty rare for me to get out without all four of them. You've only met half the family.' She smiled warmly at

314

Jess. 'Make sure you come on Saturday. We're noisy when we're all together, but I know everyone will want to meet you. Don't let Daniel keep you hidden away.'

Daniel helped to get the boys into the car. 'I haven't kept her hidden. I just don't want to scare her off with all of you lot.'

Jess laughed at the boys as they called out from the back seat of the car, 'Uncle Daniel's got a girlfriend!'

Belle yelled at them to be quiet before starting the car up. 'See you both on Saturday.' Daniel and Jess watched as the car drove off, the arms of the two boys waving wildly out the windows at them.

'Well, now you've met some of the family.' Daniel turned to Jess, who was still watching the car in the distance.

'I can't believe she's got four kids. She doesn't seem that much older than I am.'

'She isn't, she's only twenty-eight, but Tyson and her have been together since high school, and I guess it was just a natural progression that they got married and straight away started a family. It's pretty much all that both of them ever wanted, although I'm not sure they realised how much work it was going to be having them all that close together.'

'The two boys are lively,' Jess said.

'To say the least.' Daniel raised his eyebrows. 'Wait until you meet the little ones. Belle rarely gets out without Lea, who won't go to anyone else, and the baby is not quite one yet, so yeah you might say it's a busy time. They love it, though. Like I said, that's what they always wanted.'

'So will all your family be there on Saturday?'

'They will be — my parents, and my younger brother, and another sister who you haven't met yet.'

'You have a big family.'

'It's not, really. It just seems like that to you. It's only four of us, and now nieces and nephews also. We're lucky that mum and dad are both still here. Don't worry, Jess, they'll all love you. It's just I haven't had anyone with me for a very long time, and you're from out of town, so they'll all probably want to know everything about you.'

'What am I supposed to tell them?' She looked worried, the idea of meeting all the family at once a daunting prospect.

'They're all the same as me. Tell them what you want, but whatever you do, tell them the truth. You'll be fine and I'll stick with you.' Laughing at her worried face, he hugged her tightly, smothering her face in kisses until she also was laughing, the nervousness of Saturday's event forgotten.

# 48

The routine of living at the van park and work life returned to normal for Jess, and she was happy once her arm healed and she could continue with her usual routine. Doctor Thomas gave her clearance to go back to work, and she'd enjoyed talking to him while Daniel once again remained outside in the waiting room. Thomas was one of those people that you just found yourself opening up to. He was easy to talk to, and when he asked about her background, she'd filled him in a little on events over the last twenty-three years.

She also told Thomas the news that she'd received yesterday, but hadn't yet told Daniel. Johnno had rung the night before. It hadn't been a long conversation because where he was staying didn't allow phones. Only one call was permitted when patients were first admitted.

She had been unsure of how she felt about the news when later in the day she told Daniel. 'He says he's in rehabilitation, you know one of those places that helps you get off drugs. Johnno told me that the rehab centre is up in the mountains, and he looks out across a beautiful valley. He sounded determined, and although it's not going to be easy, he said he was desperate and wanted to give it a go.' She looked confused. 'He's never even spoken about anything like this before. I'm not sure how it all happened, but it's good he's in a safe place. It's got to be better than where he was.'

'That's great, Jess,' Daniel said. 'Sometimes those places do succeed with even the most addicted drug users. Hopefully it might help.'

Now that she was at her appointment with Doctor Thomas, she asked him what he knew about the drug ice and what help the rehab might be to Johnno. Thomas told her about this latest drug that he said was sweeping through small regional places as well as the bigger cities. He also had seen success stories with rehab centres, although sometimes he said it didn't always work the first time. Often the addicts relapsed and then they needed to go back again. When she told him the name of the place where Johnno was staying, he said he'd heard of it and that it was one of the best around. If anywhere was going to help, then he was in the right place. They chatted for a bit longer, Thomas enjoying talking to Jess and getting to know her. It was, after all, an exciting fact that Daniel had a new love in his life.

★ ★ ★

Daniel dropped Jess back off at the van park, which always seemed to be a lot quieter than it had previously been. Jake and Edward spent most of their time out on the roads now, living in on-site accommodation, only returning to the van park sporadically in between shifts and home breaks. Cedric had returned to his wife and kids, and once he was convinced the move was a good thing, he'd slowly shifted all of his belongings back to his family. Jess sometimes ran into him in town, and he'd always give her a huge hug. Often, if time allowed, he'd buy her a coffee, and they'd sit and chat about what was happening in their lives.

Cedric winked at Jess and stated, 'She's bossy, you know the missus, she is, but I've got my act together, and I'm not getting into so much trouble with her. You know, I'm putting my stuff where it's supposed to go and doing a lot of the cooking and cleaning. She's impressed with that. The main thing is that I'm there with the kids. They were starting to run wild, so I've brought them back into line. All in all, Jess, it's been a good move, going back. I miss the van park mob, but hey, times change, and you gotta go with the flow.'

Jess loved seeing Cedric, and promised him that she'd come out and visit his family. 'Get that bloody Hoppy to bring you out,' he told her. 'Him and that Thommo have been looking at buying a house in town, you know the two of them going halves. Not a bad idea, really. At least they'd have somewhere of their own. Them two always look after each other.'

Today as they drove into the park, Charlie was packing up his ute, his swag and bag in the back. Daniel shook hands with him, watching as Charlie gave Jess a big hug. 'I'm off, Miss Geronimo. You might not see me for a while.'

'Charlie, where are you going? I'll miss you.'

'I've given notice. I'm going to follow the rodeos around for a while. Not ride in them.' He

319

looked at Daniel. 'Not at my age. Just go with them on the circuit where I'll pick up some work. I'm sick of being in the same spot and I need to be on my own for a bit. I'm restless.'

Jess gave him a kiss on the cheek, thinking how the group that had taken her under their wing when she first arrived was starting to scatter and go their separate ways.

Daniel was hesitant to leave, and the park did seem very quiet. Even Jeffery was a rare visitor. He spent every spare moment either working or with his new boyfriend. Myrtle wasn't around much these days either, choosing to spend a lot of time in town with her sister.

'It's fine, Daniel. I'm used to being by myself, plus Hoppy and Thommo are back here tonight and we're going to have dinner together.'

'I'll pick you up tomorrow night and we'll go out for dinner.' He gave her a long kiss, dragging himself away, knowing that he was due back at the workshop.

Jess and Daniel saw each other most days at work, and then he usually picked her up and they'd go out somewhere or have dinner at his place. He never minded driving her home at night, but he was worried what would happen once all of the others moved on. She'd been lucky living next to the older fellas who had become like her family, although others who moved in when they left might not be so friendly or helpful. Maybe she should consider moving into the main camp; at least Jeffery was there sometimes, and there were others who she might become friendly with.

As he drove home, he thought about how she didn't talk much when she was around people who she didn't know that well. Daniel knew that it wasn't because she was shy, but rather that she suffered an innate distrust of people who she had no connection to, or hadn't a chance to get to know. Lea's party was coming up, and he wondered how Jess would go meeting his family. She'd been awkward around Belle and the two boys, and he chuckled to himself thinking of her meeting his younger brother, Ben and sister Liz. He was looking forward to finally introducing her to everyone.

# 49

The day of Lea's party arrived, and Jess found herself undecided about what to wear. The heat of the day was settling in and she pushed the jeans and boots to the side, choosing instead her favourite dress and flat sandals. After the next pay day she was going to buy herself some new clothes, maybe another dress, and a couple of shirts to wear with jeans. Daniel always took her to different places, but she didn't have many clothes, so she often wore the same outfit. Looking in the mirror, she pinned one side of her hair back, her dark eyes framed by long eyelashes, an unhappy look on her face as she wished that she knew a different way to do her hair, or at least that she had some idea of how to put on makeup. The sound of Daniel's ute arriving forced her to take one more quick look in the mirror, and she rolled her eyes, unconvinced that she looked even half decent.

Her unsmiling face greeted Daniel as he opened the door. 'Hello, beautiful,' he said, his eyebrows raised as he looked her up and down. He kissed her softly, pulling away to take another look at her as she stood in the doorway. 'Wow, I love that dress. You look amazing.'

'Daniel, I always look the same. I just wish that I knew how to do make-up and what clothes to buy. I need Jeffery to take me clothes shopping again.'

Daniel hadn't seen her in this sort of mood before, unhappy with the way she looked, a grumpy expression on her face. She always looked beautiful to him: her skin was soft, her eyes dark, and her hair fell naturally down onto her shoulders. The floral dress she wore drew close to her body, sitting firmly on her hips, not too short but just enough length to show off the fabulous slender legs that now stretched out in front of her. 'Jess, you are naturally gorgeous.' He squeezed her knee as she sat next to him in the car. 'You don't need make-up or fancy clothes. Even when you're wearing dirty old fluoro work shirts and shorts, you look amazing to me. Now stop sulking and put on your happy face, because you're about to meet the family.'

'I will be on my best behaviour, but honestly, I need to get some clothes.'

'I'll take you shopping. How about next time I have to go into the city, you come with me. We'll have some free time in there and both buy some new clothes.'

'That'd be fun. I need someone to help me choose clothes because I don't have any idea about what to buy.'

'It's a date. I have to go in a few weeks, so we'll work out your shifts so it coincides. Perks of dating the boss.' He laughed, watching her trying to flatten her dress down as they neared Belle and Tyson's house. 'Let's meet the family.'

Thankfully Daniel grabbed her hand as they walked into the house together, the sound of kids yelling and a baby crying background noise to a rowdy adult conversation. Thomas and Robert rushed Daniel as he walked in, wrapping themselves around his legs. Giving them both a hug, he ignored their pleas for him to pick them up. Firmly holding Jess's hand, he led her over to where his parents sat, the conversation in the room stopping as he introduced her. 'This is my mum, Beth, and my dad, John. This is Jess.'

Daniel's dad stood up, his hand reaching out to take Jess's, shaking it firmly before Beth also reached out and held Jess's other hand. 'We can't tell you how happy we are to finally meet you,' Beth said, her words so eloquent. 'Belle tells us that Daniel has been keeping you hidden away.'

'I have not been keeping her hidden away,' Daniel said as he leant down and gave his mother a kiss on the cheek. 'There just hasn't been an opportunity for us to visit together.'

Beth spoke again, 'Well it doesn't matter. We're just so thrilled to meet you, Jess.'

Lost for words, Jess smiled and nodded, overwhelmed by the friendly welcome and the kindness that Daniel's parents showed her. Daniel's dad, John, had a craggy face, with large bushy eyebrows that moved up and down with different expressions. A broad smile welcomed Jess, John's tanned face lined with creases that spread out from his blue eyes, which were the same as Daniel's. His arm was around Beth, who was dressed in tailored jeans and wore the most beautiful floral shirt Jess had ever seen, the outfit complemented by an assortment of gold jewellery.

Daniel's mum looked like she'd just walked out of the hairdresser's, her hair blonde and bobbed, sitting perfectly, just the right length above her collar, her face beautifully made up. Jess noticed her perfectly manicured nails, the redness of her bright nail polish vivid against her tanned hands.

Beth and John were both in their early sixties, and since selling the property to Daniel had moved into a large house in town. They ran a machinery business that catered for both the mining and farming industries. 'Between the business, the kids, my parents who are away at the moment, and now the grandkids, there's always plenty going on. There's no time to get bored, that's for sure,' Beth said to Jess.

Daniel continued with the introductions. 'Jess, this is Belle's husband, Tyson, who you met briefly the night we went to the concert. And this is the birthday girl, Lea.' Daniel tickled the chubby two-year-old who Tyson was holding. Jess kept smiling, her head starting to spin a little, trying to remember all the names. Lea was very cute, and Jess went to say hello to her, staring at a set of serious eyes that looked into hers only briefly before the toddler turned her head the other way, snuggling into her father's shoulder.

Tyson tried to get her to look up. 'Say hello to Uncle Daniel and Jess. Look, they have a present for you.'

'Forget it.' Daniel shook his head. 'I've given up with Lea.' He turned to Jess. 'She'll only go to Belle and Tyson, and if she's in the mood perhaps Mum and Dad. It doesn't seem to matter what you do, she's just not a social kid.'

The introductions continued. Liz was the other sister, and she had two boys and a girl who were all noisy and jumping up and down, eager to meet Jess and play with Daniel. 'This is Jackson, Dylan and Jacinta, and dad is Craig.' Both the adults shook Jess's hand, Craig trying to calm the three kids down as well as offering Jess a drink as he spoke to her.

'It's a noisy family, Jess. Thank god we live out on a large property and there's no one to hear all the yelling.'

Daniel joined in the conversation, pleased to finally introduce his family. 'Craig and Liz live out the other side of town. They run a cattle property that fronts the Black River, the same as mine.'

Jess nodded, completely lost for words, the din of the noisy kids suddenly overshadowed by the yelling or supposed loud singing as Daniel's younger brother Ben burst in through the front door, balloons and a present in one hand, the other carrying an esky.

'Happy birthday to you, happy birthday to you, where's the birthday girl? Lea, happy birthday — you can talk to me today because I have a present for you.'

Tyson laughed, still holding the clinging Lea, who now wouldn't look up at all from where her head was buried in her dad's chest. Ben tried everything — peering over Tyson's shoulder, tickling her, cajoling her with the temptation of the present, but she wasn't budging. 'She's the only female I've ever known who isn't instantly drawn to me.' He bent down, giving his mum a kiss on the cheek and shaking his dad's hand before turning to Liz and Belle, who were pulling faces at his mention of his supposed charm on females.

'Oh please spare us, Ben,' Liz said as both the women hugged him, the noise in the room getting louder as they all flung comments back and forth, the two sisters obviously used to Ben's inflated ego about the impact that he thought he had on females. Tyson was shuffling the kids, moving them outside, the noise deafening as everyone spoke at once. Beth handed the baby back to Belle and spoke to Ben. 'Daniel has a friend here, Benjamin, so please use your manners and don't embarrass us.'

Ben squeezed his mother tightly. 'Ah, Mum, as if I'd ever do that.'

Daniel stepped forward and shook Ben's hand, the two of them hugging roughly, Daniel making the introduction. 'Ben, this is Jess.'

Daniel looked her up and down, bringing Jess's hand up to his lips and kissing it. 'My god, you're too young and beautiful for him. Ditch him right now — he's so boring, and I'm much better fun. You've picked the wrong brother.'

Jess could feel her face turning bright red, and she had no idea of what to say or do. Belle pushed Ben out of the way. 'Don't listen to him at all. He's full of himself, and everything he says is meant to impress. Ben, can't you just be serious for once?'

Daniel laughed, his arm wrapped around Jess as she tried to take in what everyone was saying. They were all talking at once, and she nodded as Ben apologised. Taking her arm, Liz steered her away from where the two brothers had started talking about machinery and mining.

Jess was trying to be confident, but it was difficult to be comfortable when she was so worried about how she looked. Normally she felt good about herself and didn't take too much notice of what others were wearing. But today she couldn't help but take in the clothes of the other women. Beth, of course, was immaculate, and had handed down the same dress sense to the two women, Belle and Liz, who both looked neat and well-dressed, even with a tribe of kids hanging off of them. Both had their faces made up, their hair was styled and sleek, and their clothes matched and looked elegant, shoes and jewellery all co-ordinated and finishing off their outfits. Jess realised that she didn't even wear fingernail polish, and her nails were short and broken from the handling of machinery and carrying parcels around.

Liz handed her a drink, sensing that the younger woman felt uncomfortable. 'Don't take any notice of Ben; he's always in trouble with the women. We just wish that one day he'd meet one he'll stay with. He's what you call a player. I'm allowed to say that because he's my brother. We love him dearly, but he gets himself into all sorts of trouble, and it's usually Daniel who has to bail him out. Anyway, we're so glad that you've come with Daniel, although it's a bit chaotic when you meet us all together.'

'Thanks, Liz. It's nice to come and meet Daniel's family.' She sipped her drink, wary of imbibing champagne at such an early time in the day. Belle and Beth came over to join them, and soon Jess was listening and laughing along with them as they talked about the kids and their husbands. After a while Daniel joined them, his arm around Jess, making her instantly feel more at ease. 'So, Jess, have they talked your ear off yet? These women love to chat.'

Tyson and Craig yelled out from the shaded area outside the house, signalling that lunch was ready and for everyone to come and sit down. Ben tried his best to sit next to Jess, stating his desire. 'I should sit next to the special guest.' He winked at Jess, who was a bit taken aback at how much he and Daniel looked like each other. Ben was a younger version, perhaps a bit shorter and stockier, but the same chiselled face and blue eyes. Beth promptly sat on one side of Jess, and Daniel, who pulled a face at Ben, sat on the other side.

'Leave her alone; you're embarrassing her. Don't worry, Jess. You're safe here between mum and me.'

Jess laughed as Ben, always having to have the last word, concluded, 'Well it was worth a try. I'm telling you, Jess, you'll be sorry. He's as stubborn as a shitty old mule, and it's his way or the highway.'

Beth spoke sternly, giving her youngest son a harsh look. 'Benjamin, watch your language. Jess is a young lady and she might take offence at your swearing.'

Daniel and Jess looked at each other, both laughing. 'Oh don't worry about that, Mum. Jess can match it with the best of them.'

329

Jess added in, 'I only swear when I lose my temper.'

Daniel was dishing out the food onto their plates. 'Oh she's got a foul temper also, puts me in my place sometimes.' He prodded her playfully in the ribs, ignoring her wide eyes and the look on her face begging him to be quiet.

'Nothing wrong with that, Jess,' Beth said, as she passed the food around the table. 'Sometimes these men need to be put in their place. I always taught my girls that you need to be your own person, independent, and don't let anyone push you around.'

Tyson and Craig groaned loudly, looking at each other in mock sympathy, Craig talking while trying also to keep Jacinta from pushing her plate over the edge of the table. 'There's no chance of that, Beth. Tyson and I know exactly where we stand.'

Liz chirped up, 'Oh you poor things. They make out like they're so hard done by. You fellas get it good. I don't think you can complain about too much.' She stood behind Craig, wrapping her arms around his neck, giving him a kiss on the cheek.

'Righto, you two.' Ben was busily filling up his plate. 'That's enough of that around here. You fellas need to learn to put a woman in her place. Don't let them rule the roost.'

'And is that why you're here by yourself today?' Belle juggled Lea, who was clinging onto her, as she helped Tyson pass the plates around to Thomas and Robert.

Daniel watched Jess's face, wondering what

330

she was making of all the banter and laughter. She looked up and smiled, overwhelmed but enjoying the busyness and noise. The table was covered in delicious food, kids chattered and laughed, while the adults served and made sure everyone had plenty on their plates.

Daniel's dad sat at the head of the table, eating quietly while viewing his family. Occasionally he joined in or laughed at something, often talking quietly to his wife who sat beside him. They were both relaxed and gazed proudly over the noisy gathering, enjoying having the entire family together.

They were excited. It had been a long time since Daniel had brought anyone home to meet them; in fact he hadn't introduced them to anyone since the divorce. There was a gap in the chatter, and John leaned back, turning to Jess. 'So is your family this noisy, Jess? I think most families are the same when they all get together.'

'Um, I don't have a large family.' She paused, unsure of what to say, the room now silent apart from the quiet chatter of two of the younger boys.

Daniel sat up and put his arm around her. 'Jess only has a brother, and they were both raised in foster families and homes.'

Beth interjected quickly, 'Oh my goodness, so you're not used to a large family. God, you must think we're all crazy. They're a rowdy bunch here so you're going to have to learn to be loud and yell over the top if you want to be heard.'

'I'm enjoying the noise, actually. It's nice to see a family together like this.'

Ben added in, 'We don't get together like this too often, thank Christ. Maybe once a month. It's the women — they just don't shut up, and they talk over the top of everyone. You're better steering clear of them.'

Belle threw a serviette at her younger brother. 'It's you, Dad and Daniel when you all get into the rum. Then see who makes the most noise.'

Everyone laughed and Jess joined in, relieved that Daniel had spoken for her. He was right, she needed to just get used to saying it how it was. She hadn't done anything wrong. It was just how life had been. It was just her and Johnno, and there had never been anything in their lives like this sort of family gathering. She felt like she could just sit all day and listen to the chatter, the kids calling out, crying when they fell over, the women looking after them, making sure everyone was fed, and the husbands constantly picking up kids, toys and bikes, all left where everyone seemed to trip over them.

'It's always mayhem like this,' Daniel said to Jess as they sat together. Everyone was full after lunch and sat relaxing in comfy chairs in the backyard, the kids playing with the various toys scattered across the lawn. 'It didn't used to be so bad before all the nieces and nephews came along, but now it just seems noisier and busier.'

'I love it. You have such a beautiful family, and everyone cares so much for each other, plus you all get along.'

'Oh, don't be fooled. Sometimes we have arguments with each other, and both my sisters have gone through times when they've ended up out at my place because they're not talking to their husbands. It always looks rosy from the outside, but when you get down in the thick of it, we're just the same as every other family, ups and downs, happy and sad times, arguments and then reconciling. Most of all it's good, but life's never perfect. You're only seeing the good bits today.'

'What about your brother, Ben? He seems a bit different.'

'Yep, he is. I couldn't count the number of times I've bailed him out. Always doing the wrong thing with women he goes out with, often owing others money. He must be thirty this year and he's still playing around like he's twenty. Plus, he's been in trouble with alcohol and drugs over the years. You think he's just starting to calm down a bit and then he goes and does something else that's stupid. But that's family. We're all close and we support each other. Mum and Dad are like the base, see how they just sit back now and watch. They can only let us learn from our mistakes. I tell you what, they think you're all right.'

'They're both friendly, and your mum is so elegant, and your sisters.' She looked over at both of them. 'They just look so beautiful and neat and tidy. Everything matches.' She pinned her hair back again, straightening her dress.

'I told you Jess, you look great, so stop worrying.' He bent over and gave her a kiss, thinking how lovely she looked; her hair was a bit messy, her face flushed now from being kissed in front of everyone.

'Ease up, you two.' Ben came and sat down next to Daniel, handing him a beer, his esky never far behind him. 'You know what?' Ben turned to Jess also. 'And now I am serious. You know, Daniel, I haven't seen you looking so happy in a very long time.'

'Jess is special to me, Ben.'

Ben yelled out loudly, drawing everyone's attention, raising his beer high, waiting until everyone else raised their drink. 'To family and new friends.'

They all raised their drinks. 'To family and new friends.'

# 50

The chatter continued after Ben's loud toast, and Jess sat listening as the two brothers talked, her eyes following the kids who ran wildly around the yard, playing happily while the adults talked and relaxed in the shade. The birthday girl, Lea, played with the other kids for most of the time after lunch, turning the other way when Ben tried to talk to her, and crying loudly when her Aunty Liz tried to pick her up. 'It's just a stage,' Belle told them. 'Just ignore her, she'll get over it.'

Now as they all sat talking, Lea came back from playing with the others. She had chubby little legs and arms and was the cutest little girl Jess had ever seen. Lea stood back from where the adults sat, her arms wrapped around a post, her toes wriggling in the dust where she stood. Their eyes met, and Jess smiled at her, thinking that she must be looking for Belle, who along with the others was deep in conversation, enjoying the break from the kids.

Lea looked up one more time at Jess and then walked towards her, holding up her arms for Jess to pick her up. Climbing onto Jess's lap, she snuggled in tightly, her tiny body pressed up hard, so close that Jess could feel her little heart thumping against her own chest. The girl's legs wrapped around Jess's waist and she snuggled in. Jess held her awkwardly, not sure exactly what to do. She was so busy looking at Lea and trying to work out if she was holding her right that she hadn't noticed that everyone's conversation had stopped and they were all watching, as the little girl closed her eyes and nestled in closer.

Ben threw his hands in the air and shook his head while the rest of the family stared at Jess. 'I've been trying to win her over since the day she was born. What did you do?' Daniel said to her.

'I didn't do anything.' Everyone was listening as Jess spoke to Daniel. 'Am I holding her right? I've never held a baby before. She's pressing up really hard against me. I can feel her heart beating.' Jess had tears in her eyes. Something was aching in her body, and she couldn't work out why she was getting so emotional.

'Are you okay?' Daniel could see that she was upset and leaned in as she whispered to him.

Her voice was shaky. 'Johnno and I used to push up against each other like this when we were little. We could feel each other's heartbeats.'

Belle and Tyson were standing in front of them, watching Lea, her eyes closed, the thumb in her mouth and her little body relaxed and happy as she snuggled in.

Jess looked up at them. 'This is how twins often lie together when they're little. I can feel our two heartbeats together.'

Belle looked a bit upset and Tyson put his arm around her, speaking quietly to Jess, 'Lea was a twin. The other baby died before they were born. He was a boy and we called him Lucas. He never took a breath.'

'I'm so sorry, I didn't know.' Jess could feel the tears rolling down her face as she tried to wipe them away with her hand.

Daniel talked softly, but loud enough for his family to hear, 'Jess's brother and her are twins, and they always tried to stay together even as kids. His name is Johnno.'

Belle spoke, tears also running down her face. 'It's funny that you say about the twins, because often it's like Lea is looking for something or someone. That's why she never settles that well, and she just doesn't go to anyone else, well not usually. God, Jess, you don't sound like you've lived a very easy life. Do you see your brother much?'

'He's in rehab because he has a drug problem. We're very close, but his problems push him further away from me all the time. It's not easy for him.'

Daniel looked closely at Lea. 'She's sound asleep. I can't believe you, Jess. We'll never hear the end of this.'

The chatter resumed and she relaxed, enjoying the feeling of the baby's warm body snuggled into her own. After a while, Lea's body becoming heavy as she fell into a deep sleep, and Tyson carefully lifted her up. 'I'll put her in her cot. I haven't seen her sleep so peacefully before; she's taken a liking to you.'

John stood up. 'Righto, you lot, it's getting late. It must be coffee time. I think, Daniel, you need to make Jess a good cuppa. What a great day it's been. We're pleased you came with Daniel today, Jess. Make sure you get him to bring you around again.'

# 51

A cup of tea and more chatter took the focus off Jess, and Lea and Daniel eventually signalled that it was time for them to leave. Beth and John came out to the car and they both shook Jess's hand, hugging her warmly, telling her how lovely it was to meet her and that they hoped to see her again soon. John looked at her warmly, his voice kind as he opened the car door for her.

'You want to watch out. Belle and Tyson will be lining you up for baby-sitting, because there's not anyone else they can leave that little Lea with. You'll be top of the list, Jess.'

'Thanks. I enjoyed today, and the kids are so cute. Thank you once again.'

Daniel gave them both a hug, his mum smiling broadly at him, speaking so Jess couldn't hear her. 'She's lovely, Daniel. I haven't seen you look at anyone, ever, like that before.'

'You don't miss anything, Mum, do you?' He gave her a kiss on the cheek. 'Jess was quiet today, but it's only because she doesn't know you yet. She can be chatty and lively once you get to know her.'

'She has a very gentle nature about her.' John gave Daniel a hug. 'I've seen her out and about delivering things in the ute. I didn't realise you two were an item.'

'It's still early days and I'm just taking it

slowly. We'll be out to visit again soon. Thanks for the day.'

Jess was quiet as Daniel drove through town; there were many things going through her mind. 'So you enjoyed yourself?' Daniel was watching her, wondering what she was thinking. 'I still can't believe that Lea came to you like that. Ben and I have been competing as to who can win her over first, but she won't have anything to do with either of us.'

'It felt special that she just came to me like that. She's so cute, and it brought back memories of when Johnno and I were little.'

'Have you ever thought about having kids, I mean when you're older?'

'I've never really thought about it. Actually, that's the first time I've ever held a baby. It's such a huge responsibility, and I'd be worried that I wouldn't do a good job. I mean, look what happened to Johnno and me, all because no one looked after us. There's too much that can go wrong.'

By now they had reached the van park, and as usual it only looked like a couple of the men were inside their vans, the rest of the park quiet and deserted. Daniel walked Jess to the door, kissing her as she stood on the first step, his arm wrapped around her waist. 'I'll pick you up tomorrow afternoon. It's my turn to cook.'

Jess replied, 'I'm going to make something special for dessert. I've got everything here ready to make it.' She smiled, watching as he got into the ute, giving her a wave, before making his way out through the driveway.

That night she lay awake for a long time, mulling over all the conversations and funny events that had happened during the day. Everyone was so friendly, and they all obviously adored Daniel and wanted to make her feel welcome. Even Ben, with his handsome looks and flirtatious manner, had shown his better side, asking her about her job and how she liked living out in the bush rather than the city. Beth and John were a little intimidating, particularly Beth, who reminded Jess of Rosalie, immaculately dressed and groomed, her words pronounced just right, her posture always straight and just a little imposing. The women and their families had all been busy, but they had also managed to make her feel included and tried to put her at ease.

New situations always felt awkward. Large, noisy families who constantly bantered, teasing each other but overall showing a closeness and affection for each other, hadn't been part of her life previously, and she'd loved watching the inter-actions today between all the different family members. Sighing loudly, she lay back, looking out through the side window where she knew she could get a glimpse of the starry sky.

Today made her think about Johnno, and she wondered how he was going. Was he back out on the streets and back where he started, or was rehab helping him? Tonight she missed him terribly, the quietness of the park after the noise of the day making her feel isolated and lonely.

She tried to push her thoughts to the side, telling herself that tomorrow she'd be out at Daniel's for the afternoon. She could spend time

340

with the dogs, and then he was going to cook her dinner. The following day was a public holiday, so he'd probably come back out and pick her up again, no doubt with somewhere in mind to take her. She lay restlessly, tossing and turning, until Hoppy's relentless snoring from the van next door, jumbled up with her thoughts of the day, faded into the background, her soft breathing the only sound as she fell into a deep sleep.

# 52

Three of the men and Jess sat outside, all enjoying having their lunch together. It was rare these days, but Hoppy, Thommo and Jake were all home for the day, so they decided it was a good time to make steak sandwiches and sit together, filling each other in on what they'd been doing.

Jess was devouring a huge sandwich laden with tasty steak and salad, plus fried onion to top it off. 'I went with Daniel yesterday and met all of his family,' she said to Thommo.

Hoppy passed her a drink. 'How did that go? There's a few of them when they all get together, plus a bloody heap of kids those two women have now.'

'Well they're all nice, and his mum and dad were lovely to me. It's just, you know, it's not easy meeting so many people at once.'

Thommo passed her another roll. 'They're a great family. I've known John and Beth for years and they're honest, hard-working people.'

Jake spoke in between mouthfuls, 'Did you make a good impression? They'd be all checking you out, because it would have been a long time since Daniel brought a woman home.'

'They were all so welcoming, his younger brother is funny, and both of his sisters were friendly.'

'Ah, that Ben. He's been in a bit of trouble

from time to time, but he seems to hold down a job these days. Yeah, they're a good family, Jess, and you'll feel more at ease with them once you know them a bit better.' Hoppy grinned, knowing that the day would have been an entirely different experience for her. 'That looks like Daniel driving in now. What time was he picking you up?'

'He's early,' she said as she stood up, brushing the crumbs from her shirt. 'I'm not even changed yet.' She looked down at the crumbled shorts she wore, her feet dusty as she stood in a pair of old thongs, tying her hair up.

The men watched her, Thommo breaking into laughter, the other two soon joining in.

'What?' Jess looked at them, wondering what was so funny.

Thommo spoke in his deep voice, 'Who'd have ever thought, you two together.'

Hoppy stood up to greet Daniel, whispering to Jess, 'It must be love. We've never seen you worry so much about your appearance.'

'I thought he said he was coming later. I look a mess.'

'You look fine, love. I don't think he's worried about what you're wearing. G'day, Daniel,' Hoppy called out as Daniel waved and came over to where they sat.

'Sorry, Jess, that I'm a bit early. I had a job to fix in town, hence the mess.' He looked down at his dirty work clothes. 'So I figured I'd pick you up on the way back out home.'

'I'm not ready, but I'll grab my clothes and get cleaned up out at your place. Just give me a minute.' She strode off, wondering what on earth she was going to wear. Grabbing a dress and some underwear, she threw them in a bag, pushing her sandals on top. A few minutes later she reappeared, eager not to hold him up. Daniel looked tired, his clothes were covered in dirt, and she knew he would be keen to get home to clean up.

'Seeya, fellas. Thanks for the burger,' Daniel said as he finished off the end of a hamburger that he'd somehow managed to eat in the short amount of time that Jess had taken to grab her gear. 'I hate to rush you, Jess, but it seemed silly to drive out and then back again, and then I'd be dropping you back again tonight.'

'It's fine. I can play with the dogs while you're getting ready. Just as long as you leave enough hot water for me, I'll be happy.'

# 53

Daniel called out to Jess once he'd showered and changed. 'Shower's free. There's a clean towel hanging there for you.' He watched as she ran around the yard, the two dogs chasing wildly and then finally catching up with her. She lay on the ground, letting the excited dogs jump all over her, her shorts and shirt now filthy from the dust. It was like watching a kid play, and he reminded himself how young she was.

It was one of her qualities that he loved most, her childlike exuberance and excitement about so many things that seemed quite ordinary to him. Her enthusiasm was infectious, and he often found himself letting go of his own staid ideas and instead looking at them through her eyes, fresh and young. This afternoon, though, he did not feel like he was young. The morning's work had been hard and long, and it was only the fact that he wanted so badly to see Jess that he had driven through and stopped at the van park. The comfy couch in the lounge beckoned and he lay down, closing his eyes, thinking that he would rest while she was in the shower.

The next time Daniel opened his eyes, the room was dark and through the open window he could see that the sun had set. A small amount of light filtered through from the hallway, and footsteps padded softly across the timber floor. Jess sat down on the edge of the lounge next to him. 'I just let you sleep. You were so tired, and you've been asleep for hours.'

'Sorry, Jess. I just rested for a few minutes while you were in the shower.' He rubbed his eyes. 'This morning and the entire week have been full on.'

She wriggled in next to him, her back against him as he wrapped his arms around her. 'It's okay. I cleaned up a bit and then read for a while. I'd eaten those burgers for lunch, so I wasn't that hungry.'

His face nestled into the back of her head as he spoke. 'I ate a huge breakfast, and then Hoppy gave me a burger also. Maybe we'll just have something light for dinner.'

Jess turned her body around so she was lying facing him. 'Daniel, can I ask you something?'

'Sure, what do you want to know?' He could see her eyes in the dimness looking straight and seriously into his own.

'Um, I'm not sure how to ask this, because it's a bit personal, but . . . ' She took a deep breath. 'I just wondered if you're sexually attracted to me, or maybe you're not? It's OK if you're not, but I need to know.'

Now she could tell she had his full attention, and he sat upright, leaning on his elbow, his face looking down into hers. 'What sort of question is that? Did you just ask me if I'm sexually attracted to you?'

Jess continued, 'It's just that, well, you've never asked me to stay over. You always drop me home. I don't mind if you're not interested in me in that way, it's just that it makes me nervous trying to work out, if you know, like I said, if you're attracted to me in that way.'

Daniel chuckled. He could tell she was serious and trying to weigh up the situation. 'Do you want me to answer you honestly?' He looked into her worried face, sensing her nervousness, waiting for his reply.

'I'm confused, that's all.'

'Jess I could make love to you right this very moment, and on this narrow, bumpy couch. Am I attracted to you sexually? My god, I've wanted you from the first time I kissed you. Your face, your body . . . every time I watch you, I ache with the thought of touching you, having you close to me.' He caressed her cheek, running his fingers across her lips. 'But I wanted to make sure about your feelings for me, and also, I am trying to take everything slowly for your sake. I didn't want to send you running in the other direction.'

'Not knowing how you feel is making me nervous.'

Daniel's words were spoken softly. 'I want this relationship not to be all about the physical side. I'm a bit old-fashioned and wanted to make sure that you were ready for that part of it.'

'Well, I don't want to go back to the van tonight. I want to stay here with you.'

'Jess, that's fine. You've stayed here plenty of nights before.'

'No, tonight is different. I don't want to sleep in the spare bedroom.' She spoke so quietly he could barely hear. 'I want to sleep in your bed with you.'

Daniel laughed. 'Well, here I was trying to be the gentleman, and all the time I was just making you nervous waiting. Well we can't have that.' She pressed up against him, her face flushed and worried. Daniel kissed her gently, their bodies close as they balanced on the narrow couch.

'I don't think the lounge is such a good idea,' Daniel said. He sat up and took her hand, leading her to his bedroom. Jess was quiet and he sat on the edge of his bed, holding her hands as she stood in front of him. 'Jess, are you sure this is what you want? Because I'd wait for however long you need.'

'I don't want to wait.' She stood between his knees, and his hands wrapped around her waist, the warmth of her body coming through the thin fabric of her dress.

His hands ran over the back of her dress, feeling for the zipper. 'Don't tell me this dress doesn't have a zipper,' he said as his hands moved to the front instead, trying to undo the tiny buttons that ran down it. 'Jess, would you be angry if I just ripped this dress off you? These buttons are killing me.'

Pushing his hands to the side, she started to undo the buttons herself, their eyes drawn together as he watched her open each one. His hands found the backs of her legs, and he caressed them gently, her dress dropping to the floor as she leaned in towards him, her mouth finding his. Wrapping his hands around her bare waist, he gazed appreciatively at her slender body. 'Your body is just as beautiful as I knew it would be.' He held her at arm's length, his eyes soaking in the sight of her as she stood nervously in front of him.

'Should I take everything off?' Her voice was a whisper.

'Just stand there and let me look at you.' His hands touched the back of her legs again, making her squirm. 'Jess you always have the best underwear. I noticed it that day in the lift.'

'You told me you didn't look.' She laughed nervously. 'It's the one thing I've always loved.'

His hands moved over her body. 'I used to see it hanging, drying in the kitchen when you stayed here during the floods.'

She giggled. 'You looked at my underwear?'

'It was right in my face, hanging in my kitchen, drying in front of the stove. I also love beautiful underwear, but I like it better when it's off.' He pulled her in closer, feeling her body quiver under his hands. Soft lips travelled over her stomach, kissing across the fabric of her bra, making her squirm where she stood between his legs. Daniel pulled his shirt over his head, her skin rubbing up next to his, her hands on his chest, as he pulled her down next to him on the bed.

She lay on her back, her body next to his as he ran his hands gently over her. Running his fingers around the edge of her bra, he watched her breathe in sharply, her eyes never leaving his.

The touch of his hands sent sensations through her body, and she squirmed, pushing up against him.

'Jess, can I ask you how long it's been since you've slept with anyone?'

349

He could barely hear her answer, his hand touching under her bra, finding her nipple, rubbing gently across the top of it.

'Since I was a teenager. I'd have been about fifteen; we were kids and it was only a couple of times.'

'No wonder I made you nervous,' he said, reaching behind her back, unclipping her bra. 'My god, you're beautiful,' he said before his lips closed down hard on hers, her body writhing with unfamiliar sensations.

Daniel's hands and lips moved over her, their bodies aching for each other. He groaned loudly as her arms pulled him towards her until he lay with his body covering hers.

Time stood still as her body moved forward and she pulled at his arms and back, calling out as they joined together.

# 54

The first touch of sun lightened the bedroom, the early morning birds a background chorus as Jess and Daniel woke up. It took Jess a moment to work out where she was, and then her mind eventually registered that it was a day off, and she didn't need to get ready for work. Strong arms held her and Daniel's leg was thrown over her, her face pressed into his chest. Looking up, she took a deep breath, watching as his eyes opened, the blueness of them looking directly down at her, his face soft and handsome in the early morning light.

Wriggling closer, she enjoyed the feeling of her breasts up against his body as he kissed the top of her head. 'No work today, Jess. How good is that?' His hands stroked her thighs and he enjoyed watching her squirm as he tickled up and down her legs. 'Did you sleep all right?'

'I slept soundly. I think you wore me out.'

He laughed, moving his leg so that he could look at her body. 'I just wanted to check that I didn't imagine last night.' His hand stroked her, watching as she responded, her nipples darkening as her body pushed up against him.

'How do you do that?' she said.

'What, make you ache?'

'How did you know that?' Her breaths grew shorter, and she tried to stop her hips from moving as he ran his hands over her.

Daniel moved quickly as she pulled him towards her, the feelings from the night before still close to the surface, her quiet pleas for him to make love to her again all too much.

★   ★   ★

They lay together, enjoying the aftermath of long intense lovemaking. Her hands touched his face, moving over his lips, smiling as he sucked on her fingers. Jess whispered, 'That has to be the best feeling in the world.'

'I don't know how I'm ever going to let you out of this bed.' He rolled her onto her side, holding her tightly, kissing her gently. 'Tell me; describe how that felt for you.'

She spoke slowly, 'It's like climbing a mountain, slowly, and then picking up speed as the slope got steeper.'

'Go on.'

'Then you reach the summit and time stops.'

'My god, I didn't know you could describe things so well.' He laughed as he stroked her face, his eyes never leaving hers.

'Then it was like flying, as if I'd left the world behind, except for you, like we were flying, as if it was never going to end.' They laughed together, her lips moving over his neck, her hands caressing him.

She closed her eyes, looking for the right words. 'It's hard to describe that feeling.'

Daniel twirled her hair with his finger. 'I like the feeling of sliding down the other side of the mountain, until you reach the soft grassy slopes below, together, and here we are lying in that soft paddock of grass now. I feel like we're the only two people on the planet.'

Swirls like butterflies in Jess's stomach pushed up under her chest as she looked at Daniel's eyes gazing into her own.

He spoke slowly, making sure she could hear clearly each word. 'I want you to stay here with me. I don't want you to go back to the van. Come and live with me, Jess. I think about you constantly, and I want you here in the morning when I wake up, and I want us to go to bed together at night. Think about it, but I want you to come and live with me.'

Her lips pressed to his chest, her voice shaky. 'That's a huge move for me. I'd have to leave the park. It's a long-term decision, don't you think?'

'It is, and I told you earlier that I wasn't into short-term relationships. I've known for a long time how I feel about you, but it's a big change for both of us, so think about it, and when you're ready, let me know and I'll come and move you in here with me.'

'So it's okay for me to have some time to think about it?'

'If that's what you need.' He looked down at her, his face calm, his hands stroking her body as they lay talking. Daniel closed his eyes, the morning going over in his mind, the sensations still sending tingling feelings over his body.

'Daniel, are you awake?'

'Sure, I'm awake.' He opened his eyes.

'I've thought about it,' Jess said.

'About what?'

'About moving in here with you, I've thought about it.'

'It's okay. Like I said, take your time. It's a big decision for you.'

'It's a huge decision, and I've thought about it. I worked out what I need to do and what I want to do, and I'd like to move in here with you.'

'Are you serious?' His eyes were wide open now as he propped himself up on one elbow.

'You know me. I have to be absolutely sure when I do things, but once I make a decision I go with it.'

'You amaze me. It was only the other week you tried to get me to leave you alone. You wanted us to end.'

'I said that, but you know that I never meant it. I'm used to working everything out with no complications or help from others, particularly about Johnno. If I can concentrate on myself, I'll manage to somehow get through everything.'

'Well, now, Jess, you've thrown yourself in, because once you move in here, it's not just you, it's you and me. And your problems become mine and vice versa. You know . . . ' He laid back, running his hands through his hair, looking up at the ceiling. 'It's not just a big decision for you. I've thought long and hard about this, because I've been let down before and I don't intend going down that track again.'

Jess sat up, her voice steady. 'You can trust me, Daniel. There's no way I'd come and live with you if I wasn't sure about how I feel. I completely trust you with everything I have. I'm not sure about all the other emotions that I'm experiencing at the moment, but I'm just going with my gut instincts.'

Daniel's pushed her gently back onto the bed, his mouth closing over hers, his kisses passionate.

# 55

Jess was eager to talk over the new arrangements. 'I want to pay for half of everything, like the food, and some rent. You know I don't have anything to offer in money terms because everything I've ever saved has gone on Johnno. I'm twenty-three years old and . . . ' Daniel stopped her by pressing his fingers to her lips.

'Money means nothing to me. I know you don't have much, but you do have your job, and we'll just take it as it comes. I've worked all my life, and I've been very lucky. My family always supported me when I was younger, and the business is good. You won't have to worry about any of that.'

'I will want to put in for food and electricity, or any other costs that might crop up.'

'Okay, if it makes you feel better you can chip in for food, but that's it. Maybe this is a good time for you to save some money, put it away, then when we go on holidays you'd have your own money to spend.'

'Holidays?' She sat upright, Daniel's eyes lighting up at the sight of her naked body moving in front of him. 'What do you mean by holidays?'

His hand ran down the front of her body, moving from her chest down to her hips and then playfully stroking her legs. 'Well, I've been thinking for a while how much fun it'd be to go away somewhere together, for a holiday. Just do nothing but lie around, soak up some sun, maybe somewhere that we could swim.'

She lay back down, her eyes closed, enjoying the sensation of his hands over her body. 'I'd love that.'

'I think we need to get up and do something, otherwise . . . ' He kissed her roughly up and down her neck, her giggles and squeals making them both laugh. 'Otherwise, we're going to be in this bed all day.'

'It's so lovely to be in this big bed.' She sprawled out, watching Daniel as he picked up the clothes that had been thrown around the room the night before. 'I can't believe I'm going to sleep in it every night, and with you.'

'It's going to be special for me, too.' He tickled up and down her slender legs. 'Now get up and come with me. Let me see if I can share the shower with you without dragging you back here.'

# 56

It hadn't taken them long to load Jess's belongings into the back of the ute, Daniel surprised at how few possessions she owned. 'I guess I just learnt to live with the minimum, because when you move around a lot or don't have a permanent address, there's no use buying or keeping things.'

'You're right. Besides, we do have too much. There're lots of things in my house that I never even use.'

'You have nice belongings, though, Daniel. All that furniture that was your parents', and items that have been passed down from your grand-parents. At least they have some meaning for you.'

'Do you have anything Jess? Anything from your mother?'

Jess reached into one of her bags and pulled out a thin cardboard box. 'I have some photos.' She passed them to Daniel one by one. 'This one is of my mum, Johnno and me. We were six, and that was our first day at school. I know that because I can remember the photo being taken.'

'You look unhappy.' Daniel peered at the small photo, a gaunt dark-haired woman, her legs and arms covered in tattoos, holding tight to the hands of a small boy and woman.

'I lost my temper just before the photo was taken, because I didn't want to be in it. I remember throwing a huge tantrum. Johnno was just sad. He never seemed to know what was going on.'

'You're both so little and thin,' Daniel said, looking closer at the photo. 'You're very cute, but holy hell, what a scowl. Why were you so angry?'

'She didn't buy us school uniforms. Look at what we're wearing, both of us. Scruffy old clothes, second-hand from Vinnie's.' Jess took the photo back from Daniel. 'Apart from the fact she'd probably spent all her money on drugs or alcohol, she could have organised something for us. All she needed to do was talk to the school. As soon as the teachers worked out that she didn't have any money, they organised some second-hand uniforms for us. I remember being cold going to school in winter. Johnno and I, we'd huddle together, waiting for the bus because neither of us owned a jumper.'

'That's rough. I can't imagine what that must have been like.'

'After a while, the teachers realised that we didn't have jumpers, so they got some second-hand ones for us. She should never have had kids. No one should unless they're going to care for them properly.' Jess handed him the rest of the photos, all similar shots, both Johnno and her, always skinny and in scruffy clothes, with shoes that were obviously too big for them.

The last photo they both looked about ten, Jess's hair was long, her arm around Johnno, neither of them smiling. 'I think that's the last photo I have of either of us.' She stacked them back neatly in the cardboard box.

'What's that?' Daniel pointed to the other item in the box.

Jess picked it up fondly, holding it in her hand before passing it to Daniel. 'It's just a cheap piece of jewellery. Two love hearts joined together. Johnno gave it to me on my sixteenth birthday. He might have stolen it, but I didn't care. It's my only possession from when we were young.'

Both of them sat in the front of the ute, Jess taking a big breath before packing the items back in her bag.

'I'm disappointed that none of the fellas are here to say goodbye. I guess I'll just catch up with them through the week.'

'You can ring them when we get home, and once you have a chat with them you'll feel better.' Daniel could see that looking at the photos, as well as the fact that no one was there to say goodbye, had left her feeling dejected. 'It's not a bad time to leave, Jess, because these guys are all about to go their separate ways. We'll have them all, as well as Jeffery out for dinner sometimes.' He squeezed her knee. 'Ready?'

Sitting up straighter, she took one last look at the van. 'I did love living here. It felt like the first home of my own, and everyone was good to me. I've been lucky.'

'Time to move on, though,' Daniel said as the ute moved forward, travelling up the dusty road. 'This time, you'll have me to look after you, and you'll also have those two dogs to care for. It's going to be a new life for all of us.' He turned to look at her. 'I want to make you happy, Jess. You

360

need to feel comfortable, and for the house to be your home also. Most of all, we'll be able to spend time together, although you also need to have some space of your own. A place where you can do your own thing, actually do something for yourself.'

'Thanks, Daniel. You're always doing extra for me. No one has ever done that before. I know I always managed fine by myself, but it's a good feeling to have someone else, just sometimes, make a decision for me, or point me in the right direction.'

'I'll try not to boss you around too much.' He grinned, and Jess could tell he was excited at the prospect of her moving in.

# 57

For the rest of the trip they were quiet, both lost in their thoughts, Jess surprised at the decision she had made so quickly, while Daniel was thinking ahead, working out how to move furniture around so she'd have somewhere to put her clothes and belongings.

Before long the ute was parked in front of Daniel's house, both dogs barking from the top of the stairs. He carried her bags, laughing as both dogs whirled and barked boisterously around Jess's legs. As he placed her bags on the veranda he caught a glimpse of her face. 'Come here' he said, taking her hands and wrapping his arms around her. 'You look worried.'

'I'm fine.' She gave him an unsteady smile.

'I've seen that look on your face before. It's Johnno, isn't it?

She looked down and ruffled Rosie's ears. 'Sometimes it just eats at me. It's like a wrenching feeling in my gut, pulling me towards him.'

Daniel's lips pressed down gently on the top of her head. 'He's okay, Jess.'

'I keep telling myself that.'

'Once you're settled in, we'll go and visit. You can spend some time with him.'

'I'd like that,' she said quietly, a worried look still on her face.

'Right,' Daniel said, 'let's go in and get you

settled.' He picked her up, laughing when she squealed in delight as he carried her in through the front doorway. 'Welcome to your new home.'

# 58

Living together seemed to suit them both, and the days and weeks floated past, filled mostly with busy work days, cosy dinners together at night, and spare times used to attend the usual family and social events that were commonplace in the tiny town.

Mornings were a special time for both of them. Daniel usually woke first and would lie on his side, watching her sleep, his hands running softly over her body, reminding her that it wasn't a morning for sleeping in. It was a work day, and she needed to wake up. It took all of his willpower to get out of bed and ready himself for work, often having to ignore her pleas to spend just that extra few minutes cuddling together.

This week was going to be busy for both of them, and tomorrow Daniel was going away for a few days, travelling out further to another mine whose managers had requested some advice from him. 'I'll be back Friday afternoon. You've got Belle and Tyson's number there if you need, and I'm not that far away if you want to call.'

'Daniel, I'll be fine. You forget that I've always looked after myself.' She kissed him, and his arms wrapped around her, lifting her off the ground, her body small in a fluoro work shirt and tiny denim shorts.

'Just as well you don't wear those shorts to work,' he said. 'Because nobody would get anything done.' He put her down, holding her at arms' length, looking down at her legs. They were thin and long, and the work over the previous months had given them and the rest of her body a lithe, supple tone that Daniel found hard to drag his eyes away from. 'Jess, there's not much to these shorts.' His fingers ran around the edge of them, touching her underpants. 'They feel silky. Christ, why do you always wear beautiful underwear? How am I supposed to resist?'

She laughed, familiar with the look in his eyes. 'You're supposed to be getting ready to leave, not thinking about my legs or underwear.' They both stood still, suddenly aware that the dogs were barking, and someone was coming in through the front door.

'Righto, you two. Sorry, I hope I didn't interrupt anything.' Ben bounded in through the door, thumping Daniel on the back and tousling Jess's hair before heading to the fridge. 'Belle wanted to drop some fruit over for Jess, and I thought I'd come and give my commiserations to her for moving in here with you.'

An apple Ben got out of the fridge was soon being crunched noisily, and he jumped up, sitting on the kitchen bench, tutting and shaking his head as he watched Jess's face turning red. 'Don't be embarrassed, Jess. You need to train those dogs better. I could have caught you both out big time,' he said as he looked from Jess, who was trying to straighten her clothes, over to the doorway. 'Here's Belle, and of course the tribe, one, two, three and four.' Robert and Thomas, as usual, ran up to Daniel before stopping in front of him, both of them scowling at Jess, who leant back against Daniel, his arms wrapped around her.

'Say hello to Jess and then I'll let her go.' He shuffled her, moving her from side to side, both of them laughing, watching the two boys who were unsure how to get the person their favourite uncle was hugging out of the way. Belle passed the baby to Ben, who continued to talk noisily while still eating the apple. Robert and Thomas reticently said hello to Jess, and Daniel kissed her playfully before letting her go.

'Yuk, Uncle Daniel, women have got germs.' Thomas clung onto Daniel, who picked them both up, sitting them on the bench next to Ben, who was now concentrating on holding the baby, who had started to cry. Lea was on Belle's hip and glared at them all before hiding her head in Belle's shoulder.

'I've just about had enough of this one,' Belle said as she hitched the little girl up on her hip. 'I feel like I have an attachment to my body.'

Belle tried to sit Lea up on the bench with the others, but she clung tighter to her mother, refusing to let go, her little hands and feet curling around whatever part of her mother's body she could reach. Daniel had given the boys a biscuit and drink each, and placed one for Lea on the bench next to him. It was obvious to all of them that Belle was worn out from the demands of four small children, who all wanted a part of her, none more so than Lea.

While Daniel concentrated on supervising the

drinks that the two boys were tipping into their mouths, Jess stepped forward towards Belle.

'Righto, Lea, come to Jess.' She pulled two hands from Belle's shoulders, grabbing the little girl under her chubby arms before lifting her up and away from her mother. 'We're going to see what those two dogs are up to.' Jess smiled as she felt Lea attach herself to her side, her tiny face with the most wondrous eyes and chubbiest cheeks looking up at her. There wasn't a smile, but at least the scowl disappeared. 'We'll be outside if anyone needs us.' Jess smiled at them all before walking out through the door, leaving Daniel and Ben shaking their head in bewilderment

The baby in Ben's arms squirmed, and he stood up so he could rock her slowly. Belle passed a bottle to him, which he started to feed her with. 'What's she got that we don't have? That kid won't let Daniel or me within ten feet of her,' Ben said.

Belle sat down, relieved to not have anyone hanging off her body. 'She's the only person Lea will go to apart from Tyson and me. Jess is lovely, Daniel, and we're all pleased that she's moved in here with you. It seems a pretty serious move to me.'

Daniel wiped up some spilt drink before lifting the two boys down from the bench. 'My whole life has changed, and we get on great. You know, you're never sure until you live together how it's going to go, but I know it's going to work out.' He smiled. 'I'm the happiest I think I've ever been.'

Ben shook his head at them. 'You two are old romantics. Jesus, Daniel, I'm not sure what's been going on these last few weeks, but you look about ten years younger. What have you been up to, brother?'

Daniel threw a tea towel at him. 'That is none of your business. Now concentrate on what you're doing. The baby's been spitting out that milk for the last few minutes; she's full.' Daniel grabbed both the two boys' hands and led them outside, the sounds of them yelling and calling out to the dogs soon audible to Belle and Ben, who sat inside, Belle enjoying the quietness and some time to talk to her younger brother.

'Daniel seems happier than I've ever seen him,' she said. 'He's in love with her, and I'd say she is with him.'

'Who knows,' Ben said as he sat the baby upright, rubbing her back. 'She's a lot younger, yet in some ways, she seems older than her years. I tell you what, Belle — I give her the tick of approval. She's a stunner, no doubt about that, although he tells me she has a foul temper. You only have to see the way she looks at him, and him at her, to tell they're both lost causes. Just watch; there'll be a wedding around the corner. He won't be letting her go.'

'I think you're right, although I do think she's a bit fragile and sometimes it seems like her thoughts are elsewhere.'

'Fragile? Bullshit, there's no fragility about her. You wouldn't want to get on the wrong side of her. I reckon she'd let you have it. She might appear quiet, and she's only small, but I wouldn't want to mess with her.'

'I didn't mean fragile in that way. I just think, well, she doesn't have a family, apart from her brother. Now she's living here, it's like Daniel wants to look after her, protect her. You know what he's like. He's always been such a giving person, and he's always looked after all of us.'

'He did tell me that sometimes she disconnects. He reckons she's thinking about her brother, that it's like they're joined still, even though they're miles apart.'

'That's what I just can't work out about her. She's different than we are. It's almost like sometimes it's all too much for her, all the family stuff.'

'Yeah, she wouldn't be used to all of that.' Ben look through the window. 'We're pretty close, all of us, and we do a lot together. Plus you know he's going to have to learn not to try and take control all the time. I heard him the other day telling her how to do something. I mean she conceded and did it his way, but I got the impression that she was just keeping the peace and agreeing with him.'

The two of them talked, the baby sleeping blissfully in Ben's arms. Belle relaxed, enjoying the time with her younger brother. The sounds of the boys whooping noisily outside drifted in through the open windows, and Daniel yelled as he chased both of them around, the noise broken sporadically by Jess laughing, all of them enjoying the coolness and the last of the light of the summer afternoon.

# 59

Although Jess kept busy while Daniel was away, the house seemed big and empty and the hours in the afternoon and at night were quiet, even with the two dogs demanding her time. Wandering from room to room, she tidied and dusted, pulling down books to read, opening them and reading only a few pages before returning them to their space.

The bed seemed huge without Daniel to fill his side, and she slept with a pillow against her body, often waking throughout the night, listening to the noises of the old house as it creaked and moved in tune with either the heat, or the chill of the early morning coolness. She counted the days, and on the last afternoon drove over to the workshop, knowing that Daniel would have returned a couple of hours before.

As she neared the shed, she could see him through the large doorway. He waved as she pulled up outside. Jess jumped out of the car and ran towards him, throwing herself into his arms, her legs wrapping around his hips as he lifted her up. His lips pressed down on hers. 'I've missed you so much; it feels like you've been away for a year,' she said in between his kisses.

Daniel laughed loudly, his eyes sparkling. 'It's only been three days, and um, Jess, I'm not here by myself.' He looked over to the side where two older men stood, both of them grinning broadly as they walked over to where Jess stood, both her feet now firmly back on the ground.

Her face burned and she knew the colour of it would be bright red. Daniel introduced the older man first. 'This is Geoff, CEO of Seelo Mining, and his offsider Pete. Both of them just came back with me to look over some machinery before I drop them back at camp. The men, who were both in their sixties, shook Jess's hand. Geoff laughed loudly before asking, 'And this young lady is?' He looked at Daniel, whose arm was still around Jess's shoulder.

'This is Jess. She's our courier driver as well as, obviously, my partner.'

Jess shook their hands, her face still burning and with no idea of what to say. Pete shook her hand, laughter in his voice as he spoke. 'Christ, Daniel, I wish my wife welcomed me like that. You make a lovely young couple.'

'I'm sorry, I didn't realise anyone else was here.' She stumbled over her words. 'I'd better get going. Daniel, do you want me to pick up your mail while I'm in town?'

He reached into his pocket, giving her the post-box key. 'Thanks, I'll see you back at home in an hour or so.'

'Pleased to meet you both.' She nodded to the two men, before spinning around quickly making her way back to the ute. As she drove off, she groaned, wondering what it must have looked like to them, the sight of her running and throwing herself at Daniel. Always getting caught out, she thought. No doubt they were still laughing and making jokes about it.

It had been so good to see him, even for that short time. His clothes were dusty and dirty, and she knew he was tired from the long days at work. Pulling up at the post office, she thought about how much she loved him when he looked like that, his face rugged, his strong arms that of someone who worked hard, often grease or dirt smudged on his face. When they went out he always dressed in well-fitting jeans, shirts that showed the toned shape of his body, those piercing blue eyes that seemed to take in every part of her body.

She blinked several times. *Stop it*, she told herself, trying to remember why she was sitting in the ute outside the post office. *Christ, he's in my head*. She shook it, trying to focus on what she needed to do, and that was to pick up his mail, not dream about how Daniel looked or the way he looked at her.

# 60

Heavy footsteps that made the stairs creak signalled to Jess that Daniel was home. Before long, his solid frame filled the doorway and he threw his bags onto the floor. Dust and dirt covered his clothes, and even his hair looked messy as he grinned at her as she sat at the kitchen table. 'Don't I get the same welcome again, or is there too much dirt on me now?' He stooped down to give her a kiss, surprised when she pulled away from him. She looked directly at him and he could tell that she was angry, her words taking him by surprise as she stood up, waving an unopened envelope in front of him.

'What the fuck is this, and why do you have it?' She pushed the envelope towards him. He looked closely, the printed name of the sender clearly embossed on the back of the envelope. 'Read it out to me. I want to hear you say it, and I want to know why the fuck you have that letter.'

Finally he spoke, his eyes squinting at the writing. 'Right, I can see why you're wondering why I have this, but Jess I'm exhausted at the moment. Let me have a shower and we can sit down and talk about it.'

'No, you fucking tell me right now why you have a letter from that place. You fucking tell me all the time not to lie to you, and now when I see this, I just know that you've been leading me on, telling me lies all along. Read it out.'

He could see she was getting angrier by the minute, her voice loud, her movements agitated as the words spilled out, expletives hitting him with every second word. 'Jess, calm down. Yes, OK, it says The Mountain Drug Rehabilitation Centre, and I guess . . . ' He turned the envelope over to where his name and address were. ' . . . it does always have Johnno's name on here, care of my name. It comes every month, and I know exactly what it says.'

She snatched it back off him, her eyes glaring, cutting through him like daggers as she became even angrier, her language more coarse. Daniel eventually sat down. He was tired from work, and could see she wasn't going to easily calm down. He listened patiently until her accusations of meddling and lies started to wear thin on him.

'Jess, I said before, I'm exhausted. I'm nearly asleep on my feet and I don't feel like talking about this right now.' Jess's arms moved angrily and her feet kicked at the table legs. 'OK, I think that's enough,' he said as he reached for her arm. She pulled away from him, the look in her eyes enough for him not to try any contact with her at the moment. 'OK, I pay for Johnno's rehab. I talked at length to Dave and found out some of his background details. The police have it all on file, probably things you may not have even know about.'

'He's my fucking brother, and he has nothing to do with you. I know more than anyone what he's been through. To them, he's just a number,

374

another homeless druggo, and it would be easier for them if he was dead.'

Daniel continued, 'When I went to Brisbane, I tracked him down and met up with him. I told him how I felt about you. I worked with him to get him into the best place, and then last time when I went back, I visited him to check on how he was going.' He looked at Jess, hoping that his words would calm her down, but they hadn't.

'How dare you.' She paced aggressively and then came back towards him, her hands clenching the side of the table as she tried to find something to take her temper out on. 'He's my brother, and you've gone behind my back. Johnno has nothing to do with you. How could you lie to me? All this time I felt good because I thought that he was getting help, and that perhaps there was a chance.'

Daniel stood up, towering over her. 'You're not thinking straight.' His voice was also was raised, and she realised that she wasn't the only one who was angry. 'He's getting help, and maybe there'll be a chance of coming clean. He told me he wanted to get off the drugs and to be able to see you, to have a job, to lead a normal life. There's only a small window of opportunity when an addict calls out for help, and I can tell you right now, unless you've got money, there's not much help out there. You're part of my family now, and that makes Johnno part of it also. I didn't ask your permission because I know how stubborn you are, and I was worried that you'd go against me. It's about Johnno. All of this is about him, not you. Now I've had enough of your foul language and hysterics. I'm going for a shower.'

'Fuck you, Daniel, always thinking that you can control everything. Well, you can't control me. I don't need you or your help. I can look after everything and my brother myself.' She went to walk past him, heading towards the kitchen bench, but Daniel was quick and he grabbed the ute keys just before her hands reached them.

'You're not driving, and you're not going anywhere, either. You can go outside and rant and rave, but you walk away from here, and I'll come and drag you back.'

Jess was taken aback by the harshness and severity of Daniel's words. He was clearly furious, his look cutting as he stared at her one more time before heading off to the shower. His heavy footsteps echoed on the timber floor in time with the pounding in her head. She stood for a moment, her eyes full of angry tears, her hands clenched so tight that she felt like she had broken bones in her fingers. Exiting through the back door, she slammed the old wooden door so hard that it felt like the entire house shook. The reverberations echoed in her ears, and a foggy angry feeling tightened in her head.

Rosie and Red followed her as she stomped off through the dusty backyard down towards the river, her thin legs striding out, arms swinging angrily by her side.

Watching her through the window, Daniel tried to control his breathing, his anger still simmering under the surface, the exhaustion from doing sixteen-hour shifts for three long days shortening his patience. Christ, she'd fired up, snapping like a tightrope. He'd known sooner or later that it would come out that he had not only found Johnno and persuaded him to agree to rehab, but was also paying his costs, a promise he made that he'd keep for however long it took.

When he was in Brisbane last time, he'd visited Johnno at the rehab centre that was set on the edge of a mountain. The vast grounds and buildings were surrounded by rainforest and peaceful views across the valley, and he could tell that even in that short time Johnno had changed. His malnourished body had filled out and some colour had returned to his face, no longer the sallow grey complexion, but instead a healthier tanned look, proof of the hours of gardening and yard work that were therapeutic to his recovery. It was a complicated process to try and save Johnno, who was a long way down the track; a lifetime of abuse and dependency now thrown into chaos as the staff worked with him to try and make a clean break.

When Daniel had first looked for Johnno, it hadn't been difficult to track him down. The police kept records of where the vagrants, particularly those with a criminal, history were living, and he'd found him camped near the city, sleeping off a previous nearly lethal week on ice, his latest addiction. The two of them talked for hours, and Daniel soon realised that Johnno was at a stage where he was desperate for help, asking, pleading, and willing to accept the funding, anything, hanging on to tiny threads that might just see him crawl out of the dismal abyss that had always been his life. A tiny light at the end of that tunnel was not only the hope for his own future, but the dream that one day he might be able to be back with the only person in his life he'd ever truly loved: Jess.

And now there was someone else who loved her just as much, but in a different way than he did. Daniel told him that he considered she was now part of his family, and therefore Johnno was like his own brother.

When Daniel left the area where the group was squatting, Johnno had picked up his small bag of belongings and left with him. For some reason he felt this guy Daniel was honest. Perhaps it was the way Daniel spoke to him and looked him in the eye, or the way he was so direct with what he wanted him to do. Whatever it was, it was rare, because Johnno couldn't remember the last time he actually felt like someone was trustworthy, or had an answer for him.

He knew that this was probably his first and last chance. A lifetime of drugs and alcohol was not going to be easy to shake, but since the conflict in the van park with Jess, his mind had been turning, wrestling even more than usual with the thought of what it must be like to live some sort of normal life.

Daniel had already spoken to the rehab centre, and once he'd met with Johnno, he recognised that narrow window of opportunity, just the chance that there might be a sliver of hope for him.

It was, of course, going to cost thousands of dollars, and that would be ongoing. Daniel told the centre and Johnno that he didn't want just a quick stay, it could be for months, a year if needed whatever it took, he was up for the support both financially and emotionally. Although Johnno's mind was muddled and his body physically depleted, the talk with Daniel had penetrated the barrier of hopelessness that surrounded him, and he vaguely recognised that this could be his one chance. Surrounded by filth, death and mental illness, along with the ongoing violence and depraved sights and sounds that surrounded each and every hour of his life, he was convinced by Daniel's words, offering him a place at one of the best centres in the country, with a chance to turn his life around.

Daniel had driven Jess's twin brother through the early morning traffic, the roads becoming less choked as they cleared the suburbs and made their way up into the distant mountains. Johnno closed his eyes and visualised Jess, a woman with big brown eyes who always tried to save him, to help him, who over and over told him that she loved him and that she'd always be with him. Always her and him, together. Him taking every crooked road and bad turn there was. Jess tagging along behind, following him while always keeping on the straight and narrow, working, supporting him.

He winced, thinking of all the times he'd taken her money, pleaded, begged until she had given in. And then the last visit to her van, the final straw, he squeezed his eyes tightly trying to get rid of the vision of her lying injured on the floor, the shocked look in her eyes. And now it was her boyfriend who was secretly supporting him, and ordering that she was not to know yet, just in case she didn't want him to be involved.

Daniel watched the younger man, his features so similar to Jess's, but his face etched with years of hardness. His eyes were closed, the tears streaming down his face, and Daniel knew that he was thinking about her, the other half of him.

When they parted, Johnno said his goodbyes, his voice soft and shaky. 'I know that thank you is not enough,' he mumbled, and Daniel leant forward to hear him, the same brown eyes as Jess's staring straight back at him. 'It won't be in vain.'

'It's all good.' Daniel shook his wiry hand, small and bony against his own strong grip. 'Just come back to us all, because when it's all over, there's an entire life waiting for you, and Jess.'

'Be good to her, man,' Johnno said, and then cracked a small smile. 'Watch out for her, though. She has a deadly temper.' He finally let go of Daniel's hand, turning and walking slowly back into the centre, his stance slumped, his feet shuffling and head down.

# 61

Soft footsteps and the yapping of the dogs on the veranda let Daniel know that Jess had returned. It had been dark for a couple of hours, and he'd resisted the temptation to go and find her, to drag her back, kicking and swearing. Deep down, he knew that she needed to learn that she couldn't just run away every time there was an argument. They had talked about that when she had moved in.

As tired as he was, he had paced up and down inside the house, watching as the sun sunk lower in the sky, listening to the sound of galahs flying across the paddocks, the squawking noises fading into the distance, the quietness of the still air as the day turned into night. He began cooking the night's meal, and after a few hours breathed a sigh of relief when he heard Jess outside. The daybed on the veranda creaked and the dogs shuffled around on the mattress outside, the clues that she'd returned easing the tension that filled him.

At least she had come back to the house. So far she hadn't come inside, but he knew that even returning was a big step for her, and he was relieved to know exactly where she was. The veranda was good enough at this stage, and he figured that she'd curl up on the daybed, the two dogs probably nestled in beside her. There was no way he was going to go out to her, having made the decision not to give into her at every step. Jess was going to need to make her own decisions in regards to their relationship.

He left her dinner on a plate in the fridge, going about his routine before finally falling into bed, trying not to think about the empty space beside him. Resisting the desire to go out to her, he tossed and turned, thinking about the mosquitos that would be biting outside and the lumpy and uncomfortable mattress on the daybed. The last few days work, along with the emotional strain of the previous couple of hours, took their toll, and he fell into a deep sleep, only stirring slightly when hours later he felt her sliding silently into bed. She turned on her side away from him, minutes later her soft breathing an indication that she was sound asleep.

★   ★   ★

The room was dim, early morning light just beginning to filter in through the slit in the drawn curtains. Daniel slowly opened his eyes, his first thought that it was the weekend and there was no work today. Aching joints and sore arms reminded him of the different type of work he'd done over the last few days, and although the physical side of the specialised work was enjoyable, he acknowledged that these were not muscles that he normally used.

He glanced over at Jess, who lay under the sheet, still dressed in the clothes she'd worn when she'd left the house yesterday afternoon. Watching her sleep so peacefully, her delicate face pale, dark eyelashes splayed out on her cheeks, he questioned how such vehement words and anger could come from someone who appeared so sweet. Her lips were parted slightly and she breathed softly, her hands tucked under her head as she lay on her side facing him. Stretching out his tired muscles, his foot touched hers and she opened her eyes, looking directly into his. For a while, neither of them spoke; they just lay looking at each other until Jess shut her eyes, blocking him out.

Last night she had so badly wanted to walk away and keep walking, to never come back. The fury that consumed her had boiled inside, and she'd still been angry with him when she returned to the house. The dogs had cuddled up to her for warmth, but the mosquitos were ferocious, and she could feel some bites itching on her legs as she lay in bed, her eyes closed, pretending to be asleep.

Finding the envelope with Johnno's name on it had gutted her, and her rage as usual had boiled over, directed at Daniel for interfering in her life. Once she'd lost her cool, any level-headedness or logic just flew out the window, and language which she tried so hard not to use anymore had flowed easily from her mouth, the gutter words and mean arguments she'd thrown at him probably not acceptable in his world. Cringing, she imagined if his sisters or mother could have heard her. They were always so in control, their words chosen carefully, articulate, like those of civilised people, not words like those used by a person from the streets who as soon as they became angry lost control and reverted to foul language.

Sitting by herself on the riverbank, she had watched the sun set behind the trees, the amber light throwing its hue across the countryside in front of her. The anger that had engulfed her was briefly forgotten and she watched the beauty of the outback light as the dust swirled up in whirly twirls from the riverbed, spiralling and fading into the darkness that began to filter across the plains.

The sky above had been covered in a million sparkling stars, the galaxies strewn across the emptiness of the outback sky. Thoughts whirled in her head and a persisting anxiety churned in her stomach. It never went; like an invisible umbilical chord, an attachment to a brother that stretched and ached, no matter what the distance between them was.

Jess thought back to when she had first started working for Seelo, and how Daniel had ignored her, never once going out of his way to help her settle in. The lies that she'd told at the interview had always been on her mind, and it had been a massive weight off her shoulders when she had finally come clean and told him the truth. Lately there had been times when he'd made decisions for both of them, and the fact that he was older and assertive had for a short while been a relieving factor, taking away responsibilities that had weighed her down since a very young age.

And now he had taken on the care of Johnno. It was too much. Daniel had no idea how long it would go on. Johnno's problems were ongoing, relentless, they never let up and they never improved. How much money had Daniel already paid out? Why hadn't he told her? She could feel her chest heaving and an overwhelming fear that she was losing control of her life. Picking up some rocks from the ground next to her, she had pelted them as hard as she could up against the trees, their leafy silhouettes faintly visible in the darkness near the river. The rocks bounced off and plopped into the river sands, the echoing sounds of them sometimes landing in the water doing nothing to alleviate her anger. The recurring image in her mind of the envelope and letter from the rehab caused her to take deep breathes and clench her fists, and she sat by the river a bit longer, soon the darkness heavy, the stars high in the sky.

A numb feeling enveloped her and she began making her way back, the light from the house guiding her in the right direction. Rosie and Red had bounded in front, delighted at the unexpected long walk so late in the evening. Rosie, sensing her distress, kept coming back, licking her hand and pushing at her legs with her nose until Jess bent down and patted her. A desire to turn around and keep walking in the other direction nagged at her, but deep down she knew if she didn't return that Daniel would come and find her and make her come back. Besides, all her belongings were now at his house.

This morning, though, the anger had dispelled. Instead her stomach churned, and she felt so upset that tears welled in her eyes and she struggled to stop them running down her cheeks.

She hopped up quickly, Daniel listening as she made her way to the bathroom, the sound of the shower running sending him back to sleep.

When he awoke a couple of hours later, his arms were wrapped around her as she slept up against him, a large t-shirt covering her body, her back to him and the warmth of her body emanating onto his own. His hand slid up under the t-shirt, resting on her breasts, his face nuzzling into the back of her head as she stirred, nestling back against him.

They lay together, Daniel eventually pulling her over towards him. Her eyes were still closed as he looked down at her. 'I know you're awake, Jess.' He rested on his elbow, waiting for her to open her eyes. 'Look at me.' His hand rested on her stomach, his leg thrown across her body. Slowly, her eyes opened, and she looked straight up into his face. 'C'mon, Jess, you're going to have to talk sooner or later.' He waited for her to speak, but she closed her eyes, her head turning away from him. 'You need to talk to me. Nothing will get solved unless we talk to each other.' His hand touched her chin, turning her face back towards him.

Opening her eyes, her voice was quiet when she spoke. 'I can't believe you didn't tell me what was happening. Johnno is my brother. He's the other part of me.'

'I know that, but at the time my priority was getting him sorted, and I wanted to see if he went all right. There wasn't much use telling you when I wasn't sure if he was going to stay or not. I didn't want to get your hopes up, plus I knew you wouldn't want me paying for him.'

'So you went ahead and did it anyway, when you knew I wouldn't agree.' Her eyes closed and she took a deep breath. Tears welled again in her eyes, and she used everything she had to try to control them, to not let Daniel see she was upset. Crying was not something that she often did, and apart from the day she'd cried in front of Daniel's family, she couldn't remember doing so since before her mother had died.

Tears had always come easily to Johnno, and she'd spent most of her life trying to cheer him up and stop him crying. Growing up and trying to look after both of them, there had never been time for tears, and she'd developed a tough exterior, instead holding everything inside, bottling up the sadness until eventually it was pushed to the background, a base for the next round of sorrow that built up on top of it. Now with Daniel, she had lost the ability to control her emotions. The fact that he was angry and probably annoyed at how she had reacted was upsetting her.

His voice was terse, and he spoke abruptly. 'I told you that I was in this for the long term, and I could see that Johnno was the most important person in your life. He is your only family. If I want you to be happy, then we need to at least try and get him some help. Maybe, just maybe, there's hope. That centre is the best in the country, and if anywhere is going to help him, it'll be there.'

'But what about all the expenses? We can't just take your money.'

'Why not, Jess? Why not? It's money, that's all it is. I've made so much out of the mining, and for what? I can tell you right now, money does not bring you happiness. I'd rather try and help Johnno, and not only because he's your brother, but also because now I've met him a couple of times, I think he's a pretty good bloke. Helping him is what money is for. He's never had anyone help him, and maybe this will be the break he needs. You two are only young still, and money means nothing to me. You're the only thing that matters.'

Jess closed her eyes again, afraid to speak as her chest tightened, her tears close to the surface.

'Did you just listen to anything I said?' He spoke slowly, annoyance evident in his deep voice. 'Are you listening at all, or just waiting to abuse me again? Because I'm feeling all talked out. I'd rather that you yell and swear than this sulky silence.'

The bed creaked loudly as she moved her body away, sitting up, about to get out of bed. But Daniel was not letting go, and he pulled her back towards him, his grasp strong on her wiry arms. 'No you don't, don't walk away from me again. I've just about had enough.'

Jess burst into tears, her hands covering her face as muffled sobs stopped the words that Daniel was about to utter. His face softened, and he pulled at her hands, tears streaming down her cheeks as she tried to turn away. It was not the reaction he was expecting, and for a moment he sat in shock, knowing that it took a lot to upset her to the point of tears, and now she was not just crying, but sobbing as she tried to tell him something.

'Jess, get your breath. Don't talk, just calm down. It's not that bad; we're both angry, that's all.'

Wiping her face with her t-shirt, she managed to get some words out. 'I can't stand it when you're angry with me now. It really upsets me.'

'Well you're bloody frustrating sometimes, because you just don't listen.' His hands rubbed her back, still trying to calm her down, unused to tears from her, his anger towards her now dissipated.

'I don't know what's wrong with me. I never cry. I just get angry.'

Pulling her towards him, he hugged her tightly, her face wet against his bare chest. 'I guess I expect a lot from you,' Daniel said. 'I'm so used to calling the shots, making all the decisions. Perhaps because you're a lot younger than me, I just assume that I know best. But I probably should have talked to you about Johnno and what was happening.'

Wiping her face again, her words came out calmer this time. 'Do you think it will work?'

'The people at the rehab centre seem confident, and so does Johnno. He hasn't been on ice for that long, so that's one good point in his favour. The other positive is that he's determined to come clean on everything, and he wants to have a second go at life. And I've told him, Jess, that I'll see it through, no matter how long it takes.'

389

The tears started rolling down her face again. 'I miss him. Sometimes we'd go months without contact but I'd always eventually talk to him, even if it were over the phone. He and I were all each other had for the last twenty or so years.'

'Well now you also have me, and — ' He sat upright, looking out through the bedroom window. ' — and damn it, my family also, because wouldn't you know it, that's Ben's car that's just pulled up.'

The noise from the dogs barking came closer, and Daniel kissed Jess quickly before jumping out of bed, hastily putting on some clothes. 'He's early. Doesn't he realise that people like to sleep in on their days off?' A persistent knocking on the front door caused Daniel to call out loudly, 'Hang on. I'm coming. Stop banging on the door.'

Jess also jumped up, throwing on her shorts before eventually joining them both in the kitchen.

'Good morning to the beautiful Jess,' Ben said as he placed a large cardboard box on the table in front of her. 'Mum has sent me over with these things. She said she picked them up in the city for you and some other stuff she thought you'd like.'

'It's bloody early, Ben.' Daniel leant against the kitchen bench, Ben observing his tousled hair and crushed t-shirt. His eyes moved to Jess, who was sitting down looking at the box from Daniel's mum.

Ben looked closely at her, raising his eyebrows, before frowning at Daniel. 'You two have been

390

arguing, haven't you? I can tell. Jess is upset.'

Daniel answered him gruffly, 'We've just sorted out something, that's all. There's no need for you to know everything that goes on.' Daniel glared at Ben, trying to get him to be quiet.

'Oh god, you poor thing, Jess. I hope he didn't use the deep angry voice, because he's bloody scary sometimes. I used to be more scared of him than the headmaster at school. Just ask Belle. Daniel was always going off at us two, always telling us how to do things, always wanting to organise our lives. Don't you let him rule the roost now.' Ben squeezed Jess's shoulders. 'Belle and I will always be on your side, so if you have any trouble with him, you come and see us. We could never win over him, so we'd sympathise with you, that's for sure.'

'Jesus, Ben, the number of times I've saved your arse and supported Belle. Thank god Liz has some practical sense and seems to have everything under control.'

'Just remember, Jess, we'll back you. We're all family and always right here for each other. Don't let him win every argument.' Jess didn't say anything, but listened as Ben and Daniel bantered back and forth. She thought about how Daniel's family had, from the first time they'd met her, accepted her and made her feel welcome. Ben treated her like he did his own sisters, and he'd picked up immediately this morning that she was upset, sensing there'd been some sort of disagreement. A dull ache thumped in her stomach. They were always there for each other. There was always one of them that would help the other out. No one was alone.

Daniel placed a cup of tea in front of Jess. 'You know, I'm always the first one they ring, the whole lot of them. As soon as shit hits the fan and one of them is in trouble, who do you think they ring?'

'Mr Dependable. Just don't let him win every time, that's all.' Ben pommeled Daniel, the two of them boisterous and noisy as they flung comments at each other.

Daniel had the last say. 'Jess can stick up for herself, Ben, don't worry about that.' Daniel moved away, opening the box that his mother had sent. Holding up each item, he read out the labels on the packets before placing them on the table. 'This must be for you, Jess, because it's all smelly stuff, you know, moisturisers and all those creams you women put on your face. It says it's all natural, nourishing, rejuvenating. Maybe I should use some of this.'

'Ben, are you sure this is all for me?' Jess asked. 'There are a lot of things in here.' She pulled out a short summer dress, then a bright t-shirt, followed by a floral blouse with beautiful colours and patterns splashed across it. 'These are amazing, and they're expensive items.' Jess pulled out some more clothes, all beautifully packaged, folded and packed neatly in the box.

'Yeah, yeah,' Ben said. 'She said to tell you that she picked them up for you when she was in the city last week. Said something about how she just saw them and thought of you. She bought a heap of stuff for the two women as well, oh and I think there are a couple of shirts in the bottom for Daniel. She bought me some stuff as well. The old lady, she loves the shops. Gotta spend Dad's money somehow.'

Jess looked at Daniel, amazed and shocked at the generosity of his mother. Daniel held up a blouse, looking at the brand on the label. 'Yep, good old Mum, nothing but the best. Get used to it, Jess. She loves to buy beautiful things, and she does have impeccable taste. She'd have loved choosing all this for you. You're going to have to learn just to accept it, because she will get offended it you don't.'

'I don't have anything like this. I'm not sure what to do with all these beauty products.'

'We'll go and see them tomorrow, Mum and Dad that is, she'll explain it all. Don't ask me,' Daniel said.

Ben stood up, ready to leave. 'So do you need me to sort him out for you Jess? Belt him up, make him less bossy?'

'I think it's time you left, before you get yourself into trouble. Thanks for bringing the box out from Mum.' Daniel steered him to the doorway and out onto the veranda, the two brothers laughing and joking, as Ben said goodbye.

'See you both soon. Remember, Jess, don't let him win every time.'

The stress from the earlier situation lifted from Jess's shoulders, and she waved goodbye, watching Ben's car speed off through the property gates.

'He doesn't always give the best advice.' Daniel straightened up, his hand shielding his eyes as he followed the path of Ben's car, zigzagging wildly up the dirt road. He shook his head as the car completed a three-sixty circle in the loose dust, the horn sounding loudly as the vehicle made its way onto the main road.

Jess remained silent, her mind ticking over, hands clammy as she leant on the wooden rail, watching the trail of dust left behind.

'You're deep in thought.' Daniel looked at her, sensing her unease, a disquiet pervading the stillness on the veranda. 'What's up?'

It took her a long while to answer, her gaze wistful as she looked over the paddocks towards the green ribbon of trees that designated the line of the river.

'You've all got each other. There's always someone close by to help the other sister or brother out.'

'There is, and you're part of that now.' His words came out slowly. 'I know what you're thinking, Jess.'

'You say it yourself, you all support each other.'

'We do, and we'll always be there for you also.'

'Johnno's got no one.'

'He's got the staff working with him, that's what he needs at this stage.'

She turned towards him and looked down at the veranda as she spoke. 'He's got no family with him. I'm a long way away.'

'He's better without anyone there. He's got trained professionals looking after him. Don't do it, Jess.'

'I think I need to leave for a while.' Her eyes met Daniel's, neither of them speaking. Daniel closed his eyes. He had sensed it, felt it coming.

Turning at the same time, they looked towards the river, Daniel eventually breaking the silence. 'It seems like a long time ago that you rescued those pups from that flooded shed.' The dogs looked up as if they knew they were being spoken about. 'A lot's changed since then, for both of us.'

'For me especially,' Jess said. 'Maybe it's all just too good to be true.'

'I've told you before, sometimes things do work out and often people lead happy lives with just the normal ups and downs.'

Tears welled in Jess's eyes and she leant back on the veranda post, closing her eyes and making sure that her words came out evenly and calmly. 'I need to go to him, and — ' She held up her hand as Daniel went to interrupt. ' — I need to go to him by myself.'

'We could go together.'

'I want to go by myself. I need to stand alone. I don't want to depend on you or anyone.'

'It's not about depending on me, it's more about doing things together, supporting each other.'

'I'm sorry, Daniel. I just know that I need to be near him.'

'Where will you stay? He's in rehab. You can only visit him. He's not allowed to leave, only to have occasional visitors.'

'I'm not sure yet, but I want to work it out for myself. It's not good for me to become dependent on you, Daniel.'

Daniel ran his hand through his hair,

exasperated with her decision. 'I can make it so easy for you. We could go together, make a holiday of it, and I can find you somewhere to stay close to the rehab facility, if that's what you want.'

'I don't want you to do anything more. You're doing so much already, paying for him and organising all that you have. I need to be my own person.' She swallowed hard, surprised at how mixed her emotions were.

The invisible ties with Johnno had tugged hard and last night down at the riverbank and she had felt the incredible urge to take off to him in the middle of the night; to disappear without going back to say goodbye to Daniel or anyone else. But a strong feeling that was new to her, a feeling of trust and connection to Daniel, forced her to go back in. To face him and be honest with how she felt and what she was going to do.

'I need you to understand, Daniel. I need you to know that I have to control my own life and the choices that I make. It's been like that forever.'

'I do understand that, but we can do this together. I want us to be here together.'

'I have to go.' Her voice was small, and she bent down to pat the top of Rosie's head. 'I'll organise it with work tomorrow and leave as soon as I can. I'm going to try and find work and somewhere to live near to where he is.'

'You've given this some thought by the sounds of it.'

'I've felt the urge to go for a while, but I wasn't sure about where he was. It's been nagging at me, but I kept telling myself to be thankful for everything I have here. But last night . . . ' She closed her eyes for a moment before looking straight at Daniel. 'I decided last night. I can't not go. I'm sorry, Daniel.'

'How long will you go for?'

'I'm going to stay near him for as long as it takes. He needs to know that I'm nearby, that someone cares for him.'

'You're going to give up everything for this. You could lose your job.' He paused for a long time. 'We could lose each other.'

'Sometimes you have to make hard decisions.'

'What if his recovery doesn't work? What if you throw everything away for nothing?'

'We're brother and sister, Daniel. Wouldn't you give up everything for one of your family?'

Daniel looked at her, the confusion over-whelming, the feeling that he was losing a battle, his sinking feeling contrasting with the resolute, determined look on her face. 'I would never give up on you for anyone.'

'I'm all he has.'

'What about us?'

Her voice trembled. 'I need time.'

Daniel ran his hand through his hair, the arguments to keep Jess with him whirling in his mind. Deep down, though, he knew that he was going to have to let her go. That if he tried to stop her, she would go anyway, and then if he really tried to stand in her way, she might not come back.

He reached out and grabbed her hands, pulling her body in towards him. Wrapping his arms around her, the tension in her body disappeared and she pushed her head into his chest. He stroked the top of her head, squeezing her tight and wanting to keep her next to him forever. But he could feel it — there was sadness in her voice and her tears dampened the front of his shirt. He knew deep down that he was going to have to let her go.

# 62

A pink haze filtered over the brown paddocks as the morning sun peeped over the distant horizon. The warmth of the summer rays didn't take long to heat up the inside of the ute where Jess sat, Daniel in the driver's seat beside her. Enjoying the warmth of the sun on her legs, she smiled at the thought of how white her legs had been when she'd first arrived in the small outback town. Daniel's thoughts were also drawn back to the first day when Jess had arrived. He had been skeptical from the start, and her stand-offish attitude hadn't done much to make him think otherwise.

As he looked over at her now, he thought about how his feelings towards her had changed over the last year. Her long brown hair hung loosely on her shoulders, and he watched intently as she looked out the side window of the car.

He had sensed her decision coming, and when she had finally said the words, it had felt like the air was being drawn from his body. Every option he could think of had been thrown in her direction, but eventually he had drawn back, realising that she had made up her mind.

The last few days had been a rollercoaster of emotions. At times he would have snippets of understanding of the decision she had made, but then he would be filled with the desire to keep her with him, to organise visits to the city for her and even go with her. He'd offered for her to fly back and forth to work with him when she came back, and then go back to be near Johnno. He'd come up with every practical idea he could think of, but in the end he'd had to stop.

Jess had listened to all of it, but had remained resolute.

# 63

Charlie and Hoppy had visited yesterday. Charlie had wrapped his arms around her and hugged Jess until she begged him to stop. 'Don't make it harder for me, Charlie.'

'I know, Mrs Geronimo. Daniel told us your mind is already made up. You're leaving all of us for the big smoke. I hope that brother of yours realises what you're giving up.'

Tears welled in her eyes, and she wondered how long before she would see the two men again. Hoppy shook his head, pushing in front of Charlie. 'Gawd's sake, get off of her. It's a wonder you didn't break her skinny ribs.' He also gave her a hug before the three of them walked towards the veranda, where Daniel sat on the top of the stairs. He watched the two men with Jess, wondering if she realised how important she was to all of them.

Rosie and Red sat obediently next to him, their tails brushing excitedly across the dusty veranda as they waited for the word that would allow them to greet the visitors in their customary manner. 'Off you go' he said, smiling as he watched the dogs twirl around and bark excitedly at Charlie and Hoppy.

He had gone to see the two men yesterday while Jess was busy in at the office, sorting out the paperwork needed for her to finish up as well as saying an emotional goodbye to Jeffery.

Hoppy had understood Daniel's predicament, nodding and shaking his head as Daniel explained the situation. Charlie, however, had wanted to talk to Jess.

'How 'bout I give her a stern talking-to? That brother of hers will do whatever, no matter if she's there or not. Sometimes, Daniel, you just gotta put your foot down with these women.'

'I don't really think bossing Jess around is going to do any good. I've given her every idea and option I can think of, but it's something she feels she has to do.'

'But what about you and her?'

Daniel had taken a long while to answer. 'That is going to be a wait and see. She's adamant she's going to find work near where Johnno is, so she can contribute as well as be there for him if he needs her.'

'You hadn't thought of going there with her? I suppose you can't just up and leave the business?'

'I can't, and besides, I just can't live in the city. Bottom line is, though, Charlie, she doesn't want me to come. She wants to go by herself.' Daniel stopped talking, the control he was trying so hard to maintain betrayed by the shakiness of his words.

'So you're breaking up?'

'She said she needs to sort out everything. Being near to Johnno is driving her away from here, but she's also unsure about her feelings.'

'Feelings for what? For shit's sake, you can give her everything. What's there to think about?'

'It's not that easy for her. She's used to doing everything herself. She's not used to sharing her life with anyone else other than Johnno.'

Hoppy had chipped in, casting an admonishing look Charlie's way. ' 'Fraid to say, but Daniel, you gotta let her go. There's no two ways about it.'

'I know. She's still young, although years older in other ways, but I don't know if she feels a bit trapped here. I'm not sure, but I wonder if having to deal with the closeness of my family as well as moving in with me was a bit overwhelming. She wants time to think about us.'

'Main point is, she wants to be near that brother of hers,' Charlie said. 'I still think I should talk to her.'

'Leave it, Charlie. You gotta remember that those two kids survived together through stuff you and I never experienced.' Hoppy stood up, holding onto Daniel's arm to steady himself.

'Are you okay? Daniel said, a concerned look on his face as he steadied Hoppy, who swayed from side to side, his arm clutching tightly onto Daniel's.

'Just this old ticker. I'll be good as gold in a sec,' Hoppy muttered.

'Is you heart playing up again? Have you been to see the doc?' Charlie asked.

'Yeah, yeah, it's all good. Just got a bit dizzy for a moment. I'm fine.'

'Maybe you should tell Mrs Geronimo that Hoppy's crook. That might keep her here.'

'Stone the crows, Charlie. It's nothing a few good ales won't fix tonight, and . . . ' He paused to get his breath. 'Don't you dare be saying anything to Jess. I think we all need to let that woman go.'

# 64

Hoppy's words resonated in Daniel's mind now as he drove with Jess past the caravan park where she had first lived. The rusty chain that once held the park sign had fallen down, and weeds and litter were strewn across the yard. The vans all appeared vacant and the washing line drooped, its ropes sagging lifelessly without the flapping of fluoro work clothes once pegged tightly to its lines.

Daniel slowed down and they peered across the paddock towards the van park. She kept looking out the window. 'It seems so long ago. So much has happened.' She paused for a long while. 'Do you hate me, Daniel?'

'That's a silly thing to say. Of course I don't hate you. I just want you to come back to me. I don't want to lose you.' He noticed a tear trickling down her chin and he reached over to wipe it away.

'Just make sure you come back to me, Jess.'

# 65

Even as Jess walked to the tiny plane that would take her across the dusty plains to the bustling city, Daniel still could not believe she was really going. He stood on the tarmac, shielding his eyes against the rising sun, watching as she found her seat, her face looking worriedly through the window. He held his breath, hoping that miraculously she would open the plane door and come running back towards him, her mind changed, asking if she could stay. But she didn't, and he watched as the propellers whirred and the small plane begun taxiing across the tarmac, the pilots visible behind the curved glass of the cockpit.

Jess lifted her arm and waved through the plane window, her eyes connected with his until the plane turned and sped up, its wheels bumping and grinding across the runway.

Daniel stood motionless, watching the plane, shards of morning sun flashing off of its silver plates until it became a dark speck and then no longer visible.

★ ★ ★

A swirl of dust sped across the tarmac, sucking scraps of litter and leaves into its spiral as it headed off in the same direction as the plane. Daniel's shoulders slumped and he continued to watch the sun rise higher in the sky, the whirling dust becoming slowly distant until it also was no longer visible. The pink haze in the sky began to fade and light blue colours in the sky took on a darker shade, preparing for the onslaught of the unrelenting summer sun. Daniel gazed around, taking in the vastness, the dry colours and dusty tones of the outback that he loved so much. In the distance he heard the dogs barking from the back of his ute, where he had left them. They would miss her, and he wondered if she'd whispered to them perhaps about returning one day.

He took one final look towards the horizon before turning and making his way back to the ute. Back to his house, the work sheds and the property that he loved. For now, he was going to have to make the best of what he'd had with Jess, and as Hoppy told him, he'd just have to hang in there. He had let her go, reassuring her that he understood why she was going and that when she worked things out, he'd be there for her.

Rosie and Red looked up at him, their eyes anxious, expectant he thought, waiting for what he didn't know. He stroked their heads and tickled under their chins, noticing that they were both unusually quiet and still. Rosie's nose rubbed up against his hand and Daniel talked to them, his voice a shaky whisper.

'We have to be patient. I've let her go and we have to believe she'll come back.'

We do hope that you have enjoyed reading this large print book.

Did you know that all of our titles are available for purchase?

We publish a wide range of high quality large print books including:
**Romances, Mysteries, Classics**
**General Fiction**
**Non Fiction and Westerns**

Special interest titles available in large print are:
**The Little Oxford Dictionary**
**Music Book**
**Song Book**
**Hymn Book**
**Service Book**

Also available from us courtesy of Oxford University Press:
**Young Readers' Dictionary**
**(large print edition)**
**Young Readers' Thesaurus**
**(large print edition)**

For further information or a free brochure, please contact us at:
**Ulverscroft Large Print Books Ltd.,**
**The Green, Bradgate Road, Anstey,**
**Leicester, LE7 7FU, England.**
**Tel:** (00 44) 0116 236 4325
**Fax:** (00 44) 0116 234 0205